Rachael Treasure lives in Southern [...] her two children and their farm anim[...] Barbara Gordon. She is the co-founde[...] Healing Hub and uses regenerative agricultural and natural sequence farming principles to restore farming landscape. Her first novel, *Jillaroo*, blazed a trail in the Australian publishing industry for other rural women writers and is now considered an iconic work of contemporary Australian fiction.

Rachael is a rural business administration graduate of Sydney University's Orange Agricultural College and has a Bachelor of Arts in creative writing and journalism from Charles Sturt University in Bathurst. She has worked as a journalist for Rural Press and ABC Rural Radio. Rachael currently supplies holistic farm product to the online farmer's market, Tasmanian Produce Collective. *Milking Time* is her eighth novel.

BY RACHAEL TREASURE

FICTION
Jillaroo
The Stockmen
The Rouseabout
The Cattleman's Daughter
The Girl and the Ghost-grey Mare
Fifty Bales of Hay (short stories)
The Farmer's Wife
Cleanskin Cowgirls
White Horses
Milking Time

NON-FICTION
Dog Speak: Daily Dog Training Tips for You and Your Family
Don't Fence Me In: Grassroots Wisdom from a Country Gal
Down the Dirt Roads: A Memoir of Love, Loss and the Land

OTHER
Fifty Shades of Hay: Adults Only Agricultural Colouring-in Book

Rachael Treasure

Milking Time

HarperCollins*Publishers*

HarperCollins*Publishers*
Australia • Brazil • Canada • France • Germany • Holland • India
Italy • Japan • Mexico • New Zealand • Poland • Spain • Sweden
Switzerland • United Kingdom • United States of America

HarperCollins acknowledges the Traditional Custodians
of the lands upon which we live and work, and pays respect
to Elders past and present.

First published on Gadigal Country in Australia in 2024
by HarperCollins*Publishers* Australia Pty Limited
ABN 36 009 913 517
harpercollins.com.au

A catalogue record for this book is available from the National Library of Australia

ISBN 978 1 4607 5759 8 (paperback)
ISBN 978 1 4607 1127 9 (ebook)
ISBN 978 1 4607 4592 2 (audiobook)

Cover design by Louisa Maggio, HarperCollins Design Studio
Cover image by Ilya/stocksy.com/2581490; map of Tasmania by Adobe Stock
Typeset in Sabon LT Std by Kirby Jones
Printed and bound in Australia by McPherson's Printing Group

MIX
Paper | Supporting
responsible forestry
FSC
www.fsc.org   FSC® C001695

For the cluster of cells, enlivened by Spirit, that is You
&
for my skirt-raising soul sisters in seed and soils

'The Valley Spirit never dies.
It is named the Mysterious Feminine.
And the doorway to the Mysterious Feminine
Is the base from which Heaven and Earth sprang.
It is there within us all the while.
Draw upon it as you will, it never runs dry.'

Tao Te Ching

'Raise the skirt: reclaim your power.'

Catherine Blackledge, 2020

'There are currently 171,476 words in use in the Oxford English
Dictionary. In comparison, there are over 20 million names
for chemicals. Every three seconds a new chemical is invented.
Who knows what impact they'll have on the environment or on
people.'

Nicole Masters, Agroecologist. *For the Love of Soil*, 2019

Prologue

My name is Connie Mulligan and this is the story of my awakening. It's drifted into your hands momentarily, like a cloud drifts past and you think the cloud has no meaning to your life. But it does. That cloud, like this story, is part of you. How? Read on, and maybe you will come to remember sooner than you might.

'Remember what?' you may ask.

Remember that you have visited this blue green Earth before, sheltered under the Milky Way, time and time and *time* again, but you don't recall. Or do you? In your remembering, you will come to know you are as powerful as the universe. Just like me, when I remembered. So come with me on this journey, and when we are done, you too can re-write your story anew – milking this time of your life, joyfully and fearlessly, for all that it is worth.

Chapter 1

Dad is doing my head in with his rigid ideas about tits. I keep telling him he's been brainwashed by some marketer's idea of perfection, but he just mumbles that my fancy mainland boarding school and Hobart's university down south has turned me into an uppity, know-it-all bitch. When Dad says crap like that, I want to lecture him on sexist microaggression like Ms Shroud taught in Feminist Studies 1, but that would just add fuel to his already smouldering dung pile.

As Nick-nack and I trudge behind the despondent stragglers of the herd of cows – 'the troublemakers' as Dad calls them; 'the rebels' to me – I swivel to adjust my undies that are steadily being consumed by my bum inside my waterproof pants. A silky black crow perched in a dead gum echoes my undies-induced moan.

'Nothing wrong with being a bitch in your case, is there, Nick-nack?'

Reaching around, I fish my Bonds out of my butt. Nick-nack wags her border collie tail like a pageant flag, improving my mood. Then my sock begins slipping down in my gumboot, the makings of a blister stings my heel.

This whole tits argument started yesterday with yellow tag, cow number 1761; a big black and white beast who sails like a ship across the paddock. She's a beautiful creature, but Dad is fixated on the fact she has this one little extra teat that pokes out the back. As if she's giving you the finger, but upside down.

He likes a cow that has four neat teats, like an upturned milking stool. Faster to get the cups on that way, more hygienic with the auto teat-dip, plus less confusing for the milking relief staff, he reckons. But now he wants to cull her ... just because of that. Just for having a fifth little teat. *Idiot*.

I trudge on through the mud, cow shit and rocks that's supposed to be a well-drained road, which never got finished. The money didn't stretch beyond the new over-designed, tech-infused rotary dairy. Plus, there were my legal fees after all that awful Austral University business. These days I find it's best not to think about uni, but my mind has other plans just as the crow calls again.

Professor Turner flashes into my brain – his wavy Hugh Grant hair, the conformity of his Tasmanian old scholars' tie, countered by his zany socks peeking out from his corduroy trousers. I used to long for that gaze of his. Eyes that would ice me blue from behind deceptively jazzy glasses that he changed as often as his socks to match the bright-coloured elbow patches his wife ironed onto every jumper and jacket he owned. He thought he was cool and sexy. I thought he was cool and sexy. Now he's my worst nightmare. Or should I say was. Past tense.

Nick-nack looks up at me with her doleful violin-playing eyes, reminding me I'm thinking about Professor Turner again, and I'm to stop.

'Thanks, Nick-nack.'

No worries, says her tail wag, but really, Nick-nack has lots to worry about. The poor bitch has had a litter of pups pretty much every time after she's been in season. You'd think she'd be over it by now. Each time Nick-nack comes on, I say to Dad, 'It would be a good idea to fix her.'

'Yeah, Connie.' He'll roll his eyes. 'You're full of good ideas.' Then he ignores me, and old Paddy-whack gets to pumping his pelvis with Nick-nack yet again and soon more half-useless pups are handed out in the district like excess zucchinis. Talk about give a dog a bone!

Still, she always digs deep to find a tail wag.

'Don't you Nick-nack?'

See ... tail wag! For a moment I fall into the universe of her rich-soil eyes, specked with golden flecks. I reckon you can find God in the eyes of a dog. Makes total sense. Dog is God, only spelled backwards. No judgement. Just like God. Every Sunday, bloody Mum and Dad choofed off to Mass to listen to what old Father Morris had to say about God. That was before the diocese sold off the church to some mainlander wanting a tree change. But Father's sermons didn't seem to do them much good. Mum and Dad didn't seem to get the part that says 'Do not judge, or you too will be judged'.

I look to the docked-tail, freeze-branded rear ends of the sullen cows, labouring up the last steep pinch to the dairy, wading through mire. There's tail paint on a few, ready to be hunted into the crush to get up the duff again with Dad's expensive semen straws, bought from glossy catalogues selling bull spoof from all over the world. He does it year in, year out, despite the poor conception rates we have around here. That includes Mum. She wanted more than a brood of two of just me and my loser brother, Patrick. But Dad just didn't do the job.

I sigh thinking of her. Mum: Mary Mulligan nee O'Reilly, last sibling in a litter of eight, married thirty years to a hard-arse bloke – Finnian Mulligan. A man with a plasticine bald head like Wallace from *Wallace and Gromit*, but it's his blue eyes and square jaw that lead him to think he's still a fancy rooster around town. A real chest-puffer when he's out with his fellow farmers, and a stomach-churning flirt with 'the ladies'.

Last night, when I was telling Mum about Dad's tits bias and his stupid semen selection I said to her, 'Dad's being conned by the marketing men, the same as Patrick ... only it's the porn marketers who've got Pat. They've convinced him and his gross mates that plastic versions of women's tits are solely for their viewing pleasure and nothing to do with sustaining life. Ms Shroud said, in terms of brain function, he'll never be able to relate to a real woman, and probably won't function normally in sexual relations.'

'Connie! Enough!' Mum barked angrily, holding up her hand as if directing traffic to stop. She'd turned back to her magazine, grinding her teeth. To be fair, I think she was overly stressed that *Woman's Day* had alleged Harry and Meghan were calling it quits.

Over the frosted fence line, dragon breath huffs from Traveller's nostrils, feathered hooves drumbeating as he trumps across glistening white pasture towards me. His dappled coat is the colour of a rainy day, yet he still delivers me sunshine. He lowers his head over the fence and rumbles a greeting.

Stopping, I lay my palms on Traveller's big disced cheeks and press my forehead on his long grey spiralling forelock.

'Hello, handsome.'

Nick-nack looks up at me, worry in her collie-dog expression that the cows are marching on and away. I know Dad will be pink-faced in the dairy, underway with the pre-milking germicide spray, impatience bulging the veins on his neck. If only I could shake Dad from my head. Dad, like Professor Turner, tangles my thoughts like electric wire run off the spool.

My therapist, Doctor Dorothy Cragg, says my mind is like quicksilver, that I overthink things. She reckons medication is the only way. Now things are getting this rough at home it could be one way, perhaps? But would it really help? When I'm fetching the cows, I'm meant to be focusing on which may be lame or noticing the tail paint splodges to see who's coming on heat after we've injected them, but I've given up on Dad's inefficient, myopic system.

Instead, my mind is captured by the absolute beauty of the world that no one else seems to see – the sunlit spiderwebs trailing a mesmerising silver net across the heads of the pin rushes in a creation of perfection ... I fall into a trance, and then I sort of just ... *leave*. Like I'm about to now, forgetting the herd of disgruntled cows who are swinging angled back legs around burgeoning udders towards the bugle yard. I shut my eyes. In breath. Out breath. Slow. When I do this, I feel as if I have access to time, past and present. To a whole universe that leads me forwards and backwards, and up and down and within. I don't feel like me. I don't feel like the Connie Mulligan who everyone mocks, or ignores, or yells at. Instead, shining threads tug my mind away – thoughts hurtling along the silver skein of my daydream. There's no stopping me now. Even the sound of Lilyburn's SAND FM blaring from the dairy radio about their Hump Day Giveaway can't drag me back.

Standing in a creamy-sheened gown, the hem circled with mud, I look up at the knight. He is plated in polished metal armour, towering over me from the back of Traveller, the horse's broad chest draped in chain mail. His hands, gloved in gauntlets, lift the reins to steady Traveller, then he unhitches a scarf from a belt slung around his fauld and offers it to me. The scarf is spiderweb-silver and is perhaps the most beautiful thing I've ever felt drifting through my fingertips.

'Pretty gifts will get you nowhere,' I say, tossing my long dark hair over my shoulder. Something deep inside me swirls – I fear him, but desire for him lifts within me.

But there comes that sensation, like a thistle in my sock. The sudden prick of painful awareness that something is wrong. Very wrong. I'm not certain where I am ... I can feel the silk scarf pressing a hard knot on the nape of my neck. Saliva from my own mouth seeps into its fine fabric as it savagely draws back the sides of my mouth. And here I kneel. Gagged. Silenced. There is a hissing voice behind me. 'Whore,' the voice says, as rough hands grope under my petticoat. 'You witch, you shall burn for making me want you.'

As I blink back into the real world, I become aware the tail-ender cows have begun their slow procession into the forcing yard of the dairy, hassled along now by Nick-nack who has decided to go it solo. I know somewhere in the dark ponds of my mind, the back gate needs to be swung shut and another gate opened so the latecomers can shuffle into their spots behind the rest of the herd, their collars triggering the automatic feeder for their ration, ready to have their cups jammed on.

Dad's yelling voice comes to me like a slap. I startle awake. 'Get a grip you stupid bitch,' I hiss to myself in *that* voice. The critical voice that sounds a bit like my mother, a mocking voice, like Professor Turner. A voice that lands me back to the here and now on Sunnyside Dairy Farm.

A crash above the mindless radio banter jolts through me as Dad slams the gate, causing the cows to startle.

'For fuck's sake, Connie Mulligan, you bloody idiot!' he yells, the embers of his resentment towards me quick to ignite. 'Wake up, Australia!'

'Oh shit, Nick-nack,' I say, noticing the way her tail is jammed up to her guts, her ears flattened with concern. 'What have I done now?'

Chapter 2

Dad's cheeks are crimson. He's standing at his cups-on station, like he does most days, captain of his ship. But a ship run aground. The slow turning platform of the new 1.5-million-dollar rotary is eerily still, mid-milk. Restlessness is spreading in the cows. Some are kicking at cups. Others, out of feed, are drawing back from the constraint of the head bails, flicking back their hocks in frustrated kicks on railings. The ones yet to be milked in the flow-through yard are head-butting each other and jostling about.

'Lights are on but no one is ever bloody home!' Dad shouts, a set of cups dangling in his gloved hands. He indicates a cow along the curve of the milking stations. She has more tail paint on her than party people from a B&S ball and her udder has been sprayed with a giant red X, faded overnight thanks to the damp winter air.

'Oh, her,' I say. 'Yes. I forgot.'

In the background, on Lilyburn's SAND FM, Marjory from Maybrow is screaming, 'Oh my god! Oh my god!'

She's won herself a two-hundred-dollar Woolies gift voucher and free tickets to the latest Samuel L Jackson movie at the new Plaza on the outskirts of Lilyburn, making me wonder how a radio prize can elicit such extreme ecstasy. Doesn't Marjory know most supermarket fruit and veg is nutritionally deficient? And possibly laced with glyphosate and its chemical companions, plus as a Tasmanian quarantine measure, blasted with fumigant methyl bromide against fruit fly? I'd learned that at uni. Suddenly,

Professor Turner invades my mind and I'm slipping back into the past again.

It's my first semester. Turner is perching one buttock on my desk in the library, arms folded, leg swinging, eyes twinkling in amusement. Today's socks are patterned in colourful fish, and his glasses have royal-blue frames. I gaze up at him, knowing my adoring eyes are as melty as a Jersey heifer.

'So you want to specialise in alternative dairy systems for this assignment? Why?'

'Because humans really are stupid,' I said definitively. 'Cows are infinitely smarter.'

'Are you sure about that?'

'Yes. For starters, cows don't put dangerous cumulative poisons on their food … instead, we do it for them.'

'Is that so?' Professor Turner's eyebrow cocked, eyes twinkling like a summer sea. 'I'd like to see you dig out some science to show this, Connie. Otherwise, it's just personal speculation.'

He nudged me, winked, then said, 'We'll make a scientist out of you yet.' He walked away, leaving me short of breath and grappling with the notion that I, the normally invisible Connie Mulligan, was increasingly winning his attention – over all the other first years. Just the day before he'd called me 'exceptionally clever' – my young heart swooning.

'Connie!'

Dad is marching over, his short stocky legs savagely flinging out his heavy PVC dairy apron. I return to the here and now and shrink inside myself.

'I told you to draft her out! You know we jabbed number thirty-seven with a giant antibiotic dose last night! Mastitis! You were there with me! Remember, Connie?'

'Yes. I was. I did. I didn't,' I stammer. Then I frown. Why is this always my fault? I glance over to the forlorn-looking cow. Her hairy bag has been trimmed in a jagged buzz cut. Like poor Five Teats, her cards are stacked against her. Dad not only dislikes uneven teats, he also won't tolerate a bushy udder.

The cow lifts the stub of her docked tail. Manure gushes out like rotten celery soup splattering noisily on the concrete below. Another black mark – Dad hates cows that shit in the pit. The chunky electronic collar that records her milk data clangs on the trough as she hoovers up her ration while Dad seethes. Then I feel my mind slip again.

I'm inside the cow, tumbling in the disrupted universe of her bloodstream and her toxic gut gumbo. Disc-shaped blood cells crash along a crimson Doctor Who tunnel bumping with glowing green antibiotic blob-aliens that are killing everything within sight. Good bacteria lay slain alongside the dark slug-like bacteria that caused her infection. I see the mayhem the man-made drugs and the synthetically fed pastures have created inside her. Her inner war zone.

'Connie!' Dad's voice cuts again into my headspace sharply. I come to. There he is before me, his face heavy with blame.

'Hang on a minute,' I say in a low voice. 'I did forget, yes, but *you* were the one putting the cups on, Dad. Isn't that clever new computer system meant to sound an alarm … or have you forgotten to input her treatment, or enable it properly like you did last week?'

Dad looks set to explode, his fury capped by his shit- splattered terry-towelling hat dragged down over his blockish head. He looks skyward as if something beyond the freshly cobwebbed rafters can help him with a daughter like me.

'You've probably ruined the whole fucking batch! We can't afford a milk quality discount, let alone a milk dump. Not now. Especially with the banks … the loan …' Dad's voice has a frightening lightness to it, like a little boy who's scared.

'Moi?' I reply. Lately, I don't know why, I've defaulted to speaking in faux French when I'm nervous. He takes this as up-myself sarcasm and inches closer, begins shouting. The vibration of his fury reverberates deep within my body.

'You *know* the company's been putting the screws on us! Our cell counts have been too high for too long in the tests. You know we're borderline with them! It's because of you that we're in this mess!'

An image of the quality-control checklist stuck on the back of the old dairy door with browning sticky tape and rusting drawing pins flashes in my mind. Big red X's beside a list of ways antibiotics can get into the bulk milk; dosed fresh calvers, dried off cows, footrot- and pink-eye treated beasts and test bucket overflows. In my mind on that poster, my name, Connie Mulligan, is on the no-no list, also marked with a big red X. Sunlight flickers in the corner of my eye. My mind flickers too. I try to grasp at some of Doctor Cragg's techniques when I have these 'episodes', but, like an out of reach lifebuoy, I feel myself start to sink again.

'Connie!'

I blink from the bite of Dad's voice. Yes, I think to myself, maybe it *is* time for medication.

'Excusez-moi, Papa, really très, très sorry,' I squeak.

He sucks breath in through his teeth. 'Fucking excuse you fucking what?' His volcano energy erupts again, impacting the cows. One kicks angrily, dislodging the suction cups on her teats. Paddy-whack and Nick-nack slink out to hide under the ute.

'What's the bloody point! Get the rest of the cups off,' Dad barks. Once I've scuttled over to yank them from half-milked swollen udders, Dad hits the release button on the head bails.

'Get her out! Tip the milk! Clean the vat! Then we'll bloody well start all over again!' He begins bullying the shocked cows out of the dairy. They slide and swerve out of reach of his anger, bumping each other and calling out, as if the world has gone mad.

I want to say, *Dad, you're overreacting. The milk's contaminated anyway by the tubing, suction cups and plastic bottles, but because you were too tight to spend more on non-phthalate alternatives, why lose your undies over a little bit more contaminant in the milk?*

But I know if I do, I'll get more of the talk ... about my weird 'greenie' ideas. About the debt, about the supermarket contracts, about the inflated costs of inputs, about the newly internationally owned milk company's murmurings that Sunnyside Dairy Farm is too far up the mountain to warrant a pick-up anymore ... then he'll start on his brother and the crap Larry's caused, then land solidly on the subject of my ineptitude and the fact I'm a lowdown liar, bringing shame to the Mulligan name.

Watching the sad creatures go, I want to yell at him, *No wonder they give crook milk!* But my words remain trapped inside me, held captive in a little dark childhood cupboard. The place where I learned it is safest to shut my mouth. To never speak the truth. I don't mean truth in general, because that's a subjective thing that wavers like grass in the wind from person to person. What I mean is, truth with a capital T. *Truth.* But it seems no one around me can see what that is. I spoke the Truth at university, and look how that ended.

I'm blasted with the jolting beats of 'Eye of the Tiger' as SAND FM's local celebrity DJ Dean-O declares, 'Here's a tune to help you over hump day!'

The DJ's deep voice reminds me of the bulls we go to see each year over in Shepparton during International Dairy Week. I wonder if radio shock jocks drink steroids with their morning coffee. Sounds like it. Right now, I wish I had a set of giant balls dangling between my legs so I could challenge Dad's male world domination of this farm and dairy. But I don't. My female shame gathers in me and melts, pooling uselessly and hopelessly on the concrete floor under my gumboots. My gender within this family renders me mute. An inexplicable flood of sadness deep within my being blurs my vision.

'C'est la vie,' I whisper as I jet-blast shit into the drain.

Dad continues clanking angrily around the dairy as the roar of the four-wheeler nears, the engine noise serenading my sense of sinking doom. Patrick is coming.

Outside on the brittle winter grass, my brother swings his long legs off the bike. Striding into the dairy, he is encased from head to toe in waterproofs, looking like a murderous blue Teletubby in big white gumboots. Fresh from moving the electric fences on the river flats, his cheeks are the same shade as Dad's and his red mullet curls up from his beanie like a duck's tail.

'What's the bloody muppet done now?' he asks, sensing the mood.

Dad looks glad Patrick's arrived. It must've been the same on the day of his birth. Six generations spanning back to Irish emancipated convict settlers, a dairy farm passed from eldest son to son to son, until I was born, a girl. How defeated Dad must've been in that moment, standing over the swaddled baby wrapped in impossible pink. Like I was a bad omen. The end of the line ... until twenty months later when Patrick was born. What relief for Dad to see that little male clone of himself – initially as bald as him, until Patrick started to sprout the traditional red Mulligan curls.

With Patrick as his audience now, Dad begins the rant. Not an accurate account of the morning's cock-up, I'd argue, but this isn't the inter-university debate. Each time Dad turns to me, shouting and gesticulating wildly like an inflatable sale-day clown, Patrick pulls faces at me behind Dad's back.

I can feel it coming. That tidal surge swamp, and my vision flares, specked and white. How on earth did I get here, into this family, and what the hell is wrong with me?

Abruptly my legs are propelling me from the milking pit, through the yards, running in a ridiculous galumphing gumboot gait back along the lane. Kookaburras laugh from the dying gum tree by the new effluent pond.

'You'll give yourself a wedgie running like that, you friggin hippo!' Patrick calls at my back.

I'm sobbing as I run. I know what's coming. More silence from Dad. More lectures from Mum. More shit from Patrick. More hour-long sessions with Doctor Cragg, leading me nowhere, except back to that terrible time. The time of Professor Turner.

Chapter 3

Half an hour later, my crying subsided, I apologise to Nick-nack for using her white ruff as a hanky and emerge from behind the woodshed. At the tacked-on back porch door, I find Dad's and Patrick's boots and Paddy-whack lying on the mat licking his balding balls. Nick-nack, with her therapy-dog duties done, wanders away to the silver birch to chew on a calf hock that belonged to one of the many male poddies that Dad donked on the head, deeming it too small to bother with. The men's milking outerwear is hanging in the mudroom, but I'm in too much of a daze to peel mine off. I steel myself before entering.

Inside the kitchen, the wood heater is mumbling to itself in the corner. Patrick, in his CAT socks and camo hoodie, is at the bench devastating a bowl of Corn Flakes. At the head of the table, Dad sits behind the newspaper, the bill folders out with the cheque book and unopened mail ready to deliver the bad news. With no internet this far up the mountain, accounts day is a tiresome, tedious affair that always ends in tears, with Dad storming off to the Rootes-Stewarts next door with a memory stick to use their internet and email our accountant in Burnie. Now though, Mum is wiping the island bench in her pink washing-up gloves, humming tensely and wearing her lavender tracksuit and matching windcheater, makeup on, giant fake drop-pearl earrings dragging down her lobes, her smile fixed.

'Don't come inside in work wear, Connie, darling. How many times ...?'

Ignoring her, I point to Patrick's raised spoon of cereal and say, 'You do know they grind up old cars and put the iron shavings in that shit and call it fortified, just so they can label it "added iron".'

Patrick shovels more into his mouth, his middle finger raised at me, one glowing yellow flake sticking to his bottom lip.

'Well, you would know, Miss I'm So Edu-me-cated university brainbox. Can't even draft out a flamin' cow.'

'Patrick,' Mum cautions. Dad clears his throat and rustles the newspaper pointedly.

'Lucky you did a two-year bogan certificate at TAFE to learn how to grow a mullet and smoke pot,' I counter.

'Connie,' growls Mum.

'Fat lot of good education did you, Miss I'm-Oh-So-Private-School!' Patrick sing-songs.

Mum pauses the perpetual motion of the dishcloth. 'You two, stop!' Her bark causes us both to flinch.

Dad lowers the paper, looking over the top of his two-dollar Shiploads glasses that have a Dame Edna two-tone edge to them.

'Patrick, drop the school thing. You know the milk prices took a dive the year we were going to send you.'

'Good thing they did,' Patrick sneers. 'I wouldn't be caught dead at boarding school with all those snobby shitheads. Look how they turn out.' He waves his spoon at me, his eyes narrowing.

Mum rumbles a growl scarier than a wet cat about to attack. 'Language, Patrick.' Her makeup seems shinier and thicker today. The determined sparkle she normally enforces upon us all is particularly manic. When she turns, I see her perfect domed hair is still pillow-parted at the back. Things must be slipping.

'Well, she's most likely sunk the farm, Mum! Especially after what she did ...'

Dad slams the paper down, looking at us both as if we are offensive strangers and not of his loins.

'Stop!'

It's then that I notice Mum has the Massey Ferguson teapot out. Normally we just use the John Deere pot for weekdays after milking, but for some reason the Massey Ferguson is out. I frown suspiciously. We only ever use that teapot when someone important like the agronomist or milk-audit man comes over, or when somebody dies, like when Grandad and then Granny did. The kettle screams, *A storm is coming*, then switches off abruptly.

Mum clears her throat, setting the cups out. 'Just now, while you were out sulking, we've had a talk. Dad's come up with a suggestion and now's the time to have a family meeting.'

'What about?'

On the wall behind Dad, the round-faced clock with gold Roman numerals set upon a photo of a striking stud Holstein cow, swings its persistent pendulum, ticking like a bomb timer. The clock was presented to my parents just a month before I was born, for winning Tasmanian Dairy Farmer of the Year sponsored by Impetus Fertiliser.

Beneath the oscillating pendulum, a silver-framed photo captures the moment my parents received the garish timepiece trophy. My eyes settle on the image of my heavily pregnant mother, smiling in an oversized bright green dress, the colour of improved pasture top-dressed with nitrogen and glowing after rain. As I stare at the photo, it's fascinating to think I would've been able to hear the clock as I floated inside the warm red otherworld of her womb.

Time, I think dejectedly. It's always time for something in our house. Time to get up. Time to go to bed. Time for milking. Time to catch the little school bus at the end of Mulligan Lane to get to Lilyburn Primary School. Time for me to go to the airport to fly back to boarding school. Or in Patrick's case, time to walk the long steep pinch up the drive to the little shed and wait for the bus to the local high school, taking him out from the shadow side of the valley and an hour along the road to Burnie.

The clock ticks and time moves on. Time for Patrick to go to TAFE to do his Certificate in Dairy Production. Time for me to leave uni right before I ought to have finished my degree because I had monumentally lied to my parents and caused the biggest stink in the history of the Austral University Faculty of Agriculture, and Professor Turner had done what he had done. Then it was time for me to get a job. But because of the uni scandal, no one would touch me ... and so time has ticked on and on. Recently it's been time for me to get a mental health plan. The clock ticks.

Mum pulls out a chair and pats the frilled floral cushion. Apparently, it is now time to sit. I plonk onto the chair. *Tick. Tock.*

'Dad, I'm sorry,' I begin.

He raises his hand to silence me. 'Connie, your mother and I have ... we've ...' He stops, rolling his eyes upwards again, as if the ceiling has answers.

Mum straightens her back, soldiering on, on his behalf.

'Connie, we've decided to sack you,' she says abruptly.

She looks to Dad. Her eyes are panicked, like she's just pulled a trigger and accidentally killed something she only half meant to.

'The sack?' My heart beats in heavy pulses, more insistent now than the clock.

'Yes. It's not ... it's not working out. After all that university business, we find we simply can't ... trust you. And your mind's not on the job. This is not easy for us, but, Connie ... we've decided to let you go.'

Patrick smirks at the milky bottom of his empty cereal bowl where I know a cartoon grinning cow is winking back at him.

'Let me go? But I'm your daughter. How can you *let me go*? How can you give me the sack on a family farm when I was never officially employed here in the first place?'

They look at each other helplessly, mouths opening and closing noiselessly like introduced carp as they try to swim in their muddied family waters. A roar rises to my throat, but it catches there at the gag. All the pain, all the fury, all the rage trapped there in my throat. I swallow it all and I can feel it firing, zinging the cells of my gut, making me want to heave.

I stand, spinning from the room, dragging on my gumboots and propelling myself out across the back porch.

Mum calls after me. 'Don't run away again, darling. Connie? Shall I make another appointment with Doctor Cragg? To help you cope?'

Over the white pebble driveway I run, my heavy plastic outerwear rustling loudly like a body bag, even though I know there's no place to run, because everywhere I go there's me ... me and this toxic world, and *him*. Professor Turner.

Chapter 4

The thing about dairy farming is, apart from the changing moods of the cows set by the weather and their cycles, every day is pretty much the same. Except on days I make monumental stuff-ups ... and get the sack! It's childish to seek refuge on the steps of Granny Mulligan's old cottage as if I'm hiding or sulking but I need to think ... or not to think – I'm not sure which. Mum's words hammer in my head. *The sack. The sack! In my plastic daks!*

There's a savage splinter needling my bum which gets me contemplating the size of it. My bum – not the splinter. It's handy being able to hide my body shape for at least some of the year in men's size waterproofs. That way I get to forget that I have an arse 'the size of the Stanley Nut', as Patrick puts it.

'Glad I can be compared to an interesting geological feature,' I'd joke to him, burying the hurt deep inside me.

At my back, two windows mask empty rooms, old blinds drawn half down, the fringes like sleepy lashes. The cottage faces the plunging valley running all the way to Bass Strait that glistens in the far distance. Sometimes the evening sea mist rolls up the river to kiss the boundary fence on the expansive flood plain in a beautiful horizontal column of cloud we call the Lilyburn Jerry. All the locals know the cloud is likely laced with agrichemicals that have washed from the farmland into the river and on out to the sea, only to be lifted up by evaporation and sailed back in over the land as mist and rain. Deep down we know it could be the link between the sicknesses infiltrating our lives, but no one ever says or does anything about it. They just keep collecting it on their roofs and drinking it, watering their veggies with it and washing their clothes in it. Apparently, the lack of reaction is because of our cognitive dissonance. I learned the term in an additional psychology subject I took on in first year.

Professor Turner finds the chink and enters my mind. In he comes, this time with black arched-back cats on yellow socks. We are in his spacious office going over my Year One, Semester Two submission. To my left, framed degrees and awards take up one wall, and to my right, plinth-sized academic texts form pillars surrounding the temple that houses Professor Turner's gigantic intellectual presence. My chair is pulled up at his desk and he's leaning over me, running his index finger over my citations, so close his tie is brushing my bare arm. The tie is old scholar stripes in magenta and the same yellow as the cats. Groovy deep purple Specsavers perch on the end of his aquiline nose. No man, other than Dad or Patrick, has ever been this close to me. And no man has ever radiated whatever it is Professor Turner is radiating into my space. My heart seems to thump out beyond my chest.

'And how is my little genius going with her sloppy referencing this time round?' he asked. 'You must get this right, girl. Brief author-date citations in brackets in the body of the text and full citations in the reference list. And what's all this about cognitive dissonance in your paper? How is that relevant to your odd choice of topic about Transgenic Crops and Recombinant DNA Technology?'

'How is that relevant?' I echoed, sneaking a glance at him. 'Well, after my psychology component, I'm finding it's relevant everywhere. Take this faculty and the culture of this university for example.' I swept my hand towards the vast window revealing the tops of the gum trees dozing in weak sunshine outside the large ag science laboratory block. 'It's my observation that cognitive dissonance is impacting everyone here and what's taught on the syllabus. Chemical agriculture and industry have humanity on a slippery slope towards Earth's sixth mass extinction when combined with economics-only policies.'

'I beg your pardon?' His voice usually had play in it. Not now.

I cleared my throat, then reached for my folder.

'Look,' I said, removing the newspaper clipping within. 'Front-page news reporting Lilyburn's "chemical cocktail cloud".' I put it under his nobleman's nose. 'The leaders in our local ag sector are denying this. So is the medical board. Local council has gone silent. Of course, it doesn't help that our mayor owns a rural supply business and sells some of the chemicals that the local doctor found in her water testing and patients' blood samples.'

Professor Turner squatted beside me instantly, turning me in my chair so I was forced to look at him square on. His eyes, arctic blue, framed by magenta. The fierceness of him pumped my heart harder.

'But, my bright young thing,' he said tightly, 'are the doctor's studies peer-reviewed? Did you ask that? Was your lady doctor practising and referencing rigorous science? Have you cross-referenced this? Or are you caving in to media speculation and conspiracy theorists and climate-change fanatics who just want to block industry progress? How else do we feed the world without modern chemicals and technology? Mmm?'

His nearness was unsettling, his intensity like a sudden volt of electricity, burning my cheeks. Yet, I couldn't help a hungry rush of desire from between my legs – an unfamiliar, disturbing feeling, but thrilling all the same.

'But ...' I stammered then stopped. Then I said with certainty, 'People can't see what they won't see, and they don't know what they don't know, so how could they know? You know?'

I watched him as he reined in his irritation, snorted in amusement, then swept his flop of black hair back from his eyes. 'Oh, Connie,' he said, 'I thought you were about to shine as a star student by the end of this year. But you've really shown your immaturity in this draft paper. You've taken on a complex area of science that's beyond you.' The disappointment in his tone, a dagger in my heart. He stood abruptly, his crotch perilously near my face, then laid a hand on my shoulder. 'Please don't let me down, Connie. I've got you pinned as my first-year dux.'

I dragged my eyes up to look at him, his gaze creating tingles over my skin.

*

Traveller snorts loudly in his meditative graze, so I'm able to shudder Professor Turner away. I look out to the Lilyburn Jerry, the damp air draping over the exposed skin of my face and hands, feeling like an unwanted touch.

Reaching for my coat pocket, I pull out the spiral-bound notebook – the one I pretend to keep notes about the cows in. Withdrawing the pencil from the wire coil, I flip through my miniature sketches of anything that may have caught my eye: wind-bent trees, a double-petalled flower, the dogs twisting to solve an itch, a cow with a peculiar mid-brow swirl, the unusual shapes of the people I sometimes watch from my car at the Plaza carpark when I lose the nerve to go in.

'That's where you get it from,' Dad said once when he'd caught me sketching when I was meant to be tractoring silage to the cattle. 'Bonkers, like your Uncle Larry. He fancied himself an artist once too.'

I gaze now across the river to where Uncle Larry has holed himself up for the past twenty-five years in an old apple-pickers cottage, locked in his bitter feud with Dad. I find a blank page and begin outlining the familiar curves of the valley that wrap around Uncle Larry's place and the giant old apple-storage shed that adjoins it. Despite the massive size of the vintage shed, it's dwarfed by the vast, lumping mountain range that sweeps towards Tasmania's western wilderness. Thinking of Larry makes me think of the long-gone GP, Doctor June Amel, who used to drive up the sunny side of the valley to check on him. Mum and Dad hated her for it.

Doctor Amel's cool grace and calmness comes to me now.

We are in her consultation room, her slender dark hands delivering such care as the pads of her fingers press gently upon the tender glands in my throat, a frown between her elegant black eyebrows.

'There's some mysterious illnesses arriving,' Doctor Amel said to Mum. 'Ones I can't pinpoint. Certainly in the case of your daughter.'

Mum rolled her eyes and looked away to the chart of the human skeleton as she mumbled, 'So you've been saying.'

'I'd suggest a water filter in your home, and feeding her organic unprocessed foods, along with lots of rest,' Doctor Amel said. 'And keep her indoors if your husband is spraying on the farm.'

'Rest,' Mum said bitterly. 'I wouldn't know what that was if it fell on me. Oh well. At least Connie will get to rest.'

When the article was published in the local paper about Doctor Amel, Dad had slammed it down, causing his Vegemite toast to leap.

'Says here her Lilyburnian patients were presenting with –' Dad squinted to read from the article '– a "greater incidence of skin rashes, unexplained malaise and, increasingly, certain types of rare cancer and Parkinson's disease compared to the national average". What a load of rot! Cancer's on the rise everywhere. Told you she was a hysterical woman and a hopeless quack. She was never able to fix Connie.'

'Nothing could fix Connie,' Patrick added.

After the media storm the article prompted, Doctor Amel closed her clinic and returned to the mainland. The newspapers cited 'rural funding cuts to outlying GPs, and consolidation of services' apparently. Regardless of the reason, she's now three years gone and there's a brand spanking new medical centre up at the Plaza that streams people into pallid-looking doctors every fifteen minutes and out the other door with scripts, in a system as detached as a commercial chicken hatchery that gases baby boy chicks.

I tap the pencil on my bottom lip. Despite Doctor Amel's alleged agri-toxins, I still think the cloud's beautiful as it haunts its way up the valley. This morning, it's so crisp the cloud is almost cartoon-like, puffing perfectly against the purity of the ultramarine sky above a land of white frost. Smoke trails sleepily up from farmhouses dotting the whitened view below. I mimic them on the page.

Once the frost has melted, I know the valley's vast green hillsides will glisten and glow, curving like big bosoms, cleavaging down into a deep river and then upwards again, rising to the wild jagged mountains that drape shadows over the farmhouses and sheds. Tourists say it's beautiful, but since university and my self-directed study, I only see the biodiversity decline, the over-grazing and the erosion.

'You don't know what you don't know, about what you don't know,' I say out loud to no one.

The mountains above Uncle Larry's are blushing pastel purple like a bruise and I wish my grey lead pencil offered more options. In an instant, the rising sun blasts the face of Uncle Larry's cottage, the windows and the clerestory panes of the apple shed light with gold, and yet where I'm sitting here, at Granny Mulligan's cottage, remains deep in shadow. If my forebears faced the cottage the other way, the lifting sun could soothe the skin on my face and defrost my clawed, clutching hands. But they didn't think of that, did they? On this side of the valley, the sun's gentle warmth is short-lived. Soon it will slide behind the high, gum-treed hill and fail altogether to reach our house and parts of the gushing, dark, late-winter river below.

'Sunnyside Farm is a joke,' I say to Traveller who is ambling over drifts of daffodils the colour of free-range egg yolks, to rub his face on what is left of the formerly white picket fence that is now flaking grey. The early spring bulbs hint that this was once a proud Granny Mulligan garden. And those of the Mulligan women before her, from three generations ago, who had moved from a wattle and daub hut on the other side of the valley beside the river.

'Do you think Larry and I have inherited our bonkers-ness from long-dead great-great-great-Granny Mary Mulligan?' I ask Traveller. He turns to nuzzle an itch on his flank.

'Was she as unhinged as me when the men moved her from the sunshine side of the valley into the shadows, I wonder?'

Three crows wing past, air pulsating audibly through their feathers.

I'm sure I remember the Mulligan women's pain. They say it takes three generations to forget, but I'm certain the cells of my body still vibrate with their lives in cold shadows with nothing but cows, snakes, dark crows, and cold, blue-lipped babies. The mud and indifference from the men. Men who were busy with their single furrow ploughs, their poison and the swing of their axes ringbarking the majestic riverside gums, pushing on, even when increasing numbers of rabbits gnawed at their endeavours and snow blanketed and burned their crops.

I turn to the closed cottage door. The paint peeling, sun faded now to the gentle blue of starlings' eggs. I long for my Granny Mary Mulligan. She died when I was young, and I still miss her. My heart feels as if it has shrunk to the size of a walnut and is lodged now in my throat. Her once large food and flower garden, home to hundreds of birds and insects, is now fenced into a one-acre square by bland hinge joint wire and regimented treated-pine posts. Traveller is the lone caretaker of what's left of the space, sharing it with just one gum that is slowly dying of solitude.

Granny was not long dead when Dad bulldozed her diverse fruit tree orchard into heaps, muddling the branches with those of the old pine hedge which he toppled too, just so he could make room for his new concrete pad and effluent pond for the Starship Enterprise of all dairies. I had watched him on that day, taking on the hedge like it was the Great Wall that had kept him too long from enjoying the spoils of Grandad's dairy empire. The funeral pyre of my dead grandparents' garden is still there, now home to rooting rabbits as it slumps, waiting for Dad's match.

As Traveller rubs his face on one of the old picket fence posts, the rotted wood snaps. He startles slightly, then exhales, and wanders to the cottage weatherboards to use instead as a scratching post.

I shove my notebook away, unfold my cold limbs and go to him. 'Got the itches, mate?' He vibrates his nostrils as I rummage my fingers on his warm neck under his mane. As I do, the soft golden morning hue on the land fades and the shadows gather.

I seem to have caught Traveller's itch, so I pull my shit-splattered 'I Love Cows' cap from my head. Cold air bites my scalp and presses bitterly on the nape of my neck. Mum has cut my hair too short again.

Thanks to Mum, I've never been to the hairdressers. But not her. Every month she heads off to Roxanne's Hair She Comes in Lilyburn for a neat blow-wave and bronze dye job, hair-sprayed into the immobile shape of a World War II shelling helmet. Hair that never messes itself up, no matter what the wind or life is doing on the day. She pays for her hair by making her own 'just for her' money at the monthly market at the Lilyburn Hall, selling cakes, biscuits, quiches or her perfectly pressed clothing cast-offs and her special order footy club knitted items – that is, when Dad gives her a leave pass to go.

She'll be inside the house now, her forever moving hands dusting, picking up, straightening, plumping, scrubbing and wiping. She'll be extra tense because she's not only sacked her daughter, but also because it's 'accounts day'. The end of the month, when Dad writes her a cheque for the 'housekeeping' once all the bills have been met. It's the day when Dad's monologue about Mum's spending and my education fees, then the legal bills, rolls on like a runaway train picking up speed and adding more carriages of complaint. Prices going up and up. Milk payments going down. The supermarket squeeze.

A choking sensation comes again. Was my mistake this morning the last straw for Dad? Am *I* the last straw?

27

'Shit,' I say, closing my eyes, and fingering a crusted bit of cow manure in my hacked hair. My body starts shivering.

I'm lying in a bog of icy mud and manure beside a cow barn, whimpering. Air swirls on the crown of my shaved head, my scalp and neck, naked and exposed. From where I lie, I can see the high round grey-dappled rump of Traveller and his thick cascading tail. I go to call after him, but he is moving away, across a fog-covered moor, weaving through drab heather. The knight upon him has his broad-shouldered iron-clad back to me. His armour no longer shining but looking dull like the plated hide of a rhino.

There's a gag in my mouth and a river of blood coming from a wound between my ribs, staining the deep green cloth of my heavy woollen dress deeper still. I try to cry out again, but the gag silences me. I feel myself falling into death. Out of the blue there's a hand on my neck, fingers pressing gently but firmly on the side of my throat, then freeing the gag. I open my eyes long enough to see a Claddagh ring on the little finger of a man's hand. The ring is crafted as tiny golden hands cupping a heart, and upon the heart, a crown. My eyes scrunch shut. The Claddagh. Friendship, love and loyalty.

When my eyes flash open, I'm still here amid the daffodils at Granny Mulligan's cottage, Traveller has wandered off to graze. I've learned not to get so frightened when these visions come, but sometimes they are so real they set my heart racing, my palms sweating, my body searing with pain. They make no sense. But as I look down the boggy lane to the house, I realise that life here makes no sense either. If only I could just get my head together.

At the fence I reach out to touch the electrified wire. All three thousand volts jolt in one angry kick as my arm flies upwards. A guttural cry escapes my throat. *She's mad our Connie,* I hear my mother's sneer. Shock therapy. That might help.

Tears gather like weepy mountain clouds. When I reach this point, I know there's only one thing that will soothe me.

Chapter 5

My vision blurred by tears, it's as if I'm reaching through Vaseline as I grab Traveller's rope halter from the gate post. Dragging the noseband over his whiskered muzzle and fixing the knot under his beard as makeshift reins, I lead him to the cottage steps and clamber noisily onto his bare back in my wet weather gear. *The sack, the sack, in my plastic daks*, loops on repeat in my head.

Traveller adjusts his old bones under my weight – considerably heavier since 'the Turner days'. Through the narrow cottage gate we go, Nick-nack following, plunging down the zigzag dairy lane, battling the slurry, his feathered hocks sinking into green-black sludge. Shame and regret sit with me, like impossibly burdensome saddlebags. Placing my palm on his bowed neck, seeking my grey touchstone of calm, I try to reach beyond my impossible situation.

Silently crying, we set off across Dad's 'renovated' pastures. The rich scent of fermentation fills my nostrils as we pass the silage, spread for the returning cows in unappetising rows. On the river flats, the modern cultivar pasture that promised rich rewards in a catalogue looks anything but tasty now, like the advertised version of a pristine Big Mac.

As we trundle over Dad's expensive green desert I notice bare patches of hard-capped soil where the residue chemicals and fertilisers have pooled. There's a yellow tinge of ill health in the plants that are struggling to grow there. In my research at uni, I learned that weeds aren't weeds – that's just what humans call them. Mother Nature knows which plants to recruit to heal the sickened system. I tried to tell Dad things I've learned like that, but he just looked at me as if I'm bonkers.

Nick-nack scouts ahead, investigating an algae-smeared shallow drain with pin rushes offering scant cover for a lonely bush chook, who takes off like a ground missile. Nick-nack flops to the ground and green-stripes her white ruff with native hen shit.

'Nice one, Nack,' I say, envious of her dog's life where joy can be found rolling in stink. I nudge Traveller onwards over what was once Grandad's river meadows, where proud ancient swamp gums used to shade native pastures beside wetlands. They've all been dozed away now, but I remember the thick stands of flowering tea tree that brought birds and bees to the cool of the clear meandering mountain river.

The old chain of ponds, once a secondary tributary to the river, would flush during winter and lay cool and inviting during summer. But now they have been bullied by Dad's expensive machines into a single efficient deep gouge, and shallow straight-line drains crisscross the flats. The once majestic old blue gums with cartwheeling petticoat flowers are felled and lie in heaps on the edge of the rise. The flattened ploughable paddock is now ready for two more giant centre pivots. Dad and Patrick couldn't be more excited by it. The bank also, given the interest they'll charge on the loan.

Patrick and Dad think this tidy straight-fence farm is modern productivity playing out. But they are deceived. I remember standing beside Dad and the agronomist, Dad nodding, arms folded across his body as the young man gave his recommendations. Me squinting against the sun, hat pulled down hoping the agronomist didn't recognise me from the nightly news clips of me rushing down the Hobart courthouse steps amid a media scrum. Case dismissed.

'That's insanely expensive,' I blurted.

The agronomist cleared his throat.

'Connie,' Dad warned.

'But Dad, why dump nitrogen on the pastures when only three per cent is actually used by the plants? The rest of it ends up in the river! No wonder Lilyburn's babies are being born with fish lips and munted hands and feet.'

Dad casted me a cold look, but I hadn't been able to stop my mouth running away. Turning to the young agronomist, I said, 'Have you seen the science on it? The more nitrogen you put on synthetically, the more the plants have to chew up carbon, taking the organic matter out of the soil.'

'Connie!' barked Dad. 'Haven't you got work in the calf shed to do?'

Now, as I glance behind me to the sharp lift of the riverbank that tiers up to our ugly misplaced 80s era orange-brick house, I know my family won't be following me to offer comfort. They never do. I feel so utterly abandoned, a panic tightens in my chest and I feel myself slip.

The winter sun is swallowed by the mountains, and the shadows come. The stench of rotting, burning human flesh invades my senses. Around me, the groan of men, some with severed limbs, weakly pulsing blood onto savaged battlefield mud flats. Bloodied swords, once shining silver with the polish of men's egos, now lie impotent on the ground. I pick my way through the fug and smoke of burning upturned wagons, dead horses and bodies. I know we must get on and away before night. Struggling, heaving my foot up from the mud, I urge Traveller to follow. I try to speak kind words to encourage him on, but the only sound that comes is a guttural noise from the back of my throat. With a jolt I remember my tongue has been cut away. Warm tears fall over my freezing cheeks as I press my hand to the curved grey warmth of Traveller's neck, praying for help. Even if that help is death for us, freeing us from this living hell that my fellow man has created all around me and where women who speak their minds are not welcome.

Wailing calls of black cockatoos bring me back. I look skywards to see five of them flying low and close, lilting their call of *wee lah, wee lah*! Their beaded black eyes on me, tails spread beautifully revealing the underside paintbrush strip of modest yellow. These meadows used to drift with clouds of tiny moths and other insects, bursting upwards with every step, birds swooping in front of me, diving for a feast from an abundant, magical, biodiverse banquet. Now, Mother Nature's been captured and marched into Dad's imprisoning system of iridescent, overgrazed rye grass and white clover.

At the broken bridge we turn upstream from the bastardised river flats onto the old track, entering the bushland. A cathedral canopy of ash, stringy bark and peppermint gums domes over us. Traveller's steps soften, weaving between poas, tussocks and gentle ferns as beside us, the river sings. A wavering track leads us to my secluded horseshoe bend – a remnant of the farm that has escaped Dad's machines.

Last summer, after the university storm, I'd rediscovered this place, setting Traveller loose to graze on the sweetest of grasses. I'd pressed my belly and breasts to the warm river sand. Nearby, burbling water caressed rocks the colour of tiger's eye agate, smoothing to deeper ponds that held the secret of native fish and tadpoles amid wavering water plants.

It was Granny M who had shown me this place, ages ago, and said, 'It's a place away from the men.' She tapped her nose with her index finger and insisted I take off my boots and socks to stand in the icy mountain waters.

'But Mum will …'

'Shh!' She squeezed my hand, then lifted her round face upwards, shutting her eyes. 'If you listen to the river's music, a great mystery in your heart will be eased and your troubles washed away.'

I stood in the idyllic stream with birdlife harmonising above Granny and me, wondering if she was telling the truth.

My fresh uni humiliations were still within reach when I rediscovered Granny M's spot. In the wooden dock of the hushed courthouse, Turner's team of lawyers had torn me apart like

Tassie devils ripping into a carcass. And so, last summer I had stood in this magical river, ushering in Granny's words, but I'd found no solid ground or relief.

Today 'our beach' is cold and darkened by the winter chill and Granny M is gone. For a moment I wish I hadn't come here. Traveller is ripping up fresh pick, snorting as he settles to graze. I lie upon his old bones, his power and warmth rises through my body. Nick-nack settles on the grass where the sun lands strongest, her paws crossed, narrowing her eyes in a doze. Closing my eyes too, inhaling Traveller's scent, the cold air chills my back. I wish the river sound could rinse me clean with its sparkling gold and silver music. But instead I'm left with the blackness and the bleakness of my mind. Sacked. Sucked. Fucked.

'C'mon buddy,' I say bleakly to Traveller. 'Home.'

We pass the near-forgotten Forestry road that heads off on the other side of the river from the half-washed out rickety wooden bridge, slanting sideways like a shipwreck. It used to be the way to Uncle Larry's old pickers cottage but a flood, plus years of damp shadow have rotted it to an irreparable state, much like Larry and Dad's relationship.

'He should build a bridge and just get over it,' Patrick used to jibe when we passed the bridge, and Dad would chuckle bitterly and continue on with the family narrative.

'Round here it's not a good idea to be as "happy as Larry",' Dad would mumble. 'Miserable prick.'

Not wanting to linger at the base of the hill where my crazy uncle lives, I leg my horse but he suddenly baulks.

'What is it?'

He's glued to the spot, head high, ears pricked, nervously snorting.

'What's up your bum, mate?' I ask.

Nick-nack also sniffs at something on the breeze and takes it upon herself to wade over the rocks, across the fast-moving but shallow river. I whistle her back, but she pretends she can't hear me over the river's ruckus.

Traveller and I scrabble through the shallows after her, the noisy water masking all other sounds. Heaving up the grassy riverbank, I squint at something in the clearing beside a fallen tree. A bright orange something? Keeping my leg on him, Traveller approaches crablike with caution. The orange shape becomes a chainsaw, left beside scatterings of cut logs. Wood-hookers I suspect. I look about, thinking they may have seen me and scampered.

Illegal wood-getting is rife in the upper reaches of the state forests. It's one of Dad and Patrick's favourite role-plays – that of bounty hunters and boundary riders, keeping the wood thieves off the place. I'm about to turn my horse to leave when I notice something behind the base of the fallen skeletal grey trunk. I swallow down dread when I see what's on the ground. The body of a man. Clad in an old oilskin coat, lying face down. Felled like a tree. And deathly still.

Chapter 6

I've always dreaded finding a body, but here I am. They say what you think about, you bring about. After jumping from Traveller's back, I rush to the man with wild white-grey hair, his tatty Akubra lying beside him.

'Uncle Larry?'

Crouching beside him I gingerly touch his pallid cheek. Cold but not dead-cold.

'Uncle Larry?'

When there's no response, I look wildly up the steep hill towards his cottage, then back to our farm.

'Fuck a duck,' I say, realising that if I get Dad for help, he's likely to finish Larry off with a block splitter himself. A memory flashes of Granny M's funeral outside the church. The sudden scuffle when Dad realised Larry had shown up. The badly swung punches and shouts. My mum twisting a handkerchief in her fists, crying and begging them to stop for fear of losing face in front of the church ladies.

'C'mon, Uncle Larry.' I shake him slightly by his shoulders, then more roughly. 'Larry!'

Nick-nack leans in to sniff at him. It smells as if he's pissed himself, or maybe he smells like that all the time?

'Get out of it,' I say to Nack sternly. 'Not helpful.'

Hesitating for a beat, I begin to gently slap Larry's face.

'Uncle Larry? Larry?'

Eventually, his pale lips part, stretching strings of spittle between. He murmurs something unintelligible.

'You stay here,' I say superfluously, and then roll my eyes at myself. 'I'll go get help.'

His eyes flash open. Dark brown pupils made eerie with yellowness in the whites of his eyes, rivered with burst blood vessels. Teamed with his feral grey eyebrows, thick frosted stubble and manic hair, he seems more horror movie werewolf than man.

'No!' his voice rasps.

'I have to go get help. I'll go get Dad.'

'Over my dead body,' he mutters, trying to push himself up, but flopping down again.

Through the treed canopy, the blue sky swims above me. What to do? When I look at him again, I feel a simmer within. It's hard to pinpoint what the feeling is, but as I let it rise, I realise it's anger. Fury. He and Dad have been at it all my life. A couple of blokes who can't sort themselves out. Pathetic.

'Oh, nice. Over your dead body,' I say, folding my arms. '*I'm* the one over your dead body. At least I thought you were a dead body when I first saw you. Do you realise what it's like to stand over a dead body? Do you? Huh? It's not nice. So, you better bloody well live. Otherwise, you'll send me even more over the edge than I already am. So, get over yourself and get up!'

Eyes closing, he lets out a hefty exhale, and for a moment I think, fuck, I've killed him with my Mulligan-man-hating bile that I've learned from Mum. But then I realise he's just resting and must feel really crook.

'Well,' I say a little more gently, 'it wasn't nice thinking you were a dead body. So, I don't want you to die. I'll admit it's purely out of a selfish place, but I'm not dealing with a dead estranged uncle today. I will seriously lose my shit. Even more than I've already lost my shit. Okay?'

He doesn't answer. But he does open his eyes to take me in more fully.

'Okay?' I repeat with a firmness to my voice I haven't heard for a long time, if ever.

'Ooot,' he grunts.

I frown. 'What?'

'Ooot.' He lifts a curled finger and points up towards his cottage.

'Oh! Ute! You want me to get your ute!'

'Eeeeessss,' he wheezes.

'Okay. I'll be back.'

Stepping onto a decapitated log I swing onboard Traveller, urging him up the steep zigzagging track, pants rustling like plastic shopping bags. Nick-nack falls in behind. Rounding a steep sharp bend that curves around a majestic white-trunked gum we find ourselves in the prettiest native meadow. The open natural terrace is the first of a series of paddocked steps that rise up one after another towards the steeper slopes of the bush-slathered mountain.

At the meadow's centre is the hand-split timber cottage with its two windows either side of a squat faded blue door. The same colour as Granny M's. It's the cottage I've stared at since I was young, absorbing the family folklore of two bitter brothers with a river between them and a broken bridge.

I take in the tall vertical-board shed that adjoins the cottage. According to Dad, it once buzzed with busy apple-packing teams in the 60s when orcharding added to the Mulligans' farming income. That was before England joined the EU and stopped buying our apples overnight. Trees pulled, lives destroyed and Mulligan men made more surly.

Getting off Traveller, I set off around the buildings and soon find the ute parked in a lean-to on the southern side of the cottage. The old Hilux, once white, is now a bit like Larry's eyes, off yellow.

'Hop up on the back,' I say to Nick-nack, reefing open the door. She leaps onto the tray as if she's a movie dog on an important rescue mission. I pull the bale twine loop that serves as an interior door handle, and climb into the cabin, which looks like a naturalists' museum gone wrong. There's all kinds of paraphernalia on the dash – skeletons of dead birds, the dehydrated head of a blue tongue lizard, a possum skull, the curling horn of a Merino ram, hawk feathers bound by leather hanging from the rear-vision mirror. An unconscious shudder shivers my shoulders. Dad had always warned us off Larry, saying he'd likely slit our throats if he caught us on his side.

Reversing out, with Nick-nack not knowing she could be in grave danger and still excitedly wagging her tail, I set off down the steep bush track, leaving Traveller to graze, spellbound by the fresh mountainside grasses. I wish I could share my animals' exuberance about the situation, as I bounce the ute down the impossibly steep track towards where my batshit crazy uncle lies.

*

It takes all my strength, a massive groan of effort and a small involuntary fart to get Uncle Larry into the ute's passenger seat. There he lists like a ship, undecided as to which way to roll sideways and sink. Thankfully he sways towards the passenger door, which I'm grateful for as we jolt up the track. Up close, he really does stink. Pulling up outside the cottage front steps, Traveller looks alarmed as Larry and I topple out of the ute, hulking ourselves like a four-legged human beast up the front steps and in through the door that moans loudly as it swings wide for us.

Larry indicates a room on the left. We swerve and sway into a bedroom, made cosy with old floral wallpaper from a long-ago era. Spinning, as if in a mad barn dance, with our backs to the bed, Larry lets go, falling onto the mattress with a groan. I haul off his boots, trying not to inhale the urine that has seeped onto the front of his pants.

'Let's get your coat off you. Get you more comfortable.'

It takes some time to get him settled, and I'm even brave enough to peel away sodden trousers from his lean, yet muscled, pale legs, looking away from his private bits, telling myself nurses do this sort of shit every day. After I've layered him with blankets and tugged thick dry socks onto his feet, he's now shaking uncontrollably. Rubbing his shoulder vigorously, I say. 'Hang in there. You'll warm up soon.'

Gathering his clothes, I go in search of the laundry. And a hot water bottle, perhaps? Maybe some food or something? The kitchen at the end of the hall is a cute add-on within an old veranda, neat and tidy with everything in order. Cups on hooks, draining board empty, sink wiped down and tea towel folded primly at the wood stove. The view up the mountainside from behind the old lace cafe curtains is breathtaking. But I must not get distracted. The laundry is just off from the kitchen, so I drop his clothes into the concrete sink to deal with later.

Hunting through the creaking wooden cupboards for some food, all I find is crockery, a heap of dried herbs and a tin of peas. There's nothing but some old cheese in the fridge, a few apples and a bottle of some homemade tomato sauce – the breadbin empty. No wonder I could feel his ribs under his oilskin when I heaved him inside. Instead, I boil the kettle and make some sugared tea. The canisters are lined up on a shelf above the kettle: Blue Wren for Sugar, Magpie for Tea, Wattlebird for Coffee. Nice.

Returning with a tray, I prop him up, helping him drink. Next, I get to work lighting the small open fire in his room. There's plenty of dry bark stored neatly beside the hearth in an old tea chest, so it takes only a moment for the fire to crackle to life, the perfume of eucalyptus fizzing a release with each lick of the flame. As I set the matches back onto the mantel, I look up to see a portrait of a woman painted in thick oils of sumptuous plum and rich royal blue tones. The background is dark, so her face is almost luminescent. It's beautiful. She's beautiful, with her ski-slope nose, deep rich reddish-brown hair curling to her bare shoulders and lips as pretty as a pink rose petal. She's draped in a thick green cloak, yet one shoulder is seductively exposed. Her expression is strong, yet sad. Giant hazel eyes stare out. I'm not sure if she's wanting to come or go in the painting.

Looking around, there are other miniature portraits on the walls. Sketches too. All in an assortment of old frames, all by what looks like the same artist. All of the same sad, beautiful young woman.

Larry hacks up a cough, dragging my attention away from the artwork, but the question lingers – *Who is she?* As Larry's face turns bright red, I scamper to his bedside.

'Let me know how I can help.'

Again, his clawed bushman's hands point to a dresser. I catch my image in its mirror. Me, still in my dairy-pit gear, hair jagged like a prisoner of war mostly hidden by my dirty cap, my cheeks pink with stress. Next to me, the man I've only known as 'mad old Uncle Larry' is looking frighteningly similar to me. The madman who my family have taught me to fear.

'Shripts,' he rasps.

'Shrimps?'

He rolls his eyes, coughs again and gestures more vigorously towards the dresser. 'Shripts!'

On opening the dresser drawer, I find an envelope addressed to L M Mulligan. Inside is a series of prescriptions and a handwritten note.

Dear Larry

I hope you are feeling better. Please find enclosed your scripts with six months' worth of repeats. I shall expect a letter from you reporting on your full recovery. Also, do find some help. One thing I've discovered – forgiveness, of both ourselves and others, is often the only thing holding us back from a healthful life. People can die from broken hearts you know. You can heal yours.

Please write back. Please let me know how you are going. I miss your wise counsel and care.

Yours sincerely, and with love,

June Amel

Doctor Amel? My mind fires. Uncle Larry, seeing me holding the scripts bobs his head.

'You need me to get these?'

'Esss,' he wheezes.

'I'll be back,' I say, setting a larger log onto the fire and putting the guard in place. 'I'll be as quick as I can.'

Before I close the door, I add, 'Oh. And please don't become a dead body while I'm gone. Hang in there, will you? Please? For me.'

Chapter 7

Wipers screech, shuddering maniacally back and forth, as I try to clear grime and tenacious frost crystals from the windscreen. Beside me Uncle Larry's scripts sit like a guilty secret. I'm grateful no one was about when I put Traveller back in his paddock and dived for my car, nicknamed Poo Brown.

Driving out, I peer through a clear patch on the windscreen to see a sharp bend veering towards me. Fishtailing on corrugation, the landscape blurs beside me, the road's gravelled edges crumbled like brown sugar and ice as the tyres slide. Dropping Poo Brown back into second, before glancing in the mirror, I swing onto the sealed road to Lilyburn.

I don't give a shit that I'm driving too fast. If the balding tyres slip and I careen through the fence, down over the steep eroding paddocks and into the blackberry-filled gully, tough titties. It would be doing my family a favour. A ragged spurt of bitter laughter erupts from me.

They've sacked me! What the fuck now? *Stupid, stupid bitch, Connie.* That same voice in my head. It's best for the world if I die. My family don't want me. No one does. But then I remember Uncle Larry. If I die, he might die. If he dies, then Dad wins whatever the fucked-up game is that he's been playing with his brother. I don't want Dad to win. Like I didn't want Professor Turner to win. But those men always do.

42

To distract myself from the march of my miserable thoughts I turn up the volume on the tinny car radio.

Dean-O climaxes in an Elvis song, back-announcing with a terrible impersonation. 'Thank *youuuu*. Thank you very mush. Wish somebody would love *me* tender ... Hope you've had a *goooooood* morning, *Lillybuuuuuuurrrrrrn*, doing it with me, DJ Dean-O! It's news time and I'm outta here. See y'all tomorrow!'

He sounds as lonely as me. Changing up gears on the short downhill straight, I realise that I'm still head-to-toe in my outerwear, which I'll have to strip off in Poo Brown's tiny interior, wiggling out of it like a maggot, before I go into Mr Crompton's pharmacy. With horror I think I may have left my wallet at home, but I reach under my seat and there it is. One of Mum's cast-offs. Fake snakeskin in a hideous hot pink and tan.

'Waste not want not,' she said after she gave it to me. 'I've saved enough to get myself a new one. Not that I've ever got much to put in it.'

'Thanks for the vinyl, Lionel,' I said sarcastically, but Mum didn't smile. She never gets my bitter jokes. I'm sure they threw her sense of humour into the hospital incinerator with my placenta the day I was born. I remember now inside the wallet is my own script, compliments of Doctor Cragg. I hope I've got enough money for both our prescriptions. Worry clutches in me that I won't. I'm desperate for an iced coffee, a chicken curry pie and a lamington from the bakery. If I raid the parking metre money in the ashtray, I know there'll be enough for a few dimmies, a wing-ding or two and a couple of Rotary fundraiser mini Snickers from Greasy Joe's at least. Then I remember I ought to buy Larry food too.

Thinking of his bare cupboards, I conclude those Mulligan men must all be tight arses. Dad's always finding ways out of paying me – bartering with me for fuel from the farm bowser, then my board and keep, saying I 'owe' him for the legals so he's taking that out of my pay to cover my 'outstanding loan'.

I roll my eyes, passing Waterbright Dairy, home of the Lilyburn royals – the Rootes-Stewarts. Their new gold letterbox stands out like dogs' balls next to an ageing bus shelter they put up for their daughter, Nikki. The family name is garishly swirled upon the letterbox in regal purple, sending the message they think they're a cut above the rest. I raise my middle finger at it. The almost new, two-million-dollar roadside dairy is empty, milk in the vat awaiting the tanker, cows out on pasture neat enough for the Lilyburn Lawn Bowls Club. Perfection. Typical of them.

David Rootes-Stewart gives Dad a run for his money on all things dairy. They try to outdo each other all the time, from the tidiness of their fences and pastures to the stats on their Balanced Performance Index and top-priced semen straws during each round of artificial insemination, even to how spruced up they can appear on Tas Irrigator meeting nights, even though they are as bald as each other and both spout more bullshit than a busted sewerage main. In Mum's opinion, David wins hands down in neatness and efficiency, saying it's the Dutch blood in him. Dad just says he's full of stinking hot air like a Dutch oven under a doona.

While David Rootes-Stewart is Dad's rival, his wife, Raylene, is Mum's bestie, but in that weird competitive way that some women have. Their monthly book club meetings end with them firing more bitchy bullets at each other than a Gallipoli sniper fending off the Turks. On Saturday mornings, when it's not a market weekend, to keep themselves trim, Mum and Raylene walk down by the beach in sandshoes whiter than the sand. They never go *on* the beach. Far too messy. Instead, they walk the brand-new strip of concrete the council laid unimaginatively beside the defunct railway line, tut-tutting the dog owners who don't pick up after their dogs. Tut-tutting the things not done in their gardens or houses. Tut-tutting what their husbands did or didn't do, and in Mum's case, tut-tutting 'what Connie has done/hasn't done now!', but never tut-tutting themselves, or Raylene's perfect daughter.

I feel my jaw clench at the thought of Nikki. Mum constantly reports what she's up to in her job with the Rootes-Stewarts' international dairy-semen company, Global Genetics, or mentioning the holidays that Nikki's perfect Ken Doll–style husband, Tobias, is planning for her. Nikki imported Tobias from the mainland with a genetic freshness that can't be found here in Lilyburn. Now Mum won't shut up about the fact they have their first baby on the way.

'It will be physically enhanced, no doubt, thanks to the father's outsourced genetic input,' I'd joked, but neither Mum nor Dad found that funny. Like most things I say.

Rounding the big 35 kph bend, I slow. Like a celestial being, Bass Strait blares into view in all her sparkling, spreading, dancing glory and shunts Mum and Nikki from my mind. It's a shame the view's magnificence is ruined by the depressing sight of the Lilyburn outskirts, with its old iron-ore mine chimney stacks and underwhelming cluster of same-same grey-brick housing that sprung up when the mine was alive in the 70s. My stomach rumbles. Relief is near. I know soon I can eat my way to a soothing place like I do when I get like this.

When I arrive, the main street is chockers with seagulls and not much else. Since they shut the school and built the new Plaza out on the double lane bypass closer to Ulverstone, Lilyburn's virtually a ghost town. I splutter Poo Brown past the now dilapidated elegant buildings from a bygone era. The beauty of the old tiled butchery glints in the sun beside the now closed haberdashery store with the leadlight windows. It stayed open for a time for the oldies who couldn't adjust to internet shopping or the mainland clothing chain stores that have invaded Tassie like a virus.

I drive past Hair She Comes. Currently closed. Roxanne only opens when her clients need her nowadays ... old customers like my mum who refuse to do Plaza Juzt Cutz. 'Hair She Infrequently Comes,' I'd joked to Mum to prompt a smile, but the smile never came.

The only main-drag shops that seem to be thriving are Dawn and Dick's Real Estate Agency, next to Greasy Joe's, and at the far end of the street just before the bypass, the Ever Peaceful Funeral Home. It used to be Cooper's Garage, but now it's busy with human bodies not car bodies, thanks to whatever Doctor Amel was cottoning on to.

I reckon our current real estate boom is also thanks to the corporate-funded investment company and overseas farm buy-ups that the government are allowing. And since a few wanky foodie shows have been on the telly, we've had a rise in unfulfilled mainlanders coming here seeking their 'tree and sea changes', leading to more cul-de-sacs and concrete paths and less trees.

I park outside Mr Crompton's Pharmacy with the elegant sandstone shopfront framing timber-paned windows. The sparkle of the frosty morning is gone and now even Bass Strait is matching my mood – the sea grey, broody and bitter as she roughly swells against the giant boulders on the foreshore at the end of the shopping strip. Kelp gulls call a sobbing yelp as they sail, black wings outstretched, coasting on the updraft of bombora waves that pound the rock embankment on the point. It's coming in so rough I opt to leave my waterproofs on.

Shoving the scripts into my pocket, I'm thankful that Mr Crompton's old Lilyburn pharmacy is hanging in there, just, and I don't have to freak myself out at the Plaza like a war veteran with PTSD. Mr Crompton has enough elderly clients who haven't died off yet to keep his doors open, along with weird people like myself who can't do shopping centres. I swallow down nerves as I draw my jacket around me as small comfort from the grey winter bite. I know I have to do this, but when I get to the door my resolve dissolves when a *Back in 15 minutes* sign stops me in my tracks.

'Fuck a duck,' comes a voice from behind, making me jump.

'The old bugger likes to have a little catnap these days 'n' that. Who wouldn't at eighty years of age?'

It's Slugs Meldron's mum, Shirley, rugged up in a Richmond Tigers polar fleece and a hand-knitted plum-coloured beanie sending her blonde curls cheerfully upwards like fresh wood shavings, her fondness for me evident on her friendly pink face. She never fails to remind me Slugs was my primary school boyfriend in Grade 6. My only boyfriend – ever. And apparently, I was Slugs's only girlfriend. Ever.

'Hello, darling coulda-been-my-daughter-in-law.' She beams. 'I haven't seen you in yonks. How's it going after all that awful university biz, love?'

I look to the toes of my gumboots where this morning's cow shit is drying.

'We all thought you was studyin' to be a teacher. Least that's what your mum told us.'

'I was, but I didn't. I'm finished now. Well and truly ...'

'Ah. You always was a very clever girl.'

'Not really. I didn't actually manage to graduate from anything.'

Shame tingles my face. I never told Mum and Dad I quit my teaching degree in the very first week of uni. They'd have lost their lolly if they'd known I switched from safe-as-houses teaching to ag science and social psychology. It was a lie I'd kept for the best part of three years.

When the Turner effluent hit the fan, instead of graduating as an employable primary school teacher, all I had was an unemployable mishmash of academic learnings, like a cake with too many ingredients. Mum and Dad were ropeable. Out of pocket. Out of luck with a daughter like me. Then came the scandal.

I look at Shirley, thinking of my incongruous mix of studies leading me to academic nowhere. But at the time, nothing could diminish my appetite for environmental science, soil ecology, feminism, psychology and a dash of non-affiliated mainland university holistic ag management. Nor, it seemed my appetite for sexual tension and illicit encounters with my lecturer, a man twenty years my senior. Me with my voracious appetite to learn *everything* about everything. Like an addict. I just couldn't stop, lust-induced carpet burn on my knees and all.

'It all went a little pear-shaped,' I say to Mrs Meldron, feeling as if I'm choking.

'Yes, so I read in the paper. Not to worry, ducks. That professor sounded like a total tosspot. What a scumbag scammer with what he done with those uni funds too. Honestly! Some men.'

She steps closer. A deep look of concern. Her voice softens. 'And how are you now?' She nods at the pharmacy. 'Everyone well, I hope?'

I scrunch the scripts tightly in my hand, shoving them deeper into my pocket where last week's empty Twisties packet rustles.

'Right as rain, we are,' I answer, my voice taut like a wire about to snap. 'And you?'

For a split second a cloud crosses her expression. 'Oh, us? No point complaining,' she says tightly, but proceeds anyway. 'Since those foreigners bought all of North West Land Holdings, our business is buggered. They reckon our milk tanker run needs "consolidating", whatever that means. Barry's being a prick about it. And Nigel, well, he just goes bush more often these days. Running feral he is.'

Nigel? It takes a while for my brain to catch up that she's talking about her son Slugs, dubbed so ever since he was given a slug gun from Santa, and shot one of the little peppercorns into his sister's bum, which had her spending Christmas Day at the Ulvie medical centre.

'Hardly ever home, he is, like his father. Least I still got me chooks. I love me chooks.' Shirley shrugs, then suddenly brightens, holding onto my forearms. 'I know! We've both got time to kill until Mr Crompton wakes up. Let's go grab a cuppa together! Catch up on the old days. Remember when you and Nigel was in Grade Six ...'

Next we're walking down the street towards the bakery, and she's covered the historic boyfriend/girlfriend bit and is now rabbiting on about Slugs's sister, Nicole, who has 'a number two on the way'. As I rattle my brain into place to understand she's talking about a baby, I send out a silent apology to Uncle Larry. I hope that while I'm having a milkshake and a pie, he doesn't up and die.

Chapter 8

As we cross the street, Shirley is so busy talking about the Richmond Tigers' likelihood of making the finals and their 'hot ruckman', she doesn't initially see the newspaper taped all over the bakery's old wooden bay windows, tugging at the door perplexed as to why it won't budge.

'It's closed,' I say, pointing at the sign.

She grimaces. 'Not having much fucken luck in Lilyburn are we?' She reads from another sign, printed in 1930s movie-reel font. *Coming soon! The Happy Chappy Vegan Cafe! Watch this space!*

'*Vegan!*' she screeches. 'You're fucken kidding me! *Here?* In Lilyburn?'

A seagull lands at our feet, squawking angrily as if in agreement. Clearly since the bakery's been closed, there's not been much crumb action for the insistent silver gulls. My mood plummets as I think of the now unobtainable beefsteak pie and iced coffee that has so many times saved me.

The vegan sign switches my uni brain on, and with it, my runaway mouth. 'Strictly speaking, a one hundred per cent vegan diet is deficient in iron, zinc, vitamin D, calcium and omega-3 fatty acids. Also, due to Vitamin B-12 deficiency, it can lead to irreversible neurological effects. Not to mention it's become a giant money-making industry and marketing boom, supplying over-processed products to ill-informed people, who don't understand the lack of holism in most agricultural systems. The plants used in vegan products are generally grown in the most toxic and deadly forms of agriculture man can manufacture.'

For a moment Shirley looks at me like I'm an alien, then grins affectionately, squeezing my arm. 'Oh Connie, I love your knowledge vomits! You always was such a little brainbox bookworm, driving Miss Prinkle mad with your professor questions in Grade One. You're a born genius.'

At the mention of the word professor, a panicked surge lifts in me. In desperation I seek out a Doctor Cragg breath. In breath. Pause. Hold and exhale. Repeat. The seagulls lift, circle and scream as Professor Turner arrives, looming out of the blackness of my mind. It's halfway through my third year. I'm walking into his office.

'Ah, Connie Mulligan,' he purred from behind his desk. 'My A-one student. Come in.'

Since I'd received his email that morning saying he'd wanted to see me, I'd been jittery with hope. Hope that this draft paper I'd worked on day and night for months would reinstate me as his golden (and gropeable) student once more. Standing at his desk, I hoped that this could be our turning point, back to how we once had been, back into his affections. But his smile had turned to a sneer. Picking up my spiral-bound draft thesis, he slowly rubbed his fingers over his clean-shaven clenched jaw. The room turned cold when his eyes met mine. Chill factor, forty below.

Next, the thesis flew through the air. Despite ducking, the end of the spiral-binding caught the soft skin below my eye, slicing it, blood trickling onto my hoodie. The sudden shock of red on my fingertips and the slow drips blobbing onto the white pages of my fallen thesis held me. I stared at Professor Turner in disbelief.

'What the fuck is this?' he shouted. 'Lies! Falsity and female hysteria! Re-submit.'

'Connie? Connie, love?'

I shudder, searching for an anchoring place in Mrs Meldron's friendly blue eyes.

'It's not that bad about the vegans, is it?' she comforts, squeezing my hand with concern. 'You okay, love? Shall we try Greasy Joe's, huh? He does a shit coffee, but it's better than nothing.'

She points over the road next to Dawn and Dick's Real Estate Agency. Linking her arm in mine she walks me over the pointless traffic island, seagulls stick-legging out of our way.

'Aren't vegans just angry vegetarians?' she asks. 'Some of them seem to be so fucked off about everything. I'm not sure these happy chappies will be all that happy.'

Her comment prompts a small laugh from me, and with her caring touch and the prospect of food at Greasy Joe's, I feel myself ease within. A dim sum or two. A chicken wing-ding or three. Washed down with a choccy milkshake. I wonder if Uncle Larry might like some chips and gravy with chicken salt? A go-to of mine when I'm feeling down. When we reach the door, we discover that Greasy Joe's is also closed. Shirley swears about ducks again. My stomach tumble-turns. We peer through the window.

'Where the fuck is Joe?' Shirley exclaims.

The place has been gutted. There's no sign of Joe Andrianakis in there anymore.

'Who'd want to buy this place?' she asks. 'And what the frig is goin' on? Surely the vegans haven't bought this as well? Bloody Joe didn't mention a word he'd sold. Why's he done a runner, do ya reckon? Twenty years he's been here. We welcomed him as our own. He could've said goodbye!' She squeezes my arm tightly. 'So much for a coffee, huh? All we're left with is the friggin supermarket cafe at the Plaza. I'm not goin' there ... not if it means bumping into *them*.'

I'm not sure who she means by 'them', but a scowl arrives as hard as cold steel and when she glances at me, I recognise a shared sadness in her eyes. Her social niceness draws away like the tide and we are both left high and dry on the depressing lonely beaches of our life, staring at each other.

'Oh, Connie, it's so damn good to see you,' she says in a quavering tone that I've never heard her use before. Tears fill her eyes as she pulls me into her ample breast. My face is smooshed against the Richmond Tigers emblem so firmly I'm sure I'm going to have the logo imprinted on my cheek. She holds on to me like I'm a lifebuoy in her day, and without me, she would surely drown. I'm about to ask what's wrong when Dawn from Dawn and Dick's Real Estate Agency zips up in her little red bubble car, the driver's door declaring: *Don't be a Dick ... sell with Dawn & Dick.*

Out Dawn gets, dressed Hillary Clinton style in a red suit with black patent-leather, high block heels and giant gold loop earrings that look as if they could perch a couple of parrots on them. As she inserts a key into her office door, she says, 'What's the place coming to? First vegans. Then that.' She waves at Joe's.

'Yes, what is with that?' I ask, thinking of my chips and gravy no more.

'Bloody Joe sold privately. To some mainlander. For cash. So, it was out of my hands who it went to. God knows how they got council approval.'

'They? Approval for what?' Shirley probes.

'Oh, I don't know.' She waves her hand about as if she has flies annoying her. 'It's going to be some kind of shelter. Or women's gathering place?'

'Shelter?' Shirley and I echo.

Shirley's eyes widen again. 'Not fucken cats! I hate cats. Nigel shoots them.'

'No!' Dawn says, rolling her eyes. 'Not cats. For women.'

'A women's shelter? *Here?*' Shirley asks.

For a moment I remember my sacking, the impossibility of my family, and wonder if they'd have room for me.

'Now I've got this ... right next door to me!' Dawn says, clearly disgusted.

I frown, wondering what's so wrong with a women's shelter.

Dawn notices my expression. 'Well, not exactly a shelter. But some kind of women's support thing. Don't you see? Bloody do-gooders turning up bringing bad with them. It's going to lower the tone of the whole town.'

'How?' I ask as I look up and down the desolate street.

Dawn, exasperated by my question, ticks the answers off on her fingers as she speaks. 'It could possibly bring in drug addicts. Violent men turning up at all hours. Disturbed women having spats. Mullet-wearing, undernourished kids in hoodies out on the street, thieving. It's just not on.'

'Why are you so certain that will be the result?' I challenge, back at the uni debate. 'And why would you assume it's only women from lower socioeconomic demographics who need support? Don't you realise domestic violence permeates all sectors of society?'

Dawn looks at me like I've said something overtly offensive. 'I know about you, Miss Smarty Pants,' she says coldly. 'We don't need you to stir up more trouble here.'

'Leave Connie's business out of it,' Shirley defends. 'She's right. How is a women's centre so bad? Sometimes we all need help when things get rough at home.' She sniffs with distaste at Dawn, then gestures at the empty, tired old street. 'You say Connie's trouble. Pot calling the kettle! This place wouldn't be so deadbeat if you hadn't sold out to the bigwigs who built the Plaza and then started selling up all the family farms to foreign owners.'

Dawn looks like she's been slapped. 'Enough, Shirley! You stick to your business, I'll stick to mine.' She glares at us with her thin pinched face, lined heavily from a life of smoking cigarettes, then she goes into her office and slams the door.

'Hypocrite,' Shirley says, watching her through the window. 'Her business *is* my business. She's selling off so much property to blow-ins that we're about to lose our milk tanker business. Making a motza she is. It's what started all the trouble with Barry.'

I watch her swallow emotional pain. She pats my hand and I wonder if I'm expected to ask, *What trouble with Barry?*

But the moment moves on.

'C'mon, love. Let's forget the coffee. I reckon Mr Crompton has had his little grandpa nap and will be open by now.' She leads me back towards the pharmacy. 'A one-dollar cuppa from the machine at the servo is our only option now. Not even I'm depressed enough to do that.'

'Me neither,' I agree.

Chapter 9

I've been standing here for ages in the servo on the Lilyburn bypass, desperate for food, but the young Indian guy restocking the Pie Face warmer has failed to notice me despite the taser-like door buzzer. I glance at the bain-marie, not sure why pies need faces and why we need different pies in Tasmania when the good old Nationals have done us fine for decades?

I rustle my dairy waterproofs loudly, cough politely, then dump the cluster of junk food from my arms onto the counter, knowing I have to get back to Uncle Larry soon with his medication. Pie Guy has AirPods jammed in his ears, so when he finally sees me, his black eyebrows shoot upwards as if I am wearing a balaclava and carrying a gun.

Aarav (as his badge says) walks over and starts beeping everything through the till. Eyebrows scrunch, searching for the barcode on the mint-choc carton. He has the most impressive nose I've ever seen – it's huge. But teamed with the eyebrows, it kinda all works and he's very handsome.

I'm so taken by those thick brows and aquiline nose I almost forget that my world and my mind is falling apart, and I've been given the sack, and I've seen my first dead body, even though he wasn't dead. And I'm about to go on medication that I know is likely to offer me more side effects than solutions.

'I'll grab a pastie too, thanks,' I say to Aarav, thinking Uncle Larry could do with eating something with vegetables in it.

After he's tonged Larry's pastie into a bag along with a sachet of tomato sauce, he asks, 'Is that all for today? No fuel?'

I drag my eyes away from his brows to the dark chocolate fondue ponds of his eyes, wishing I could whip out my notebook and sketch him right now. He is utterly beautiful.

'No, thanks. No fuel,' I confirm, and I realise that's the truth within me. No fuel. It's as if I have no energy in my being-ness. Nothing to keep me going in my body. Nothing to get me revving. I'm empty.

I pass him my last fifty-dollar note, forcing myself to stop staring at him as I wait for my change.

'Thank you,' I say, wondering if it would be politically incorrect and downright Tasmanian-ignorant of me to start up a conversation with him about cricket or Bollywood movies. He avoids my gaze, looking absently out to the bowsers as he drops a lonely coin in my hand. I realise he's not here anyway, not really. Half in his iPhone-world, wishing he were somewhere other than the Lilyburn servo. I wave the coin at him.

'Ten cents short of a dollar, eh?' I say, tapping my temple.

He tilts his head, perplexed, and the magnificent brows pull down but he says nothing.

'Okay then. See ya round like a rissole,' I say, tucking Mum's tacky wallet under my arm, dragging the weight of my body out through the auto doors, the plastic bag making *swish-swish* sounds against my pants.

Outside, the main highway sustains a constant roar of spud trucks and commuter cars headed towards Burnie, except for one dirty white van, pulling out from the stream, blinker flashing as if winking at me. I hurry to my car, cranking open the stiff door and diving inside.

Two young men in the van roll to the bowser, cut the engine, high-five each other. Coloured wristbands on one. Snazzy red watch on the other. The driver's smile is framed by a dapper black handlebar moustache, not unlike one of Aarav's eyebrows. The other man's smile shines into the world with extra-white teeth, surrounded by a sandy-blond on-trend beard. His 'look' is made even more chirpy with an offset yellow beret. From the rear-vision mirror, a Green Tara goddess swings between them cheerfully amid a string of paper flowers. They bring such a different colour palette compared to the local one of hi-vis green and orange that I forget my haste to return to Uncle Larry. I can't take my eyes from them. They're unlike any of the men in Lilyburn I know. These guys might as well be from outer space ... or more likely the mainland.

I slump lower in my seat, ripping open my Samboys like I'm at the movies about to watch a really good film. My spirits lift when my fingers clasp a doubled-over curled chip. They taste better than the flat ones, I swear. Fat and salt glide over my tongue, easing things for me. Stealthily, I lower the window slightly to catch their conversation.

'How lucky were we?' laughs Moustache-man.

Aren't his ankles cold, I wonder, looking at the large gap between pants-leg end and his green felt mule shoes? Definitely mainlanders.

'I know, right!' says Blond-beard man. 'We should've filled up when we got off the ferry. But the old girl made it!'

A mud-spattered navy 4WD rumbles loudly from the highway, giant silver spotties on the roof looking like a rack of stage lights lifted from a musical theatre. From the dead wallaby, possums and roo hanging on the back rack, I know exactly who it is as he pulls up at the diesel bowser. Shirley's son – Slugs Meldron.

I slump down further and put my rigid plastic hood over my head. Slugs – my Grade 6 boyfriend for a week. He was Joseph and I was Mary in the nativity play back in the day. I know I must get going, but something keeps me watching as he rolls his short round body out and salutes a 'g'day' to the tourists.

Like me, he's been in good paddock too since I last saw him. Ruddy red cheeks, puffy hands like rising white pastry and a tummy rounding out like he's eight months gone. He's balding over his brow now but has let his black hair grow long at the back so it rests over the collar of his forest-scape hunting jacket, mullet-style. Only not. Due to his balding brow, it just looks like all his hair has slipped backwards. I can't believe I ever held hands with him in the room where we kept the art smocks and bags! A groan escapes me.

The van men stare at Slugs's grim cargo.

'What youse lookin' at?' Slugs asks, yanking the nozzle out of the cradle.

'N … nothing,' falters Blond-beard. 'It's just they're … so beautiful … and so, so … dead.'

Slugs, who never possessed the calmest of tempers (think truck-chucking in sandpits), has puffed up to twice his size. 'Course they're fucken dead. Wouldn't you be if you'd had a bullet put in ya head?'

Waving his hand towards the tannin furred carcasses, Blond-beard says. 'Sorry, mate. It's just, we're …' He stares at the roo. 'We're vegan.'

'Vegan? Shit. You poor bastards.' Slugs shakes his head. 'What you're lookin' at is pet food. And skins. Would be wasted otherwise. Crop protection for your fucken salads.'

Not helpful, Slugs, I think. Memories from long ago rise up: Slugs crying round the back of the toilets because he'd found a roadkill wallaby with a joey on the way to school. After morning assembly, the teacher had told him he couldn't keep the joey in his underpants anymore, and took it from him saying she'd keep it warm. The tiny pink hairless thing had died by recess, wrapped in a few tissues and tucked in the lost property clothing. Slugs had lost the plot at the teacher as the cold flaccid little thing lay dead in his palms. He'd been suspended for a week.

'You bloody vegans are all nut jobs,' Slugs sneers. 'Goin' on about meat is murder. How many dinosaurs you murdering there with that van of yours?'

The mainlanders back away a little.

'We don't want any trouble,' Blond-beard says holding up his hands in surrender. 'We'll just pay for our fuel and be on our way.'

Slugs shakes his head and says sadly, 'You got no clue. You lot. No clue. Now fuck off back to where you came from.'

He shoves the nozzle violently into the diesel tank, turning his back. The moment is over. Moustache-man climbs into the van, and Blond-beard jogs in to pay. Then, they drive away in their farty, greenhouse-gas emissions van that clearly needs an oil change and a tune-up. They won't be going back to where they came from, I think. I reckon those two are the happy chappies and they are here to stay.

As Slugs watches them go, he shakes his head again then lumbers like a lazy bear to pay. I drag my seatbelt on, remembering Uncle Larry on his potential deathbed. There's still time for me to see my first real dead body today if I take any longer. Or I may even become a dead body myself if Dad finds out I'm helping Larry. I start the engine, and as I struggle to undo my mint-choccy milk carton, a loud tap on the window startles me. Milk rivulets down over my wet weather gear. Outside, Slugs is sipping on the same. He grins, his straw between his teeth. I lower Poo Brown's window all the way.

'See that?' Slugs asks indicating where the van was.

I nod.

'Bloody mainlanders.'

'Yep, bloody mainlanders.'

He slurps his drink. I slurp mine.

'Vegans 'n' all! Probably on their way to camp up a tree and shit from great heights onto a bulldozer.'

'Probably.'

I slurp. He slurps.

'So,' he says, 'whaddya been upta?'

'Not much. And you?'

'Shootin'.'

'Right. Shootin'. Good. Yep.'

Another pause as a loud dual-wheeled Deutz with a spray rig rolls by.

'I'm president now,' Slugs says, with a bit of a sniff. 'Of the Duck Shooters Association.'

'Oh. That's nice,' I say, thinking it's not nice for the ducks. A crow flies over, cawing insistently, as if to say, *Thank fuck I'm not a duck.*

'Yep. Got some new mainlander mates in it. Really shook the old fellas up. Mr Rowenbotham is spewin'.'

Another long pause and a fertiliser-spreader truck rumbles past, tank-like.

'Oh. Good. Just saw your mum.'

'Did ya?'

'Yeah.'

'Did she tell ya?'

'Tell me what?'

'Oh ... nothing.'

Silence. Slurping.

'Right then,' Slugs says, flicking one side of his mullet back over his collar. 'Good chattin'. See ya round.'

'Yep, see ya.'

Slugs climbs up into his kangaroo hearse and drives away, and I'm relieved he didn't mention anything that he'd heard about Professor Turner and me on the news.

Finishing my milk, I shove both fundraiser Snickers bars in my mouth in succession, then bunny-hop out of the servo thanks to my big fat gumboots and Poo Brown's busted little clutch plate, wondering if Uncle Larry has a microwave. His pastie has gone cold.

Chapter 10

Pushing open Larry's cottage door, kicking off my gumboots, I rustle my way into the narrow hallway.

'Helloooooo,' I call gingerly, puffed from my ride with Traveller back to Larry's, as I peer into the bedroom. The bed is empty, the sheets are flung back, the fire almost spent.

Nobody. And, thankfully, no *body*.

'Uncle Larry?'

I find him in the kitchen, recently showered and shaved, his damp hair combed down, old woollen dressing gown on, feet in tatty ugg boots that have seen better days. His face is pale, knuckles white as he leans on the table, clearly in discomfort. Behind him in the laundry a washing machine clicks over to spin. He looks up at me, as if shocked to see someone in his house.

'Ah! There you are,' I say in a too-bright voice, like I'm Mary Poppins or someone equally as sucky. I take in his lean, long and deeply lined face, searching curiously for the likeness of his brother. I find a faint similarity around his mouth, but that's all. He's nothing like my dad. Instead of being proud-chested, large and loud, he's lean-muscled, small and quiet. Mulligans must have such slippery genes, I conclude. Patrick with his orange hair and blue eyes. Me with my dark brown eyes and black hair. The thought of genomes makes me think of university. Professor Turner promptly appears in my mind's eye.

I'm standing in one of the bland classrooms, reading my study synopsis out to the entire tutorial group, Professor Turner gazing out the window, his hands clasped behind his back, jaw clamped as he listens to me.

'Since agrichemical companies began gene-editing back in 1995, seemingly ego-maniacal geneticists have been inserting these "slippery genes" throughout the plants we eat and the animals we consume, without any consideration for the holistic impact, or any consultation with the wider community. Take for example, the fast-track genome work supported right here at Austral University in CRISPR Cas-9 that underpins the corporate interests–'

'That will be enough!' Professor Turner's voice thunderclapped across me sharply. The whole class startled. Tilly Gutherson, a first year who was clearly being fast-tracked by being invited to be part of our third-year group, glared at me. She added to Turner's icy river stare that swept me out of the room on the strong current of his anger. As the door closed behind me I was left in the bubble of my enforced silence, humiliated.

I shake the memory off and look to Larry who is sitting, staring at me. I clear my throat. Dumping down servo shopping bags, then drawing out the prescription medication, I say, 'Good to see you up and about!'

'You took your time.'

'It would've taken me another half hour if I'd driven up via Irishtown seeing as your bridge is bung, so I rode my horse up again. Plus, Mr Crompton was snoozing and I don't do the Plaza.'

At the sink, I take a glass from the shelf, fill it from the tap then push the box of tablets across the table to him.

'Thanks,' he rasps, hands shaking as he opens the box then presses two from the foil.

'I got you some food too,' I say brightly, dragging out the ratty looking pastie and a half-eaten packet of Skittles.

It's then I sniff the air and notice a pot beginning to bubble on the stove. Beside the sink, a scattering of papery garlic peelings and chunky pumpkin skin pieces lie on a chopping board next to a knife, along with a pile of freshly chopped parsley.

'Where'd you get that?'

'Supermarket,' he says.

At my frown, Uncle Larry points to the small window. Outside, along the vast sun-capturing north-eastern wall of the shed is a large, fully flourishing vegetable garden with a tapestry of colourful pollinating flowers. I gasp at its beauty and productivity, even at this bleak time of year. Instantly I'm reminded of Granny M and her patch of paradise that she would immerse me in on days when Mum was tired of me, which was every day.

'Oh, wow,' I say, a little deflated that I thought a pastie and Skittles would cut it. I turn back to him. 'Here, let me finish making that. I'll bring it to you. Go back to bed.'

He looks at me for a long, silent time, studying my face. As he does, self-consciousness burns within me. I think how I must look, with my shit-splattered 'I Love Cows' cap jammed on over my jagged dark nothing hair. The ugly mole that mocks me every day in the mirror.

'Ya got a bit of cow shit there,' I hear my brother's voice taunt. Patrick's said it ever since we were little and never seems to tire of the joke, and my hand never fails to lift to run a fingertip over the bump. Mum says I need to get it lasered. She reckons it's all people stare at when they first meet me – that, and my large backside when I depart.

Once, when I was little and at Granny Mulligan's cottage, I saw a black and white photo of Marilyn Monroe in a magazine – parted lips, seductive half-closed eyes, and that mole of hers – in *the* exact same place as mine. I'd gasped. For a moment, in a single glimmer in time, I believed I was movie-star gorgeous like Marilyn. Granny saw me staring and running my finger over Marilyn's mole, then my own.

'Here,' Granny M said, taking up the scissors, 'let's cut her out. Then you can take her home.'

With delight, I'd stuck the picture to the bathroom mirror, then found Mum's lipstick and applied it, copying the Marilyn pout. I stared at the photo, then stared at my image in the mirror. I was beautiful. I could see my beauty radiating from me, like liquid sunlight, only whiter, brighter. I'd sucked in a breath, smiling at myself and the wonder of it. I may have had short dark hair, not halo-blonde like Marilyn, but she and I shared that same mole. It marked me as gorgeous, like her. As I did a little girl twirl, Mum came into the bathroom. She looked to the counter scattered with her makeup, then to my face. The slap was savage.

'Connie Mulligan! Don't you *ever* touch my things again. You hear?'

I can still feel the bite of her fingertips on my upper arms where she'd shaken me and the scratchy burn of tissues as she angrily swiped lipstick from my mouth, and it seemed, tried to wipe the mole away with the makeup too. Then she'd marched down the hall to phone Granny M, who was barely five hundred metres away in her cottage, and tore strips off her for putting 'lofty ideas' in my head.

'She'll never be beautiful,' my mother had hissed.

Now as Uncle Larry stares at the round chub of my face, I think he must be looking at that mole, which is darker, larger, these days. Nothing beautiful about it. Self-hatred ignites.

'It's no trouble really,' I say. 'I've got nothing much better to do.' The thought of going back to the house almost crushes me. His head tilts ever so slightly, as if trying to solve the puzzle of me. I'm about to scrape the vegetable peelings into the rubbish bin beside the sink when his voice jolts me.

'Chook bucket,' he indicates a chipped white enamel bucket with a cobalt trim. 'And the seeds go on the sill.' He points to where other seeds are drying on paper towels in a sunny spot. I smile. Granny M is back in the room with me. Once he sees I'm on track, he lifts himself up gingerly from the kitchen stool, grimacing.

As he passes on his way to his bedroom, he pauses.

'Thank you.'

He speaks the words with such gravity, that tears pool in my eyes. I go to the stove, pick up the wooden spoon, and tell myself it's the steam from the pot making my eyes continue to run. With the soup ready, I go in search of a bowl and find a sliding door I'd not noticed before. Entering, I discover roof-high shelves of stored food. Apples under hessian sacks. Onions and garlic plaited and hanging next to dried herbs. A giant chest freezer murmuring.

Opening it, I see cryovacked meat within. Labels on the packages read, Barbara, Molly, Glen, David. My mind flashes with images of shallow graves, bodies in wheelie bins, skeletons in cellars. I grimace, shutting the lid quickly and backing away. I must've caught too much of Dad's true crime telly, I tell myself.

When I take the soup and the pale pastie blobbed with sauce into Uncle Larry on a dented tray, I tell myself to get a grip about the names on the bags in the freezer. I half expect him to loom out at me from behind the door with a hatchet. Instead, he's in bed dozing. I set the tray down. Am I feeding a serial killer? Keep things normal, I tell myself, knowing that normal is not my forte.

Outside the window, Traveller lets down a snort, drawing Larry's attention. My big-arsed grey is gorging himself on the fresh wallaby grass that rolls down towards the river amid the trees.

'The old fella's in good nick for his age,' Larry says. We both gaze out the window to the horse.

'Pa put in his will that Dad wasn't to sell or shoot him. That he was to be kept on for me.'

I feel an awkward silence engulf the room.

'Sorry!' I add quickly.

'What for?' He lifts a spoonful of soup with shaking hands, blowing gently on it, his deep brown eyes locked on me.

'For mentioning the will.'

'Why would you be sorry for that?' he asks, taking his first mouthful.

'Well. With you and Dad … and all that?' I wave my arm in the direction over the river towards Sunnyside Farm.

'All what?'

I twist my mouth, knowing I'm digging a hole and maybe Larry is encouraging me right into it.

'Well,' I begin, 'the fact that Grandad left Dad the main farm, and you only got this side – the less productive, steep block, you know, even though you're the older brother.'

Larry sets down his spoon. He clenches his jaw, his eyes narrow. 'Is that what he told you?'

I stop my nervous prattle to study his face. His expression is angry. Murderous in fact. In an instant I remember that this is a man I'm meant to be scared of. The one who would fire shotguns off randomly over the river any time of the night. Blast our house in a blaze of light at 3 am with spotties. Uncle Larry, who has apparently sent threatening legal letters repeatedly to Dad for decades, costing Dad in lawyer's fees.

'Yes. It's what he told me.'

'Is that so?' he replies coldly. 'Well, we all have our own version of the truth.'

I'm left standing in a pool of confusion. The burning wood on the revived fire behind me bangs like a gun. I jump. Nerves fire throughout my body.

'Look, I'd better get going. Milking time,' I say, swallowing the lie.

'Yes. You'd better get going.' It's then I notice the shotgun leaning up between the old wardrobe and the wall beside his bed. I remember the skulls of dead creatures on his dash. And I'm out the door faster than a rat up a drainpipe. Dad was right. Larry is loop-the-loop cray-cray.

Chapter 11

'Where the bloody hell've you been?' Dad glances up from his laptop, the bank statements, cow production input sheets and bills spread over the table. 'Your mother's been getting on my back, fussing and worrying.'

Sceptical, I look over to her where she's savagely taking her secateurs to the indoor plants as if she's de-nailing hostages, furiously sucking in her frustration at the untidiness that Dad's dairy debt is creating in her space. Patrick is on the lounge reading the *Tasmanian Country*, absently twirling his duck-arse mullet.

'Out and about,' I say, relieved none of them noticed my mini adventure across the river to the dark side. Having shed my gumboots and waterproofs I can smell my own sweat, my guts rumbling from all the crap I've eaten. If they knew I'd been helping Larry, they'd be seething. Tugging down my navy Sunnyside Holstein logo top, the fire murmurs to itself as they look up at me blandly, then turn back to what they'd been doing as if I'm not even here.

Down the hallway, my bedroom offers no comfort. It's a nauseating conglomeration of Mum's taste. Apricot quilted bedspread, floral fabric pelmets in plum tones, frilled curtains looped up on gilded hooks. Another veil of tizzy lace obscures the farm views as if Mum wants to pretend she lives altogether somewhere else. The soft toys Mum's given me over the years glare at me from a large armchair as if they too are disappointed with who I've become.

I flop face-first onto the bed into Mum's carefully arranged mountain of cushions. I watch the crazy film of my day so far from behind closed eyes. The cow stuff-up. The sack. The nearly dead mad uncle lying in the bush. The colourful newcomers to town. As I think of the happy chappies and their vegan-ness, memories of my university research fires in my mind. The day I discovered the necessity of having ruminant animals on cropping farms and the role they play in closed carbon cycles. It was contrary to everything the media was reporting about cows and climate change, and everything Turner had been teaching me.

I'd been smitten by him, but what I was learning made me see beyond his declarations about technology saving the Earth and feeding the world. The more I discovered about the dangerous genetic meddling of plants he'd been involved in before he became my teacher, the more my desire for him began to fray and unravel. His hot breath in my ear saying I made him horny began to feel like nerve gas oozing toxically into my cells.

My mind is fizzing and sparking, and I know I'll be carted off to those dark days if I don't stop now. To fend off the memories I begin humming 'Green Green Grass of Home' over and over.

I really ought to shower. But I have no energy, so I roll onto my back. As I look at the pink fluted light shade, the room starts to spin. I can't get in a breath. It's as if Dad has his gumboot pressed on my sternum. Then I begin the slip. The slide. I'm going again.

I'm huddled in a small dark hut, air thick with peat smoke. My knees ache, pressed on the cold dirt floor, back damp with fevered sweat, fingers and toes numb. Ice. So cold. Unpeeling my coarse woollen shawl, my long dark hair falls over my shoulder as I look down to the baby I'm cradling. My baby. It's then I freeze. Fear clutches my chest. Outside I hear soldiers.

'Cailleach,' one taunts at my door. 'Witch,' he hisses as he piles old dry thatch under my hessian door.

A drip of flame from a torch and my raw throat catches a scream. 'No! Please!'

The men laugh as they drunkenly lurch away. Flames crackle upwards, heat sears my face. The thatch above me roars. Through the haze and fury, a figure emerges in the doorway. Standing firm, silhouetted, like a burned tree trunk. He has come again. His raised arm shielding his face. The Claddagh ring reflecting the fire's flickering light.

When I wake, it's dark. Sweat lies in the valley between my breasts and my temples pulse. My Care Bears and other toys on the armchair regard me silently.

Outside, the day is trying to turn to night but the biggest moon I've ever seen is sliding upwards into an indigo sky, bathing Mum's garden in cool blue shadows and silver light. The bedside clock tells me milking time is over and Mum will now be cooking our dinner, always on the table at six thirty. Sharp. Just in time for us to eat and watch the devastating, brain-dead TV news, plural.

When I stand, the plush apricot carpeted floor feels like it's tilting. Palms on the walls to steady myself, Mum's voice comes into my head, *Don't you mark my clean walls with your grubby hands, Connie.*

It's not until I get to the kitchen that I remember Uncle Larry. I wonder if he's okay. Smells of our standard fare of steak, spud, gravy and steamed veg greet me. Maybe I should have prepared another meal for Larry? Even if he is potentially a serial killer. Dare I go back? But then I think of the letter Doctor Amel had written him. So tender and filled with compassion for him. If he's such a crazed violent man like Dad has said, why would she be nurturing him from afar? She's clearly not getting her hefty doctor's fee for her troubles.

'Make yourself useful,' Mum barks when she sees me, her cheeks red as she tongs steak onto a plate to rest. The clock ticks onwards to 6.35. She hates it when the men are late. Diligently I gather cutlery from the island-bench drawer and begin to set the table.

'Now go ring the dinner bell,' Mum says, as she slings dollops of mashed potato onto the plates, chucking carrots on beside them.

For a moment I wonder if she's laced them with 1080 poison like Dad does for the wallabies and possums after the oats start to sprout. On the porch, I begin tugging the bell's cord hard, jolting old Paddy-whack awake from the clanging. The four-wheeler fires and Dad roars along from the dairy just as a silhouette of Patrick emerges from the brightly lit calf shed, bucket in one hand, dead calf in the other as he drags it by its back hocks, Nick-nack following hopefully. I pout. Another little calf-soul gone.

Inside, I take my place at the table. The clock ticks. Soon, with Patrick and Dad seated, the meals are plonked in front of us. Dad huffs when the TV news reports another large Tasmanian dairy farm sale.

'First the Canadians. Now the Chinese. Is the government that stupid?' Dad says, sawing angrily at his steak. An ad break comes on. Dad mutes the TV, silencing the skinny woman with insanely white teeth spruiking probiotics for gut health.

'Now you're out of a job, Connie, maybe the big companies might give you work on one of their farms – cleaning dunnies?' Patrick lays the bait.

Dad stops chewing, warns him off the topic. 'Leave it, Patrick,' he says, like he's commanding a dog.

'Well, they may not have heard about her and y'know …'

I stiffen as tears rise. Not this again.

Mum sets down her knife and fork. 'If only you'd done teaching like we said …' She rolls her eyes. 'I suppose it'll be up to me to help you, again.'

'I don't want your help!' I say with such sudden ferocity even Patrick stops chewing to look at me.

'Well, if you won't take help from me, you could start by helping yourself,' Mum says. Her voice has the sinister calmness of a flooding river, its glazed surface belying the dangers below. 'I mean, look at you!'

She waves her hand at me. Still in my clothes from this morning, my belly sticking out from the too-small polo top, my thighs overhanging the small kitchen chairs like I'm wearing a pair of old-fashioned jodhpurs and my socks grubby.

'You could've at least tidied yourself up a bit before dinner. I mean, who'd give you a job? Other than us.'

I push my plate away, knowing the knot in my throat means it will be impossible for me to swallow anything right now. I look at them. The clock ticks. The past haunts.

I think of today. Uncle Larry's artful clutter. His beautiful vegetable garden. The peace on that side of the river. A place where nature is given free rein. Then the men at the service station. Their colour and freedom. Happy chappies. And Shirley's loving motherly hug.

It's then that something snaps in my brain. An idea arrives. The insistent clock ticks driving the moment and my idea on. I gather up my plate and stand abruptly.

'Sit down and eat your dinner, Connie,' Mum says.

'After what we do on modern farms, why would I eat any of this supermarket-bought crap? What's so wrong with having a vegetable garden? Like Granny M used to?'

'Says the junk-food queen,' Patrick quips.

'Well, if you want a garden so badly, get off your arse and grow one yourself,' Dad adds. 'I'm the one who pays the bills around here.'

A tidal surge of emotion like a tsunami lifts within me; there's no holding it back.

'You? Pay the bills? That's a joke,' I say, glancing at the unpaid piles set aside for next month. 'It's your management that's the problem. Nothing is functioning on the land anymore! Have you noticed there's bugger all birds nowadays, let alone a bloody bee – not since you cleared for the new pivots and began spraying your expensive chemical piss everywhere like uppity tomcats?

'You get Fanta Pants here to spray the pre-emergent herbicide, then a broadleaf spray after germination, then you order seed coated in neonicotinoids and at least six fungicides later, along with a final spray of atrazine to desecrate your grain crop at harvest, you then feed that shit to the cows and proudly say you produce healthy milk! *Really?* C'mon! No wonder we're broke, spending all that money on warfare against the land we live on! You need to sack yourself, Dad, not me!'

Dad rises from his seat. 'That's bullshit, Connie!'

Blood pulses in my ears. 'Bullshit laced with a chemical cocktail,' I say shrilly, my heart hammering. 'Don't you get it? It's why the cows shit kryptonite goop and slip their calves each year! This supermarket shit is not even fit for the dogs! I'm going to chuck it in the shit pond.'

Plate in hand, my truth spilled of all the things witnessed, observed, and yet shoved down into my silent female core, I head to the mudroom door, slamming it behind me.

Chapter 12

Outside, the moon's domination of the sky is subduing the stars. Elated for having spoken my truth, and victorious for having flogged a plate of dinner for my banished uncle, I set off in the otherworldly blue light.

Nick-nack is led by the dinner's scent as we walk towards the dairy. I need to find something to cover my awkward cargo now that I've committed myself to going back to mad Larry's in the dark. The contents of his freezer flash in my mind. Frosted bags with people's names written neatly upon them. Am I being paranoid? Have I watched too many episodes of *Vera* on the telly to make a sound judgement? Am I as crazy as my family tell me I am?

In the dairy I switch on the light, set the plate down and a memory arrives. There's me, high on professor infatuation hormones and exciting new-found knowledge, lecturing Dad and Patrick in the dairy pit about plastics in the food chain and the innovative solutions.

'Did you know that American scientists are making cling film and other packaging out of *milk*! Soon we'll be able to have our cheese and eat the wrapping too!'

'Whoop-de-do,' Patrick said. 'So fucken what?'

'So what? You knucklehead, don't cha know the actions of humans over the past forty years have caused the extinction of over *half* the planet's living species?'

'Wish someone would extinct you,' Patrick said as he pulled the cups off what I would deem an over-milked udder.

'Connie,' barked Dad, 'get your head out of your arse. Calf shed. Now!'

I shelved my natural-plastics excitement and slunk off to my daily task of scraping the putrid-smelling shit and straw from the floor of the calf shed, while around me the black and white babies cried and died.

Looking about now I spy the box of food-hygiene hairnets. That'll have to do. I stretch a couple of them over Mum's 'good' china plate, mushing the potato downwards.

'There. Happy as Larry,' I say satisfied, grabbing a torch on the way out.

Riding a horse and carrying a food-laden dinner plate may not be the best idea, so with a deep breath I set off on foot, the moon at my back, my shadow leading me forward down the track to the rushing river that seems louder at night. The cows camped around a hay ring in one of the grazing strips stand, stretch, and sniff the air, surprised to see me on foot at this time.

'It's all right, girls,' I say. 'Just going for a moon walk.' I spin about and do my best Michael Jackson backwards steps in my gumboots, hoping humour will calm myself, but it doesn't.

At the river, the torchlight on the wonky bridge enhances deep treacherous shadows and illuminates the manic rapids below. Staring down at the gaps, I teeter across, jumping solidly onto the riverbank. The soft soil, blanketed in native pastures instantly brings calm. Inhaling damp night-time bush scents, I walk up the magical track bathed in silver-blue light and gentle shadows. Soon the steepness of the hill claims my breath, and I have to stop several times to suck in air. Soldiering on up the last sharp incline, the cottage appears. The apple-storage shed seems giant from this angle, and my gaze is lifted further to the tiered paddocks that give way to moon-drenched bushland of mountain ash and leatherwood, the ferny glades between hillsides patterned in silver. I'm entranced by this place, iridescent tonight, until

I remember I'm going to see my mad uncle who has bodies in his freezer.

Knocking lightly on the door, then gently opening it, I call out gingerly. 'Uncle Larry? Hello? It's me … I've brought you some tucker.'

There's no answer, so kicking off my boots, I enter. From the sound of Larry's gentle snores, I know he's still alive. The bedroom fire is glowing gently. Rather than wake him, I sweep the torch beam along the hallway to the kitchen and place the dinner in the fridge, looking around for a pencil and paper to leave a note, but there is none.

Another door from the kitchen could lead to an office so I open it. A small hallway takes me to another door, where I find myself in the cavernous space of the apple-storage shed beneath high tree trunk beams, cut decades ago from the surrounding bushland. Luminescence from the clerestory windows floods the space.

I spotlight my torch around, gasping. I'm in what appears to be a professional art studio with giant canvases, paints, rags, tins, paper and brushes scattered over huge trestle tables. On the walls hang massive canvases, unframed – vistas of the very same moon-blue mountains I've just admired. And in each one is a woman. *The* woman. Her heart-shaped face, wavy auburn hair. Pale skin shining. I scan the torchlight about and painting after painting reveals the same woman: standing among hens, arms wrapped around a white enamel bucket. Riverside on a grey horse, surrounded by silver-green.

The paintings are so beautiful, tears prick as I fall into the timelessness of one after another. Some time later I shiver, feeling voyeuristic and intrusive, so I haul myself back to the task of writing Larry a note. I drag open a drawer. Inside is a pencil and a notebook. Taking it out, I notice the cuttings from some yellowing newspapers shoved in a folder. I slide out the first article – it's headlined *Tassie artist Mulligan makes big in NY*. There's a photo of a young, strikingly handsome Larry and the same woman

75

who's in the paintings. She and Larry have a startled flashbulb look to their eyes even though they're smiling. He has his arm around her, protectively, his chiselled looks movie-star worthy; she, boho beautiful in a 70s suede coat.

The photo caption reads, *Rise to International Fame – Tasmanian Artist Mr Mulligan and his unidentified travelling companion.*

I read on.

It's been a crazy ride for dairy farmer turned artist, Mr L.M. Mulligan. From the backblocks of Tasmania to the spaghetti junctions of Los Angeles, he's the talk of worldwide towns. Mr Mulligan has enjoyed solo shows in Galway, Istanbul, Montreal and Sao Paulo. His South American exhibition moved from Brasilia to Rio de Janeiro and his gallery show opens in New York this month. In just a few short weeks, Mulligan's work was attracting crowds of unprecedented numbers. Meanwhile solo shows are planned for the UK after Mulligan takes the US by storm.

'It's unbelievable for a Tassie dairy farm boy to wind up on the global art stage,' said Mulligan.

I flick to the next clipping. What I read troubles my heart.

At the top of a brilliant career, artist L.M. Mulligan has disappeared without a trace. Despite his absence, the exhibition of his extraordinary work opened in New York, drawing crowds of up to thirty thousand flooding through New York's famous Clandenberg Gallery.

The exhibition will move to London later in the year. Mulligan's work is expected to attract six-figure sums at auction, and many speculate his sudden disappearance is a promotional stunt to inject mystery into his work, and perhaps help the auction hammer fall upon higher sums.

Inside the folder, more clippings are held together by a rusting bulldog clip, but I tell myself I'm being a snoop. Instead, I scrawl a note, my mind rushing like the river below as I try to absorb what I've just read.

> *Dear Uncle Larry,*
> *Dinner in the fridge. Hope you're recovering.*
> *Connie M. X*

As I turn to leave, a small watercolour captures my attention. Her portrait again, the same drape of green from a shawl over a bare shoulder, like the one in Larry's bedroom. She's resting her chin upon her hand and wearing a ring. The Claddagh. I shudder as I feel time swirl.

'Who are you?' I ask, picking it up and staring at her in my torchlight. Glancing about and feeling dreadful for doing it, I carefully roll the small sketch into a tube and place it in my coat pocket. Surely he won't miss one?

In the kitchen, I put the note on the table, quietly settle another log onto Uncle Larry's fire, replace the screen, and leave him snoring. As I trudge down the zigzag track with the beautiful woman in my pocket, there's something in my gut that tells me things are not adding up. Slippery genes, these Mulligans.

When I get to the bridge, I don't want to cross. I don't want to return to my life on Sunnyside. Looking up to the moon, I send out a prayer that something big will shift me forward, to some place new. The moon is higher now, her brilliance darkening the shadows. Where she lands upon the surface of the water, a reflection beams back with such illumination, I feel as if my whole being is permeated by it.

On Larry's idyllic side of the river, there's a foot track downstream. I set off along it, hopeful it will take me to the concrete bridge the timber companies put in a few years ago to get their heavy machinery to the upper reaches of the mountain range. Up on Dad's side, Nick-nack must sense me out and about and barks from her kennel, the sound echoing across the valley.

Above me, the house and dairy sheds and their normally bright lights are tonight paled by the moon, but her gleam can't reach the black wall of a sheer cliff face where the river is eroding on Dad's side like a gaping wound. A territorial night-time plover calls indignantly. Inhaling the plant perfumes I listen with delight as wallaby and paddy melon thud into bracken fern, and possums scuttle up well-worn vertical pathways on tree trunks. A magpie, confused by the moon, warbles as if it's morning.

Amid this Eden, a peacefulness settles for the first time in years, the smell of the landscape like a balm to my brain. My hand roams to my pocket, where the energy of the mystery woman seems to pulse in my palm.

At the forestry bridge, knowing it's time to cross back over, my mood slumps as I step onto its solid concrete surface. It still holds echoes of the insistent rumble of log trucks coming and going from the pine and blue gum coups in the formerly secret glades of the Great Western Tiers. Making my way up the wide gravel road, I stop. Parked on a pull-over spot, canopied by dark gums, is our neighbour Raylene Rootes-Stewart's car.

What's she doing here? Has her uppity navy Volvo broken down? Then I spot Dad's four-wheeler bike parked beside it. I puzzle seeing it. His 'accounts day' is running late. The Rootes-Stewarts begrudgingly allow Dad to use their internet for the small fee of a bottle of Scotch each quarter, but he never stays for socialising to share it with them.

Why is his bike here? My mind bolts with a collage of catastrophes that something terrible has happened to him. Walking faster towards Raylene's car, my breath quickens. Then I notice the car is moving. Not rolling forward, but rocking. Peering through the dappled night light, it appears as if two people are struggling, wrestling each other, windows fogged. Are they having a fight, I wonder?

As I squint in deep moon shadow gloom, I realise with a jolt – they aren't struggling, they're screwing.

Chapter 13

Shouldering open Granny M's stubborn cottage door, I stumble into the darkness, floorboards creaking. My mind is enmeshed in panic as I digest the knowledge that my dad is rooting Raylene Rootes-Stewart! My god! Raylene roots not David Rootes-Stewart, her husband, but instead roots Finnian Mulligan, my dad! My breath comes hard from my power walk up the hill via the paddocks onto the main road, hurrying away from the grubby, incomprehensible scene.

Traveller lingers, both curious and unsettled by the new face of the cottage with its open door. It's been years since I've been inside. Mum forbade me to enter after Granny M died, based on 'hygiene and safety issues', and Patrick had convinced me it was haunted.

I remember Mum standing right here in the doorway the day after Granny's funeral, hands on hips, face pinched in distaste.

'I'm not helping you clean up this rubbish tip, Finnian,' she'd said to Dad, flicking her rubber gloves at the hallway. 'Your mother lived in squalor. If you ask me, the whole place needs a match.'

Dad's face had turned that piglet colour and he'd walked with hunched shoulders back along the overgrown pathway muttering, 'I'll do it myself then, in my own time,' before disappearing into the dairy. Nearly ten years on his 'own time' is still coming. The cottage remains shut up and silent.

I switch on the torch armed with its Super Heavy Duty battery. 'Ever ready and no longer unsteady!' I declare following the eerie narrow illumination deeper into the cottage. A musty smell rises up, along with the taint of rat urine. In the dimness, I can see Dad's half-arsed attempts at packing up Granny Mulligan's things, with suitcases stuffed with old clothes shunted against the hallway walls, next to boxes stacked with papers and books.

Passing the lounge room, I gasp when the torchlight captures Granny's red woollen coat draped over her Sunday Mass dress, laid out on the armchair, her shoes set on the floor. It's as if Granny has been deflated in her chair, like a red balloon. Was it Dad who placed the clothes there like that? Tears prick painfully. I can still see her in those Sunday clothes, standing on the veranda next to me, looking down at her heeled red shoes.

'I don't actually like these shoes,' she'd confessed. 'Dreadfully uncomfortable after a lifetime in boots. I only wear them to stir the other old biddies up on a godly Sunday.' She'd winked, taken my hand, bent over and whispered conspiratorially, 'God doesn't care what shoes you wear or if you have knots in your hair, Constance. You're loved by the Great Power anyway. But c'mon, darling, let's tidy you up before Mass so your mother might approve of you.'

'Oh Granny,' I say in the darkness, every cell of my body warming with a tingling of love. But what if she were actually still here? What would I say to her? *Hey Granny M, I've just seen your son with Raylene Rootes-Stewart bonking in the back of her Vulva.* I shake the thought away and move on, shining the torch into the kitchen.

Here, Dad has again made a half-hearted attempt at packing up Granny's artful yet organised clutter. His grief-filled rummaging all those years ago, mixed with the inexplicable anger he seemed to have for both his parents, has left the room chaotic and sad. I pick up a bottle of sauce from one of the boxes. In the shaft of torchlight, the use-by date shows it should've been slathered on a sausage eight years ago. I roam the light around, so it captures flying china ducks on the wall. The old kitchen wood stove, silent as if in hibernation. Granny's old radio that used to play the *Country Hour*. The small round table prompts memories of summer lunchtimes, Granny serving me up crunchy straight-from-the-garden salads and cold sliced roast mutton, from meat that Grandad had cut up himself in the killing shed. Then in winter, her homegrown dish of tomato, onion and zucchini bake topped with crunchy breadcrumbs and homemade cheese, dobbed with her heavenly melted handmade butter from her house cow, Audrey. Memories flood. My heart beats with hope that maybe I could create a life like that again. A life that Larry has somehow retained, even if in a sideways, hermit kind of way on the other side of Sunnyside.

At Granny's bedroom door, I linger. It doesn't feel right invading it tonight. Plus, it's a little creepy, like I might find her ghost sitting up in bed, reading her Somerset Maugham like she used to before Mass. I journey further along the narrow hall that swoons and sways in the darkness. Creaking open the spare bedroom door, I discover the little bed that Granny would tuck me into, singing her Celtic songs from the old country – songs and stories that were passed down to her even though she never went to Ireland. In fact, she never left Tasmania in her lifetime, going to Hobart only once, and Launceston just three times to see Pa in hospital before he went. I'd listen wide-eyed as she spoke of the little people and told tales of the wise old women who people believed were witches. The bed slumps and sighs when I sit, sending up a puff of mustiness.

Outside, Dad's four-wheeler revs upwards from the mountain road. Quickly, I flick off the torch, racing to the window to peer through the curtains. He rides the bike to its normal place in the skillion shed beside the discarded silage wrap, and gathers up his laptop bag from the milk crate on the back of the bike. Head torch on, pointless with the moon, pants now in place, he walks towards the house.

Watching him get around in such a normal way, I realise this Raylene Rootes-rooting could've been going on for a while.

He's been logging into more than Raylene's wi-fi for some time now I suspect. Professor Turner threatens to emerge in my head and shame looms. But I won't allow him in ... not here ... not in Granny's cottage. And somehow, amazingly, he doesn't.

Lying down, I pull up an old blanket crocheted in a mishmash of Granny's leftover wool. Sleeping in a cold, dark, dusty cottage is preferable to going home to sleep under the same roof as my philanderer of a father. It takes an age for sleep to find me despite the enormity of my day. At first, I think I am dying, pain and panic paralysing my body, heart racing, body sweating, breath short, but eventually I sense Granny's and Grandad's presence, and for a moment, part of me feels comforted, loved and safe.

As I slip into sleep, I'm with Granny Mulligan holding my little hand, wading through high corn and a symphony of summer plants in the veggie garden.

'Growing food is all about making love, Connie. Creating love,' Granny Mulligan says. 'See these plants ... they need to pollinate. To share their love dust with each other. The breeze or the insects are their cupids, helping the plants fall in love. Then, under our feet there's a universe of love – worms, and tiny things like bacteria, good viruses, fungi and our original cell ancestors. We can't see them with our eyes, but we can feel them, all talking their silent love talk so that when we eat the food, we eat love. And they roam around our bodies, in love, and we stay healthy!'

Granny leads me out to the orchard where hives buzz with honey love-making bees. My heart feels full and blooming, as if I too am an open-petalled flower, light pouring out of me, ready for those love bees. In that moment, I see that same light of love reflected back at me in Granny's eyes and as she looks from me to beyond the orchard, where Grandad waves from the old Herringbone dairy ... and watch the love dust, like pollen, blowing between them, some of it falling on my head, so I know I am blessed and also that this is how life can be.

*

The next morning, brilliant winter sunlight spills through the window, slicing through dust particles. Outside lies a cracker of a frost. The cottage is so cold my breath comes out as steam. My freezing nose must be the colour of a raspberry and my toes feel like ice cubes. Staring at the pressed-tin ceiling, the paint peeling like lace, I see how welcoming the room is, despite its abandoned state. The old curtains are now threadbare, sun-thin and lank, but still pretty, stitched by Granny M herself.

It feels good to be here even though there's a mummified corpse of a possum in the corner, one toe-claw curved in the air, as if it's making a dying proclamation. Granny M's cottage could really do with a clean-up. Dad had once suggested renting it as a farm stay or B&B, but Mum had hammered the idea down like a post-rammer on a treated-pine log.

'I'm not a chambermaid or a servant to tourists! And I am certainly not anyone's breakfast cook. Or a bed-maker for people other than my family,' she'd insisted. 'Besides, who would want to stay in an old dump like this?'

I realise now why she's always so bitter. She must have known all along that Dad gets about the district like a randy ram who's jumped the fence.

Father Morris leaps into my mind, fist banging on the pulpit, warning in a low voice, 'The man who commits adultery with another man's wife, even he who commits adultery with his neighbor's wife, the adulterer and the adulteress shall surely be put to death. Leviticus 20:10.' Clearly that bit was glued into my brain when I was eleven years old, but Father's dire preaching must've never stuck to Dad's.

I wish I could erase all that unhelpful religious scripture from my brain, keeping only the good parts that Nick-nack seems to live by, Granny herself would say they deliberately kept the best bits out, with twisted lies and buried truths on women like Mary Magdelene. My belly rumbles. I haven't eaten since the servo, so I sit up swinging my legs out of bed thinking of bacon and eggs, wondering if I should just go home. Then, in the silence of the sleepy cottage, I hear the word, or at least sense the word – *Stay*.

Did I hear it, or think it? I panic, and my eyes dart about the room for a source. But there's no one else here besides me.

Stay. I swear, I can hear it again. I think of Doctor Cragg. Maybe it's time I listened to her advice and started that medication? This is too crazy. Even for me.

'Stay?' I say aloud.

I shut my eyes tightly. Can my life get any weirder? Can *I* get any weirder?

Outside the cows are calling as they make their way to the dairy where SAND FM's Dean-O is cranking through the top ten manufactured pop tunes. Then Dad fires up the ute, Patrick the bike. For them, it's just another day on Sunnyside Dairy Farm, but for me, everything has altered. The world has tilted sideways.

'Holy Mary Mother of God,' I say in my best Irish accent.

As I propel myself up from the bed, I realise despite everything, this is the most buoyant and alive I've felt in years. Something? Life? It seems lighter now, particularly being here, and after spending time on the other side of the river, where the natural world still rules and Uncle Larry has nestled into his art and garden for solace. Traveller snorts outside the bedroom window and begins rubbing his sizeable backside on the weatherboard walls. I love that he's so near. My guardian.

'Okay,' I declare in the empty room. 'I'll stay. I will stay!'

Stretching my arms up and over my head, I breathe in the largest breath I've taken in years, relaxing my diaphragm, flowing air deeply into my lungs. My thighs are sore from last night's walk but it's a good kind of pain. For a moment the little cottage feels happy. I feel happy.

When I stand, my foot lands on the carcass of a dehydrated starling. It sticks to my sock, and I shake it off, chuckling and promising I will clean the place from top to bottom, starting today.

Unexpectedly there's a banging on the door.

'Constance? Constance Erin Mulligan? Are you in there?'

Instantly, my nervous system fizzes at the sound of Mum's voice saying my full name. Twice. It's never good when she does that. Hearing her shove the front door open, I shuffle into the hallway, boots in my hands. She's standing on the threshold in her sorbet-lemon pants, polyester puffer jacket of floral tangerine and Persian blue. She hasn't sacrificed her 'town shoes' to come find me. Instead, she's in her bright orange gumboots, her makeup and hair done to perfection.

'God, girl! You had me worried! I thought you'd strung yourself from a rafter or something. Don't you *ever* do that to me again!' Steeling herself, she strides in, stiffly hugging me, the scent of Imperial Leather lingering around us. Holding me at arm's length, she looks into my eyes, her frown deeply grooved between her pencil-perfect eyebrows.

'When I saw you hadn't slept in your bed ... I thought the worst, given your current state. I knew you couldn't have gone to a friend's house.'

'You needn't have worried,' I say, her barb about Connie no-friends snags.

'Is that all you've got to say? I've sent your father and Patrick out looking for you all over the farm and in the sheds. And here you are holed up in this cesspool! Your father's late for milking. He's fuming and in a foul mood, which he takes out on me. The only reason I knew you were here was because of your horse.'

She gestures to Traveller who has wandered around from his spot dozing outside my bedroom. He flicks his ears forward when he sees me. Mum rolls her eyes at him then looks back at me.

'I've got you an emergency appointment with Doctor Cragg. You'll need a shower. I've put your clothes out on the bed.'

My throat clutches and I freeze. 'No!'

Mum looks at me as if I've just pooed on her best rug. 'No?'

'Yes. I mean, no. I'm not going to Doctor Cragg. I'm going to spend my day here, cleaning this place up, because ... I've decided I'm moving out! Moving in. I mean, I'm moving out of your house and moving into ... here.'

Mum folds her arms, putting on her cat's-bum face, then her expression morphs into amusement.

'Oh Connie! You are such a silly girl.' She gestures inside the cottage, narrowing her eyes. 'Don't you realise, the power's been cut off for years? It will take weeks to get it reconnected. And then there's the cost! Who's going to pay? And look at this place ... for all we know the tanks leak and the plumbing's shot. You really don't think, do you? Have you even thought to check the water tanks? This place is anything but livable.'

My resolve shrinks. Maybe I hadn't thought it through properly. Maybe Mum's right. And maybe she'll need me in the house, with the business that's going on between Dad and Raylene.

The voice comes again as clear as day. *Stay.* I watch for Mum to react to gauge if she heard it also, but she remains immobile in front of me.

Mum glances at her watch and taps it with her red nail. 'No arguments. We are going to Doctor Cragg. You are not moving in here. That's final.'

For a brief moment I want to break her, to smash her life to pieces by telling her something that will bring her Queen of the Faux Castle fantasy down. The power of knowing that Dad is having an affair with Raylene rushes in my brain like a violent windstorm. My cheeks burn hot as I clench my jaw and fists.

Mum takes a step back to regard me more fully. 'Connie? Are you having another one of your episodes?'

Behind Mum, in the clear blue sky, five black currawongs wing past. Their call of *kar-week-week-kar* rings out as they circle and land amid the early daffodils, shuffling about on the frosted ground, squeaking and mewing. They look curiously at us through their bright yellow eyes. Rough weather is coming. They always arrive before the coldest, darkest snowstorms high on the ranges.

My eyes lock on one bird. He's particularly large, glossy and handsome, with his shining dinner-suit feathers contrasting his vibrant white wingtips and tail points. He seems to be muttering to me, as if he's saying I take life too seriously and it doesn't have to be this hard. That it's okay to just be. I breathe in, and feel an energy rise in me just as all the birds give flight, calling loudly, winging away towards a solitary giant gum down on the flats.

'Listen,' I say in a voice that is not like my own. 'I'm staying here.'

'No!' Mum says sharply, cutting me off.

She looks set to slap me. The past burns on my cheek. A flash of memory and the hiss of 'you little bitch' comes back to me. Then a succession of slaps, rolling forward through time. Slapped for spilling milk, slapped for dirtying my white school socks when I'd wandered out on the path to pat Paddy-whack, slapped for burning toast. Slapping me now with her energy. And now I know, slapping me because she's burned up with fury because deep down, she knows Dad is a cheating liar.

'I'll meet you in the car in twenty minutes,' she says, and walks away.

And all my defiance leaks out of me, just like that.

Chapter 14

An hour later as I sit on Doctor Cragg's over-cushioned couch, she asks flatly, 'Moving out? Starting a vegetable garden? Making friends with vegans? As a –' she consults her notes '– rebellion against your family?'

She drags her designer tortoiseshell glasses down to pincer her nose into a small triangle of skin, which I swear is a deliberate move to stop her nostril flare of judgement.

'Um ... well, it's more of a reclamation.'

I think of the voice I heard in Granny's cottage.

'Didn't you say a better diet and exercise would help me with my –' I point to my head and swivel my finger around my temple '– y'know ... noggin.'

I look brightly to Doctor Cragg. 'Just mentioning the vegetarians and vegans almost pushes them over the edge. Once, when Mum told Dad they now have "Like Milk Unsweetened" in the Plaza Woolies, he blew his stack. So I bought him some as a joke, but he didn't find it funny. Dad hates vegans more than he hates Collingwood.'

For Doctor Cragg's benefit, I list the ingredients of 'Like Milk' on my fingers. 'Water, salt, pea protein isolate, solubilised proteins precipitated at their isoelectric pH and collected by centrifugation. It's a bit different from how cows simply create milk protein via plants.'

Doctor Cragg looks at me poker-faced, says nothing, so I bumble on. 'But seeing as my family's sacked me from a farm that is broke and environmentally brutalised, and I've got bugger all to do all day, I reckon starting a garden at Granny's and eating more veggies would help.' I wave my hand around to wake Doctor Cragg up a little. She looks bored.

'It'd also be my own little uprising against corporations cashing in on people's ignorance about modern food systems. People don't know about the mass production of chem-drenched monocrops that destroy soil, guzzle water and push nature out. They think by being "plants only" people they're saving the planet. They don't know billions of living things are annihilated just for a bag of salad. But, when you see what Dad does to the cows and the land, I get what the vegans are on about. Some livestock farming is as questionable as all get-out, like massive grain-reliant feed lotting. Most of our food systems have been hijacked by morally bankrupt but filthy rich and powerful businessmen. And governments. Control the food, control the people. Y'know.'

I stop, not because I've run out of things to say, but because I've run out of breath.

Doctor Cragg frowns. 'That's quite a lot you're dealing with in your head, Connie. Do you think by focusing on so much negativity, it's exacerbating your anxiety?'

'Anxiety! Of course. There's so much to be anxious about! Don't get me started on 5G electromagnetics and pharmaceutical industry agendas!'

'Is this kind of thinking making you paranoid perhaps? Are you starting to fixate on conspiracy theories, maybe?'

'Conspiracy theories!' I sit back in my chair, stunned. Professor Turner used those exact words to dismiss me when I found the sinister agri-corporation link he'd been trying to steer me away from. Doctor Cragg's suggestion is like pouring petrol on my already crackling flames of anger. I narrow my eyes, raising my voice in exasperation.

'If people knew the soil-microbe murder that goes on for their fruit and vegetables, which in turn murders their own health, they'd be horrified! Do you know the lengths those corporations, those men, go to, to keep crap like Dicamba, 2-4D and glyphosate in the western world's food system? If vegans knew about that, they wouldn't eat plants either – there'd be nothing to eat! But they don't want to know. The human brain is so powerfully manipulated!'

In my distressed mind, Professor Turner promptly arrives at my shoulder, hissing in my ear to *shut the fuck up*. Shuddering, I twitch him away.

'When you say, "those men", Connie, who do you mean? There are female scientists and industry leaders who work in the same spheres. Why "those men"?'

I pause, knowing where she's trying to lead me.

'Were these the types of issues you were investigating at Austral University under Professor Turner?'

Another shudder runs through me and I freeze. *Under* Professor Turner quite literally, I think, full of shame. And before I can stop myself, I have a memory of lying in his office, his hands pinning my wrists to the floor as he rubs his rock-hard erection over and over the crotch of my jeans. His breath is hot in my ear. 'Does my little genius enjoy a little frottage on a Friday?'

In the gap of my silence, Doctor Cragg asks, 'When you say the human brain is powerfully manipulated, are you including yourself here? Can you see your own confrontational behaviour with your family?'

She looks to her notepad as if she doesn't really want to hear the answer. I think she just wants to keep me talking long enough so I dig myself back into the hole that confirms I need medication. I clear my throat.

'No! I see things clearly. I think. Well, I did. Before ...'

'Before what?'

'Before they backed *him*.'

'Him? Are you referring to Professor Turner? And the court case? The fact he was acquitted?'

I swallow down the humiliation. 'On both counts,' I say,

looking bleakly out the window. 'Human insanity just keeps rolling on … The patriarchal, capitalist systems keep retaining their power, which will bring us to extinction, so what on earth is the point of *anything*? What's the point of living?' I realise tears are streaming down my face.

There's a long pause. The clock ticks.

'So, you're having suicidal thoughts, Connie?'

'No!' I say, shocked at her suggestion, but prickles of misery rise behind my eyes. Am I? My nervous energy monologue derails and comes to an abrupt halt. The slight lift of Doctor Cragg's eyebrows and the tilt of her head tells me she's analysing me, deeply. On the wall the clock ticks. What is it about me and ticking clocks? Always being boxed in by time.

Tick.

Tick.

Tick.

Doctor Cragg draws in a long slow breath, as if she is trying to find the stamina to endure her hour with me.

'So, Connie, do you think what you're doing at home is helping yourself? Giving you power? Or can you see it as another form of self-sabotage? A disempowerment. A way of confirming to yourself and your family that you don't belong?'

I shrug so as to look indifferent, but my cheeks burn.

What if I don't want to belong with them and their vacuous hearts? I think, but I keep the words shut inside me. Resentment rises that I'm having to sit in Doctor Cragg's nest of on-trend cheap polyester cushions.

'I belonged when Granny and Grandad were on the farm,' I say with a smile, hoping to put her off her sniff for suicidal signs. 'Grandad always said he'd only produce as much milk as the season and the land allowed. To do anything more would be greedy. He and I would move pigs around on the hillsides to keep the blackberries in check, and he had a few sheep that grazed the flats among the cows, along with Granny's chickens. They said all those animals kept the food cycle of the soil and plants going.

Then, when the plants in the bush and the air on our skin told us, Grandad and old Uncle Dougie's dad would do a circular burning of certain places in the bush. He wouldn't let me come. Said my legs were too little yet. But I'd watch the slow smoke from Granny's veranda with her. She said there was a rhythm and a cycle to the days. That life ought to be taken with a slowness. And it was never, ever, *all* about money, but it sure was about richness. So,' I say to Doctor Cragg with finality, 'I don't belong. Not now. Not now I've seen the other side.'

She pauses, her head still tilted. 'The other side? Are you referring to death?'

'No.' I laugh. 'The other side of the river. Over there, it's how it should be.'

Emotionally exhausted, I stare at one of the cushions. It's covered in a black and white photographic woodland scene. I assume the cushions are meant to instil a sense of calm and comfort in her patients. Instead, I feel panic about my life and the state of the natural world swirl in me, and find myself falling out of my body again, out of my mind and into the forest cushions.

I am walking through sepia winter woods, the fallen leaves soft and damp under my slippered feet. Rich scents of forest floor decay lifts with every step. A fur cloak is draped about my shoulders and snow is beginning to fall in a world of silence. Beside me, Traveller walks, his warm breath on my forearm as I lead him by the reins. I'm searching through a grey curtain of snow that blankets a seemingly endless stand of dark leafless trees. Limping, I carry on, following the smell of death and the lift of black smoke above the treetops. Searching for him. For our home.

'Connie? Connie!' Doctor Cragg says sharply, startling me awake.

'Yes,' I say, sitting up like I'm at the principal's office.

'Your mind went again, didn't it?'

I nod, fear lifting in me.

'Where did you go?'

'I don't know.'

'Were you hearing voices?'

'Yes.'

'Are they negative? Aggressive?'

I shrug. 'I guess. I don't know.'

'You either do know, or you don't know. You need to tell me.'

'I don't know!'

'Do you want to talk about what happened?'

'Where?'

'At the university.'

A piercing pain shoots through the crown of my head. 'No!' I turn my face from her.

The clock ticks.

'Look, Connie,' Doctor Cragg says gently, 'these episodes are a form of post-traumatic stress, that's led to a type of psychosis. I believe they are getting worse. More frequent. I recommend we refer you to the hospital for an MRI to check there's nothing physical going on, and then I strongly suggest you utilise that script. It's time.'

'Time,' I echo.

I pause to look out the window, which frames a view of the abandoned Blockbuster video store and the old Service Tas building before they moved the centre to Ulverstone. Psychosis? MRI? As Doctor Cragg gets up and goes to her computer to write a referral and another script to take to the pharmacy now, fear sizzles behind my eyes and my vision clouds.

She looks over the top of her glasses, tapping her pen on her bottom lip as she regards me.

'Time's up,' she says abruptly in a lighter voice. 'I'll see you in a fortnight.'

Chapter 15

From Mum's car, I look blankly to the wind-streaked clouds that are spilling over the mountain tops, shredding the winter cerulean sky. Rounding the last upward corrugated bend before home, Doctor Cragg's diagnosis hammers in my head: *Psychosis. Diagnosis. Psychosis. Diagnosis.*

Nearing the dairy, Mum opens the window and the cold mountain air blasts inside, slapping my too-hot cheeks. Dad is clanking in the undercover yards to the roar of SAND FM's mainland syndicated afternoon show. The city-centric comedy duo's inane banter about *MasterChef* spills out over the barren paddocks.

'Dinner will be early tonight,' Mum calls to Dad. '*MasterChef* final.'

He waves at her and turns his back.

I look to Mum, wanting to be cruel to her.

'You do know that your heroic master chefs are also dishing up dioxins that bind to animal and human fatty tissue and bio-accumulate in the food chain. But who cares … let's just stick to our cognitive disconnect, industrial capitalist systems and mindless media addictions.'

Mum stops the car beside her empty fake wishing well.

'Oh Connie! Stop showing off with your stupid university brain. You're not smart at all. Look at the messes you make. Of your life. Of mine. Help me with the bags.'

'What? Those awful polypropylene things.' She cuts me with a

94

look. My inner dialogue marches me along the path: *Holy Moses I've got psychosis. What a diagnosis! Holy Moses …*

After I'm done putting the hideously over-packaged products into Mum's OCD pantry, I mutter that I'm going to my room.

'Here,' Mum passes me the crisp paper bag containing the medication. 'Might as well get stuck in.'

I head to the bathroom, splash water on my face and look into the mirror, swiping angrily at the familiar mole.

From the drawer, I take out the crumpled box of medication I'd already bought yesterday and hold both light-as-air packets in my palms, sensing their pharmaceutical denseness. Sitting them on the sink, I fill my bathroom cup with water. Leaning in towards the mirror, I gaze deep into my reflection. There are specks of gold in my dark brown eyes. I think of Nick-nack. I look down to the pills, press a tablet out of the foil.

Chills run over my skin. Hastily, I wrap the tablet in a tissue, ram it in the bin and shove the boxes back in the drawer. Staring into my eyes again in the mirror, I immediately know I have to get out of here and back to the cottage.

Skedaddling from the bathroom, I almost collide with Patrick.

'Doctor Cragg sorted your Skippies out?' he asks, tapping the side of his head.

For a split second I want to tell him about Dad and Raylene, but the sneering look on his face stops me.

'At least the medication she's given me is legal,' I counter. 'Not like the shit you shovel into yourself to numb your feelings. You're just as bonkers as me, Patrick. Who wouldn't be, with parents like them?'

I see him flinch ever so slightly, then he gives me the middle finger and shuts the bathroom door in my face.

It's just the impetus I need to go to the hallway cupboard, drag out my old boarding school suitcase and, like a secret agent who's been sprung, start packing my things in haste. I'm so excited to be zipping up my case, I barely register the dogs barking at a car arriving.

After surveying my room for what feels like the last time, I set off down the hall, trailing the case.

As I near the kitchen, Raylene Rootes-Stewart's crisp voice buzzes near my ears like a slightly terrifying wasp. What's she doing here? Peering from behind the door, I see she's talking to my mother at the kitchen bench. Their heads bowed together.

'Psychosis?' Raylene Rootes-Stewart says in a shocked whisper. 'Are you *sure*?'

Mum whimpers. 'Yes.'

'Oh, my dear.'

Raylene's sharp pencilled-on eyebrows are unnervingly similar to Mum's, shaped by the same lady in the Plaza shopping centre booth. Raylene's lift upwards in a show of conciliation as she whispers, 'At least she's not a lesbian.'

My mother dabs a tissue to her cheek. 'Who would even know that? I'm not sure what any man would see in her? Lord knows why that professor targeted her. The second girl was far prettier. That I could understand.'

Another part of me crumples inside. I know I ought to stop listening, but I hang near the doorway.

'Hopefully the medication she got from Doctor Cragg today will help. I'm exhausted, Raylene. Exhausted. She exhausts me.'

Not as much as Raylene exhausts your husband, Mum, I want to say, bursting through the door. But I don't.

'Well,' Raylene says, 'I reckon our plan will work. For now. Don't you think?'

Plan? I wonder. Deep breath. In I go. Leaving the case in the hallway, lurking like a forbidden lover.

'Bonjour, Maman. Bonjour, Raylene! Comment ça va?'

Raylene looks at me blandly. Large half-sphere earrings dominate her lobes, like she has two half apricots stuck on her ears. Her top is striped in the same fruity colour with white – pristine – like her trousers. Her boat shoes, also white, are tied with laces tipped in gold, the eyelets matching her bracelets, rings and the chain that loops to her glasses. All I can think of is my dad having sex with her. I shudder.

'Ah Connie! So lovely to see you,' Raylene says, but looks me up and down and sniffs as if I'm roadkill on the turn.

'Connie, dear!' Mum says, her smile stretching thinly upwards. 'You'll never guess what? Raylene has come to tell us the most exciting news!'

That she's banging Dad, I think grimly. When I don't respond, Mum fills the gap.

'Raylene's Nikki is going on maternity leave!'

A Nikki-image flashes in my mind. Raylene's daughter is one of those clippity-cloppity efficient girls, always looking oh-so-proper in her neutral-tone linen dresses and her long-sheened ponytail that swishes like the silkiest of race-day horse tails.

Mum has always compared me to her – from pre-kinder play dates to Christmas camping trips with the Rootes-Stewarts, all the way through. They gave up hope of us ever being friends in Grade 1 when I put worms in Nikki's sandwich. I didn't do it to be nasty. I did it because I actually believed they would taste nice. The birds seemed to love them so much, so why wouldn't Nikki? Even Slugs had taken a bite and said it 'wasn't bad' before I was sent home and the counsellor had been called in for Nikki.

'Congratulations. That will be nice for her,' I say. 'She can nest in her last month of pregnancy.'

My mother relaxes a little. I've clearly given the appropriate response.

'Well, yes,' says Raylene. 'It's great for Nikki. But the thought of being a grandma makes me feel so old! But I believe it's *you* we need to congratulate, Connie, love.'

My eyes narrow suspiciously as I look from Mum to Raylene.

'Congratulate me? Why?'

They glance at each other. Raylene sweeps up non-existent crumbs on Mum's benchtop into her palm.

'Nikki's convinced them at Global Genetics that you can take on some of her work while she has the baby!'

'Nikki's job? But isn't she ...? Doesn't she ...?'

'Sell semen,' Raylene says brightly.

'Sell semen,' I repeat darkly.

The room spins. I don't want to slip. Not here. Not in front of Mum and Raylene. In my head, I count backwards from a hundred, like Doctor Cragg has suggested.

'Yes! But not just any semen! The best dairy semen in the world. Irish, Canadian, American, German, Scandinavian and of course, Australian. We're exporting embryos and semen to China and the Philippines now. You'll be part of it all, Connie. At least until Nikki's back.'

'But I don't want to be a semen sales rep,' I say weakly. Mum looks set to explode.

My mind races and runs screaming, smack bang into the conclusion that this is a set-up. I know the Rootes-Stewarts are majority shareholders of Global Genetics and Raylene is on the board, so she has sway. She has manufactured this position for me – a sheltered workshop role. Out of guilt, perhaps?

'Connie!' hisses Mum through a tense smile. 'You could at least give it a try! Remember when you were little, how you would go through the bull catalogues with Dad? You'd help him choose our semen.'

I nod but know she's talking rubbish. I just liked looking at the amazing names they gave the bulls and their impressive regal pictures, with combed plumed ends of tails, front legs positioned on mounds of dirt, heads tugged high in shiny leather halters.

'Of course, we'll have to take you shopping at the Plaza for some new slacks. I'm pretty sure nothing fits you anymore. A shame you can't borrow some of my clothes ...' She turns to Raylene. 'Poor Connie takes after the Mulligan women, not the slim O'Reillys on my side.'

Mum and Raylene look me up and down.

Panic grips – I think of the boxes of medication in the bathroom drawer. Doctor Cragg says it will take a couple of weeks for them to take effect.

'When do I start?'

'Monday,' they say in unison.

'Monday! But it's Friday! In three days?'

'Plenty of time. Saturday morning shopping it is.'

As much as I don't want to work at Global Genetics, I realise that with a job, I'll be more likely able to do up Granny M's cottage and get myself away from here. I think of Uncle Larry's hillside supermarket that emerges from fecund soil across the river. I could start my own garden. Fend for myself. Maybe today is the day my life turns around. Excitement starts tingling in me.

Patrick emerges from a cloud of Brut from his post-milking shower so Mum blurts out my news to him.

'Her? A job?' Patrick frowns. 'Doing what? Tearing up rags from the op shop with the other 'tards?'

Mum stiffens. 'That's not very nice, Patrick. You mustn't make fun of your sister or people with disability.'

'Same diff.' He grins.

Raylene looks smugly at us, as if she's enjoying this dysfunctional family shitshow.

'At least I'm not ejaculating chemicals all over the farm that have been scientifically proven to cause smaller penises in wallabies. You've most likely got an empty sperm-sack with munted atrazine-addled tadpoles.'

Mum reels back in horror. Instead of bright jagged lights beating like wings in front of my eyes, I deliver a wink to Patrick, and for a moment feel a beat of connectivity with him. Maybe the way we carry on is actually our way of coping with the toxicity we've both marinated in all our lives with Mum and Dad.

'I'm moving out. I'll be over at Granny M's,' I say calmly. 'And on Monday I can become as complicit as Raylene in shrinking the global gene pool down to cattle that are more inbred than the people you'd find in Lilyburn.'

Brushing past Patrick, I notice a teeny smirk of amusement on his face.

Chapter 16

The wind is slinging arrowhead raindrops that sting my mountainside cheek. As I lug my suitcase towards Granny M's, the gusting westerly picks up even sharper. Then the downpour gets heavier, buzzing my body. The saturated air carries excitement as dramatic dark clouds fold over the darkened mountains, and trees moan in the wind. Nick-nack follows, ears flattened, less elated than me to be out in the elements.

By the time we get to Granny M's door, we're soaked. Rain slams on the cottage roof deafeningly, droplets sliding from us, puddling on the boards. Nick-nack looks up at me with lit-up eyes, as if she is gazing directly at God, her tail wagging with pure joy at the potential that I might let her inside. Traveller has spotted me and is moving from his sheltered spot under the lonely gum, head tilted against the watery onslaught, ears pricked despite the deluge. He arrives at the rusted bullnose veranda roof and almost walks up the steps to me. A warmth sweeps through me along with the unfamiliar sensation of joy.

'We're home,' I say to them both. Before I shut the door on the squalling day, I gaze out across the valley towards Uncle Larry's. Through the storm-tossed trees, glimpses of his lit windows reveal themselves. I'm relieved to see the lights and vow to visit him as soon as the weather eases.

Nick-nack follows me, trailing water along the hallway. I first gather some old kindling from the wood box on the back veranda, and revive the old lounge room heater. It seems to breathe with satisfaction as it warms, the flames licking the dry wood.

In the bathroom cupboard I find some tatty, scratchy old towels and shag up Nick-nack's wet coat. She delights in the drying off, so that when I stop, she wants to play tug of war with the towel. After an intense battle where the torn towel loses, I invite her to sit on the mat in front of the wood heater. As if she's been an inside dog all her life, she sighs contentedly, curling up, tail over nose.

Her eyes follow me as I drag the old leather pouf nearer the fire and sit to undo my suitcase, pulling out my old jeans and comfy woollen jumper, relieved to be peeling off my wet town clothes that feel tainted by my visit to Doctor Cragg and the pharmacy today. Tucked flat in the side of the case, I remember the sketch of the woman that I swiped from Uncle Larry's. Taking her out, I stare at her face for a time, then prop her on the mantle. It feels right that she is here.

In the kitchen, I'm relieved when the tap runs clear and easily. I recall the tank up on the stand and Grandad's sermon on the surety and freeness of gravity to serve us – not just in the farmhouse, but on the land as well. Turns out Mum didn't know what she was talking about. Slinging my already soaked jacket over my shoulders, I dart out into the rain and pluck up some mint that's gone wild along the side of the house. In the kitchen I find a small saucepan, fill it with water and throw in some leaves, setting it on the wood heater in the lounge room to boil.

After tenderly moving Granny's coat and dress back to her room, I flop into her old armchair, a cup of mint tea warming my palms, the old worn chintz chair wrapping around me. Looking about the room, I know I have days, even months of back-breaking, nail-tearing, arm-aching, neck-crunching, knee-crushing work ahead of me to lift the cottage to somewhere near livable, but my heart feels happy about the task. The rain on the roof thrums, the fire crackles, Nick-nack snores and I stare into the flames and whisper a prayer of gratitude to the Mulligan women who trod these old floorboards before me.

Good girl, Connie, I can almost hear Granny Mulligan's voice in my head.

Good girl? I feel my mind prickle. The notion can't seem to land. Me? Good? Me who learned I am bad, messy, lazy and naughty. That I am shameful, fat, ugly, useless. And yet ... maybe I *am* a good person – at least I have good intentions.

I look up to the old print above the fire of Ayrshire cows grazing in a meadow as low sunlight spills over the gentle trees. Memories of Granny M flood my mind.

I am in the kitchen, Vegemite jar in hand, black goop all over my hands and clothes. Granny and Grandad's Jack Russell, Spades, is also covered in the salty dark smear, swivelling to lick it from his coat.

'Connie Mulligan! What have you done?' Granny exclaimed, coming into the kitchen and dumping down an armful of silverbeet.

'I'm turning Spades into the Ace of Spades,' I said. 'Black.'

Granny Mulligan stood in her boots and house dress, belly jiggling up and down, laughing, hanky pressed to her mouth, eyes creased.

'Grandad! Grandad! Come see your new dog!' she called out. Spades, catching on to the mirth, began to twirl and yap.

As Grandad arrived and they'd stood there chuckling, they hadn't called me naughty or shouted that I'd made a mess or wasted good food, but instead Granny M had called me 'inventive' and Grandad said I was 'creative'. Soon after, with Spades in the deep concrete laundry tub, brown salty bubbles lathering from his coat, Granny M explained: 'Spades wasn't named after the spades on the cards. He was named that because he dug up my garden a lot when he was a puppy.'

'Spades, you're naughty!' I said, looking into his little chocolate-sultana brown eyes.

'Oh darling, he wasn't being naughty, that's just what puppies do! They dig! Grandad and I made a game of it and trained him that he could dig all he liked in some areas of the garden, but not others. He just needed some creative freedom. And someone who could speak his language.'

I realise now she was trying to reach me. To say that my parents didn't speak my language. Dear Granny.

*

Getting up from my chair, I wander to the laundry to the same concrete sink. Spades is long gone. Just the drifting shell of a dead daddy long-legs spider hanging from the tap. If it had been my mother who had discovered my Vegemite dog desecration, she would've smacked my legs with a wooden spoon and showered me in cold water, before locking me in my room.

I stare out the water-streaked windows to Grandad's workshop and machinery shed. I watch my little seven-year-old self trailing Grandad across the grass, a clean Spades following me. Inside the shed, he set up a piece of wood in a vice and passing me a hammer and a nail, said, 'Here, have a crack.'

As I tentatively swung the hammer, he said with a glint in his turquoise eyes, 'I can tell you have the Mulligan practical gene, Connie. It's no good just being clever, you need to be both practical and wise. You have that in spades.'

He had no sooner said spades, when Spades appeared, tail wagging, sump oil smeared over his back, dabbing footprints over the shed floor. Grandad had groaned and then laughed.

'Back to the tub for you,' he said.

*

Now here in the cottage, I feel fed by them. Sheltered by them, and a return to a self I'd forgotten all about. I turn the laundry tap on, listen to its splutter, and wash the old dead spider away.

You're a good girl, Connie, I hear again as if the water is carrying words through the pipes from a time long ago. I turn the tap off and go back to the fireside chair that offers so much more than just warmth.

103

Unexpectedly, there's a knock on the door. In the cold dimness of the afternoon, stands my mother under her orange umbrella, her face drawn and tense.

'Are you ready to come home?' she asks. 'Your father's going off his rocker.'

'I am home.'

'Please, Connie.'

It seems she has no energy for anger or fight. And here in the cloistering of the cottage I have no energy for fear of her.

'No,' I say firmly again, in a voice I barely recognise.

She looks at me with sadness, then eventually she shrugs. 'Suit yourself. You'll be back in a day or so. Once you realise what living with no power is like.'

'I've got a wood stove. The dunny flushes. Got warm water to wash myself. What more does a woman need?' I reply with bravado.

Mum shakes her head. 'All that money, wasted on formal private schooling. Then the shame of what you did. And this is how you treat me.'

She turns and stalks towards the gloomy glow of the farmhouse through the rain. I shut the door and sense, more than hear, Granny Mulligan's voice.

Good girl. Stand your ground.

*

That afternoon, I set about cleaning and decluttering, room to room, Nick-nack trailing me about as I sort stuff into piles. Op shop. Waste recycling centre. Or chuck. When I venture onto the back porch I notice how the back rooms' floors lean like a listing ship. Out in the rain, I look underneath the house to find two of the cottage's foundation stumps have rotted away. Remembering there's a couple of Grandad's old metal truck jacks in his garage, I think to myself that tomorrow I shall bribe Patrick with a box of beer to help me prop the old girl up on her underfloor bearers again so I can close the toilet door. Level.

A few hours later, the mummified animals removed, floors mopped and candles in place for tonight and the bed made with clean yet musty sheets, I step out onto the veranda to enjoy a moment of stillness. The rain has eased so magpies warble on the grass, strutting about for worms that have risen in the sodden soil. My stomach grumbles hunger.

Pulling on my boots, I call Nick-nack to my side. 'Larry'll have some tucker for us.'

The rushing river below the cottage is sending frenetic energy into the damp atmosphere. The low winter sun emerging from unburdened rain clouds tells me there's not much daylight left, so to save time I head to the machinery shed. With my Ace of Spades in my pocket, knowing I've got the card of all cards in my deck to deal to Dad, I pinch his four-wheeler. As I rev away down the track, Nick-nack perched behind me, I think, Dad can go off his nut at me. I don't care. That will only force my hand. I will play my card, so he knows *that I know!*

As I fishtail over Dad's cultivation obsession, the rain has turned our soil into a puree of diarrhoea. Leaving the bike beside the river, Nick-nack and I cautiously cross the wonky old timber-getter's bridge, watching the rush of energy below.

Stepping onto the other side, instantly I'm soothed by the intense bushland fragrance released by the rain. Before I know it, without too much puff up the steep track, Nick-nack and I have arrived. We find Uncle Larry in his rain-soaked vegetable garden, one boot up on a garden fork digging out spuds stored in the cold winter earth, his cheeks pink.

'Hellooo, Uncle Larry!' I call, leaning over the high fence so I don't startle him and give him a heart attack.

'*Fuck!*' I roar when the fence bites me on the chest. I'm the one about to have a heart attack. I look to the plain wire I'd failed to see that is insulated by black keepers along the top of the fence.

'Possum wire's on,' Larry says, not halting in his spud-gathering, a subtle smile on his face.

'Well, it's working,' I confirm.

He stoops awkwardly to gather up a wooden crate.

'Here,' I say, rushing around to the gate, 'I'll get that for you.'

'No need,' he says as he makes his way slowly through a patchwork of winter flowers and vegetables, greeting Nick-nack with a quiet, 'G'day dog.'

It's then I notice a fresh-dug patch beside the garden gate. Old timber paling has been nailed into the shape of a cross. Lettering on it says *Frida Kelpelo*. Larry sees me looking.

'My last kelpie. She was a good one.'

'When?'

'Just last week.' The heaviness of his loss carries with him as we walk to the house where he pauses to kick off his wet boots and asks abruptly, 'What do you want?'

He doesn't wait for my answer, but instead goes through the side door to the kitchen. Hastily I dislodge my boots, tell Nick-nack to wait. She settles beside my gumboots as I follow Larry inside.

'I don't want anything,' I say to him.

He sets down the box. 'Well, what are you doing here?'

'Checking that you're okay. That you don't need anything.'

He pauses. He looks younger today. Perhaps it's because he's cut his hair, has shaved, and his blood is circulating around his body once more.

Then he narrows his brown eyes. 'What could you possibly offer me?'

I look down to my socked feet. I bite my lip. Tears threaten.

'Nothing. Actually. I have absolutely nothing.'

As I angrily swipe a pesky tear that has escaped, I feel him regarding me intensely. My cheeks begin to burn. Eventually he speaks.

'Well, while you're here, you'd better make yourself useful.'

He chucks me a potato peeler, rinses rich soil from the largest potato I've ever seen and rolls it across the table to me, leaving a muddy trail. Neither of us speak as we get on with peeling and chopping spuds. Then we start on the giant leeks that he pulls from the crate. Soon he gestures to the side pantry behind a sliding door that I'd failed to find on my first visit.

'Onions. In there.'

Entering, I find the bounty of stored apples, dried herbs, plaited garlic and onions neatly hanging from an old ladder. When I re-emerge and quietly begin on the onions, the bellows of Dad's cows rise and the tractor revs. It's silage time. I can hear Dad screaming his guts out calling for Nick-nack. And for me.

'Far out, he's noisy,' I say. 'Even without his bike.'

'Tell me about it,' Uncle Larry says. 'Always was a mouthy, loud bastard. You can set your watch to his racket.'

'Sorry,' I say.

'What for?'

'For that,' I say, pointing hopelessly in the direction of Dad's angry cacophony.

Larry shrugs. 'It's not your doing.'

He sets the pot on the stove and fuels the wood oven.

'Hungry?' he asks as he takes a billy can of fresh milk from the fridge and sets it beside the stove. A swell of tears pool again in my eyes, and I know it's more than the onions.

'Yes. Starving.'

Larry looks at me with a furrowed brow, shrugs, then finishes peeling. As I swipe scraps into the chook bucket, Larry begins cooking the soup. I glance up to a painting of the woman above the wood stove's mantel, this time she is painted amid springtime daffodils. I can't help myself.

'Who is she?'

Larry stops stirring. 'Who?'

I gesture to the painting and then to the smaller oil portraits on wooden boards that are propped on the old dresser. 'The woman in the paintings.'

He looks back at the pot, staring into it as if the answer is in there, the muscles in his jaw firing. He turns to me slowly, his eyes narrowed bitterly. 'You'd better ask your father that.'

Chapter 17

The next day is Plaza day. Any comfort found in Uncle L's soup and Granny M's cottage dissolves as I sink captive in the leather seat of Mum's pristine RAV, swerving around thick concrete columns, following yellow lines to find a park. The Plaza's underground carpark roof looms low. Fluoro lighting flickers in the corner of my eye. Any resolve to be calm is smothered by the sheer weight of the huge shopping centre complex, concreted heavily above us. Mum's fury at me moving into Granny M's fills the car to the point where I feel as if I can't breathe.

'We should've got here earlier,' she complains. 'Saturdays are always extra busy.'

A cluster of shoppers glide trolleys out from an illuminated glass tunnel, making their way to their cars. My heart kicks, my palms sweat. Each time I look at Mum's sharp profile, images of the rocking Volvo dance into my head. Then arrives the woman's face in the sketch and Larry's words, 'Ask your father.' Dark pasts, these Mulligans.

We get out of the car in Red Section 4 – Mum has me repeat it to her so we don't lose the car. Every muscle in my body fires.

'Stand up straight, Connie,' Mum barks as she gathers up her orange tote bag and zaps the car locked.

Walking through the auto doors, I'm sent into heart-racing sweats as we slide up the escalator. Advertising light boxes show off the latest in lingerie for impossibly skinny youths, and the best-value bundle of addictive fat and sugar that can be had for just four dollars.

'Don't touch the rail, Connie. Germs.'

'Stop treating me like I'm five,' I say.

'Stop acting like it then.'

The moving ramp glides us past another teen model's bikini-clad crotch and we are spewed out into the shiny, slippery first floor. As I leap nervously off the escalator, the tiles feel as if they're moving too. The sound-soup of humans floods my mind with a dull panic. Under the maddening lighting, I acknowledge the sad irony of the fake plastic plants that fail to photosynthesise and freshen the artificial air that is pumped through dust-lined ducts. As I wipe my damp palms on my thighs, I recall Doctor Cragg once instructed me to take the Plaza on. 'Tell your primitive part of your fight-or-flight brain that there are no lions or tigers here.'

'But,' I retorted during that session, 'there are dangers that lurk there. Real dangers. Predators of the worst kind. Worse than lions and tigers. The giant corporations. Forever ravenous, eating up younger and younger victims. From the window posters of computer-smoothed models in porno, come-shag-me get-up, to the fast-food outlets selling blob chickens in oil to DNA-altered Oompa Loompa kids, to the phone shop that charges a hundred bucks for pieces of wire and plastic because people have to have the latest iGadget and don't seem to mind brain tumours from increasing levels of electromagnetic frequencies that waver through their skulls unseen!'

I'm sure after my monologue that Doctor Cragg only just stopped herself from rolling her eyes. 'It's common for people to experience panic attacks in busy places like shopping centres, Connie. That's all that's happening. The rest is in your mind.'

Mum is now browsing ten-dollar factory-sweatshop flannelette shirts outside Blowes Menswear. Glimpsing the fruit and vegetables in Woolies, my wired body picks up on the seemingly perfect produce that belies the invisible chemicals of warfare that are infused within them, grown in deadened soil destined for desertification. This place is genuinely a horror show to me but it seems no one else in Lilyburn sees it. Let alone calls it out. Cognitive fucking dissonance!

My body shudders and my overloaded brain tries to cope, but the centre is too busy, too noisy, *too everything*, and my vision blazes white. As I look at the seemingly plastic produce, my brain begins to chant: *Pesticide. Herbicide. Fungicide. Insecticide. Suicide. Genocide. Infanticide. Homicide. Pesticide, herbicide, fungicide, insecticide.* The words loop around and around until I blurt out, 'Cide! Latin for kill!'

'What?' Mum looks at me critically, knowing I'm slipping.

'I can't be here,' I say. My lips are tingling, the left side of my face is numb and my arm is zizzing with pain.

Mum groans. 'For goodness sakes, Connie! Stop being so dramatic. You put this on every time! Come on! I haven't got all day. I think we'll start at Millers. They ought to have plus sizes. You may have got to that stage, don't you think?'

Her words are like soggy two-minute noodles in my ears as I try to settle my system with some Doctor Cragg breaths. My body jumps when a loud voice comes over the speakers.

'Goooooood morning, Lilyburn! So great you're here to Do it with Dean-O this morning, right here in Shopright Plaza where it's Shop-a-holics Saturday! Hooraaaaay!'

'Oh! It's him!' Mum looks around excitedly.

His voice, surround sound, comes again. 'There's loads of great giveaways and fantastic tunes to get you in that shopping mood! So come on down and see us on Upper Level One, opposite Wendy's Donuts.'

Dean-O flicks a switch so we're instantly suffering an 80s revival, piped throughout the Plaza, where The Bangles are having a 'Manic Monday' even though it's Saturday.

'That explains why it's so busy,' Mum says. 'I've always wanted to meet him. He sounds so lovely on the radio!'

The flush of a lovestruck maiden blooms on Mum's cheeks, her eyes shining bright. Grabbing my arm, she hauls me up another escalator and on towards SAND FM's leading guy, DJ Dean-O.

SAND FM's mixer desk is flanked by radio display banners and two skinny promo girls in cat-slink black, illuminated by long platinum-blonde hair. One dazzles a smile, passing Mum an *I do it with Dean-O every morning!* bumper sticker.

'Oh! Thank you!' Mum gushes. 'May I have a second one for my husband's farm ute? He does Dean-O in the dairy, *every* morning.'

Her cringeworthy fangirl gush is enough to cure me temporarily of my Plaza panic as she lets out a little squeal and starts waving both hands at him.

'Helloooo! Oh Dean-O! Hello! Big fan!'

Mum lunges as Dean-O shines a massive cosmetic dental bill smile. He steps forward in a black bomber jacket, denim jeans, white t-shirt and runners, on-trend retro glasses, and rat's tail in place on his shoulder.

'May I shake your hand?' she purrs.

'You can do more than shake my hand, madam, if you like,' he says, smothering her hand with both of his. Mum blushes and looks away.

'What's a lovely looking doll like you doing in a Plaza like this?' he smoodges.

Mum presses her red lacquered fingertips onto her chest in false modesty, and laughs again. 'Oh just a bit of shopping. I'm buying my daughter some slacks. She starts work on Monday.'

Dean-O looks me over. I can tell he feels sorry a glamourpuss like Mum has a daughter like me.

'Oh? Work doing what?'

'Selling semen,' Mum answers proudly.

I want the floor to open up and swallow me. When you are as into cows as our family are, it's nothing to talk about scrotal circumference, nice tits and semen straws. To us it's like talking about the footy score or the weather. But what Mum fails to realise is, not everyone understands what she means by selling semen, as Dean-O's horrified face would testify.

'We're dairy farmers,' I say, trying to be helpful. 'So it's bull semen she's talking about.'

Dean-O looks relieved. 'Yes! What other semen would she be talking about!' He laughs too loudly, awkwardly. 'Interesting job,' he finishes. But I can tell he doesn't mean it.

'With Global Genetics,' Mum adds to impress.

'Ahh yes! I think I've heard of them,' he charms with a white lie. 'Well, duty calls.' He gestures to the mic. Before he presses the 'on' button, he calls out to Mum. 'A pleasure to meet you Mrs …?'

'Mulligan.'

'Mulligan,' he confirms as if he really wants to remember.

'You can call me Mary,' Mum says.

His eyebrows lift. 'Mary, fair Mary!' He pats the place of his heart and swoons his eyes upwards. 'You're a fine, fine woman! Your husband is a lucky, lucky man! An absolute pleasure to meet you, *Mary*.'

Dean-O hooks on his headphones, fades the song and blares out another round of 'Goooood Morning, Lilyburn Plaza!' pistol-shooting an index finger at us as he does.

Walking on towards Millers Fashion, Mum's like the cat that's got the cream.

'Oh, he's so nice. Doing it with Dean-O in the morning will never be the same again!'

Life, post Raylene rooting Dad, will never be the same again either, I think as I follow her, dragging my gloom along behind me like a dead possum on a bit of bale twine.

*

The change room is impossibly small and I'm onto my sixth pair of pants, averting my eyes from my winter-white post-Turner trauma body. It's almost unrecognisable to me under the harsh lighting – like it belongs to another person.

'Have you got them on yet?'

Mum begins to draw back the curtain. I hold it fast in place.

'No! Just a sec.'

'Could you be any slower?' Mum huffs.

As I stoop to step into the trousers, I daren't look at my face in the mirror. If I do, I'll see the hideous dark mole above my lip, and the jagged short dark hair framing my blocky, bleak face. It's not so much my face I want to avoid, but my eyes. My haunted eyes. As I haul the awful elastic-waisted polyester pants up and over my backside and gut, I feel as if I can't get a breath in. Vertigo spins me.

Professor Turner appears. He's at his computer, his back to me. I've just knocked on his door. He drops his head when he sees it's me.

'What do you want?'

'I came to see you about something.'

He propelled the chair forward with his feet to its place behind his main desk. The desk he used to sit me on. The desk where he had parted my legs and rubbed his unzipped erection against my inner thigh, whispering in my ear that I was his curvy little genius. I remembered the last time he'd done this his socks had been peacock blue with toucans on them. Today his socks were purple with yellow fish on them. Elbow patches red, and deep brown–framed glasses. Not his best choice.

'Yes?' he hissed.

My heart scrunched. I knew the documents I held in my hands were dangerous.

'I found this on the internet while I was researching, and I wanted to ask you about it,' I said, spreading the American Food and Drug Administration release document out on the table.

'Researching what?' he asked.

'Researching you.' I tapped one of the documents. 'I've been reading up about the FDA's green light for Baker Earth's Dicamba and Round Up tolerant corn. And cotton, and canola and sugarbeet and soybeans. Over several years.'

I ran my finger over the referenced list of scientists who, by law, had to put their names on the papers that supported the global brand of agrichemicals.

'Surely there can't be two Simon S Turners who work in this field?'

He looked at me with a chilly ominous air but said nothing.

'You were working in America around this time, weren't you?'

'So?'

I pulled from my folder the printout of the small news clipping I'd found in a local US newspaper, reporting scientists had allegedly skewed the research results leading to the release of some of the deadliest toxins to be used on patented seeds and crops.

'You've always taught me to research thoroughly ... well, I discovered just how many US universities are financially influenced by big pharma and chemical companies. Including the university you were working at in the States. So, not surprising it would be in a scientist's best interest to lead the results in a certain way if there was big money offered?'

Turner narrowed his eyes and I matched him back.

'Does Austral know?' I asked, waving the article at him.

'Know what? It was that line of research and my contacts that made them so keen to have me home. You do realise you're firing blanks, Connie. Those ridiculous allegations were all cleared years ago. What's this got to do with anything?'

'It's got to do with everything!' I said, thinking of the way he'd built me up, torn me down, played with me, groomed me for his own pleasure.

'Connie,' he tried to soothe in his old tender tone, 'what's this really about?'

'It's about the F's you keep giving me. And I'm not talking Fucks, because you've been careful not to go that far. You told me science was meant to be impartial. But it's not, is it? Because if you were skewing your results to make it okay to dump deadly water-soluble toxins into our food systems, for advancement, for tenure, for money or your career or whatever ... then it's not impartial. But this article explains why a man of your, let's say, scientific calibre, is hiding out in your hometown at a small-time university where the only power you can now wield is over your gullible female students.'

He stood from his desk. 'I've had enough of you! It was a mistake to mentor you.'

'Mentor me? Is that what you call it?'

'If you expose me, I expose you. Little whore,' he hissed. 'What would your parents think of you? The way you prick-teased me. As if anyone would believe someone like you.'

*

'Connie!' Mum barks. I startle and see my eyes in the change-room mirrors. Deep. Black. Stupid. Whorish. I have to get out of here! I drag back the curtain. Mum looks to the pants critically.

'They look a bit ... a bit dowdy. But they're the best so far.'

Emotion arrives in a tidal surge, sobs threaten like dark storm clouds. Tugging the tag off with the barcode, I shove it into her hands. 'Here. These'll do. I'll pay you back later. I'm going!'

'Going? Going where? Connie? Stop! *Wait!*'

I'm running again, over the slippery tiled floor in my socks, leaving my boat shoes adrift in the change room with my old pants, and my mum standing open-mouthed watching me go. My shame following me like a terrifying haunting in the darkest of woods.

Chapter 18

Outside the Plaza on the highway verge, cars roar by slushing oily droplets onto me. My socks are sodden. My heart, limp. Mum will be pissed off I've got my new semen-sales work trousers dirty already. The frost-clear morning has gone, like the currawongs at Granny M's this morning said it would, and now dark clouds are rising over the far-off mountains, the wind at my back, rain falling. A jacket would be good right now. I'm already soaking from the long grasses the council will, come springtime, blast with glyphosate again. My feet are freezing, my scalp cold, nose running. Tears and snot. A great look. I hear a crow call, but there are no crows out in this heavy rain. It's then I know I'm slipping.

The dark bird swoops, winging its way over the people gathered in the bleak cobbled village square. I look in horror to the gallows where a coarse rope dangles the heavy pendulum of a yet-cold woman. Despite the frosted air, sweat trickles down my back.

'Witch!' shouts someone next to me in the crowd. I feel I'm about to crumble to the earth, when a hand lands firmly upon my arm. A Claddagh ring on the little finger.

'Tar anseo. Come here.' He pulls me to his chest, bends his head and whispers, 'It's not safe here for you. We must leave.'

Then everything falls to black.

A massive petrol tanker moans past, the driver blasting the horn, startling me back. I long for the hug of Granny M's cottage

116

around me. To revive the stove in the kitchen and get it breathing warmth again. Or to find that sliver of hope I discovered with Uncle Larry in his quiet cottage in the bushland. The rumble of another diesel engine nears, and I turn to see Slugs Meldron with his indicator light on, pulling over beside me.

'Okay then, Universe,' I say, surrendering into the moment. Slugs leans across and opens the passenger door. My unlikely knight is wearing a camo jacket and baseball cap on backwards that kicks out his mullet, and is chewing on a Macca's burger.

'Oh. Hello Slugs,' I say.

'Need a lift?'

'I guess.'

'S'cuse the mess,' he says, as he swipes waxy thick-shake cups and other food packaging from the passenger seat.

'No worse than my car,' I say, shutting the door. I'm instantly comforted by the warmth and the sound of his stereo playing Lee Kernaghan and The Wolfe Brothers' version of Slim's 'Lights on the Hill'. Everything feels a bit more normal. Boxes of bullets on the dash. Scope digging into my thigh on the seat. A peeling *I love bush pigs* sticker on the glove box. It's Tassie as, and I feel safer. Not like being in that fucking Plaza with all its mainland same-same plastic factory-generated crap.

Slugs looks over at me as I click on my seatbelt. 'You okay?'

'Yep.' I nod, stroking my palms over my sodden navy slacks. 'Just doing a bit of shopping. Nice to have this rain.' I nod towards the sparkling drops.

'Sure is,' Slugs says, looking down at my socked feet, his brow knitted with concern as the rubbers screen back and forth. His eyes linger on me, then he shrugs, checks his side mirror and pulls out on the highway. As we drive he does his best to cover over the madness my unexplained shoeless wandering brings.

'Mum said she liked seein' ya in town the other day.'

'Ah. Yeah. Good.'

'She didn't tell ya, did she?'

'Bout what?'

'Bout Dad. And them splittin' up?'

I spin a look at Slugs in shock. 'Your mum and dad are splitting up? No way!'

'Yeah. Nah. Yeah. True.'

I find the notion incomprehensible. Milk Tanker Barry and 'She'll be right Shirley' are such a fixed sun and moon in our Lilyburn world it's impossible to think their orbits have more than a wobble in them. We drive on, the wipers filling the silence.

'She never said anything,' I say.

'D'ya know why they're done and dusted?'

'No?'

Slugs has one hand draped casually on the top of the steering wheel, but there's nothing casual about his expression. His jaw is clenched, a deep frown. He swiftly eradicates a tear with the sleeve of his camo-fleece hunting shirt and fixes his eyes on the road.

'Whole town knows. Whole fucking district knows.' He thumps the steering wheel. We drive on, the wheels flinging up water from the road.

'I don't. But that's no surprise. Connie no-friends.'

'You can count me as your friend,' Slugs says quietly, staring ahead.

'Thanks. But why'd your dad up and leave? Your mum's awesome.'

'Let's just say Dad wanted a new wife.'

'A new wife? But he has your mum?'

'Not anymore he doesn't. He's getting a divorce so he can marry Anong.'

'A nong? You mean a young 'n' dumb one?' I ask.

'No! Her *name* is Anong. He ordered her on the internet.'

'He ordered her?'

'Well, you know what I mean. One of them Thai dating sites. He's been over there 'n' all. Left Mum 'n' me to deal with all the crap the corporates have been shoving at us – about pushing us out.'

'*Fuuuuck*,' I say remembering Shirley's devastated face outside Mr Crompton's. 'I'm sorry.'

Slugs grimaces and glances away, scrunching his face to stop the tears falling.

'You know … maybe it's for the best? Some things are in the long run.'

'Maybe,' he says, 'if the big guys don't bugger the business first. That's where the shit began. The stress. Arseholes.'

'Yep,' I say, thinking of the money-grabbing, morally vacuous Turner. 'Arseholes.'

The distance to Lilyburn feels like stretched rubber bands as we travel along the highway in silence.

Eventually Slugs says, 'I read in the paper about that guy at the uni. And how you … you know … tried to tell people about his dodgy science, and how he … you know … with … you … and that other girl … y'know? And then what them uni cockheads done to ya.'

I swallow. 'Yeah. Bit of a shit time.'

'Sorry. Shouldn'a brought it up.'

In the silence of wiper-swishing, I find myself stemming tears too. Then I have an overwhelming urge to share with Slugs my discovery that Raylene Rootes-Stewart is rooting my dad. I'm about to open my mouth, but then Slugs glances over at me.

'Where ya headed?'

I pause, knowing I need time for my body to settle so I can think straight. I have a headache. I have a body ache. I have a heart ache. I have a *world* ache. I begin to wonder how on earth I might be able to get back up the mountain to Sunnyside Farm, but at the moment I don't want to go back home.

'Cafe, I guess.'

Slugs glances at me as if I've just wiped snot on his glove box. 'Cafe? Not the vegan one?'

'Yup.'

'No way! Fucken vegans. They're all bonkers.'

'Fair enough. I get it. You can just drop me outside then?'

The conversation slides to an end after that.

*

In Lilyburn, Slugs steers his big-rig ute around the war memorial roundabout where the clock has been permanently stopped at 3.11 for as long as I can remember. The seagulls lift and scatter as we pass.

Nearing the real estate agency, former bakery and Greasy Joe's, I notice a gathering of council work vehicles. Out of their vehicles, the men are clustered together in their hi-vis work gear on the traffic island, looking like stranded neon penguins.

'G'day fellas,' Slugs says as he rolls to a stop, a gearstick flick into neutral so the engine idles like a docking ship. 'What are you doin' off your arses on a Saturday? What's goin' on?'

The men look out from the hoods of their big work-issue rain jackets, dripping, looking miserable.

'Flash flooding from all this rain,' one says.

'Been putting out the Water Over Road signs,' adds the young one, as if he's quite buoyed by the task.

The biggest council guy points to Greasy Joe's shop that is now shining with lights on the dark winter's day. There's a blonde woman moving about inside. Then Big Guy gestures to the old bakery opposite.

'We was just tryin' to get lunch. But it's only fucken women's centres. Or fucken vegans. I mean, what the fuck?'

'Yeah! A fella'd starve around here,' says the skinny wizened one, who looks like he's already halfway there.

'Tell me about it,' Slugs said. 'You blokes work on council … how'd they pass it? How'd they let this happen in Lilyburn? Fucken mainlanders, buyin' their way in.'

The men catch Slugs's wave.

'Hell yeah! It's like back in the eighties when them mainlander greenies turned up for the No Dams, and never fucken left,' Big Guy says.

'Yeah,' adds Junior, who's following their lead. 'What's it their business being here?'

I frown, the tension of the morning building up and spilling out of me. I open my mouth before I can stop myself.

'Is it really a serious community threat to have either a women's support centre or a vegan cafe in Lilyburn?' I lean forward, my voice cracking like a whip.

The men seem startled, as if they've noticed my presence for the first time.

'I mean, surely at this point in humanity's journey where we're on the brink of mass extinction, you can see that conservation is entirely necessary? In the eighties it wasn't just the mainlanders who were worried about protecting the wilderness of this place. There were plenty of Tassie people – small sawmill owners even – back then who predicted that the small parochial parliament run by the good ol' boys of Hobart was going to bugger up the place. Which they are. Take a look at salmon farming. The tree plantations. The big inefficient irrigation systems. The chemical ag. The offshore land sales. All founded on shitful governance that provides no meaningful regulation. Tassie locals are all poorer for it.'

Slugs shifts uncomfortably in his seat. I plough on. My mind and my panic that no one can see the truth is running my mouth, like it used to at uni.

'The sons of those old school ties are *still* chasing power and money – still selling our land to foreign investors, cramming the place with tourists, clearing bush for more houses, blasting land to quarry blue metal for more roads, destroying ecosystems for more corporate farms! Those same governments are backing deadly supermarket systems and encouraging chemical cocktails to be sprayed on our tucker. Killing river health and poisoning our seas.'

My voice is winding up, like a northwest coast wind turbine in a gale, but I can't stop. Rivers of frightening research floods my brain from uni days, and such is my desperation for these people to truly see the truth, I keep on talking even though I can see their steel-cold faces glaring at me.

'Take you boys, for example, your local government, your council, is fine with having you spray all the roadsides and kiddies parks and schools with toxins. I can see some of you are past your breeding prime, but for those of you who aren't ...' I look directly at Pimpled Junior who has surfer blond hair escaping from his rain-soaked hood. 'You oughta know the sperm count of Aussie men has dropped more than fifty per cent in less than forty years! If that's not a message that we're jet-skiing up shit creek then what is? Targeting vegans and stressed-out mums ain't gunna help ... If you fellas want jobs and growth here, we need to let in new people, new ideas, new economics – in a system that factors community *and* nature, not just money and big swinging dicks.'

I stop. I breathe. I can feel my heart trying to shatter my ribs from the inside out. Slugs's cheeks have gone a flame red. The men have shuffled back uncomfortably. When they don't respond, I add mildly, 'They do an okay pie out at the servo. It's not a National by any stretch, but if you're hungry?'

I suck in a breath, looking through the rain-smeared window to the lovely old double-storey bakery that's getting a makeover. There's a battered skip bin in the lane between it and the pub, and the shop's doors are cast open, despite the roar of waves and wind-driven rain. Outside, only just hanging in against the gale, tethered to a post like a skittish horse, are a couple of chalkboards. The specials sign is advertising so many specials, it seems nothing is special.

In large font the other board shouts:

CRUELTY-FREE MEALS
LUNCH SPECIALS
Lentil and Cauliflower Pilaf
Vegan Shiitake Scaloppine
Dairy-free ice creams

'Thanks for the lift, Slugs,' I say, abruptly getting out of the ute. As coolly as I can in my socks, dorky slacks and soaked clothing, I saunter over the road.

As I go, I hear Slugs say to the men, 'She's got a few roos loose in her top paddock since that uni business.'

Chapter 19

I've no sooner set foot inside the Happy Chappy Vegan Cafe, when someone calls out, 'Hello beautiful. Here for some lunch?'

Beautiful? I look around to see if Nikki or someone is standing behind me. Eyes adjusting to the light, I recognise Moustache-man emerging from the kitchen swing door, drill in hand.

'You'll have to excuse the mess, we are open but we're still renovating.'

His voice is friendly and bubbly. He's wearing denim overalls, leg cuffs rolled up revealing yellow stitched Doc Martens. A bright green soccer top hugs his sculpted shoulders. While I'm looking him up and down, he's looking me up and down too.

'Have you forgotten to take your socks off, or have you forgotten to put your shoes on?' He grins at me.

I look down to my sodden socked toes. 'Um, I'm not really sure.' I pull a silly smiley face. He must think I'm mental. If he does, he's not far wrong, but he's not showing it.

'Socks off I say!' he declares brightly. 'Barefoot grounding on Mother Earth is the healthiest thing you can do for yourself. It's to do with Earth's magnetics. It's one of the reasons we moved here. Too much electromagnetic and air pollution and concrete in Melbourne. Horrendous. Vernon is terribly sensitive to it. It's good to be grounded.'

'Is someone talking about me?'

Blond-beard emerges, wiping his pale thin hands on a tea towel. Today he is beret-less and his hair is gelled up with product.

'Always,' says Moustache-man. 'Let's introduce ourselves to this lovely young woman.'

Lovely young woman?

He points to Blond-beard. 'This is my fiancé, Vernon Dawkins. And I'm Fenton. Fenton Plannery as in Tim Flannery, but with a P. And you are?'

'Connie. Connie Mulligan.'

'Connie Mulligan! Great name! Irish right?'

'From generations back. The Irish bit stuck, mainly thanks to the Catholicism I reckon.'

'Oh, how lovely,' says Fenton. 'About Ireland, not the Catholic bit. They've not been too keen on people like us historically.' He pulls a face.

'Nor people like me,' I add wryly. 'I think historically it has something to do with having ovaries and, in my case, strong opinions.'

'Touché, sister!' Vernon says. 'I've never thought of it that way. You may be interested in what our amazing Megan's planning over the road. She's wanting to run empowerment courses for women.'

I'm tempted to express my relief that the old greasy isn't going to become a cat shelter like Shirley first thought, but they strike me as 'cat people'.

'Have you ever been to Ireland?' Fenton asks, drawing us back to the start of our conversation.

'No. I've dreamed of going. One day, hopefully.'

'Us too,' Vernon says.

The pair lock eyes and begin to sing. 'When Irish eyes are smiling, sure they steal your heart away! When Irish hearts are happy all the world seems bright and gay!'

They laugh.

'Ireland will be a long time coming for us after biting off more than we can chew here!'

Fenton sweeps his hand around the new-look cafe. The bakery's cheap white plastic tables and chairs that used to scrape loudly over the tiled floor have been replaced instead with warm timber trestle tables and long wooden bench seats. The dreadful brown tiles have also been evicted, revealing original dark timber boards. Where the fizzy drinks fridge used to be now stands a large rustic kitchen dresser. It gleams graciously with a collection of shining silver antique teapots. And where the white bread rolls were, as fluffy as candy floss, there's now an old wooden butcher's table on industrial wheels. Upon it is a beautiful cluster of vibrant green herbs in terracotta pots. The wall above the old counter that advertised pies is now covered with a giant blackboard framed by old paling timber. The menu chalked there reads like a foreign language to me.

Suddenly, the sound of a revving engine outside shatters through the building. Tyres squeal. We turn to see Slugs roaring the guts out of his ute on the wet street, spinning the bikkies on the spot. Diesel smoke rising up in the rain. He's giving the vegans the middle finger while the council workers try not to look amused.

'Go back to where you came from, ya veggie burger bastards! Ya fucken whack-job mainlanders!'

Dropping the clutch, his giant off-road wheels squeal away, fishtailing as he sounds his *Dukes of Hazzard*'s Confederates horn.

Fenton and Vernon watch in shock. A woman in a flowing skirt with long wavy blonde hair emerges from the old greasy, disturbed by the commotion, and looks out through the rain. The council workers scamper away, not wanting to seem part of Slugs's social protest. As the council workers drive away, and the woman goes back inside, I wonder if the men are headed to the service station for a pie. At least it will give Aarav something to do.

'You know him?' Fenton asks.

'Yes. He was my boyfriend.' I swallow, regretting my truth-telling. 'In Grade Six. For a week,' I add hoping that makes it seem better. 'Just ignore him,' I reassure. 'People just don't like change around here.'

The buoyant mood has faltered. The rain is so loud on the corrugated awning it swallows every sound.

'Food,' I prompt, pointing inside to the bain-marie that has an assortment of designer foodie goop.

'Yes, of course!' Vernon exclaims brightly, trying to get us all back on track. 'We have cauliflower cheese-like bake!'

'Cheese-*like* bake?' I inquire.

'Yes. A dairy-free alternative from Europe, made from No-Muh Blue Classic by Vegusto, which is Swiss-style and a hundred per cent plant-based gourmet.'

He's clearly been rehearsing his foodie spiel for a while, smiling proudly from behind his sandy buzz-edged beard. I feel compelled to respond enthusiastically, but as I near the food, steam lifts and the scent greets my nostrils like a melted plastic bag. He gestures at what could be mistaken for an anaemic cow poo on a stainless-steel surgery pan, topped with a pea shoot. His colourful plastic bangles jangle around on his wrist as he gives a shopping channel wave of his hand. 'Can I tempt you?'

'Um, are the caulis spray-free?' I ask, thinking of Uncle Larry's vibrant veggies. No point taking some to him if they're not. Larry'd been dubious about giving his chooks the servo pastie calling it 'toxic waste'.

'Sorry, no,' Vernon says, deflated. 'Organics are a bit hard to source around here. Ironic given this is the veggie-growing capital of Tassie!'

It's the cue I need to go all 'uni' on them. I point out to the green treeless Lilyburn hillsides that rise above the shop rooftops across the road.

'Have you seen the giant food company storage complexes up there in them thar hills? Armies of trucks that come and go carting neon carrots and the like? It's a factory system. Not a farming one. That fulvic red soil out there is deceptively depleted. If you tested it, it's likely contaminated with all kinds of post-war agricultural inputs and has very little carbon and living biology. Even the organic farms don't have living, thriving soil.'

I throw Vernon a smile because I know I sound slightly paranoid and incredibly bleak.

'Really!' he exclaims, pressing his fingertips to his chest. 'You seem to know so much about it!'

'Waaaay too much. Put it this way, when I was at uni, I had a hobby of midnight trawling through the Australian Pesticides and Veterinary Medicines Authority website. My game was to learn the super-dooper long chemical lists for vegetable growing – even in organic systems. Bit of fun, to chew up the long, lonely nights when my roommates had headed off to the uni bar, or the rugby, or to have sex with one another.'

'You learned chemical lists? While everyone else partied? Whatever floats your boat!' Vernon laughs.

'It was better than watching *Love Island*.'

He throws his head back and laughs again. 'Oh Connie! You're too unique! I just love you!'

'Take those cauliflowers for example,' I say, gesturing to the bake. 'I know they're dosed with Imidacloprid and Spirotetramat! How yummo does that sound? My endocrine system is going to really go for that!'

'With *what*?' Vernon asks, looking worried, glancing from me to the food and back. 'I didn't know that.'

'Most folks don't. Most of our plants are grown in chemically boosted soils and sprayed with things that are likely carcinogens, suspected hormone disruptors, neurotoxins, developmental or reproductive toxins, and of course honeybee toxins. That's some kinda salad dressing!'

I feel Vernon's energy droop, like a glyphosate-sprayed broadleaf plant.

'Geez, Connie, you sure know how to kill an appetite.'

'I know,' I say, bracing myself for the same rejection that I get from most people.

Fenton waves his hand across the food offerings. 'Well, if not the cauliflower, maybe you might like to try our mung bean fettuccine with organic borlotti and adzuki bean sauce, topped with a Cheddar Flavour Dairy-free Delight? The Cheddar Dairy-free is registered by the Vegan Society,' he adds reassuringly. 'Plus it's not only free from dairy, but also free from gluten, soya, lactose and palm oil! Or try some jackfruit pulled pork with Australian rice? Not one single piggy was harmed in the making of your meal. You can pig out guilt-free!' He too has been diligently practising his waiter spiel.

I feel dreadful deflating his balloon, but I can't help it.

'Did you know,' I say gently, 'that rice needs *triple* the amount of water as other cereal crops to produce the same dry weight? The multinational companies that grow rice in Australia seem to be guilt-free though because our Australian river systems are dying, if not already dead in places, and yet they still insist on growing it inefficiently.'

They look shocked but encourage me to go on.

'On top of that are the methane and nitrous oxide that rice crops emit. Globally, rice fields are adding gases into the atmosphere that are equivalent to twelve hundred coal-fired power plants.'

The boys pull 'holy fuck' faces.

'Oh, this is terrible,' Fenton says.

'But this is stuff we need to hear, Fenton!' Vernon insists. 'The whole reason we became vegan was to help save the environment. We're aiming to be as Earth-friendly as we can in our business. Fenton here spent ages researching eco-packaging for our takeaways. So ...' He turns to me. 'What do you suggest we do, Connie?'

'What do you mean, what do I suggest?' I ask. No one ever *asks* for my opinion, let alone a solution.

Vernon looks pleadingly at me. 'How do we find farmers who, as you say, can supply us with food grown from a living, thriving soil?'

I realise I've found some people willing to hear the truth about food – more unpalatable than the actual product made from it. The men are looking at me with genuine interest, and with hope that I actually might be able to help them.

'Well ... you could learn about the universe of life in the soil and its minerals and its relationship with plants and your stomach microbiome. You could get a worm farm, grow your own? Once you feed worms that are going to feed your garden you really start to think about the whole food web. Or you could be like me and just eat junk because you give up, knowing we're all fucked.'

The chink of cheerfulness that I'd momentarily found with the happy chappies closes over like a cloud blighting the sun. Once again, I become the hopeless, hapless creature, Connie Mulligan, beaten and afraid of her patriarchal world.

'Once you've seen what I've seen you can't unsee it. It's so huge and confronting you just give up!' I say, with desperation in my voice.

'Give up?' sings a voice from the doorway. There stands the curvy, blonde woman who emerged when Slugs was thinning his tyres on the main drag, 'Surrender, yes! But never give up!'

She steps closer, and I realise she's older than I first thought, but with her pretty face and long twisting blonde hair, she looks ageless wearing a gentle green cardigan pulled over a cotton floral boho dress, made warm by leggings and long leather boots. The boots give her away as not being vegan, and for some reason I feel slightly relieved by this fact.

'Megan Larkins,' she says, holding out her hand. 'From Verenda Women's Support Centre. Our hub. Just over yonder.'

It's in that moment, taking my hand, that her mouth drops open in amazement.

'Oh my goddess!' She rests her hand to her chest as if to slow her heart. 'Connie Mulligan? In the flesh?'

'You know me?'

'Oh my dear, dear girl.' She draws me into the warmest of hugs. 'Of course I know you.' When she pulls back to regard me, there're tears in her eyes.

'The *Mulligan v Turner* case! I followed it. I was *appalled* by how you were treated. Oh you brave, brave woman. I wondered if I'd ever get to meet you.' She turns to the chappies.

'Good menfolk – get this woman some lunch. It's on me. Takeaway, thanks. And would you mind bringing it over the road? Ms Connie and I have some women's business to attend to. Don't we?'

Before I can answer, she's leading me out into the street where the rain has eased and sunshine is pouring through the breaking clouds, making the street glisten, washed clean.

Chapter 20

As Megan walks me under the newly painted awning that reads, *Verenda Women's Hub*, she tells me energetically and enthusiastically, 'I was about to set up Verenda on the mainland. But my inner GPS told me Tasmania was it. So I rang the lads. We've been friends for yonks. They found out Joe was ready to go, and the rest is history ... still in the making.'

She flings the door wide, links my arm in hers, and we step over the threshold.

'Here you are!'

'Here I am!' I say. I look around the building. 'Wait. Where am I?'

The place has been totally gutted. It's hard to picture Joe in here anymore, flipping burgers and draining oil from chips.

'Visualise this,' Megan says, sweeping her hand about the empty room. 'Pull up the lino, reveal the Tas oak floorboards. All sanded and polished, and warmed with colourful rugs.'

She gestures to the wall where ice creams and yellow fried food were once advertised.

'Then here, lush cerulean wallpaper – maybe coiling with vines or peacocks, and giant urns straight from a grand colonial Indian garden. Patterned velvet chairs over here, and in the window – couches in reds, pinks, turquoise and tropical greens. Plus sumptuous cushions waiting to be sunk into. Can you see it?'

I nod, blown away not so much by her vision, but her certainty that it is happening. 'It's going to be beautiful,' I say.

'Ah, it's not just beauty ... it's about claiming and harnessing our female rage, then transmuting it into positive power. Welcome to the sisterhood, Connie!'

I feel giddy as she takes my hand and sits me down beside her on a couch covered by a workman's sheet.

'I sense you're angry deep down. Furious in fact,' she says.

I think of my mother's veneer that hides an undercurrent of savage fury. Then my own tumble-turn thoughts about Dad, my brother, and of course ... Turner and the world. I nod again.

'Me too. When I was younger,' Megan says. 'I used to be as angry as fuck. Even as a little girl. But I never knew why. Slowly I realised it was because of our culture. Our society. We're so conditioned we don't even notice the injustices. I used all that women-hating culture destructively against myself. Raging against my femaleness. Taking it out on my parents. Shagging every man in sight. Dumping the good ones, keeping the bad. Becoming an animal activist and causing chaos. For me, being a vegan meant I became a vandal, a bully and a thug.'

She chuckles at herself. 'Megan the vegan. What a dick! Part of me knew I was twisting my insides out being fucking furious at the world all the time. Meeting aggression with aggression.'

'What changed?' I ask.

She picks up a framed black and white photo and passes it to me. Two adult children with her same smile hug her, radiating family love from behind the glass.

'Sasha and Joshua,' she says. 'It wasn't until I had my babies that I gentled. Plus I got dumped on my arse by a bloke not man enough to partner a real, evolving woman. It was brutal. *He* was brutal. As a single mum, without all the outside noise, with just me and the kids, I began to slowly heal. And as I did, I realised I had the power to hold a space for other women to transform.'

She sets the photo back down.

'Our female ancestors lived it. They held their wisdom. Their power. Society was coached to worship the Divine Feminine, so that harmony was held on Earth with nature.'

Looking into her ocean blue eyes, a vortex begins to spin within them and I know that I'm falling inwards.

I am roaring, like the sea in a storm, my throat burning with my powerful sound. My weighty matted hair falling over wide shoulders smeared with mud and blood. My fist is clenched, muscles and sinews taut as I grip a stick and hold it aloft. It is perfectly smoothed and balanced as a weapon. One to bludgeon the heads of his lord's men. Beside me stands a broad blonde woman, busty and strong. She too is covered in mire, her clothing torn, her face chalked in white battle lines. She is screaming out a war cry in a tongue I can sense is that of the ancient warrior women I have known. She is making the sound a woman makes when her babies have been murdered, her forests cut down and her rivers drained. She will have no more of it.

I blink. The image goes. I look to Megan. Her inner confidence emanates from her as brightly as the shipping beacon that glows on the end of Lilyburn's breakwall on dark nights. I want to sail with her on her sisterhood seas – even if it means getting wrecked on the rocks of my current Lilyburn life.

'Wait here,' Megan says.

She returns and kneels before me.

'Your feet must be freezing.' She peels away my sodden socks with such tenderness and then rolls a pair of colourful woollen socks onto my feet. There's a reverence in her actions. She is both motherly and sisterly. It brings tears to my eyes.

Laying a hand on my knee, she looks up, right into my soul. 'What they did to you was nothing short of evil. A witch hunt, through and through …' She stops mid-sentence and squeezes my knee. 'Just know I'm here for you. When you're ready.'

'Ready for what?' I ask.

'To purge. To cleanse. To let go. And then to begin our quiet revolution,' she says with a grin, rising up.

'Revolution?' Before she can sail me further into her oceans, the chappies burst through the doors.

'Lunch for our ladies!' Fenton declares.

'We decided we'd join you,' Vernon adds, holding up an extra brown paper bag, vegan fare within.

'Lovely! I'll just quickly finish Connie's tour. You boys dish up,' Megan says.

For my benefit, she draws back a heavy canvas drape to reveal an assortment of idle cabinetry tools and swept piles of wood shavings.

'Commercial kitchen in here, so our participants can grow food biodynamically in the garden and begin to cook again, or learn to cook. Beyond that door will be a common room where the kids can hang out, and through there, consulting rooms for counselling. But not just talking-heads therapy. We'll be teaching bioenergetics. Movement, breath, dance, and embodiment work like tapping and yoga to help women come back into their bodies after trauma. And upstairs we're renovating bedrooms for emergency accommodation. Just got to get the plumbing underway, some box-ticking with council and we're good to go.'

'It's going to be amazing!'

'I aim for it to be amazing. After my partner did what he used to do to me, I know what women need. I'd turn up to shitty domestic violence support centre waiting rooms with out-of-date *New Ideas* and cold chairs, only to find the woman dealing with my case would be on long service leave, or my appointment double-booked.

'The government feeds us crumbs for funding. So I've been using all my networks ... particularly the corporate female leaders and politicians to reinvent how this sector rolls. Plus I'm good at running on the smell of an oily rag. Classy does not have to be costly,' she says.

She sees my attention is captured by a massive print of Sandro Botticelli's *The Birth of Venus* hanging above where Joe's cooker used to be. We stand before Venus's nakedness, barely covered by flame-red hair as she emerges from a seashell.

'Our Roman goddess of love, formed out of the ocean's foam, riding a seashell to land. A perfect metaphor for the women of the village of Lilyburn situated by the sea.'

'Lilyburn? A village?' I reply. 'That makes it sound far fancier than it is.' But something inside me blooms, giving a sense of the possibility that this place could flower into something altogether different than what it is right now.

'That's the point!' says Megan. 'We women are far fancier than we know. Verenda aims to give you back your dignity and help all women celebrate their form, no matter what that might be. Then there's our right to be powerful.'

There's something in her words that both lifts me up and makes me cringe simultaneously.

'But meanwhile,' she says, 'sit. Eat.'

I land at the dining room table where the chappies are laying out eco forks and lighting candles, clearly at home here.

I look to the walls and realise I'm surrounded by vaginas. There are paintings of sacred female triangles, black and white photos of stone goddess figurines with giant labias, and religious works from every culture that shout 'Map of Tassie' from the walls. I wonder what Patrick would say if he were here. Megan directs my eye away from the vajayjays and beyond the eating area to where the walls have been marked up with tape and builder's pencil lines.

'By the end of the week, there'll be two large arched windows there and French doors in between. Big beautiful old things ... a demolition find from further down the coast by Vernon. And outside are the makings of a new leafy garden. There'll be white gravel pathways edged by terracotta flowerpots, leading to a large fire pit rimmed with flat stones. All nestled under the century-old pear and walnut trees out there.'

'It's going to be truly magic,' Vernon adds.

'Yes. I didn't want some heartless predictable space that makes women feel even more beaten down by the world. Beauty and love are inextricably linked and they bring healing. Nature heals us too.'

'It's not just women she's helping,' Fenton says, spooning out lentils the colour of calf poo. 'We would have tucked our tails between our legs and left Lilyburn by now if it weren't for Meegs joining us.'

Onya, Slugs, I think to myself.

'So, here's cheers.' He raises a glass of water. 'To Verenda,' he toasts, and we follow suit, chinking glass rims.

I shovel some beans into my mouth and instantly my tastebuds are challenged by the fuzzy mush. There's an urge to slather some of Patrick's Black & Gold sugar- and salt-infused tomato sauce on the strange food. But given that I am now in the company of what feels like new friends, I tell myself to suck it up and swallow hastily.

Vernon recounts to Megan, with impressive accuracy, most of the evil food spiel I'd given him earlier so that Megan nods.

'There's a parallel for sure,' she says, looking thoughtful. 'Women, with our cycles and seasons, live against the grain of our inner selves in terms of time. We are forced to march to patriarchal linear time. And farming's no different. It's run on mankind's time. Not Mother Nature's. Women and nature exist in polychronic time, not monochronic time. That's why the world feels so out of kilter for so many of us.'

I glance up at her, amazed to hear her perspective.

'I hadn't thought of it like that. But you're right! You should see the grind Dad puts our cows under every single day,'

'Well, Connie, it makes sense. The land *is* feminine, and it is being killed by a heavily masculine, rigid system – not a circular, nurturing system.'

She looks at me with her clear tropical-sea-coloured eyes and for the first time in my life I high-five someone, feeling very unqualified in the action, but knowing I have to celebrate what feels like a blinding revelation. The land is feminine. She, like me, exists in a different flow of time. I feel my heart opening up like a daisy to the sun after months of grey.

'Is that why you have this ... um ... art?' I ask.

'Not to mention the name of her business,' Fenton adds.

'Verenda?' I ask.

'Yes,' Megan says. 'It's an old word for vagina.'

When she says *that* word, I almost splutter out my beans.

'Verenda,' I echo again, trying on the word uncomfortably now I know what it means. Mum never allowed me to even mention 'those bits down there' – certainly not at a dinner table.

'It translates as the parts that inspire awe or respect. It's a word that contains grace, gravitas and a great provenance combined.'

Megan directs my gaze to a photo of a stone carving of a woman with extremely generous genitalia, pillow-like and proud. Under the frame reads *Sheela Na Gig – Ireland*.

'I tell women that these figures used to look down from hundreds of medieval buildings. They were symbols of power. We have to remember as women we still have that power.'

Before I have time to process Megan's words, the room swirls, and Professor Turner enters my brain without permission. In my horror vision, he appears at the window in the darkening street. His tongue protruding, growing longer and longer, so that it folds in lewd circular motions around his face, then begins to smear on the window. *Little whore*, comes his voice. *Get back in your box*.

I push the half-eaten meal away. 'I'm sorry. I shouldn't be here. I mean, I have to go! It's getting late. Just. Gotta. Go.'

I push up from the table. Megan gets up too and before I can run, she encircles me in her arms.

'I've got you,' she says. 'Just breathe. Just. Breathe.'

*

Later, the lights of Megan's seven-seater sweep along Sunnyside's drive. She slows at Mum and Dad's house.

'A bit further,' I say indicating the pale shape of Granny M's cottage in the headlights. Megan pulls up.

'It looks awfully dark.'

'No power. Not yet,' I say sheepishly. On the drive up here, in the warm safe space of her car, I'd spilled my guts. All of it had tumbled out. From whoa to go. Turner. Me. The study. The sex. The court case. Mum. Dad. Raylene. Patrick. Doctor Cragg. Medication. Now I'm suffering from verbal regurgitation regret. I quickly reach for the door handle.

'Thanks for the lift.'

'Connie. Wait,' Megan says, 'I'll help you get settled in.'

Despite my protests, she's out of the car, and the moon is escorting us down the pathway. She fusses over Nick-nack and goes ga-ga over the winter warm coat of Traveller. In the cottage she helps me light candles, revives the fire and settles me onto my chair.

At the door, she pauses. 'See you in the morning.'

'The morning?'

She indicates the boxes, garbage bags and piles of stuff that line the hallway.

'Working bee. The boys and I will come help you set this place up as your haven. See you tomorrow. I'll bring coffee.'

'But ...' I begin. She shushes me, pats my arm and glides from the room. As the fire brightens, Nick-nack pads over, rests her head on my knees and gazes up at me with Divinity in her eyes.

Chapter 21

It's Monday morning and this work shirt takes some getting used to. I have a shoal of sperm swimming over my left boob and over my right, hot pink embroidery reads *Global Genetics – Dairy's Destiny.*

Destiny, I think forlornly, tugging the black shirt over my navy slacks. Is this my destiny? I'm sitting opposite Office Manager Danny Watkins as he clatters my details into a computer. The way he's twisting his mouth side to side and huffing, I get the feeling Raylene really dropped this (me) on him at short notice. I wonder if she explained that my new job was to get me off the farm so she can find her way into my father's trousers more often? I think not.

For a moment, I ponder Dad and Raylene's commandment breaches in the Bible that were drummed into us at Sunday school: 'Thou Shalt Not Commit Adultery and Thou Shalt Not Covet Thy Neighbour's Wife.'

I'd committed all ten to memory along with the terrifying passage: 'Don't profane your daughter, to make her a prostitute; lest the land fall to prostitution, and the land become full of wickedness.'

That one sentence had scrambled my eleven-year-old girl mind as I bowed my head in what I thought prayer looked like alongside the adults, my eyes glazing over at my too-white socks and shiny brown sandals. The burden of my gender had draped across my shoulders. I see now why I'm more sexually repressed than a brick and more confused than a northwest swell. And why Megan's views on the feminine Earth rippled through me like the healing sound of a deep penetrating gong.

Looking at Danny, who would've been a hunky rugger-bugger in his day, I resolve to be more charming, like the happy chappies had been as they'd moved about Granny M's yesterday, full of flirt and fun. Megan also, infusing the house with her childlike wonder at Granny's old things, cleaning and repositioning them back to beauty. Mum and Dad had skulked near their house, not game to come near 'the vegans' and 'the raving feminist'. Patrick had fishtailed the four-wheeler outside the cottage, grinning like a ventriloquist's dummy, before revving away, leaving me to my new friends and new life.

Now, while Danny's occupied, I scan the office. It's a bland open-plan space with carpet-covered cubicles and several computers swirling screensavers around like disturbed neon jellyfish. On every wall hangs perfect photos of impressive bulls and stud Holstein cows with International Dairy Week prizes and charts of their performance data. Above Danny's head, a poster reads, *Global Genetics. Your one stop shop for breed leaders from around the world* and another saying, *Maximise your semen investment!* with a picture of Nikki smiling with a cute little calf.

I can't help but think she maximised her husband's semen investment ... and now here I am. I can see where Nikki usually sits, near the window overlooking Ulverstone's Main Street. Her pot plants are in perfect health, as is her perfect husband who is photographed cuddling her, beachside.

'So,' Danny says, swivelling his body to me, that now speaks of too many beers and too much time at a desk, 'you do know what we do here?'

I want to say, *Shrink the world's bovine gene pool down to dangerously low levels*, but instead I say, 'Yes. You source the best international dairy semen and offer genomics and sexed semen selection, and in addition to your core business, you source beef semen for clients looking to supply the local F-one market with beef mop-up bulls. Then there's your on-farm services, like de-horning, freeze branding, arm service for artificial insemination, pregnancy scanning, livestock sales and export orders and supply of National Livestock Identification System tags. All delivered with local know-how, but global connections.' For my finale I use my best DJ Dean-O voice. 'Maximising your clients' semen investment!'

Danny blinks at me. 'So, you studied up on us.'

'Yes. A bit of a quick cram. I didn't know I had this job until three days ago.'

He looks at me over the top of his glasses. 'Try one hour for me. But here you are!'

'Here I am.' I'm not sure what to say after that, so Danny fills the space.

'They told me you were a brainbox. No clue with people, but a smart cookie.'

'They did?' I reply, wondering if 'they' was Mum and Raylene and if they also mentioned that I was 'a stubbie short of a sixpack' in the head.

A shoal of awful memories from university swims into my mind faster than spermatozoa racing for an ovum.

I am at the uni bar, drunk for the first time, showing the townies the spray irrigator dance and my newly invented dairy farmer cups-on rap. The night blurs until after the bar has shut, when I find myself flat on my back in a university dorm room, losing my virginity to an obese computer-science student called Byron with chronic eczema. As he lies on me, grunting, I turn my head away from his rancid breath to focus unfeelingly on the university texts on his desk.

My eyes fixed on a title: *Computer Systems: A programmer's perspective.*

Tears slid down my face as I recalled the singeing image of Professor Turner earlier that day. As Byron humped and pumped, as if he was trying to start a campfire with his dick, I realised that enduring this physical pain was easier than the image locked in my brain.

That of Professor Turner, and how I'd tapped lightly on his door and walked into his office to find him, goofy purple glasses set aside on his desk, in his office chair, head thrown back to the ceiling, face contorted. It was then I realised first-year student Tilly Gutherson was bobbing her head up and down over his crotch. I stared long enough to watch her mouth sliding up and down the smooth pink shaft of his penis, her eyes scrunched shut. Professor Turner was moaning, her ponytail in his fist, hips writhing, legs rigidly sticking out as if an electric current was running through them.

They must've sensed me. Tilly opened her eyes, lifting her reddened lips from his pink helmet. She turned her haunted gaze on me, a mix of excitement and devastation burning within them, as mine once had done. As she swiped the back of her hand across her mouth, Professor Turner's expression had morphed from blowjob-ugly to insulted indignation at the interruption to his afternoon student delight. The delight that I used to bring him. I was his ticking time bomb now. A girl about to blow his cover instead of his knob.

'Next time, knock! Now, get out!' he shouted, roughly pushing Tilly aside, coming at me, his dying penis swinging side to side, half-mast trousers inhibiting his movement. 'If you say anything about this to anyone – I'll make sure you're going nowhere in life.'

I fled, the door slamming behind me.

*

And now here I am in an office selling sperm. *My destiny.*

The phone rings. Danny holds up his index finger. 'S'cuse me a tick.'

'Global Genetics, Tassie's link to the world's best semen. This is Danny. Please hold for a moment.'

He covers the mouthpiece. 'Company policy. Nikki makes us all answer the phone that way. I'll write it out for you, till you get the hang of it.' He turns back to his call. 'Sorry for the wait.' A smile finds his square friendly face. 'Bob! How's your synchrony program going? Cows cycling? Yes, yes, the progesterone and the prostaglandin's not cheap with that vet. Best to use the other fella.'

Danny swivels his chair round so he has his back to me. I look to the ceiling, tears in my eyes. What the hell am I doing here? A place where science has taken ownership of female reproduction for the sake of industry. I think of all those cows I shoved my arm up for Dad because my arms did less damage to their bowels than his chunky forearms. I'd injected into their reproductive tracts perfectly computer-matched bull semen from America or Europe, most likely from environments that didn't resemble Lilyburn at all. I'm sure the cow would've preferred to suss out her own bull before she joined with him, using her cow wisdom that came direct from the Higher Power of Mother Nature herself. My eyes land on Nikki's plants – the only bit of nature in here – and my vision swims. Then I realise, it's my attitude that needs to change. Maybe this is the place I can utilise all that has flowed into my mind since university. Buoyed by this train of thought, I get the feeling Danny and I are going to be the best of friends!

Danny puts down the phone, makes a note in his diary. 'Right then. Any questions so far?'

'Yes.' I breathe in.

'Go on,' he says.

Excitement tingles my skin. I'm going to make a good impression ...

'When I was writing my paper for my specialist dairy unit, I discovered there are more than nine million dairy cows in the United States and the vast majority of them are Holsteins, like the ones here.'

Danny looks puzzled and slightly unsettled. Regardless, I continue. I point to the photos. 'More than ninety-nine per cent of America's cows can be traced back to one of two bulls that were doing their semen thing back in the sixties, which means nowadays, our global cows are more inbred than a Tasmanian family from Black Bob's!'

Danny taps his pen on the desk, his friendly face now stormy. 'Your point is?'

'My point is that because of this ... this ...' I wave my arms around the office. 'This commercial, production-only economic system, now out of all the male Holsteins in America there are just two Y chromosomes, making the cows so genetically similar, the effective population size is less than fifty.'

I pause, hoping Danny has got my point, but he hasn't, judging from his scowl. If I'd been telling Vernon and Fenton these facts, they'd be interested.

'Shouldn't that concern us? That Australia is following America's lead?' I ask.

'What?'

'That by losing diversity we're susceptible to possible collapse – like the Irish Potato Famine, where they used one strain of potato and the blight wiped out the entire crop. Then the people starved.'

'Look,' Danny said, 'I don't have time to sit here and talk about potatoes ... and least of all training someone who clearly doesn't want to be here.'

I shake my head. 'No! I do want to be here! At least now I do! The longer I'm in here, the more I see this could really lead to something meaningful between us. Something big! We could invest in a database of broad genetics, rather than narrow. Swim against the conventional semen stream to use a pun.'

Danny shifts in his chair as if his underpants are being disagreeable. 'Pun?'

My voice lifts in volume. I'm so desperate for Danny to hear me. To get me. To understand that what I'm saying is really important.

'Don't you get it? If Holsteins were wild animals, that would put them in the category of critically endangered species! Globally, when it comes to our cows, we're just one big inbred family, and that's dangerous! We could make Global Genetics truly global and preserve breeds for genetic diversity and for Mother Earth herself.'

Danny stands, pushing his chair back, gathering up his mobile phone and keys. 'Are you for real? Honestly, I don't need this shit. Not on a Monday. Didn't Raylene tell you, my wife's sick. Really sick. I'm going out.'

By the time he's at the door he's barking into his phone, the tone he used with client Bob altogether gone. 'Raylene,' he snaps, 'we have a problem. A big bloody problem. I need you to get down to the office now!' The auto doors slide behind his back, and he marches off down the street.

I sit. The clock on the Global Genetics wall ticks. I look around.

Tick.

Tock.

Maybe I ought to tidy something. Clean the work kitchen. Study up on the bulls they use. As I get up, my heart sinks. I'd had a similar reaction at uni when I'd passed in my Dairy Industry essay paper, only to get an F.

'F for Fail Connie,' I say to the empty room.

The phone rings at the reception desk. Hesitating, I walk over to pick it up. I smile. I breathe.

'Global Genetics. Tassie's link to the world's best semen. This is Connie. How may I help you?'

Chapter 22

'You call this food?' Uncle Larry asks, looking dubiously into the cardboard takeaway boxes that I've spread out on his kitchen table after my first day of work.

'But it's vegan,' I say frowning. 'And if you knew the chappies, you'd know it's made with love. They're so ... heartfelt.'

He looks at me with apology. 'Do you mind if I pass it on to Glennon?'

'Glennon?'

He repacks the food into the brown paper bag stamped with the Happy Chappy's jaunty logo: two cartoon versions of a smiling Fenton and Vernon, circled in a leafy vine.

'Come with me.'

'Where to?' I ask, a tingle of doom running through me. He doesn't answer as we drag on our boots, setting off towards the vegetable garden. As I follow, watching his back, I tell myself, *No Connie, he is not going to murder you, put you in cryovac plastic and into his freezer.* My mind counters itself: *But if he did, at least your polyester pants and work shirt won't break down for several centuries so there's a chance forensics may find them buried somewhere and solve the crime?*

Larry gestures to the old vertical board shed. 'In there.'

The door gives an eerie creak as it swings open slowly, enhancing my suspicions that I'm about to be done in. Inside the dark space I glimpse an axe leaning against a wall. There's a large wooden chopping block made from a giant tree stump, meat cleaver wedged upon it. Butcher's gambrels hang from a rafter. The floors are concrete, dark brown in places. Blood!

I swallow and turn towards Larry who is now blocking the doorway.

'Been too crook to push the barrow up.' He gestures to the hills above his house. 'Could you?'

He reaches for a wheelbarrow behind the door. It's laden with fresh garden waste, secured with a net.

'Hay contractor rutted the track with his tractor last summer. Too rough for my old ute, so it's shanks' pony until I find someone to get it fixed.'

'Sure,' I say with relief, taking up the barrow handles.

We trudge up a thigh-burning track, both of us puffing hard and stopping frequently, the bag of takeaway flopping about as it hangs from one of the handles. As I walk, I lament the heaviness of my body and my runaway train of a brain that wants to dramatise my life to the point where I believe Larry is a murderous madman.

It's right on a dusk of gentle violet when we reach the end of the steep track, the landscape illuminating slowly into silver with the rising moon. We are standing in an idyllic mountainside clearing, dotted with gentle green wattles and giant gums, fenced with both wallaby wire and electrics. There's a large timber and corro livestock shelter beside us and a hay shed filled to the brim with bales. Turning, I breath in the spectacular view of Sunnyside Dairy Farm and the sweep of the Lilyburn Valley all the way to the sea.

'Wow! I've never seen our place from this high up. Or your farm. It's incredible!'

'Incredibly hard to farm too,' he says as he reaches to turn off the solar electric fence unit, set on a post. 'Now I'm older. And not too flash ...'

I want to ask him what's wrong with him, but don't want to pry. I had glimpsed the prescription at Mr Crompton's and deduced his illness has something to do with his heart.

'Still. It's beautiful,' I say looking out to the darkening mauve sea far off in the distance.

Larry turns his back to the valley, facing the mountain, tilts his head back and cups his hands to his mouth calling. 'C'mon! C'mon! C'mon!'

In response, an orchestra of sounds echo out in the still evening air. Soon a motley mob of animals rush out from the surrounding bushland, gallivanting excitedly towards us. There's mix-breed cattle, sheep, pigs and a couple of goats in the combo herd. Even a turkey or two turns up out of the scrub. Larry begins flinging the carrot tops, weeds and other vegetables over the fence, so I dive in to help. The first to tuck in is a rotund pink pig with six babies milling around her.

'This is Glennon. Let's see if she's a vegan, shall we?' Larry says passing me one of the boxes. I slump the food over the fence, so it lands in a plop. Glennon downs her jackfruit pulled pork and rice in less than a second, then sets her small lively eyes upon me, urging me for the other boxes, her piglets squealing and jostling for any morsels she's left. Leaning over the fence, Larry lovingly scratches the back of the sow and grins. 'Looks like she is.'

'At least that jackfruit recipe might have saved some of the less fortunate of her kind,' I add, looking at the happy pig.

He chuckles and grunts an agreement. 'It's madness what they do to animals these days. So arrogant. Makes me ashamed to be human,' he says, pulling a remaining milk thistle out of the barrow and offering it to the sow. 'Your favourite. Isn't it, Glennon?'

Watching his tenderness towards the animal, I wonder again what Larry's full story is. Dad never pats Nick-nack or Paddy-whack, let along talks kindly to the cows. He'd always told me and Patrick that Larry was a 'cruel bastard'.

Larry gestures towards the hay shed. 'Would you mind? Stan and Stevie like their hay of an evening. They've missed out of late.'

At the sound of their names, one of the belted Galloway steers lifts his head from his turnip tops and lets out a gentle moo. We enter the well-stacked hay shed followed along the fence line by two black-faced Suffolks.

'Trev and Rodger like a slab each – away from the cows. The goats tend to mop up. And I put an extra one out for Shona.' He gestures to a ewe standing a way off with a lamb at foot. 'Shona's a little shy when she has a baby. Can't say I blame her. They do end up in my freezer now and then. All part of the cycle of life I guess.'

As I lift one of the bales, Larry pulls a knife out from his belt and unfolds the blade. I freeze. But then I blink the moment away as Larry passes the knife to me. Bending to cut the blue twine, the fragrance of the bale wafts upwards pleasantly in a scented echo of last summer.

'So, you're not a serial killer then?' I mutter, smiling to myself.

'What's that?' he asks.

'You're not fond of having them as killers then?' I say more loudly, covering my tracks.

He looks back at the animals, a frown creasing his brow. 'Not really. I get too fond of them, but everything leaves this Earth and cycles back round. It's all energy exchange. They are loved and that's the main thing. And I don't eat a lot of meat. One keeps me going for a good while. I use it to pay people for fuel and favours sometimes and people say they can taste the care. It's a good system. Suits me just fine. Maybe not the animals, but the way I figure it, they wouldn't have had a life on a meadow at all if there wasn't a need for them. Plus, how else do I keep the soil and plants healthy without them? If I didn't graze, the place would be out of control with the blackberries and gorse within a year.'

I've not heard him speak so much before. But clearly this place lights him up. It gives me courage to speak. 'Uncle Larry?'

'Mmm?'

'What do I do? About these farm systems? Like where I work. Today I talked about gene pool shrinkage. They just didn't get it. They can't see it.'

'Light the path.'

'What do you mean?'

'Suggest new things.' He points to a dumpy little mottle-coated cow. 'Take a look at Izzy. She's an old tri-purpose breed. Her ancestors supplied meat, milk *and* draught power. Heritage cows like Izzy are scrappy but can survive unmedicated outside on unmanaged pastures. They're dying out because farmers like your dad can't afford to keep them and can't see the value in them.'

'Then there's Eloise there.' I admire the pretty cow with the patched brown and white hide. 'She's a Pinzgauer. From Austria originally. They're great surrogate mothers. A single cow like her can raise several orphaned calves and give them enough milk and protect them as their own.'

'What's this got to do with Global?'

'Someone like you, Connie, someone … um, who sees things *different* could build a semen database and storage for the likes of Izzy, what's left of them. And trial different surrogate mother–calf systems with cows like Eloise. It's something we would've …'

His voice trails off just as goosebumps thrill my skin.

'Yes! That's a fantastic idea! Global could be leaders in not just our lovely but needy, greedy Holsteins, but the rare ones.'

'These old breeds are naturally disease-resistant. I just let them get on with it when they calve.'

'Not like Dad who has the vet out every other day for C-sections and infections,' I add.

'And these old-style girls can be milked well into their teens. Izzy's having her eleventh calf this year. Has kept me in milk for over a decade.'

My mind opens and as we walk down the hill I begin to feel eager about going to work tomorrow. I'm enjoying seeing how much a part of the landscape Larry is here, like he's woven into the fabric of it. Unlike Dad, who seems to want to iron that fabric flat and stand firmly upon it in his unyielding boots.

But something is missing with Larry. The woman in the paintings perhaps? Why has this quiet unassuming man been so long alone on a mountainside with his eclectic animal family and a brother on the other side telling the world he's a mad monster? The unanswered questions keep roaming around my mind until I arrive back at his cottage.

It's there, with such care and tenderness, he produces a curried vegetable pie from the oven and begins cutting me a large slice.

*

Later at Granny M's cottage, Nick-nack is waiting for me at the door in the dark, already keen for her new spot fireside. She dances inside with me, and instantly I feel wrapped in the welcoming energy of the cottage, despite the chill.

After lighting the candles, I kneel to set the fire, pausing when I sense a presence. Turning slowly, I realise Dad is standing in the shadowy lounge room doorway. The candles flicker. He's in his work clothes, beanie on and nose red from the cold of the night air. It's way past Mum's strictly scheduled 'teatime' so I realise things must be bad in the house if he's not already home.

'I came to see how your first day of work was?' He has a nervous expression reddening his cheeks, and he's hovering like he's sussing me out. There's a lid on his baseline anger, but I know there's something simmering in his quiet voice.

'Did you?' I respond, not offering anything more. I keep on with my task of setting the fire.

He's not used to my silence. He fills the gap. 'Mum's asked me to come over and find out.'

I turn to look directly at him. 'Did she?'

'Yes.' Dad clears his throat and edges his way into the room. 'Um, Raylene called from work to say you'd started well.'

'Did she?' I strike a match, enjoying the fizz, watching the flames take hold. Nick-nack watches too. There's golden-orange light dancing in her eyes. I rest my hand on the ruff of her neck.

'You'll spoil her, having her inside.'

'Will I?'

'Connie …' Dad begins, barely keeping the growl from his voice.

Does he know that I know? From his demeanour, I think he might. He moves to stand over me. Uncomfortable with his nearness, I rise, daring myself to meet his gaze. I have the Ace of Spades now. The right card to hold.

'Now, about working with Ray–' he begins, but then something on the mantel catches his eye and he stops abruptly. His shocked stare is locked on Larry's watercolour portrait. Slowly he reaches out, picks it up, then looks to me.

'Where did you get this?' he demands. 'Did you get it from *him*?'

Nick-nack flattens her ears, crouches and tiptoes from the room, tail jammed between her legs.

'Him? You mean Larry? Yes. I did. He told me to ask you about her.'

Dad's looking at the portrait, jaw muscles working overtime.

'Who is she, Dad?'

His gaze burns at me, top lip turning upwards in a sneer. 'How dare you!'

'How dare I? What have I got to do with this? This woman, who happens to be in every single painting Larry does – Dad, who is she?'

'She ... she is ... history.'

'Then who *was* she?'

He tosses the portrait into the fire where flames devour the edges of the thick parchment, consuming the woman's face to ash.

'I told you to *never* go over there!' Dad shouts.

Somehow, here in the cottage, I find my inner resolve. 'I think, given the situation, it's beyond the stage where you get to tell me what to do, Dad.'

'Given what situation?'

'You know exactly what I mean! I know you're having an affair with Raylene. And I know Mum doesn't know. Not consciously at least.'

Grabbing my wrists with his strong square hands, he shoves me backwards into Granny M's chair, and pins me there. His grip is so tight, my flesh stings. 'If you're so interested in other people's business, why don't you ask your Uncle Larry the full story about that woman? How she tried to con me?'

Anger surges in me. 'Why don't I tell Mum the full story about you and Raylene?'

Dad sucks in a breath of fury and grips me even harder. 'How dare you blackmail me. You shouldn't dare open your mouth. After everything I've done for you. For years I've put up with you and your whingeing. And you with that professor. You're disgusting!'

Veins bulge in his neck and temples. He smells of sweat, and there's beer on his breath. He's a mean dog when he drinks, which is why Mum never lets him.

'Dad! You're hurting me!' My veins are now pulsing in pain. I look to him pleadingly and all I can see is the face of Professor Turner. I scrunch my eyes shut, turning away from his booze-soaked rage.

'Dad!' I shout. 'Stop!'

'What's going on?' Patrick's voice infuses the room. 'Dad?'

He relinquishes his grip and steps backwards. 'Just the usual shit Connie creates in our lives,' he says bitterly, looking down at me as if I'm scum.

Patrick looks from Dad to me. 'Mum said tea's getting cold,' he says uncertainly.

Dad exhales a frustrated groan and pushes past Patrick, slamming the front door on the way out.

'You okay?' Patrick asks as I begin to rub my throbbing wrists. Swiping the heel of my hand over my eyes, I turn my face away, holding it all in. I flinch when he touches me on my shoulder. 'Connie?'

His rare moment of empathy releases a sob in me. I have to bury my face in my elbow, to stop the emotions surging with a wildness I know I won't be able to control.

Patrick remains near, hovering. Awkward.

'I see that he treats you like crap,' he says eventually. 'It's easier for me to be a prick like him than confront him. You're braver than me. Some mornings I could punch his lights out. But I don't. Like I say, you're braver, Connie.'

I listen, crying quietly, as he walks from the room and closes the front door.

Soon, Nick-nack stalks back in, nudging her wet nose under my throbbing hand. Drawing her to me, I hold on to her for dear life.

'Thank Dog I've got you, Nack,' I say to her before a blackness in my heart swamps me.

Chapter 23

The next day, when I get to work a smidge after nine, my eyes are still swollen, my wrists still burning, but my heart is soothed and my mind stilled. Thankfully the office is empty. Earlier, desperate, I'd knocked hopefully on Verenda's door. Megan had appeared in her dressing gown, hair a riot of curls. On seeing my bruises and my broken expression, she had folded me into her arms.

'Come on, darling,' she said. 'Come inside.'

Just an hour with Megan proved better than all my sessions with Doctor Cragg combined. 'Learn to let go of the thoughts you have written on the world,' she said. 'Change your mind, Connie.'

Thanks to Megan, I'm now robust enough to not just survive my day, but flow through it peacefully.

The phone rings and I soon find myself with my cow-poo-crusted shoes up on the Global Genetics reception desk talking to a nice but stressed-sounding young man called Paul. He's telling me how he recently took over his father's farm. Initially he was inquiring about bulls in the new Global Genetics catalogue, but it seems my questions have got him on a dairy-geek roll.

'We're sitting at about 1.8 tonnes per cow per lactation in the bail,' he brags. 'Last year we produced 96,000 kilograms of milk solids but we're aiming to push it up to 105,000 next year. And since I've taken on the management, in the last three years we've had an increase of forty kilograms of milk solids per cow.'

'Bravo you,' I say, meaning it. It would've taken a lot to push the system that hard. But then I ask, 'And how's your cows' health?'

'Okay, sort of.'

'Vet costs high?'

'A bit. Yeah.'

'I know this last season, my dad needed increased antibiotic doses in the daily feed ration. Was it the same for you?' I ask, letting him know I'm one of his kind and not just an office person.

'Yeah,' he says.

I'm leading to my big question, pausing before I ask, 'Paul, tell me – are your cows happy?'

'Happy?'

'Yes. And, more importantly ... are you happy, Paul?'

Silence on the other end of the phone.

'Happy?' he answers eventually. 'I've never really thought about it. No one's ever asked me that before. I guess the cows are happy – they're producing milk, right? And am I happy? I know the banks are happy ... and the supermarkets are happy – they've got us over a barrel. Happy ... mmm?'

'Well, have a think about it, Paul,' I advise. 'Farming is best considered from a holistic point of view. You're at the centre of all this. Now, what about your pasture management? Tell me, what's that look like?'

I lean back into the chair and swivel about. I'm enjoying this. Talking to people on the phone is easy when they don't know me, can't see me and Danny's not here – most likely avoiding me, hiding in the semen storage shed.

For all Paul knows, I could look like Justine Clarke – that cute, friendly actor from *Play School* with the dimples – *and* be a leading geneticist. All he has is the sound of my voice, which he seems to have warmed to.

'Well, I've talked Dad into a new pivot so we're doing some bush-clearing and have a three-year plan for pasture renovation,' he's saying. 'We'll sow a summer crop. We're going for pasja and millet – something high energy and early maturing. Then back into perennial ryegrass.'

'Okay,' I say, 'so you're feeding your cows that. And what are you feeding your soil microbes and doing to support your soil's fungi, viruses, bacteria, nematodes and all those good things? What are you doing to keep a living soil sustained so your cows' gut health is maximised? Cut your vet costs? Increase your calving success?'

Silence. I plough on.

'If I were you, I'd be looking for more diversity in your pasture choice. Have you heard the new science about quorum sensing and signalling between plants and soils – all that wonderful communication is triggered by loads of different plants and a living universe of soil?'

'Um,' he says, faltering. 'Our agronomist has us applying NPK … and increasing nitrogen application – I reckon we'll raise it to two hundred units of nitrogen per hectare per year.'

My body shudders. A flash vision appears of the algal blooms dragged about by lazy currents in the bays where the river meets the sea.

I clear my throat. 'Are you sure you want to throw your dollars away like that, Paul?'

'What? What do you mean?'

'Well, plants can only use about three to five per cent of the nitrogen we put on dairy pastures. The rest of it goes into the air and into the water, which is why our river system in Lilyburn is so buggered and every year there's less and less fish for the Catch a Flatty comp.'

I know I need to stop talking like this, but my desperation to convert Paul is as fierce and impassioned as a televangelist. It's crashing out of my mouth, slamming straight into his mindset – a mindset like so many – of cognitive dissonance about what we do to Mother Earth. I'm going to say it anyway!

'Do you like a beer, Paul?' I ask, with what I hope sounds like earthy coolness and not a madwoman rant.

'Beer? Yeah. I like one or two ... maybe three of a weekend if the missus lets me,' he says.

'Well, an agroecologist Nicole Masters says that spending money on nitrogen is like buying a hundred cartons of beer, drinking five and throwing the other ninety-five straight out into the skip at the back of the bottle-o. If you can wean your system off it, you'll be saving yourself a lot of money and helping the environment. This system, our farming system, it ain't pretty, Paul! We need to find other ways.'

There's silence his end so I continue.

'We have to ask ourselves what would nature do?'

'Nature?'

'Yes, nature. She would have a diverse, complex system of plants, insects, birds and other species, all supporting and being supported by a *living soil* – a soil that can access all the nutrients required for your cows and utilise all the waste in that system. Then you can slowly ditch the expensive stuff that comes in drums and overall be more profitable and be happier – even healthier.'

More silence. I can tell I've lost him. Like I lost all my lecturers and peers at uni. Like I lose Doctor Cragg. And Slugs and the council workers. In desperation I pull out my best Nicole Masters quote. 'Paul, listen ... we're inadvertently destroying the soil upon which life on Earth depends.'

'Are you saying I'm destroying my farm, and that I'm not happy – or healthy?' Defensiveness barbs his voice. I falter. He swoops.

'You bloody university types,' he huffs. 'I was just after some semen, not a bloody greenie sermon. Tell Danny to email me the bloody catalogue with what he reckons.'

The line goes dead and so does my heart – or at least that's what it feels like. Soon after, Raylene powers through the door, wearing a satin cornflower-print shirt and quilted velvet jacket with gold buttons, looking like she's been upholstered as a posh Royal's couch. She's also wearing a murderous expression on her face.

159

'Connie Mulligan, what on earth are you playing at now? You just can't help stirring up trouble, can you?'

I slide my feet from the desktop. An anger like I've never known lifts in me.

'What am *I* playing at?' I ask fiercely, my eyes narrowing.

It's as if I've found myself in one of Mum's daytime soaps. After the brick wall I hit with Danny and Paul, my body is zinging with frustration for the world and the people in it. I'm fed up with the wrongness of everything – things that no one can see! Or no one wants to see. Professor Turner was the same. The thought of him is now no longer bringing numb despair to me, but a kind of muted anger. Megan's words about the buried anger of the female collective bubble upwards. 'I think the more relevant question would be what are *you* playing at, Raylene?'

'I'm only doing this as a favour to you and your family,' she barks, 'and yet here you stand, unrepentant, insulting our clients, sending our office manager crazy within half an hour of you being here! Danny's threatening you go or he does! He's under so much pressure now his wife's sick. Honestly, how do your mother and father stand it! Especially after all that university business. The drama you caused was disgraceful. Your mother's furious with you.'

The past squarks. A dark bird flies over threatening to smother and cover me with its sinister wings. I'm back in the court room with a line-up of Professor Turner's colleagues all giving testimonials of his good character, while hand-picked fellow students and other teachers tear me down. I shake the humiliation from me.

'Enough!' I cry out, glaring at Raylene.

Her shocked expression morphs into one of inquiry as she searches my face for the Connie Mulligan she knows so well – the compliant, impotent version of me. My mother's version of Connie Mulligan. A version I feel I'm done with from this moment, now.

'How furious would Mum be with you, Raylene?' I pause, staring her right in the eye with a Clint Eastwood coldness. 'Particularly if she knew about you?'

Raylene tilts her head to one side. Poker-faced, yet there's a tiny quiver in the corner of her right eye. 'Knew what?' she asks haughtily.

'That you are fucking my father.'

Chapter 24

The next day Raylene calls me into her office. Sitting at her desk in her floral shirt reminiscent of 'springtime potted colour' outside the hardware store, she weaves her long slender fingers together, four of them ringed in gold.

'Connie, how can we help you? Anything at all.'

'Well, Raylene,' I say, 'I've done some thinking since our little *chat* yesterday. I've got a proposal for you and the board.'

'Proposal? For what?' she asks guardedly.

'Global Genetics' brand-new Heritage Breed Preservation and Diversity Semen Collection Program.'

Rearing back in her chair like a horse seeing a snake, she asks, 'The what?'

I pause, giving her a narrow-eyed stare to remind her of her tenuous position.

'Go on.'

'It's a program designed to help store and protect diversity of cattle genetics.' Zesty energy lifts in me, rolling me on. 'We're also going to establish a Holistic Dairy Practice Trial Program.'

'A what? We?'

'Let me give you some context. If most customers knew what went on in the industry, truly, they wouldn't buy our milk. There really has to be a way the calves can stay on their mothers, and we get milk. Or at least stay with a mother? Provided the mother is a nice one,' I add for my own benefit.

162

'Are you serious! We'd be blacklisted if we suggested that! Where are you going with this, Connie?'

'I'll tell you where *we* are going with this. In the next budget, thanks to your input Raylene, Global Genetics will fund some practical trials on surrogate mothers in calf-rearing, and – even more boldly – leaving the calves on their mothers. A calf-at-foot system.'

She snorts sceptically. 'That's crazy. The board will never ...'

'Oh the board will get it, coming from you. You'll be able to show them examples of farms in Europe doing exactly this in answer to consumer demands.'

Raylene shakes her head vehemently. 'You can't be serious?' she replies, incredulous. 'Our industry values production and profit, and safeguarding against food supply liability. You know that. Be a realist, Connie.'

'A realist? Me? We're already losing dairy customers in droves due to dietary and environmental impacts. A huge rethink is required. That's the reality. But I think you'll find it's you who's living in a fantasy world, Raylene, with my father.'

With my trump card laid squarely on the table, she clenches her jaw and lets me finish.

'I'm asking for a special board meeting for an on-farm trial at Sunnyside. It's about time the industry recognised the all-important social stability and education that a reliable matriarchy brings.'

'How long are you going to keep doing this?'

'As long as it takes,' I say meeting her energy. 'Regardless of what you and Dad are up to, it's a smart business choice to investigate a more natural way forward for our industry. It's the type of consumer-driven change that's here with us anyway.'

The phone rings. She grabs it up, keen to end the conversation. The news on the other end of the line turns her face white. She sets down the phone, swipes up her car key and says, 'It's Nikki. The baby's already on its way.'

*

As the weeks unfold we barely see Raylene and I'm left to free-range on my suggested projects. Whispers roam the office that something's seriously wrong with the baby.

It's lunchtime on a Friday and I'm just finishing up on the phone after tracking down a rare as hen's teeth Shetland kye breeder. I lob into the kitchenette to find the normally elusive Semen Field Team tucking into their food.

Sandy, Heath and Norman mutter their greetings in between mouthfuls. I sit down, taking out a brown paper bag filled with gatherings from Uncle Larry's garden and some nuts and vegan treats from Happy Chappy, humming cheerily.

'You're chipper,' Sandy says.

I grin. 'I'm on a roll. Raylene's given us funding for a field officer to head out next week for our next canister in Western Victoria.'

'How do you do it,' Sandy asks, 'wrap her round your little finger like that? She wouldn't even fund a box of beer for the Christmas party last year.'

I shrug, then pull out a couple of Larry's baby carrots, twisted and curved around each other like mating snakes. I smile at the remains of rich soil where they connect. Good for my gut. Good for my soul. I crunch into one, the sweetness exploding in my mouth.

'Snap,' Sandy says when she takes a thick straight carrot from her lunch box too. She taps it on mine. 'Cheers.'

'Cheers!' I laugh.

She takes a theatrical bite.

'Did you know commercially grown carrots are made straight by chemical intervention?' I say, 'And that there's a link between the sprays they use on carrots and children's arthritis.'

Sandy swallows like she's gulleting down a rock. 'Really?'

Heath and Norman stop eating and look at me.

'There's this guy who's developing a device to measure nutrient density of food. He compared a regular supermarket carrot with a market-garden carrot. He reckons you'd have to eat two hundred of your type of carrot to get the same nutrition as the one I've pulled out of Uncle Larry's garden! *Two hundred!* That's a shit-ton of carrots! You'd be pooping orange!'

I point to Norm's apple. 'Supermarket bought?'

'Yes.' His bloodhound eyes look worried.

'Ninety-nine per cent of Australian apple samples tested positive for at least one pesticide residue. Same for nectarines and peaches. A single grape sample contained fifteen pesticides! Even cherry tomatoes, imported sugar snap peas and strawberries had thirteen different pesticides in them.'

My eyes land on the hot chips Heath is devouring. '*And* did you know the average potato has more pesticides by weight than any other produce. I can show you the study if you like?'

'No!' they all chorus. We fall to silence.

'I don't mean to be a seagull, but can I have one by the way?' I ask eventually, indicating Heath's chips.

He pushes the bag towards me. 'You can have the rest.'

As I chow down on the chips, Sandy says, 'You sure know how to kill an appetite, Connie.'

'So I've been told.'

Even though there's still another ten minutes left on our break, the team start packing away their unfinished lunches and are about to leave when Raylene arrives, followed by a grim-looking Danny.

She smiles at me. 'Ah Connie, I'd hoped I'd find you here with the others. I have an announcement. Everyone, sit back down.'

'What?' I ask, narrowing my eyes suspiciously.

'Congratulations are in order!'

'Congratulations? For what?'

'You, my dear girl, have just won a trip to Ireland!' She says it like she's on a TV game show and dances on the spot a little.

'Me? Ireland? *Why?*'

Raylene looks slightly disappointed that I'm not more excited. 'Because you've won Semen Sales Rep of the Year!'

'But I'm not a Semen Sales Rep.'

'Yes, Connie, I know,' Raylene says with false brightness. 'It was actually Nikki who won the prize … I just got off the phone from our German counterpart who runs the competition. As you are well aware, she can't take the trip with a newborn baby! And you know, little Sarah is not exactly thriving. So, you're it!'

My mind races. People like me don't go travelling overseas. People like me don't have exciting things like this happen to them.

'What about Danny?' I ask. 'Shouldn't he go ahead of me? He knows the ropes. He's more of a people person.'

Danny shakes his head. 'No way can I go,' he says, holding up both hands. 'I can't even fly to Melbourne for a Bryan Adams concert without puking in a bag. I'd never make it to the other side of the world with my stomach intact.'

I know he's lying through his teeth.

'Plus, his wife needs him here,' Raylene adds soothingly.

Despite the rumblings amid the crew, Raylene stands her ground, immobile as Margaret Thatcher in her decision. It's then I realise it's all to get me out of the way. And most likely to put a pause on my rare breeds project and to help Dad from being pestered about beginning the calf-at-foot trials on his farm.

I look to the Semen Field Team. 'What about them? They've been here longer than me.'

Raylene shakes her head. 'With the Spring AI program underway and their family situations, we can't send any of our ground crew.' She gestures towards the team, who I'm sure have a green tinge of envy on their skin. 'We need them here. So, it's you or no one. Connie, we need the connections. It's just for two weeks. There's a dinner, an Expo and a five-day bus trip with other sellers to key dairy farms and bull-semen collection centres in Europe. Then home. That's it. It'll be busy, but you should be able to handle that?'

'Mais … non!' I begin to falter. 'You know what I'm like with …' I feel colour flame my cheeks. 'With people … face to face. And dinners, I can't do dinners.'

The on-farm team glance at one another.

'Nonsense,' Raylene purrs. 'You've been here long enough. You're good on the phone. I've heard you. You just need to learn to stay on topic. It's just a matter of building from there.'

Sandy releases a snort, flinging her carrot into the bin.

'You'll be fine,' Raylene persists. 'You'll represent us well.'

The room starts to spin, the pictures of the cows floating off the walls and the floor tilting, my vision flaring with white dots. Pain zings shoulder to fingertips. I try to pull in a breath.

Raylene's thin fingers grip my upper arm. 'Now come on, Connie. Into my office. We've got to get your passport application underway, pronto. You're leaving in just over three weeks.'

'Three weeks!'

'Yes! Not much time,' she says as I follow her blindly into her office and slump onto a chair. She sets herself down in front of the serious-looking forms. 'I'm assuming you don't have a passport. Jane at the post office can fast-track the documents through for us.'

'Ireland? Are you sure?'

My head begins to throb. There's a blinding flash of white light. I close my eyes to it, trying to focus on my breath, but I feel the slip, my eyes rolling back into the darkness.

In a cob stable, whitewashed within, Traveller and I stand in golden hollow stalk straw. I'm singing to him, my voice melodic like a harp and grooming his dappled rump in long soothing strokes sending dust motes dancing in a slanted beam of sunshine. I sense someone at the door, watching me. Resting my forehead on the horse's shoulder I smile. Fingertips brush the nape of my neck. Stars shimmer over my skin. My lips part in desire. His breath is warm on the skin of my neck. 'Tha mi dhachaigh, my love, you've come home.'

'Full name?' Raylene's voice cuts in, her pen hovering over the passport form.

'Um, Constance Erin Mulligan.'

'Erin?' Raylene asks. 'Erin as in the Irish name for Ireland?'

'Yes,' I reply.

'Ha!' She smiles as she ticks some boxes on the form. 'It'll be like you're going home.'

'Home,' I echo. 'Yes, *home*.'

Chapter 25

I glide through green crepe streamers stepping into Verenda where toe-tapping Irish music is playing.

'Oh! She's here! Our semen queen!' Vernon cries swooping me into a hug, Fenton pressing a glass of champagne into my hand. Hovering shyly near the recently finished kitchen is Uncle Larry who waves at me.

'Larry? What's going on in here?'

'Megan went and got the bloody hermit herself,' says Shirley, nudging him. 'We're having a Piss off to Ireland Party for you and an unofficial opening!'

'Any excuse for a party,' says Elsie, one of the first women to stay at the support centre. Outside I see the other 'newbie' women, Dannika and Claudia and their children who are playing on a swing, strung from the old floodlit walnut tree.

'Wish I could get in your suitcase and come too!' Shirley says. 'Meegs reckons time away from Lilyburn would help me get over the crap with Barry and his new bird.'

Out of the blue, Jane from Aussie Post bursts through the door shouting. 'Gatecrashing!'

'Ahh it's our passport string-puller!' I say, grabbing a drink for her.

'Well, Raylene scares the shit out of me, so of course I got it done,' Jane says, clinking her glass with mine.

'Everyone's here!' Megan says, striking a single blow on a drum. The sound illuminates the room with such insistency it reverberates in my solar plexus.

'Everything, everything is vibrational energy,' Megan says. 'That's why we're gathering to send Connie powerfully on her way to the other side of the world and open our doors with a party. Ceremony is important for the sisterhood.'

'Here she goes!' Shirley says like a little kid, excited for one of Megan's impromptu uplifting sermons.

Megan bangs the taut skin again. 'Drumming is ancient,' she says over its soundwaves. 'It helps move stuck energy, and believe me, in this culture, women have so much stuck energy!'

'Not even prune juice would shift mine!' Shirley mutters.

Megan hands us each a drum. 'By drumming, we put out a resounding call for spiritual and social renewal. The ancient priestesses did it. Why not us? Let's send Connie to Ireland with that old power activated within her!'

The sound energy swirls and lifts so that soon I can feel the thrumming rhythm seemingly reconfiguring my heart, rearranging the surface of every cell of my body and beyond. The beats get faster and faster. The room seems to blur and swirl in a colourful mix of light, like melting rainbow ice cream in a vortex. Even Larry, reluctant at first to join our circle, has his eyes shut, a look of utter bliss on his face. I find the sound river he's in, closing my eyes, only to be jolted out of my drumbeat trance when Dawn arrives looking impervious in a crisp blue suit with shoes so pointy they look like they'd serve as chisel ploughs.

'Will you keep it down!' she shouts over the remaining drummers. 'This is the third time I've asked you to stop with the banging, Megan. We agreed. Not until I've closed for the day and I'm well and truly home. You hear me?'

'Maybe it's you who needs a banging,' mumbles Shirley, so that Jane splutters and Dannika elbows her.

'Perhaps you'd like to join us?' Megan asks.

'No, I bloody well would not.'

'Do I detect some unresolved anger, Dawn?'

'Don't you try and bloody well women's-therapy me, Megan! And no, I am not angry!' Dawn shouts, her powdered, smoker's lined face pinched, ice blue eyes ablaze. 'I just want a bit of shush!'

'Can't you hear your buyers over the phone, eh Dawn?' Shirley goads. 'Are we stopping you selling the rest of our district to the foreigners and bigwigs?'

I can't help a chuckle escape.

'Best to not poke the possum,' Larry murmurs.

Dawn emits a strangled noise of frustration. 'Just keep the fucking music down or I'm calling the police!' The Tibetan doorbells jangle violently as she departs.

Megan sets the drum down. 'Some people aren't ready for higher vibrations. When they feel them they react with anger.' She shrugs. 'Well I guess it's time for your presents, Connie!' she says.

'But I'm only going for two weeks!' I protest.

'Part of a woman's healing is to learn to receive from others,' Megan says just as Shirley lays a heavy parcel on my lap. Their attention draws heat prickles to my cheeks. Peeling the paper away, shiny red gumboots are revealed. They sparkle with green faux crystals and a bedazzling of sequinned hot-pink hearts.

'Oh, very fancy!' Vernon laughs, holding one up to the light. 'They're hilarious!'

'Yep. My glue gun was running hot!' Shirley says.

'You'll get an Irish fella in those to be sure, to be sure,' Jane quips. 'You'll need these to go with them.'

She hands me a gift bag of frilly knickers, some with leprechauns on them, others with shamrocks. Laughing, I hold each design up.

Megan throws open a large wicker basket. Skirts froth out of it.

'What's with the fancy dress?' I ask, as she hands me a green one.

'This is no dress-up game. This is my ammunition supply.'

Reading the inquiry on my face, she explains, 'Women around the world have been raising their skirts in a show of power for

171

centuries. History has recorded lots of women exposing themselves to fend off entire armies of men! Even changing government policies in recent times. And stopping civil wars.'

'Vive la resistance!' I say, pulling the flouncy tulle skirt over my pants. Even Larry wears one and in no time we're dancing in pinks, oranges and purples to The Pogues. Shirley, in bright yellow to match her Richmond Tigers logo, and me in my Irish green. Vernon and Fenton wearing red and yellow over their black jeans, so they look like Toulouse-Lautrec can-can dancers. Jane's Aussie Post uniform is transformed into an Alice in Wonderland look with white sparkled petticoats. The shelter women's children catch the wave and join in.

Shirley and the chappies begin their own ridiculous version of Irish dancing and Jane starts moving like Paddy-whack when he dry humps the air. Then there's me, trying to match Megan's smooth as silk gyration, but instead moving so woodenly I feel like I look like someone trying to scratch their arse without their fingers. I'm laughing so hard, Larry catches my hands and we twirl in a joy I've never felt before. Dancing near us, Megan shimmies her black skirt upwards, the light swirling within the fabric like the universe of stars itself.

'The wisdom of the ancient, and your power is found below your navel, Connie! Embrace it. Take that ancient wisdom with you to Ireland.'

I chuckle and dance harder, revolving like a whirling dervish, spinning off my past, my parents, my pain, until I am spent. When the spin of colour dies down it's time to go. We shuffle out into the dimming daylight and for the first time I feel like I belong somewhere. And now, it's time to leave.

*

The next day, as the wheels fold into the belly of the plane and velocity from the updraft pins me to my seat. I'm leaving behind my world as I've known it – that skid-marked disaster that was my life in Tassie. I feel potential rise in me, now I'm headed for Irish green! I shut my eyes and picture the colour in my mind's eye. A stunning version that is emerald, verdant, shamrock and mint. The green of healing. A leafy land of photosynthesis. A place where love may bloom, both within me and without. Or, as Shirley had put it, I 'might get a bit of Irish sack action'.

Now, as the plane shudders upwards and away, excitement and lament all meld into one. Shutting my eyes, I pray to myself, *Let this new Northern Hemisphere version of Connie Mulligan emerge, ready for love! Ready to heal. Ready to remember my ancient wisdom within.*

The plane bumps and my eyes fly open, panic gripping me.

What if Professor Turner follows me? What if he won't fall away to the past? I sigh too loudly, scrunching my eyes shut. He can't come with me. *He can't.* I shuffle uncomfortably in my seat, wiping my sweating palms on my thighs.

The rather large woman beside me turns and smiles. 'Okay, love?' she asks.

I nod.

'Don't like flying?'

'Oh, I like flying. I don't like falling,' I say. Then I realise I may sound like a smart arse, so quickly add, 'I'm fine, thank you.'

She pauses but persists. 'Where are you headed after our stopover in Dubai?'

'Ireland,' I reply.

'Nice. Work or holiday?'

'Work. I won a trip to go,' I say as the new Connie Mulligan, smiling broadly. This Connie is the one who makes friends easily. The one who is charming. And funny. And interesting. And vibrant. Engaging. Colourful to others, not dull brown anymore. Haven't I got my new kaleidoscope friends to prove it?

'Oh! Congratulations. What work do you do?'

'I work with semen.'

'Oh, so you're in the navy? Shipping? That kind of thing?'

'No,' I laugh. 'AI'

'Ah! Artificial Intelligence! I don't know anything about computers and that sort of stuff. They have taken over the world, so I'd imagine you'd be a busy girl.'

'No!' I laugh again. 'Not that kind of AI either! Artificial Insemination. I'm talking *semen*, semen. The white squiggly, spurty stuff that's stored in testicles. We collect it and sell it.'

'Oh,' she says, eyebrows lifting then diving to a furrow. She tenses, her smile gone.

'For the dairy industry,' I add hastily.

'Oh! I see.' But I can tell she doesn't see at all. She reaches into the seat pocket for her reading glasses and pulls out a magazine. 'Well ... nice talking then. Have a nice flight.' She opens the magazine and turns away from me.

'You too,' I say crestfallen. Conversation closed.

I press the button on the seat in front of me and on the screen a little cartoon plane tracks its way over Australia, bound for the great blue of Mother Earth's oceans and a land far away on the other side. Perhaps the new version of Connie Mulligan needs more time to emerge.

Chapter 26

Hours later, crumpled and groggy from the long-haul flights, I drag the new upside-down Northern Hemisphere version of me, and mum's hideous big cat–print suitcase to the hotel check-in desk. The concierge, smiling, hands me a cardboard sleeve with what looks like a plastic credit card in it.

'There's your key,' he says in a thick Irish accent. I stare at it, coming to terms with the fact that keys are now cards, and wanting to ask him if they still unlock doors if there's a power outage?

Behind me, the burble of semen industry delegates have spilled from the buses into the foyer of the swanky Dublin Hotel, the decibels climbing as more and more arrive.

'Can I get someone to take your leopard – I mean, luggage up to your room, madam?' the concierge asks.

'Um, no thanks,' I squeak.

As I roll my giant beast towards the lift, a man starts chasing after me.

'Excuse me! Excuse me! Australian person!'

I turn to him. He has a UK Sires logo on his top and hair so thin it's combed flat, leaving blond and pink stripes over his forehead.

'Where on earth is our Nikki?'

'Our Nikki's back home.'

His fair British hedgerow brows lower. 'But why?'

175

'She's had a baby,' I say.

The man's eyebrows leap upwards. 'Really! Oh, fabulous news! Simply wonderful. Did she have a bull calf or heifer?' he jokes.

'Heifer, luckily. If it was a bull calf, they may have donged it on the head – surplus to industry requirements.'

'Excuse me?' the man replies.

'Oh, nothing. A girl. Sarah.'

'Delightful! Anyway, I'm Gavin Cumberston, current Semen Sales Rep Winner UK. And you are?'

'Nikki's sort-of replacement. Nice to meet you,' I answer, redness crawling up my cheeks, as I rush for the lift.

As the doors slide shut, I reach for Megan's belly breath to find my inner compass. But pressing the buttons over and over, the lift refuses to move. My lungs refuse to expand.

The lift doors slide open again and a woman steps in – German, judging by her dairy company logo of Besterind.

'Lost your key?' she asks.

I nod, mute. She presses her hotel card onto the lift panel. We start sailing up towards the eighth floor. After she disappears, leaving behind a waft of expensive perfume and an air of superiority, I try the same with my card, and off I go upwards. When I get to the eleventh, I'm relieved to get out of the lift, only to encounter the longest corridor of same-same doors and odd geometric carpet in black, white and greys that gives me vertigo. I rush past the maddening cloned doors to room 111. On the door, there's a panel like the one in the lift. Slamming my plastic key on it, a green light flashes and the lock gives in.

Stumbling inside, the air is as overstuffed as the pillows, and I can smell the chemical traces of the cleaning products that have been slathered over the room. I go to the window, wishing I could slide it open and step onto an imagined balcony. I want to fall into the heavy embrace of the low metallic sky with its welcoming kiss of cold Irish rain ... the only sign of nature here at this inner-city hotel. Instead, the double-glazed windows keep me trapped. I press my forehead to the glass and look to the bleak street.

Here I am, Ireland. Home? I wonder. Yes. I can feel it settle in my bones. I'm home. But I'm not in the right place. The walls and low ceiling press in upon me, like a dungeon. I fall onto the bed, eyes clenched, hands on my belly, rising and falling, until I find calm.

*

An hour later I remember the itinerary in my backpack and spread it out on the bed to review. First up is a fancypants industry dinner in the auditorium downstairs. I grimace, then remember Megan's gift of three vibrant retro 50s polka-dot scarves – one red, one green, and the other a cheerful light blue.

'To help you remember you *are* light and colour,' she'd said.

I can feel my sisterhood gifts bursting to be let loose for this new adventure. I can do this, I tell myself. Switching on the telly, I'm buoyed by the refreshing Irish accents, leaving them to lilt about the room as I head to the bathroom. Will the water drain anti-clockwise in the Northern Hemisphere, the opposite to home? Sure enough it does, and I am momentarily convinced my inner swirl can reverse, but my hope about Northern Connie fades the moment I shower and dress. Stepping from the bathroom I come face to face with my reflection in the floor to ceiling mirror doors. My short black hair looking mental-asylum jagged, and wearing an elastic fabric dress the colour of Uncle Larry's sow. Turning, I realise I look like a poorly processed sausage with all my lumps and bumps, made so clear by the hotel's glaring lights. Anger towards Mum simmers. I know she's done this to me deliberately, out of spite. She insisted on the dress when all I'd wanted was a plain black one.

Slumping on the bed, I'm unable to bring myself to go out looking like this. Besides, do I really want to go and mingle with all those semen people? Nice though they may be, they are still indoctrinated by a capitalist, mechanistic industry. I'm likely to offend them the moment I open my mouth. Bedside, I notice the hotel compendium with little gold-embossed tabs.

One reads: *In-Room Dining.*

Perfect. I dial 9, then peel off my dress and wrap myself in the white robe that hangs behind the devastating mirrors.

'Thank goddess,' I say to the empty room, knowing I'll have a steak and chips on the way to me soon. Along with the chilled comfort of a chocolate mousse.

*

The next morning, I watch from my window as the giant tour buses line up and are slowly stuffed full of chattering semen-sellers and industry reps. Soon they are pulling away from the hotel entrance and as they do, I feel a sense of calm return to my body.

I roll my suitcase out of the room, into the lift and down to the hotel desk, where I slide the plastic key to the concierge.

'Checking out, please.'

He looks perplexed but prints out my bill. I gasp at the price of last night's room service. I sign it, knowing Raylene will go off her chops, but it won't be as bad as when she finds out about what I'm about to do. Sucking in a deep breath, I exit the hotel, where my taxi awaits.

'Where to?'

'Connolly train station, please.'

Chapter 27

I'm standing at the bar of The Farmer and the Folly flanked by Mum's wild game suitcase and a golden labrador called Captain (according to his tag). The dog looks at me with melty brown eyes, beating his tail on the dark timber floor. Falling into his God-backwards eyes I feel he is a sign that I've done the right thing in running away from the conference. Embroidered on Captain's collar is *Don't Feed Me. I'm Fat Enough.* He stares up hopefully, as if I might happen to have a hamburger in my pocket.

'You're not fat, buddy! You're cuddly!'

'That's what my ex-girlfriend used to say to me,' says Patrick, the pale-skinned but cute young man before me. As he fetches my room key from the back office, humming away, I turn to drink in the cosy yet expansive pub that is filled with wooden tables, bentwood chairs and little opaque glass screens that divide the booths.

The timber-panelled walls are covered in old advertising memorabilia, Gaelic footy team photos, wooden hurling sticks and fraying pennants. There's mirrors mottled with age, patinaed wallpaper backgrounding cloudy bottles and chipped jugs, all illuminated by a clerestory window. Fading pink lacy knickers hang from a wall-mounted lamp with a sign that says *Dave, we think you left something. Grand finals 1972.* The old wooden bar has been worn smooth with centuries of laughing, yarning and crying into whiskeys and pints.

This is the Ireland I was bound for, and my inner intuitive compass that Megan has woken in me tells me I'm on the right track. I feel unstoppable – like a river bursting its banks. Tingles run through me.

'What brings you to Mountrath?' Patrick asks. I'm relieved to see he's twirling an old-fashioned metal key on his finger that will fit into a normal metal lock. He lifts a hinged section of the bar and ducks under.

'Um … I'm hoping to meet the Donovans from–'

'Donohill Dairy,' Patrick finishes my sentence.

'You know them?'

He pulls an 'of course' face. 'Know them? Dairy rock stars, they are! You're not the first to come here to see them. Some call them rebel farmers, bad for dairy business. But I think they're great.'

'Bad for business? Rebels?'

Patrick shrugs. 'It's just what folks say.'

'I just found them on the internet one day at work. They looked interesting, like the future of dairying – regenerative, chemical-free, a calf-at-foot system. Rare-breed cattle suited to the local environment; direct sell to conscious consumers. How is that being rebellious?'

'You hear a lot working the bar, mostly from folks who are stuck in the mud.'

I look to Patrick's long timber workstation with all its on-tap beers, clean bar mats out ready for the day.

'Still, it must be a great place to work. You know, I've got a brother called Patrick too. He'd like this place.'

Taking out my Global Genetics work phone, I take a few quick photos of the old-style beer levers.

'I'll send him a pic now. Can I take one of you? Show him what a proper Patrick looks like.'

'If you insist.' He happily poses in front of the bar with Captain and gives a thumbs up. 'Would your Patrick also be as cool as me?' Irish Patrick asks, doing a few supermodel hip juts.

I look to his soft white flesh, yellow t-shirt covering a little bit of a belly. His product-laden hair is spiked in rather sparse strawberry peaks. There's a twinkle of cheekiness and a large dose of kindness in his pale blue eyes.

'My Patrick is nowhere *near* as cool as you.'

'Correct answer.' He grins.

I text, *Time for a Guinness with my new Irish brother Patrick, who is way cooler*, and send the photo whooshing to the south of the globe to my cantankerous brother, who I'm feeling oddly fond of right now.

'Okay then. Follow me,' Patrick says, taking my case.

At the top of a landing, he gestures to room 8, slots the key in and opens the creaky door. Even for my short stature the doorjamb is so low I have to stoop to enter.

'Bathroom's that way down the hall on your left. Meals at six. Happy Hour's at five and goes for two hours.'

'Happy Hour for two hours?' I ask.

'This is Ireland, you know. On Saturday's we have six o'clock rock at seven.'

Chuckling, I look at the time on my phone. It's only 11.30 am. I'm yet to even contact the Donovans about visiting their dairy, which is where my plan gets a little foggy

'Anything touristy to fill in the time?' I ask.

He shrugs. 'Ginny in the kitchen can do you some lunch at twelve. Then there's a heap of old shite to look at – castles, old churches, that kinda thing. And if you like shoppin', well too bad. You'll need a car to get to the main shopping centre down the motorway. New fucken plaza. It's near killed this place. Portlaoise is worth a look, but you'll need to take the bus. The Donovans' Dairy shop and cafe's there. That's livened the place up a bit.'

'Bus? I reckon I've had enough of travelling for today. I fancy a walk.'

'Well, the only shop nearby that you might like is the antiques shop but it's only open Saturdays. Oh wait … there's

Mrs O'Brien's Little Miracles and Mercies Charity Shop. She has late-night shopping of a Thursday when there's a cattle sale on, so you're in luck.'

'A cattle sale?' I ask, my curiosity piqued.

Patrick inclines his head. 'That way. Selling starts at four. If you want to take a look, go right out the door of the pub. Left at the town monument and walk about three blocks. You'll see the cattle trailers parked there at the co-op. Can't miss it. Follow the mooing. And the smell of shite.'

'Thanks. Beef or dairy?' I ask.

'Ehm ...' Patrick thinks for a moment. 'It was dairy last month, so I reckon it'll be beef.'

'Oh,' I say, a little disappointed, but still excited nonetheless. There could be rare beef breeds that my radar has missed that would tie in nicely with my new catalogue, given the trend of dairy farmers now joining cows with beef bulls to sell on calves to the meat trade.

'Anything else?' he asks.

'No. All good. Thanks.'

For a moment he pauses. 'Did you want a cage for that thing?' He points to Mum's suitcase. I look down at it.

'Um. No thanks. I'll keep it on a leash in the corner. Just a raw steak to feed it later, if you wouldn't mind.'

Patrick snorts in amusement. 'You're funny, you Australians.'

'Tasmanian,' I correct.

'I thought it was the same.'

'So did I until I went to the mainland. We are definitely not the same.'

'Well, you're a funny Tasmanian.' He looks me over. 'Mind yourself then,' he says, and he ambles away down the stairs.

'Mind yourself,' I mutter. What is it with the Irish saying that? I fall back on the bed, closing my eyes, wondering why on earth I've done something as impulsive as this?

My phone pings. It's a text from brother Patrick: *Piss off you dick. It's nearly midnight on a milking night!*

I roll my eyes and text back: *Well put your phone on silent then, you big firkin eejit. And how are you getting signal anyway? I know you're out skanking again.*

I search for the middle-finger emoji. As I press send, I begin to wonder if this ugly banter is actually our version of love for each other. In the lead-up to coming to Ireland there'd been less taunts from Patrick. The tension in the main house between Mum and Dad seems to be eroding his bravado. On the day I'd left, he'd actually been sincere in saying, 'Have a good time.' Perhaps as far as siblings goes, with Patrick, this is as good as it gets.

I lift myself off the bed, clicking on the Donohill Dairy website on my phone, searching for a direct number. I find an email address, and a contact for the farm shop. There's a number for a Declan and Grainne on the farm. And a Devlyn and Siobhan. Who to ring? Maybe their shop number instead? As I hesitate, a string of thoughts runs through my mind – what if they won't see me? What if they do? What if I find all the answers to my dairy dilemmas? And when I do, I can't implement them at home anyway?

That 'what's the point' feeling invades so I press the screen off. I'll call later, after lunch. Or after Happy Hour. Or after the cattle sale. No point rushing. Then I look to the phone again.

'Remember, you are Northern Hemisphere Connie now! So just bloody well call them!'

The first number goes to message bank. The second one too. Then the third. I'm too shy to leave a message. Then with a sudden rush I try the first number again. The answering machine beeps.

'Um ... you don't know me from a bar of soap, but this is Connie Mulligan. And, well, I'm over from Tasmania. I work in the dairy industry, and I'd love to see your farm. If you have time. Um, call me back ... please. It's urgent ... I mean I'm urgent, I mean I'm desperate, like meeting you and visiting your farm will save my life. Shit. Sorry.' I scrunch my eyes and hang up.

'Idiot!' I shout, throwing the phone on the bed. I'll sound like some kind of nutter to them. Then I remember I am some kind of nutter. They're never going to call me back. Tears prickle. I look about the room. Given I could be here for a few days with no Plan B, I might as well disembowel the leopard. After hanging my things in the wardrobe and placing my 'smalls', as Mum calls them, in the drawers, I set the travel sketchpad and pencils that Uncle Larry gave me beside my bed. The overly generous 'pass the hat around fund' from the Lilyburn lot and Uncle Larry ought to see me through until my return flight if I spend carefully.

At a tiny rust-stained sink lit by the gentle light from the window, I gather up my tiny supply of toiletries and robe, then trek the long crooked hallway to the shared bathrooms. In the slightly grotty women's bathroom I catch myself in the mirror, sucking in a breath of surprise.

My hair is curling around my face from the dampness of the Irish air, my cheeks still rosy from the excitement of finding this lovely old pub. I look different from the person in the mirror at the hotel last night, there's no doubting. There's an unfamiliar light and life dancing in my eyes. Even, the mole is looking charming on this side of the world. And there seems to be less of my body. I consider for a moment the notion that Mum's pink dress and the blaring hotel lights had been lying.

Pulling up my navy knit jumper I see that my pre-boarding-school waist has returned. I hadn't noticed, but it must've slowly reappeared since I've been trekking up the hillside to Larry's and back, along with eating his and the Happy Chappy's food and steering clear of Aarav's. Maybe Northern Hemisphere Connie *is* emerging.

Smiling, humming in the shower, a fantasy swims in my mind of me riding the narrow lanes upon Traveller's dappled Irish Draught back, with Nick-nack at his feathered hocks, arriving at a summertime pub where an Irish beau waits for me at an outdoor table, a big smile on his face. I feel a sparkle in my body. Drifting my fingers over my neck desire rises through me like the sunshine after rain, and glints in the place where my thighs meet. What on earth has Megan unleashed in me? I chuckle. All those vaginas hanging on her wall have reminded me I have one.

Tucked in a diner's nook in the bar I tackle the giant 'on the house' pint of rich black Guinness that Patrick has poured me, the froth settling on my top lip. Sweeping my tongue to capture it, I feel a buzz that I'm actually here! Any remorse at leaving the conference is getting wiped away with the pleasure of this pub. Before me steams a hearty pastry-topped bowl of Guinness stew. When I'm done eating, Patrick arrives flourishing a bowl of 'complimentary' ice cream that is sweltering beside a warm Guinness and chocolate pudding.

'Might as well make a proper Guinness pig of yourself.'

'That's not a good idea,' I say.

'You'll walk it off. The ice cream is from Donovans' Donohill Dairy. The best you can buy.'

I stare at the bowl, then pick up the spoon. A cold cloud of creamy heaven arrives onto the pillow of my tongue.

'Orgasmic,' I murmur to myself. It's the best ice cream I've ever tasted.

By the time I leave, I'm set to burst as I trundle outside to burp a little under the hanging flower baskets.

'See you after the cattle sale,' Patrick calls from the doorway. 'The bar will be proper buzzing here afterwards. Mind yourself, then.'

As I set off on the Mountrath village street, I'm met with a low grey sky I can almost touch. The sky's drabness is mirrored in the grey concrete render of buildings, brightened by vibrantly coloured doors of teal, pink, red and green, and flower boxes bringing cheer to the mute buildings and drear of the weather. I pass an elegant old tiled-front butchery, a tacky chain-store chemist and a betting shop that seems to suck shuffling, peak cap–wearing, red-nosed men into it as they pass like it has its own punters' undertow. Twin-pot chimneys jag the skyline. I pass lace-curtained windows discreetly masking the goings-on within. The damp street shushes with passing cars. Then a rumbling convoy of farm tractors passes. I stare at the brand-new John Deeres that to my Tasmanian farmer eyes indicates government farm subsidies.

In readiness for the saleyards, I'm wearing Shirley's noisy red gumboots, thick black leggings and one of Mum's too-tight black coats belted around my waist. I've added Megan's dash of feminine colour with a green spotted scarf tied at my neck and have jammed my cherry red beanie over my curls. I'm as glammed up as I've ever been on the way to a cattle sale.

Just a few buildings away, I can see the sign for Miracles and Mercies Charity Shop hanging on a wrought-iron bracket. As I pass an antique store, I catch my reflection in the glass. Beyond my opaque image, my eyes adjust to a collection of old-time goods: woven baskets, figurines, a squeeze box, then, a full suit of armour arrests my gaze. It stands tall and sinister, eye-slits dark and expressionless, silver-fingered gloves resting on a giant sword.

I gasp. Lights flicker. My vision flashes.

I am crouching, cold, crying, lungs burning from the chase. Hearing hoofbeats, I turn. He's there again. In his armour. On my horse. Blood on the tip of his sword.

'Devilish woman,' he hisses and drops a coarse wet rope over my neck, heavy as a metal chain. He reaches up to his bevor and hinges it downwards revealing his face. For a second, I recognise that harsh, cynical mouth and in the shadows of his visor, those cold eyes. Blue. Ice. The face of Professor Turner. Him, but not him. Him of another world. Another time. The rope's length runs taut as he spins the horse on his broad haunches, making ready to ride away. My fingers fight around the noose, but I stumble, I fall, and then I am dragged on, into blackness.

'Love?' comes the gentle voice of a woman. 'Love, are you all right? Here ...' A warm hand clutches my elbow, helping me up from where I've sunk to the pavement outside the antique store. My head throbs, my breath comes ragged and painfully, and the world feels tilted.

'I think you'd better come with me, my dear one.'

Chapter 28

The old lady helps me to the door of the Small Miracles and Mercies Charity Shop and slips the key in the lock, then flips the *Back in five minutes* sign over and ushers me in. The collective smell of people's unwanted stuff, marinated with memories, prompts another giddiness overload.

'There you go, dear. Rest here for a bit.' She indicates a white wrought-iron stool with fancy legs, topped with a matted hot-pink fluffy seat, the sort Barbie would sit upon to brush her long plastic hair. In a daze, I plop down in a woozy swirl.

'You all right, pet?'

The knight's face flashes, shuddering my body. The features those of Professor Turner.

'I think I'm just having a panic attack,' I lie.

'Is that what you think?' she replies doubtfully.

Maybe she can smell the Guinness on my breath and thinks I'm drunk. She stoops, staring directly into my eyes. Shyly I study her face – oval-shaped with gentle lines of age around her eyes and sides of her mouth, her once-dark hair now streaked grey, piled upon her head with feathering wisps falling prettily down to frame her classically beautiful cheekbones. I notice she wears an expression, not of concern or judgement, but of deep curiosity. Her gaze bores into me. She has dark black-brown eyes that seem to form two endless tunnels of time to another dimension. I feel as if I could travel right into them and come out into a whole other world.

'From what I can tell, you had a slip,' she says directly.

'A slip?' I ask, massaging the back of my neck where the muscles have jammed into rigid ropes. 'No. I didn't fall.'

She waves her hand at me as if I'm being silly. 'Go on with ye. Not *that* kind of slip. The other kind. Back in a jiffy. I'll put the kettle on.'

Before I can ask her what she means, she walks with her upright posture to the rear of the cluttered shop, flips a curtain and disappears.

While I wait, I look down to my gumboots. All their jazzy brightness seems stupid now ... now Professor Turner has followed me here. I stare at the vintage jewellery in a glass cabinet beside me. The gleaming light from the bygone-era brooches, earrings and necklaces begin to fracture as tears arrive. When the lady returns she rattles a tin in front of me.

'I can't tell how many Christmases ago these are from, but you might also be low in blood sugar and should have one.'

I look down at the striped candy canes, thinking of my giant pub Guinness feast topped with ice cream less than half an hour ago.

'No, it's not low blood sugar,' I say, fear of the truth making my voice tight.

She sets the tin down and stands erect to survey me again, placing her elegant hands on her slim hips which are draped nicely in a long tweed skirt of autumnal colours. She wears a plain gold wedding band, too loose for her finger nowadays. The pretty, sheer cream silk shirt she wears is made warm by a boiled woollen vest of gentle green. Pinned at her chest is a golden horse brooch. I begin to wonder what her story is. Clearly she's wondering what mine is also, by the way she's tilting her head and staring at me.

'You're Australian?'

'Yes. Sort of. Tasmanian. People think it's the same, but it's not.'

'When did you get here?'

'Three ... no – two days ago ... yesterday, or thereabouts, I think? It's hard to tell. I'm not very good at figuring out time,' I say, thinking of the visions I have of lifetimes past.

'Do you have family here?'

I shake my head. 'I might, but we lost track, generations ago. I'm just here for work so I won't get time to–'

She cuts me off. 'You're upside down, lass. You need to ground. And I do believe you need a cleansing. You have hooks. Do you have slips often?'

'Pardon?' I reply, utterly confused about hooks.

'Outside is the best place for a cleansing.' She gestures to me. 'Come, come!'

'Cleansing?' I sniff at my armpits as I follow her. 'I've just had a shower.'

She smiles, gathering up a tartan blanket and leads me past the orderly rumble and tumble of clothes, books, cast-off shoes and children's toys, past the chuggling kettle in the kitchenette and out a crooked door, which she opens with a sharp kick at its base.

I step into the prettiest leafy garden that's embraced by the warmth of mottled ancient stone walls, coated tenderly by beautiful climbing red and yellow roses, so vibrant they capture my gaze.

'Late bloomers,' she says indicating them, before leading me to a stone bench with scroll work made more beautiful by the covering of deep green moss and pale lichen. She spreads the blanket on it and we sit. Laying her hand on my shoulder, warmth runs through me comfortingly from her touch.

'I'm all right,' I say but in reality my body hurts all over, and just walking out here felt like I was moving through thick sludge.

'May I help you take those beauties off?' She points to my boots.

I nod numbly. She stoops to lift each leg and tugs off my gumboots, and then with motherly care, rolls my thick farm socks from my feet. Goosebumps thrill.

'Walk,' she commands, and points to the grass. The lawn is so soft to tread upon, it feels as if I'm standing on a green cloud. I pad barefoot beside the curved fringes of a cottage garden. Like the roses, the garden's doing its best to hang on to summer with the remains of honeysuckles, lupins, delphiniums and sweet peas. The grass feels cold but welcoming on my soles.

'Good,' she says. 'Now breathe.'

I glance at her. 'You sound like my psychiatrist.'

'Lord above! I hope not!' She laughs, the sound as cheerful as an Irish reel.

To appease her, like I did Doctor Cragg, I heft my shoulders up for an intake of air

'No girl! No wonder the spirit in you is starved for life. Not like that. Here ...' She takes my hand and lays my palm onto my stomach. 'In through your nose, so the air pushes your belly out. See? At the same time, clench your inner bits like you're bursting for the bathroom. Hold it. Now slowly ... breathe out. Do it three more times.'

I do as she says, and miraculously my zizzing body settles.

'Better?'

I nod.

'Now then,' she soothes, 'what would a healthy young girl like you be needin' a psychiatrist for?'

I feel the blood drain from my face. Southern Hemisphere Connie looms near. I don't want her to spoil the magic that I've found here. Inside, the kettle tings off and she claps her hands.

'Ahh ... that tea. Stay here. Let the old Motherland welcome you home, child. You'll feel better in a moment. I'll be back in a tick.'

In her absence, I feel ridiculous standing here with my white feet exposed on the lawn. Backdropped by the sulky sky, a raven caws from a chimney pot before winging away to a church spire that rises high on the other side of the wall. A shudder runs through me.

'Raven mad,' I say quietly to myself. When the woman comes back, she passes me a mug with Elvis on it.

'I checked in with your soul self. Herbal with honey. You need clarity.'

'My soul self?' I ask.

She gestures for me to sit, and ignoring my question asks, 'What happened? Out there on the street?'

I swallow. 'I'm not … *well*. Or at least that's what Doctor Cragg says.'

'Your psychiatrist?'

'Yes.'

'Why does he say you're not well?'

'She,' I correct. I bite my lip, dreading to bring Connie Mulligan of the south here now. 'I'm not sure. It's just sometimes I'm here, but I'm not here. Not in this world. And I see things. Hear things. That aren't here … aren't real.'

'How can you know they aren't real?' she asks matter-of-factly.

I look at her for a moment, puzzled. 'Because they're not.'

'Who says?'

I look skyward. The raven seems to be eavesdropping. '*Everyone.*'

'Everyone? Who is everyone?'

'Doctor Cragg. My family. People at uni.'

She chuckles. 'And what makes them think *they* know what's real in this world?'

'I don't know? I guess they're normal.'

'Normal? What if they are the ones looking at the world all skew-whiff? What if I told you that what you see or sense is just as real as this world and perhaps only layers of time.'

'Time?'

I search her face. Surely she can't be saying all those things I see are real? The burnings, the blood, the violence … That man with the ring whose face I never see? The knight, like Turner, who hunts me?

'Most think time is a straight line, like an arrow. But the tender-hearted ones – the ones like you – know otherwise. Their bodies and their hearts remember. But the families they arrive into tangle up their minds. The tender-hearted ones are those who find it hard to be here, with the sleeping ones. Mmm?'

I nod blankly.

'You, m'dear, have been here before, more often than most. Part of you knows you are simultaneously on many paths. It's the old souls who recall.'

'Paths? To where?'

'To remembering you are pure light and power. Knowing you are creation. That through your heart-mind you are one of us here to create new possibilities for the world on behalf of the sleeping ones. Most people here are in a kind of trance.'

'Trance?' I echo. 'But Doctor Cragg says I'm the one in a trance when I ... go.'

I shake my head again as if to settle her words into some sort of understandable semblance. She's talking in riddles. The woman arranges her vest, pulling it around her body against the chill and clears her throat.

'What's your name, love?'

'Connie. Connie Mulligan.'

'Good Irish name! And your folks? What do they do back in Australia?' She corrects herself. 'Ehm ... Tasmania?'

'Dairy farmers.'

She nods. 'Well, it's nice to meet you, Connie.' She holds out her hand. 'Sybil O'Brien. Mrs O'Bee to most. They reckon I'm the wife of Obi-Wan Kenobi, Jedi master, because, like him, they say I "use The Force"!'

Her eyes crinkle with amusement as she parodies a *Star Wars* light-saber move. She turns to me. Those dark tunnel eyes draw me in.

'Tell me what you see, Connie? What do you hear?'

Biting my lip nervously, I try to divert her question. 'You know. This and that.'

'No. I don't know. Tell me.' There's calm command in her voice.

I fidget with a button on my coat. 'Sometimes it's a hanging, *my hanging.* Or my sister's, even though I don't have a sister. Sometimes a burning. Sometimes a stoning, a stabbing, a battlefield. There're babies. Sometimes dead or dying. And there's men. One with a ring – kind, gentle. One in a suit of armour. Always on my horse ... my actual horse, Traveller. That man is cold – cruel, brutal, murderous.' I shudder as the face of Professor Turner appears again clad in the dull silver helmet.

Mrs O'Brien remains quiet.

'You see ... Doctor Cragg says I have a form of psychosis and I need medication.'

Mrs O'Brien makes a scoffing noise. 'What a load of twaddle. Medication? Really!' She shakes her head. 'What is it with arrogant female doctors who only practise aggressive male medicine? They have lost their senses! They have lost their wisdom! They have forgotten what you are remembering.'

She takes my hands and turns to me. 'My dear girl, you don't need drugs. There's nothing wrong with your mind. You're not ill.'

'But you've just met me. How can you know that? Isn't it irresponsible to be telling me that when you're not a doctor?'

She laughs. 'My dear, out there in the world – yes, it would be considered irresponsible. But in my world it's not, because I know.'

'You know? How?'

She leans towards me and whispers. 'I know what you see. I see the same things. Or at least similar. Until I cleared it from the starlight of my cells. I saw you coming. It's time for you to do the same, so you can lead the sleeping.'

I shiver. 'What do you mean? Saw me coming? Lead the sleeping?'

'I may be no doctor. But I am a healer. A country woman who upholds the gifts of Brigid. I was shown you were on your way.'

'Brigid?'

'The Celtic Exalted One, our goddess of spring, fertility and life. I base my arts on her as a healer.'

'You mean you're like a shaman.'

'Not *like* a shaman.' She winks at me. 'I am that I am.'

'You are who you are,' I answer. 'And who I am is mad, apparently. My mum says I'm mad. So does her friend Raylene. My dad. My brother, Patrick ...'

'Connie!' she says sharply. 'Stop! What gentle-hearted woman wouldn't be mad in a world like this one? You'll feel better about yourself when you accept your gift.'

'Gift? What gift?'

'That you are a seer. You have the gift of *sight*.'

'What do you mean?'

A woman's voice calls out from within the shop. 'Helllooooo? Mrs O'Bee?'

Mrs O'Brien grins and pats my hand. 'Excuse me, dear. A customer. One of our regulars.'

I nod, my head still running with questions.

'Come in when you're good and ready. And if you get talking to the little people, get on their good side.'

I look around. 'Little people?'

She points to the flower beds. 'The sprites. The faeries. The land divas. They're all about. As are the spirits. They're waiting for you to hear them.'

'The spirits?'

'Of the Divine Feminine. Stay here in the garden and you'll see,' she says. 'You might find one they missed. One they forgot to smash.'

She inclines her head towards the rose-covered wall that separates the garden from the church. 'Oh, those brothers, how they feared our power! But they couldn't erase us completely. We are on the rise!'

She winks at me, and I'm reminded of Megan and her ability to coax a smile from devastated women using the same inner sense of fun. Laughing, head tipped up to the sky, the raven answering her, she disappears inside the shop.

The bird lifts and flies over me, calling as it lands on the rose-covered wall, eyeing me. I stare back. In the periphery, light dances in the shadowy moss-covered places. I move closer, peering into the dank green shadows. Nothing.

The raven caws again, watching me from above the roses on the high wall. It spreads its inky wings, flying off to perch upon the church spire. I'm compelled to lean in to smell the sumptuous blooms. Noticing an irregularity in the stonework behind the climbing canopy, gingerly avoiding thorns, I draw back the leafy branches. There, on the face of the ancient wall, set in a border of carved stone, is the sculpted form of a voluptuous, round-breasted woman perched on her buttocks, her legs spread, her exaggerated vulva open and prominent.

'A Sheela Na Gig.' I breathe, incredulous. I recognise her from the art in Megan's dining room. Megan had explained to me that she was a goddess from the Palaeolithic and Neolithic times when the Divine Feminine was revered – before Christianity swept across the world destroying feminine icons like this one. Here I am, face to face with her quite by accident. Or is it? Involuntary tingles sweep my body as I stare at my ancient stone lady, her tongue protruding powerfully, her exaggerated verenda, fierce.

Tentatively, I reach my fingertip out and slowly, in a downward stroke slide it over the vulva stone. A sense of utter calm comes over me. I am woman.

'Ah! You found her.' I startle at the nearness of Mrs O'Bee's voice. It's as if she's flown to my side.

She reaches out her hand and curves her finger down the deity's vulva to rest next to mine.

'Who is she?'

'Most silly old fart historians called them "architectural grotesques". The eejits called them strange, hideous, ugly and disgusting. Some said they were warnings against lust.' She turns to me, her eyes lively. 'What a load of rubbish!'

Turning back to the Sheela Na Gig she says in a drifting voice, 'This one shows us the beauty and power of all women, from the womb to the tomb.'

Megan's words about the Sheela Na Gigs return to me. They represent the life-giving and regenerative powers of the Earth Mother. I realise the stone goddess is celebrating the opening direct to the universe. The place that brings the flowering of new life.

'The old ones knew women had the power to ward off evil,' Mrs O'Bee says. 'We're not just the portal to new life, but we are meant to link mankind to Mother Earth. It's women who are meant to protect the crops, the seeds and the soil so we don't starve. Least that's how they saw it in the old days.'

I look from Mrs O'Bee to the stonework. 'So women are meant to be the leaders in food and farming?'

'We women are not just meant to be the fertility keepers, but also of the entire Universe. We are usually the first to wake and to remember we are pure light, like the stars. These days, men … many of them degrade us, keep us in our boxes … but how else do they think they got to this world in the first place? Via the feminine. They're frightened of us.'

My father and Turner leap into my mind. All the suggestions I'd made about a new path in agriculture, and how they'd dismissed me like I was nothing. But now, like a flower finding sunlight I begin to feel my petals unfurling.

I, Connie Mulligan, am and have always been more powerful than beyond my wildest dreams. And a slow dawning comes upon me. Our Earth Mother needs me to find my voice, now more than ever.

Chapter 29

Mrs O'Bee leads me back inside the charity shop, and I plonk onto the Barbie stool, my bare feet tingling and my mind firing with a million questions.

'To settle your nerves,' Mrs O'Bee says, taking the Elvis mug and handing me a fine bone china cup, dainty flowers twirling around the rim. I sniff at the liquid and my eyes widen.

'It's medicinal,' she says with a wink, and chinks a Peppa Pig mug with mine. 'Ireland's finest.' Raising her cup, she sips, shivering her shoulders. 'Ah. Better.'

Tentatively, I take my first taste of Irish whiskey. I expect flames, but instead a strange sensation of smooth warmth slides down my throat and glows in my belly, like I'm drinking courage.

Feeling oddly 'right' after the herbal tea, the whiskey and seeing the Sheela Na Gig, I begin to wander between the shelves, looking at people's unwanted vases, strings of beads, saucepans and summer hats. A flowered box with dainty faeries catches my eye. When I open it, music tinkles and a ballerina pops up on a spring, spinning slowly. I watch her delicate form and shudder involuntarily. Mum gave me a similar one for my eleventh birthday. She had loomed over me as I unwrapped it, making sure I liked it. I'd hated the perfect girl inside with all her dainty pastel pretty ... the sort of girl I could never be. It was as if Mum had given me Nikki in a box to taunt me.

I sense Mrs O'Bee at my shoulder.

'Not that one,' she tuts. 'I prefer this one. She's more for us.' She picks up another jewellery box with a blast of colourful flowers on its side. Opening it, a hippo wearing lipstick, a red bikini top and gold tutu flips up, holding aloft a yellow umbrella. From a little speaker on the side, the Weather Girls' 'It's Raining Men!' begins to razzle-dazzle the air around us with verve and cheek.

Laughter bursts from me, bringing with it a release of tension and some tears. 'She's hilarious!'

'Isn't she a craic! Better than the other boring Betty,' Mrs O'Bee says with a smile. 'She has a bit more freedom about her.'

Bursting from behind a change-room curtain, a large lady appears stomping and singing at the top of her lungs. She's got a riot of silver-grey hair and is wearing an oversized Aran woollen jumper with purple and red cable patterning as thick as shipping ropes.

'Shauna!' Mrs O'Brien gasps. 'For the love of god! You scared me! I forgot you were in there.'

'You know me,' the woman says, 'slinky as a cat.' She runs her hands up and over her substantial stomach and massive breasts, then spies the whiskey. 'Oooh! I'd love a nip! Where's another cup?'

'You're in luck,' Mrs O'Bee says, then points to a shelf full of coffee mugs and teacups right next to her. 'Take your pick. I'd recommend the commemorative one of the Pope. He looks so pumped in that photo.' Laughter dances from them both.

'Shauna, Connie. Connie, Shauna.'

I nod at the mesmerising joy-filled lady. Mrs O'Bee pours whiskey into the Pope cup. Shauna turns around, her back to me, head cocked over her shoulder coyly.

'Do you think my bum looks big in this?' She runs her hand over her jumper-covered rump.

Seeing my hesitation, she splutters mirth.

'Don't think you have to answer that, pet. I'm having a lend of ye. I'm trying it on for my husband. Believe it or not, he's even rounder than me! I think it will fit him, Sybil. He's only out with the cows 'n' pigs so they won't mind the colour.' She grins before she disappears behind the change-room curtain again. 'It'll be warm for him. I'll take it.'

Behind the counter, Mrs O'Bee flips out an old vinyl, places it on the turnstile of a record player and sets the needle down. As it crackles, she turns up the volume. Jerry Lee Lewis and his 'Great Balls of Fire' begins belting about the shop. The thrash and rhythm encourages Shauna to come out swinging from the change room. Giant jumper flying around her head, expansive hips circling.

Mrs O'Bee takes me by the hands. 'Dance it out of ye,' she cries. 'Feel the joy. Celebrate your gift! You had the presence of mind to be guided here to us.'

'What gift?' I shout over the music, but Mrs O'Bee can't seem to hear me and begins bopping and shimmying with Shauna. They are both as light on their feet as dancing birds, gripping each other's hands and flinging each other out between the men's trouser rack and the sports tops.

When the record ends, Mrs O'Bee looks at me, her eyes scanning as she puffs. 'What's say we work our magic on this young lass, Shauna?'

Shauna smirks. 'Indeed! Why not?'

'What style? What era suits her best, do ye think?'

They ponder a moment.

'I think her figure and her colouring makes her a fifties girl,' Mrs O'Brien says, arranging my curls up on one side of my head. 'That scarf looks good on her – she's got a Jerry Lee Lewis girl look about her. Why don't we keep going with that.'

'Agreed. Fifties it is,' Shauna says.

'You do tops. I'll do bottoms. Connie, you go get your kit off,' Mrs O'Brien orders, and the women begin rummaging along the extensive and tightly packed clothing racks.

Gingerly, I creep into the change room.

One whole hour and three nips later, rock 'n' roll music playing the whole while, Mrs O'Bee stoops, belting my waist tightly over a navy polka-dot A-line skirt. Shauna tugs a red cardigan over my clinging white shirt. I feel like I'm a giant dress-up doll but am going with it. Why not? Northern Connie is up for anything. I look down and feel a swell of self-admiration. My bosoms look wonderful with the red cashmere cardigan pulled in, and there's my hair, pinned perfectly by Shauna, who has also painted my lips a cherry red.

'She's got such a gorgeous figure, wouldn't you say, Sybil?'

'Indeed, I would, Shauna. I don't know why she hides it, do you?'

'If I were young and looking that way, I'd be putting it in front of all the boys. Waggling it all in their faces.'

They've been talking about me in front of me like this the whole time. Recalling their dance days, the evenings when they would do each other's hair, style each other's clothes. The young men they led on. I can tell they're enjoying using me as an excuse to relive those days. Dress after dress, and skirt after colourful skirt, along with jazzy pants I'd never think to wear and soft cardigans are brought my way, until at last there's a pile on the counter that could clothe the Northern Hemisphere Connie Mulligan for a month!

I think of the sisterhood of women I've found at home, and now with my new-found Irish friends my spirits lift so high – along with the whiskey – I twirl in one of my new outfits: a leopard-print leotard and a big wide black skirt. I'm a rock 'n' roll doll. All curves and cuteness. All hips and shake.

Mrs O'Brien cranks the music up some more so we can hear it over the torrential rain that is now sledging the street outside. Shauna dons a sombrero and begins to waltz about with the naked torso of one of the male mannequins. As I weave backwards out of her way, I collide with something big, solid and damp. Spinning about, I'm all at once face to face with a tall, stern-looking man carrying a cardboard box that is threatening to sag apart from the rain that has streaked it. He's looking down at me with his black eyebrows pulled low over dark brown eyes, his shaggy black hair sleek-shiny with rain.

'Whoopsie! Sorry!' I laugh, but I can tell he is finding the whole encounter very unfunny. He is emanating irritation. Shauna puts the mannequin down. Mrs O'Brien stops dancing and turns the record player off abruptly.

'Are you drunk again, Mrs O'Bee?'

She tugs down her vest and runs her palms over her skirt. 'Indeed no! We've only had two.'

'Three. We've had three.' Shauna titters.

Mrs O'Brien looks to Shauna and concedes. 'All right. But little ones.'

'Yes. Teeny,' Shauna says. 'Isn't that right, Fabio,' she says to the dummy, kissing his cheek and raising her commemorative mug. 'T'was the Pope's fault.'

The man rolls his eyes and says, 'You know the ladies from the Holy Trinity don't like it when you play loud music and get the customers off their noggins.'

His eyes slide up and down over me and the self-consciousness I feel in the ultra-tight top burns my cheeks.

'And you are dressing up the customers again, Sybil!'

'Yes. Well, Nick, this is Connie.'

I give an inept little wave. He barely glances at me.

'Please don't tell your mother!' Shauna says, putting Fabio down between her legs on the floor.

'Yes!' Mrs O'Bee begs. 'She whacked us with the big stick at the last committee meeting. We didn't want it in the minutes for the sisters to read that we dressed up Father Godfrey in a cow onesie. We were only having a lend!'

'You didn't tell me you had onesies,' I joke, causing the ladies to scrunch their faces, desperate to contain their mirth.

Nick sets the box onto the counter. 'Ma asked me to drop this into you on my way to work. I now know she actually wants me to check up on you.'

'Yes, of course, what your mother says goes,' Mrs O'Bee says tightly.

Nick looks at her darkly.

'Sorry,' she adds immediately. Then in a kinder tone asks, 'You off for another night shift?'

'Afraid so.'

'Any luck with the estate? Your plans?'

He shakes his head.

Mrs O'Bee sighs. 'Oh Nick, I'm sorry. We'll keep asking at the stones.'

He rolls his eyes.

'Don't be like that,' she says. 'Have faith.'

She leads him away by the arm, their heads bent over discussing something privately. When they're done, he nods a goodbye, jaw clenching before striding out of the shop, stooping his tall body into the driving rain.

'Ahh,' Shauna says sadly, watching him go.

'Aye.' Mrs O'Bee turns to me. 'Well, now we've had our telling-off, Connie, would you like to take these?' She pats the pile of clothing.

I hesitate. I'd never be brave enough to wear these clothes, but I'm not brave enough to not buy them after all the attention and whiskey the women have given me.

'It's Thursday – cattle-sale day special,' she lures. 'Fill a bag and it's all yours for five euros.'

'And Sybil can cram a bag, to be sure,' Shauna adds, gathering up her husband's shouty purple and red jumper. 'Nice to meet you, Connie. Enjoy your travels. Mind yourself.' She gives me a big hug and scampers out into the rain, plastic bag with the jumper held over her head.

'Yes, I'll take the lot, please, except maybe this one.' I look down to my leopard-print bosoms, realising I would match Mum's suitcase in it.

When I change into my own clothes and see my reflection, I feel instantly bland. Sexless and boring. After today, I want more colour. I want more life! I want more Sheela Na Gig! And, as Mrs O'Bee has told me, I am a *seer* and I get to create my world. I'm not just some mad woman my family thinks me to be. I can choose not to believe them anymore. I can change my mind. With my lips still painted red, I blow myself a kiss. Pulling back the curtain with a flourish, I pat my Shauna-styled hair, thinking that this afternoon has been the most fun I've ever had.

At the counter, Mrs O'Bee has my new-old clothes waiting for me, jammed into two swelling enormous bags.

She pushes them towards me. 'They were the biggest I could find. Ten euros okay?'

'Wow! Thank you!' I breathe. 'It's a relief to find something else to wear. I've got sperm all over my other shirts.'

'Pardon?'

'Semen sales.' I draw back my coat and flash her my Global Genetics shirt logo.

'I see!' Mrs O'Bee laughs. 'Wasn't sure where you were taking me with that one, dear!'

I'm about to set off out the door when I realise I don't want to carry the shopping bags around the cattle saleyards, nor get them drenched walking back to the pub, so I turn back to Mrs O'Bee.

'Um ... do you mind if I pick these up tomorrow? Save carrying them?'

'Of course, dear! Let me put them behind the counter. We open late on Fridays. About eleven.' She scans the rain outside. 'It's lucky you're wearing those flashy gumboots of yours. You also might need one of these.'

Mrs O'Brien pulls out an umbrella from a cluster in an old barrel. It's navy blue with pink coiffured poodles on it and a white frill at the edge. 'Complimentary. Bit of a faulty catch, but it'll see you right.'

She looks towards the street where clouds are shooting heavy silver darts. 'I'm glad you had the slip right at my door. Everything happens for a reason. Everything.'

We look to where Nick is still sitting in his grey car in the grey rain on the grey street.

'He's taking his time to get to work,' she says sadly.

'What's with him?' I ask, curious about the tension he seemed to carry with him like a cloud.

She glances at me. 'Parents. Grief. The crush of life that turns us to either powder or to diamonds. It'll be his choice.' She looks at me directly, her eyes again black, like the darkness of the universe itself. 'He's at a crossroads. Like you.'

Her voice sounds different. The air of mysterious exchange we had out in the garden earlier has returned. Questions jostle to my mind, all pushing to be at the front of the queue.

'Crossroads? About that … I'd like to ask you–'

The umbrella in my hand leaps to life, flicking open and making us shriek and jump.

Mrs O'Bee pats her sternum. 'Yes – that's the trick with that thing.'

I'm about to press her for more information when the door flies open and a young woman dashes in, spiked blonde hair glistening wet and a plastic poncho rustling.

'Christ! Could it piss down any harder?' she says.

'Niamh. It's her shift,' Mrs O'Brien explains. 'Hello, love,' she says to the young woman.

'My feet are wetter than a duck's arse. I'm going to have to change.' She hovers at a shelf of shoes. 'Do you know which aren't dead people's?' Waving the question away as too hard, she bustles to the back of the shop and disappears behind the curtain to the tearoom. 'I'll just go dump my coat in the sink.'

The spell broken, Mrs O'Brien smiles at me kindly. 'Maybe now's not the time,' she says.

Tick. Tock. Connie, always out of time.

*

Stepping out of the Small Miracles and Mercies Charity Shop, I pull my collar up against the rain. Under my new second-hand poodle umbrella Gene Kelly's 'Singin' in the Rain' starts roaming around in my head like a movie soundtrack. I can see

Nick through the rain-smear on the windscreen. I think of the crossroads Mrs O'Bee mentioned. So I cross the street.

From the shelter of my umbrella, I tap on the car window, my funny gumboots now looking bright and pretty with promise in the afternoon gloom.

Nick, surprised, screens the window down a little, grimacing at the rain entering his nice warm car. In the low light of the afternoon, I notice just how darkly Irish his eyes are, and how the peppering of stubble that prickles over his jaw has grey in it. His hair is greying too, at the temples, and he's as handsome an Irishman as I've ever met – not that I've met many so far. It's only then I realise he's been crying.

'Okay?' I ask, gesturing at the car, as if it won't start.

Embarrassed he looks away. 'Fine. All fine. Thanks.'

There's an awkward pause as the rain thrums.

'Well then ... it was nice to meet you, Nick,' I say. 'Mind yourself.'

'You too, Connie.'

As he winds his window up, I can barely believe he remembered my name. With an unfamiliar energy I can't explain, I dance my way over the street, my bright red gumboots splashing through puddles. I know he's watching, and he might think I'm mad, but I don't care. It's been confirmed by Mrs O'Bee Wan Kenobi, the local Irish Jedi mistress and keeper of the stone Sheela Na Gig, I am far from mad! I am, in this part of the world, perfectly damn well sane! I am a seer again.

Chapter 30

In the giant noisy undercover yards, I can't take my eyes off her – an enormous cow the colour of caramel pudding. She's freakish and sad. Just looking at her hurts. She's rocking like a hulking ship, swaying her weight from side to side, seeking relief from pain that must be flowing through her impossible body. The well-intentioned yard men have put some rubber matting down over the cold wet concrete, but it seems to make no difference for her. Nothing would take away the fact she's a conglomeration of human greed and grotesque genetic meddling. Dags of mud are crusting on her belly and I deduce she must've lived sunk up to her guts in waterlogged suffering soil.

The buoyancy I felt coming from the charity shop with the Sheela Na Gig, and eyeballing the dark, handsome, if not sad Irishman has completely evaporated. All around me are animals so interbred, I can see the conformation problems everywhere, in their overly bent legs, fallen hocks, sway backs and elongated spines. Distressed and mooing deafeningly, the females appear malformed. There's not much feminine about them. In fact, there's no room for femininity here. They are mostly double-muscled Belgian Blues, Charolais, Simmental and Limousins. Lady Arnold Schwarzeneggers of the cow world. Huge slab shoulders, bullish block heads and giant Nicki Minaj buttocks globing outwards as if advertising 'slice me off and eat me'. All shaped by man for man and the hungry beast of global economies. My heart sinks.

Even in Ireland, the push for Big Ag has corrupted the minds of mankind. The journey on the train from Dublin had taken me past the same mono pastures and crops of chemical-dependent plants – the same sad systems we have at home. The towering modern tractors in the saleyard carpark hitched to big solid-sided cattle trailers had dropped my jaw walking in here. Such huge equipment for tiny parcels of land, all propped up by government subsidies, telling me that corruption and conformity infuses the mindsets of the people here too.

The men are all dressed in the same muted tones. Pushing through their crush, I won't look at their faces but instead, down to my dazzling gumboots. The dung running along shallow drains either side of the walkway carries the stench of cryovac grass spurted from nervous cow guts. Their digestive systems overtaxed by fermented silage and too-rich nitrate-drenched modern pastures.

The nightmarish scenes continue, walking past impossibly huge twelve-month-old steers with giant-boned knees and wide block heads.

The spectre of Professor Turner leers near with the toxic energy of his beloved Big Tech agriculture and chemical agronomy. It seems he, and men like him have taken over the world!

As I wither within myself, I'm starting to feel the cattlemen's eyes on me. Their conversations lull as I pass by, like in a Western movie when a stranger walks into a bar. At first, I thought they were just ogling my funny boots, but the skin on the back of my neck is tingling, hairs lifting. Hostility and suspicion crackles around me, like a storm brewing. I shove my hand in my pocket, wrapping it around my phone, wanting badly to take photos to share with Patrick on the similarities and differences of Australian and Irish saleyards, but instead I shuffle on, self-consciousness boiling inside me.

The auctioneer draws the crowd in and I'm carried along on his river of sound of unintelligible words. I try to turn on my power, the way the Sheela Na Gig made me feel, but there's no circuitry in my body to find that place. Soon the crowd, like water congesting into a pipe, slows, as we drain into the selling area.

One by one, each cow is let into a ring yard, made to move about as they are auctioned. Lot number 15 – a giant square brick of a cow, is cajoled by an electric cattle prod. The digital display tells us she's over a thousand kilos and she's being sold for failing to get in calf. My misguided imaginings of quaint, idyllic Ireland and mixed farming systems shatter like broken glass. The cattle here are like the ones Global Genetics push onto the market – all designed to fit the European Union trade, not the local landscape.

The crush of people lifts my anxiety, so I look to a small grandstand rising above the selling yard. Perhaps if I can get above the throng, I might avoid the slip? Desperately I scan it for a space, and I realise with a jolt there's not a single woman here. *Not one.* It's *all* men. I search the big shed and at last spy a stern-faced lady seated high up in a gallery beside the auctioneer. She's wearing a business-like navy jumper and white shirt, entering sales data into a computer like she's firing bullets. Turning, pressing past what seems to be a wall of farm men, I scuttle to the back pens, clutching the rail to stop the slip, but I know by the way the sounds are coming to my ears like goop, that I'm already gone.

Lying on my back on a cold stone slab, leather cuffs bite my wrists and ankles. I look down, a sheer sheet of blood-soaked linen barely covers me. Beside me, the sound of a wooden wheel turning fills me with dread. As the rope shortens, my arms and legs splay wider, wider and yet wider still. My head draws back from the pain. The scream that comes from my parched mouth is otherworldly. It must've lifted the blood of one man as he fumbles under his robe and steps towards me. My world goes black.

When I come to, I find myself standing, staring at the faces of doe-eyed yearlings, fat and ready to sell. Here I am, *torn.* On all levels. My breath is shallow. I spin around to run. Without Nick-nack or Traveller I'm not sure how I can ease the panic, but then I remember the dog, Captain. I wonder if I can make it back to him. Rushing around the corner of a stock lane, I crash into the solid body of a man. My faulty umbrella flashes open in front of my chest, like a shield. Reeling back, I look up. He's the tallest farmer I've ever seen, standing like a castle turret in his heavy woollen felt black coat.

'Sorry,' I mutter, closing the umbrella, gazing up at his high-altitude face. He's an elderly man with white hair, barber-neat under a peak cap. He's dressed in his best for sale day with a paisley olive-green cravat and holding a fancy gold-topped cane. He carries an air of entitlement also.

'Easy now, lass!' he says, irritation tightening his voice.

'Sorry!' I say again breathlessly.

'What brings you here, missy? Not spying on us, are ye?' There's darkness in his tone.

I look into his eyes, pleadingly. 'No! Certainly not!'

'Well. What business do you have coming here?'

'I'm over from Tasmania. Dairy farmer.' It's then I rip open my coat and flash my logo at him.

He peers at it, leaning over me. Then shakes his head. 'Don't you make me get my glasses out, girlie.'

'Global Genetics,' I say, tapping my finger on the logo. 'I'm here for a conference. Semen sales.'

I want him to be impressed, but he leans even closer so I can see tiny red veins on his nose.

'In case you hadn't noticed ...' Slowly, he looks up and around the selling centre. 'You won't find ducks, nor hens round here.'

His comment hits like a slap. My mind rushes back to when Granny M once took me to see shearing in the Tasmanian northern midlands. As we stepped inside the shed, me inhaling the strange pungent scent of sheep and wool, the men shouted, 'Ducks on the pond!'

Granny M made a scoffing noise but pulled me closer to her side. Afterwards, when I asked her about it, she laughed.

'They were letting the other men know there were women present. No more swearing. That they have to behave themselves when the birds arrive.'

My seven-year-old self asked, 'Why can't they behave themselves anyway?'

'It's women who were the true keepers of the world. The females set the tone for society. But we've forgotten that.'

My little brow furrowed.

'Look to the cows, Connie. If your dad let the cows run with the bulls, the cows would be sorting out which ones behaved well enough to have the privilege of mating with her. Mother Nature always gifts us with her balance when you let her run the place. But when men run the show, and women aren't called on to stand up for a bit of grace, a bit of dignity, it all turns to shite.' She clapped her hand over her mouth. 'Whoops! I swore. Feck me! That'd upset the shearers! Bloody ducks on the pond, my arse.'

I giggled and she stooped and lovingly squeezed my cheeks. 'Don't tell your mother I said those bad words!'

Then she got a faraway look in her eyes. 'Oh Connie, imagine! Imagine if good-willed women ran the world. If women built cities. If women ran the farms, and the banks and the legal systems. We would all live in a totally different world. No child would go hungry. No man would rape. No forest would be destroyed. No river would be poisoned. But we don't run the world and we women are now taught to turn on each other. Women like us have to take the little victories and pleasures where we can. Fly under the radar with our wins so they don't shoot us down. Like ducks.'

In the yards now, I look to the man's cold face. There's so much ice in his gaze, I could be a frozen duck.

'You mind yourself, young lass,' he says curtly as he walks away, his back an impossible high wall to me, his mind and heart unreachable. Again, I stand, *silenced*.

I'm about to leave via a side gate, when an eruption of shouting and clanging metal spins me to the sound. The burst of noise above the cattle's cries escalate as people dressed in animal costumes and vibrant clothing swarm into the laneways. Many carry placards, the lettering in red dripping paint like blood.

Leave Animals the Fuck Alone!

End All Animal Oppression.

'Meat is murder! Meat is murder!' The chanting activists surge, swinging gates open, letting the cattle within spill out. Chaos spreads like wildfire. I watch mesmerised. Then I think of Patrick, and Vernon and Fenton and the people I want to share this moment with at home. I fumble, fish out my phone, swiping it onto video to catch the action of the onslaught of cattlemen cascading from the sales area like water from a burst dam, smashing into the protesters where a tussle of epic proportions begins. My heart hammers. The whole place has gone wild! As people shout and punches are swung, the cattle gallop along walkways, metal gates and yards crashing like iron swords. My umbrella flies open. I'm so startled I overbalance, my heel hooking on a gate rail, my gumboot ripping off. I'm already falling when the tsunami of terrified yearlings hits the gate. It swings violently towards me like a punch and collects with my skull. Then time stops.

Chapter 31

I'm riding a grey dappled horse through bright white mist, hued golden around the fringes by an unseeable brilliant sun. The mist swirls, revealing pastel rainbows all around. Such stillness. Such peace. Such light! I don't know where he's carrying me, but I don't care. All that's present is a sense of love, of safety. A knowing that all is well. Actually, it's better than well. It's perfect, indescribable bliss! I can feel a pulsing extraordinary power between my legs – the place where new life comes. The place where the Sheela Na Gig holds protection for our Earth. It's not sexual. It is sacred. I inhale and as I do I notice the entirety of my surroundings expand in a brilliant sweep of colour, like the wings of a bird lifting upwards. On my exhale comes the downdraft of misted wings. It is so beautiful. And all of it is me, and I am it. In the mist I hear voices. Women. They are singing. Singing my name. It's then I know I must turn this horse around, and ride towards them.

'Are you waking up?' I hear a deep voice.

The mist spirals like entwining serpents rising upwards and I feel myself falling backwards, grappling for the horse, my fingertips instead sweeping through his mane into nothingness. Swiftly he is gone.

A cracking pain shatters inside my skull. Behind my eyes a searing pressure, and heat roars with each loud pulse within my ears. I blink my eyes open, lashes crusty, mouth dry. I'm shocked to realise there's a tube in my nostril. To my left a small window reveals a sky of grey, muting the sinking sun. The entire vista seems so surreal and dense compared to where I've just been.

'Ahh, she's back with us,' a deep voice says.

I turn my face towards the blurred figure beside my bed and he comes into focus. I frown. My neck zings, my head throbs. Eventually, I recognise his features.

'*You?*' I ask in wonder.

'You remember me from the charity shop?'

'How could I not?' I wince. 'What's happening?'

'You've had a bit of a bump on the head. Can you tell me your name?'

Nothing comes to me.

'Where am I?' I ask. 'Am I dead?'

'You're certainly not dead. You're in hospital and I'm Doctor O'Meara. And you are?'

'Me?' I lift my hand to touch my heart space, noticing a needle taped to the back of it leading to a drip. I search for a name in the vast emptiness of my mind. When I can't find one, panic rears like a frightened horse.

'I'm not sure?'

Doctor O'Meara frowns. 'Mrs O'Bee introduced me to you as Connie.'

'Connie?' I repeat vacantly.

'And your surname is?'

Blankness. I shrug and tears pool.

'It's okay,' he soothes and lays his hand on my upper arm. 'Panic not, time will set you right. You're in the Portlaoise Hospital, just a short way from Mountrath where you were staying before the commotion.'

A thick black fog in my mind sweeps in again as I grapple for memories. 'Commotion?'

'Remember the cattle sale?' he prompts. 'You got knocked over.'

'No? How long have I been here?'

'Ahem. Let me think ... three days. Yes three. You do remember you're in Ireland?'

'Ireland?' I whisper, shocked. 'Yes of course I know that,' I lie. No! I hadn't remembered!

Doctor O'Meara's dark eyes narrow as he studies me. 'How are you feeling?'

It's this question that flummoxes me. Aside from the headache, and not really knowing who and where I am or how I got here, part of me feels altogether altered. Peaceful even. Calm. That overwhelming, overarching sensation of love in my whole being remains, as if part of me is still in the rainbow-illuminated mist with that beautiful horse. Under my scalp, a pounding pain begins and drags me back.

'I'm feeling confused,' I answer truthfully.

'Well that's only natural. Mrs O'Bee will know more. But unfortunately she and Shauna took off to the hills for one of their crazy lady things at the old stones and can't be reached, and Niamh at the shop knew nothing of you. But as soon as they're back we'll find out your full name so we can contact your relatives.'

'Relatives?'

Concern pulses so I press my fingertips gingerly to where my head hurts, discovering the bandage swathed diagonally across my skull and a large surgical pad covering my left temple.

'Don't worry,' he reassures, 'Mrs O'Bee will enlighten us. She's good at enlightenment.'

A flash vision arrives – a raven, red and yellow roses, the stone goddess on the wall. Mrs O'Bee dancing with me in flouncy skirts and laughing.

'The Sheela Na Gig!' I gasp.

'Pardon?'

'And the dancing hippo!'

'Shauna?' he asks, frowning.

'No! Not Shauna!' I laugh. 'The hippo in the box! "It's Raining Men"!'

He regards me with puzzlement, then sets a doctorly expression to his face. 'I think you'll be here for a few days longer than I thought. Can you recall any names of your relatives back home in Australia?'

'I'm not Australian,' I say, the brain fog clearing enough to know it with certainty.

Doctor O'Meara tilts his head slightly. 'You're not?'

'I'm Tasmanian,' I say with conviction.

'Tasmanian? Is that right?'

'Yes, we're Australian, but not.'

He folds his arms, surveying me as if I am an unsolvable puzzle. As he does, I take in his checked farmer-style shirt under his white coat and polished elasticised brown leather boots. For some reason, I feel relieved he's not wearing a tie. He has a wide chest, with hair that curls darkly at the V of his shirt. With his sleeves rolled up, his arms look lean and muscled, as do his thighs, like he'd stride up a hillside with ease.

'I didn't know you were a doctor when I met you, Nick.'

He inclines his head and a smile blooms. 'Good! You remembered my first name.'

'I'd never have picked you as a doctor. You look like you'd belong better in a paddock.'

'A paddock?'

'Y'know – a field, I think they call it here.'

He sighs.

'Do you like being a doctor?' I ask, staring openly at him. He tightens his folded arms across his chest and lifts his eyebrows.

'I think it's time you rested, I'll book you in for some tests.'

'I wouldn't like to be a doctor,' I say prattling on in the hope he won't leave. 'I know this friend ... I've forgotten her name, but she's always going on about modern medicine and how the world's largest pharmaceutical company bought the world's largest agrichemical company. Suss, eh?

'She says they have an evil business model that makes trillions of dollars by making people sick with the agrichemicals that produce cheap food, and then make even more money offering to fix your problems with pharmaceutical drugs.'

'Is that so?' Nick replies, eyes narrowing.

'Yep. My friend says many doctors unknowingly, and sometimes knowingly, have sold their souls to the Corporate Devil.'

I cover my mouth, as if I've burped. 'Cripes! That was a bit full on. Sorry. But she's really blunt, my friend. A bit of a pain in the arse, really. Truth be told.'

Doctor O'Meara's eyes crinkle. 'Have you been colluding with Sibyl?'

'Mrs O'Bee? No? Why?'

'She rabbits on about the same things to me. It's lucky your intense friend isn't here to join forces with her to judge me,' he says. 'I'll go order those tests and I'll get the nurse in for some more pain relief, shall I?' He grins. 'That way the drug companies can make a bit more profit out of me peddling their wares. In the meantime, you get some rest.'

'And you'll come back?' I ask like a small child.

His brows knit. 'Of course.'

With him gone, I stare out the window, displaced. The horse in the mist felt so much more real than here. Outside, five brown ducks wing across the grey sky. I'm transfixed by the orderly beauty of their arrowed flight.

A tiny pretty nurse arrives with an air of busyness. I smile at her. The nurse, however, is not smiling back. She has flame red wavy hair pulled into a tidy ponytail, beautiful arched eyebrows and a dusting of freckles over her pixie face.

'Ah! The doctor said sleepyhead's awake!' she says rather sarcastically, as she checks the time on an upside-down watch pinned to her uniform, reaching for a chart hanging on the bed. She moves to the drip monitor beside me, looks at the screen before turning her attention fully on me, her eyes the colour of a glacier – all gentle green and soft blue, but cold.

'How are you feeling?' There's a prickle in her, like the static frequency of an untuned radio and I realise that prickle is aimed at me.

'I'm feeling surprisingly good,' I answer.

'Well, I'm sure those cows that found their way onto the motorway aren't feeling *surprisingly good*,' she mutters, mimicking my accent. 'At least you have a doctor looking after you, not like the cows who only had a garda with a gun to see to them. Not to mention the poor innocent people who are in the surgery ward who crashed their cars into them.'

I look at her in horror. 'Crashed into them?'

'What did you expect? Terrified gigantic animals and busy motorways don't mix – especially in heavy rain. Doctor Nick will be back to you shortly. He's great with people who knock themselves out senseless doing senseless things.'

'Senseless things?' I ask, confused.

'Please tell me you're not faking your memory loss? Just so you aren't charged?' the nurse asks directly, frowning.

'Charged?'

'You so-called do-gooders. Can't you see you're just spreading more shite in the world with all your activism crap.'

I puzzle at her calling me an activist. I notice her name badge.

'Amber.' In saying her name, she looks at me this time with more presence. 'I have no idea'what you're talking about. All I know is I *love* cows. I love all animals, but I would never be an activist like that.' My voice is calm and holds not a shred of defence.

She purses her lips and narrows her eyes. 'Hold on. Back in a sec,' she says.

Moments later she returns with her phone.

'Look.' She types something rapidly with her thumbs, and holds the phone before me. 'You've gone viral. Four million views and climbing.'

I see my image appear in a cattle saleyard. 'Somebody was filming me?'

'It seems so,' Amber says. 'One of the yard men was suspicious of you the moment you walked in.'

I watch my moving image, and the pink life of my cheeks, my earnest large brown eyes, my red lips and the mole on my face enhanced by Shauna's 50s-style makeup. As I watch myself turn, I take in the full roundness of my rump, the curve of my waist in the belted coat. Jazzy gumboots and a red beanie enhancing rich dark curls. I smile. *I'm beautiful.* Not the fashion industry version of beautiful, but the being alive, womanly way of beauty. I wonder at my youth and strength, and I see *me* – the me from within. The light. The one riding the horse in the mist.

Yet still I'm puzzled – what did I do at the cattle sale that Amber is so tetchy about? I'm about to ask when she says, 'Keep watching.'

Discord erupts as protesters converge, flooding the space with chaos. I watch my umbrella explode, and the moment I trip backwards, gumboot flying, the hefty cattle stampeding, the gate slamming me.

I suck in a breath. To be a witness outside the experience is unnerving as the steel gate smashes into my head, my body dropping like a stone, head bouncing hard on the shit-covered concrete. The poor cattle leaping over me in terror and spilling around me as they run.

I turn my face away in horror.

Amber senses my shock at witnessing my own accident, and says, 'I'm sorry you had to see that, but you need to be sorrier for the animals and people you impacted.'

'Me? What is it you think I've done?'

Amber looks to her phone again. 'This is what they've made of it.'

She scrolls to a YouTube clip that jumps to life. A newsreader appears and says, 'A violent animal activist attack caused mayhem today at an Irish saleyard when protesters released cows and assaulted several farmers, leading to the hospitalisation of at least seven people.'

Her voice overlays footage of me. 'But the cows weren't sure who was friend or foe, taking this vegan protester as a carnivore.

After the freed cows attacked the red-booted rebel, some stampeded onto one of Ireland's busiest motorways, causing a multiple car pile-up.' The footage cuts to carnage on a highway.

'Of the seven people hospitalised, two are critical. Several protesters have been arrested. Sources say the Muck Boot Mobster is believed to be the ringleader of the attack, arriving at the saleyards earlier to help lead the protest. When the alleged activist regains consciousness, they will be questioned by guards before possible arrest. After a spate of global protests by animal rights lobbyists, the minister for agriculture said animal activism attacks such as these ought to be ...'

Amber taps the screen and pauses the footage on the stern face of the suit-clad minister. 'They've got you pegged.'

'I would never do something like that!'

'Wouldn't you?'

She leaves me then, alone in the room.

Would I?

*

That night I dream a grey horse comes to me and lowers his head between my hands. I drift upwards onto his back, riding into a misty night. As the mist clears, I find myself clip-clopping down the prettiest coastal village street beside a glittering summer sea. There's a pub painted fresh in a classy cream with hanging baskets of outrageously colourful flowers. People sit in the sun at outdoor tables, laughing and chatting, dogs lying at their feet. I stop to watch a fiddle player spilling out toe-tapping sound with his bow. There are hundreds of women following me, smiling, laughing, flinging colourful skirts from side to side, singing. When I pull the horse up someone reaches for my hand. A gleam of gold on his little finger. A Claddagh ring ...

Somewhere in the hospital comes a clatter then a cough and I wake. The warmth of the dream lingers, comfortingly, like a hug. Then I think with a jolt: *Who am I?*

Chapter 32

In the morning Mrs O'Bee arrives at my bedside carrying a big bunch of flowers, which she lays on my lap.

'Mrs O'Bee Wan Kenobi!' I say, grateful my short-term memory is returning.

'Ahh! My Connie dear! What a time you've had of it!' She leans over and pats my hand. 'I'm so glad it worked.'

'What worked?'

'Shauna and I called you back.'

'Back?'

'Yes. When we heard you'd been knocked from your body, we went up to the stones. Did you not hear us calling you? It was the mistiest night – we never thought we'd find the car again.'

Goosebumps thrill my skin and a shiver sweeps through me like a sudden chill breeze. She draws me in with those deep black eyes and pats my blanketed leg. 'You must've heard. You're back with us.'

'I did hear the voices!'

A squeaking noise in the hallway distracts me from asking more. Instead of hospital staff pushing more trolleys past, in rolls Patrick with a giant leopard-print suitcase, which makes little mouse screams with every wheel revolution. Beside him pads Captain on a lead, uncertainty in his expression about his strange surrounds. He's wearing a lady's purple polar-fleece vest, fastened with a wide white belt, with the words in texta, *Official Hospital*

Therapy Dog. Captain's look is completed with green plastic beads around his neck. Mrs O'Bee has clearly had her stylist's way with him in the Miracles and Mercies Charity Shop.

'He had to bring the beast via the lift,' Mrs O'Bee says, gesturing to the suitcase. 'It was too big and heavy for the stairs now we've stuffed it full of the clothes you bought. And lucky we did unpack the bags. We found your wallet in there with your ID. The hospital staff's just calling your family now.'

'My family?' I reply looking absently at the suitcase and wondering why I'd choose such a giant hideous thing.

'Yes. Doctor Nick said you're a bit foggy about it all. He said you're okay on the short-term memory though, so that's a blessing.'

Amber bustles in, sees the dog in his unofficial outfit, and folds her arms sternly. 'That's not going to fool anyone. Dogs are strictly prohibited in the hospital. He has to go.'

Patrick grimaces, shortening Captain's lead guiltily.

'None of us believe you for a second, Amber,' Mrs O'Bee says.

Amber's face erupts into delight, and she sets to cooing over him. 'Well, maybe he can stay a few minutes ... Just hide him under the bed if you see anyone coming, particularly Matron.'

Captain beats the air hard in waggy joy. His whole presence and demeanour is infectious. It fills the room until he's momentarily distracted by the remains of my breakfast on the hospital trolley.

'I owe you an apology,' Amber says moving to my bedside. 'I had you pegged wrong. Mrs O'Bee set me straight. You're no activist. You're one of us. I'm from a dairy farm too, you know.'

'Dairy farm?' I frown, grappling for memories. One thing is certain, I know I'm no protester.

'Well,' Mrs O'Bee says, gesturing to the flowers, 'aren't you going to see who they're from?'

The brown paper rustles as I pick up the heavy bunch, admiring the harvested sunshine of their cheerful yellow, pink and magenta petals. As I search for the card I say, 'I have a friend. She used to tell me about the perils and pitfalls of the spray-reliant commercial flower industry. Any time we saw commercial flowers, especially on Valentine's Day, she'd say cynically, "Love hurts – the environment." Then she'd carry on about people's expectation for unseasonal blooms, with air miles and refrigeration attached to their price tags, along with the health costs of sending flowers dipped in biocides and floral preservatives – all flat-packed to people who thought they were lovely when there was nothing lovely about them.'

'Gee, your friend sounds like a right craic, *not*!' Patrick says.

I feel pity for the person I've recalled. I wish she could see the intentioned message of love, compassion and care in the gift, despite how the flowers were grown. Having gratitude for the gesture is my most pressing need right now. Not judgement.

Plucking out the envelope tucked into the stems, my body tingles as I read aloud the inky print: '*Hand-tied blooms from the Wicklow Walled Garden – Ireland's best in naturally grown, chemical-free, ethical seasonal flowers.*'

My body buzz rises into a surge of joy at the profoundness of this moment. I wish my cynical friend was here so I can say to her. 'See! The human world *is* awakening. People *are* changing in how they treat this Earth and each other.'

'Well?' Amber presses.

I pull the little card from the envelope and read out the message: '*When you are back on your feet, see you soon for that farm tour. Heal fast. The team at Donohill Dairy – Devlyn, Declan & Grainne, cows, calves and kids XX.*'

'It's from the holistic dairy farmers, the Donovans!' Amber says, eyes lighting up. When I look a little blank she adds, 'The Donovans are Dairy Divas! I mean that in a nice way. Everyone goes bonkers for their butter. The queues on the street outside their farm shop on the weekend start at sparrow's fart. It's the only dairy stuff that doesn't make my little brother hurl.'

Amber takes the flowers. 'Let's get them into some water.'

'But I've never met them?' I ask, looking at Mrs O'Bee. 'To give me flowers?'

'That's the kind of people they are.'

Mrs O'Bee lays her palm on Patrick's shoulder. 'Patrick here remembered you'd said you'd come to Mountrath to visit them. So I called. We've been friends for eons.'

'They're neighbours of Doctor Nick too,' Amber adds. 'His parents own the big estate next to their farm.'

'That won't earn Connie any brownie points, being connected with him,' Patrick mutters. He and Mrs O'Bee exchange a glance, just as the man himself arrives.

I drink Doctor Nick O'Meara in – charcoal jeans, a smoky metallic shirt under his white coat, earnest eyes, his wavy black hair falling to one side over his brow. Today he looks more muso than doctor.

'What's this? A social gathering?'

'Just cheering the poor lass up.'

'Nice flowers,' he says. 'That was kind of you, Sybil.'

'Oh they're not from Mrs O'Bee,' I say, waving the card. 'They're from the Donovans at Donohill Dairy.'

Doctor Nick's expression tightens. There's an awkward silence. Mrs O'Bee clears her throat.

'Ward C Room Four,' Mrs O'Bee says clearly wanting to move the conversation on. 'Your patient – the old man in the bed by the window – he has a blockage of the heart.'

Doctor Nick shakes his head and closes his eyes. 'The man is in for a broken leg. Sibyl, you know you can't come in here dishing out diagnoses.'

'I'm not. I saw it. The life force is clogged up there.' She waves her hand around her chest area. 'That part of his body is like a mobile phone that can't get a signal. He needs to heal something that happened when he was five, and the rest of his troubles will ease. His leg will heal faster and he won't be headed for a heart attack.'

Nick groans, and throws his head back in frustration. 'Sibyl, please.'

'Oh! Speaking of phones,' Mrs O'Bee says, rummaging in her bag and passing me my mobile. 'Screen's a little worse for wear. I cleaned the cow manure off but it still pongs a bit. Being the dairy girl you are, I expect you'll like that. Patrick got you a charger for it too.'

'Dairy girl?' I echo, seeking absent answers in my head.

Patrick takes the cord and plugs it into the wall beside my bed then lays the phone beside me. I stare at its myriad of spiderweb cracks on the screen, thinking that's just how my brain feels.

'You'll be able to call your other brother Patrick,' he says.

'Other brother?' I begin to feel the room spin.

Nick steps forward. 'Now good folks, and the dog who is unsuccessfully hiding under the bed, I need to talk alone with my patient about her scan results. She's going to need some quiet now. I can see our Connie Mulligan is finding this all a bit challenging.'

Connie Mulligan?

The name washes in my mind, as if the tide of my past is about to come in. I feel suddenly faint.

'Visiting time's up,' Doctor Nick says, looking at me. 'Out, you lot.'

Patrick invites Captain out from under the bed, and taps the edge inviting him to put his front paws up beside me. 'Say bye to Connie.'

'He'd look better in a lab coat,' Nick says. 'But then if you think about it he's already in a lab coat.' He laughs at his own joke, watching the jovial labrador wagging his tail as if trying to fluff rainbow happiness into the room. Gingerly I lean my head forward and sift my fingertips through his sumptuous ruff.

'Very funny. Thanks for bringing him. My friend says you can see God in the eyes of dogs. She says, "Dog is simply God spelled backwards."'

'Your friend is right,' Mrs O'Bee says. She casts Nick a look. 'The non-believers among us – the ones who think with just their heads and not their hearts – are the ones who most need a dog to wake them up. My little ol' dog Mish can spot the sleeping people.' Her statement has sharp edges to it.

Nick clears his throat as Mrs O'Bee holds her gaze at him.

'Time's up for visitors,' he says.

Mrs O'Bee delivers a conciliatory smile, 'Of course, Doctor Nick. Give our best to your mother. But before we go, Shauna and I put something together for Connie to help pass the time.'

She lifts a backpack from Patrick's shoulder, unzips it and hands me a bundle of beautiful crisp sketchpads with tins of watercolour pencils and ink pens, brand-new and ripe with promise. There's a bundle of brushes and a box with other art items. Gratitude swells tears in me. Something in me tingles and an image appears of a gentle man on a mountainside and colours of every spectrum melded together on paint palettes. But no name. A surge of fresh panic looms, like I'm standing on the edge of a vast empty canyon.

When they have gone, I turn to Doctor Nick. 'What's going on with me?'

He pulls up a chair and leans towards me, clasping his hands. 'Now, I'm going to go a bit technical on you while I explain what your scans have shown. But trust me – it's all good news. You just need time.'

'Time,' I say, the word seems like a ghost passing through me.

As he sets about explaining his prognosis about my temporary long-term memory loss, his words fade in and out until he arrives at the end of his doctor's account of my head injuries.

'Anyway,' he says, 'it was good Mrs O'Bee found your ID. It's finally so nice to properly meet you, *Connie Mulligan*!'

When he speaks my name again, it feels to me as if someone has dropped a stone from a high cliff. For a moment there's silence, but I can hear the stone whistling as it falls, knowing that when it lands something in me will crack.

*

An hour later, alone in my room, the stone finally lands, and when it does, something within my heart shatters. I am she! *I am* my negative friend. Connie Mulligan. The very same young woman, tortured by the blindness of humans and the damage they do to Earth. I see now that I wasn't helping shift the world at all, but instead adding to the problem. Just like the angry activists. Tears brim as I turn to the quiet sky beyond the windowpane as memories of home and my sullied past jostle for attention. My phone jolts me. The word *Mum* flashes on the screen as it buzzes. Instantly my body tenses.

'Hello?'

'Connie! What on earth were you thinking? Skipping the tour like that? Raylene is livid.'

My stomach contorts. Like a tap turning on, memories of Mum's energy return. In rushes the images of Raylene and Dad having sex in the car. Then comes Turner. I feel my body wilt like a water-starved plant.

'Raylene's going to call when she calms down. But I'd say you won't be going back to work at Global,' she says.

I shut my eyes at the bitter discordant energy seeping through the phone.

'Honestly, Connie! I've barely slept. You've added ten years to my looks, I'm sure! I've been so worried about you!'

'The doctor said–' I begin.

'Yes, I know what the doctor said. I've spoken to him just now, and he told us that you can't fly home for a couple of weeks with head injuries like yours. A couple of weeks! Raylene's made it clear she's not picking up the tab! I guess your father and I will have to foot the bill. *Again.* This is so typical of you.'

I inhale and shut my eyes, but instead of apologising I remain silent.

'Connie? Connie? Are you there?'

I let the silence remain.

'Oh so you're not speaking to me now. Well, Dad's here wanting a word.'

There's a scuffling noise.

'Hello?' comes a familiar deep voice. I feel a faint tug of homesickness but it's short-lived when I hear his tone.

'What the hell were you thinking, Connie? To pull a stunt like that? We've had the ABC and the local paper giving us shit over your animal activism connections. Those bloody feminists and vegans you hang out with … it's all over town. Had to put the part-time milkers off because of you. We can't afford them anymore, not while you're on your free fucking holiday! Your mother's back working in the calf sheds and dairy. Wait till you get home,' he threatens, then stops abruptly.

Before he can begin again, I say spontaneously, 'Save your breath, Dad. I don't reckon I'll be coming home.'

*

Half an hour later, still numb as bitter memories flood back, Amber bustles in, eyes bright. 'Well, I must say your brother is quite the charmer. He couldn't get you on your phone before, so he called the ward. We chatted for ages. Matron's not happy, but what's a lass to do when a cute Australian boy says how much he loves my accent? Holy Mary, Mother of God, he sounds nice!'

'Patrick? Nice?' A flash of memory comes to me – a wedding anniversary vase lying shattered on the floor beside Patrick's brand-new birthday soccer ball. His little legs smacked red and bleeding from Mum's steel sewing ruler. Him screaming, face contorted in anguish.

'Yes, he was a cute little kid,' I say, with a sweep of compassion for him.

Amber pauses at the flowers. 'I wish some fella would give me flowers,' she says wistfully, dabbing her fingertips softly over the blooms. 'The last fella I went out with was such a shite. All he cared about was his video games and energy drinks. He was always acting the maggot with other women.' She rolls her eyes. 'Have you got a boyfriend?'

Normally this would be the time I'd say something like *I never want a boyfriend and a boyfriend would never want me.*

Instead, different words fall from my mouth as naturally and as certainly as rain from the sky. 'I think, after all this, I'm planning on allowing a man to come into my life, yes,' I say. 'And when I do, I'm aiming higher than a bunch of flowers now and then.'

'How do you mean?'

I sit up straighter, looking to the cotton puff clouds dotting the sky outside, my eyes misting with emotion as if it's happening already out there in the future.

'He's not just going to give me a bunch of flowers, we're going to grow whole meadows of them – living native wildflowers and glorious tame European flowers, you name it! Blue, pink, violet, yellow, white, red, orange. Acres and acres of them in long green grasses. And on a sunny day, he's going to lay me down in that meadow and weave the pretty little flowers all through my hair giving me a flower crown, like I'm a queen on this blue-green planet. Then he'll kiss me on my lips for so long, they'll become as plump and full as a red, red rose! And then ... some other things will become plump and ... well, you can imagine the rest!'

'Oooh!' Amber shivers, smiling, eyes bright. 'Wow! That's some wishing. In that case, I'll have what you're having too! Bugger just a bunch of flowers.'

'You're on,' I say, beaming at her. 'Let's hold each other to it!'

'Deal!' We shake on it.

Chapter 33

Six days later, I think I've made Doctor Nick O'Meara cry a bit. He's standing beside my leopard case in the hospital underground carpark, gazing at the painting I've just given him. He is speechless and spellbound. Amber had a similar reaction when I gave her painting to her just before.

I wave vaguely at his portrait and say, 'It was just a little thank you. You can throw it out if you hate it.'

'Hate it? No!' he says as sudden as a gust of wind. 'I'm just stunned. No one has ever done something so lovely for me.'

It's the way I see him. His face, serious yet kind. The line of his mouth, set shut as if trying to rein in a natural joy he's never been allowed to fully express. The gentleness of his sincere eyes set below his dark eyebrows.

'Watercolour,' I say. 'I'm just learning. I think Amber's turned out better.'

He glances at me and his doctor's persona melts away. There he stands, raw and vulnerable before me. 'Connie, I love it.'

'Well I did have a lot of time on my hands,' I say, trying to sound blasé in the presence of his emotions.

'You've made me look better than I do.'

'No. I paint what I see. The beauty within. No matter what others tell us about ourselves.'

For a moment our eyes lock and a deep understanding between us seems revealed. Both of us know we share the same pain …

We have been parented brutally to within an inch of our lives. Comply or die.

Moments later Mrs O'Bee mutters as she buckles her seatbelt. 'Not everyone gets their car door opened for them by their doctor on discharge.'

As we drive away from Nick, I think back over recent days. At the end of his shifts he would enter my room, dragging his doctor's coat from his lean body, and plonk onto the foot of my bed.

'She's impossible!' he groaned, waving his phone at me.

'Mother troubles again?' I invited, and out it would come – his mother story of the day.

Yesterday's though, stopped me in my tracks.

'She's refusing to back off,' he said. 'She's not moving one inch towards reconciliation or compensation. And now you ...'

I took in his furrowed brow and the way he was running his hands through his hair in frustration. 'What are you talking about? What about me?' I asked.

'You're off to stay with them. The Donovans! Of all people.'

'Of all people? The nicest dairy farmers in Ireland?'

'I can't believe Sybil arranged it. She knows full well they're suing us.'

'Wait? What? *Suing you?*'

'Well not me – my father, up until he died. But now Ma and I are the estate we're tangled in his mess. I've insisted Ma settle out of court with them but she won't. She's like a dog with a bone.'

'Court?' I asked.

With his name paged through the hospital speaker, he rolled his eyes and dragged his coat back on. 'Gotta go,' he said wearily.

Now the onslaught of traffic cowers me into my seat, despite the comfort of Mrs O'Bee's shaggy little dog, Mish, warmly settled on my lap. The frenetic pace of the commuters smudge in a grey blur, streaming like ghosts across the streetscape. The more I sense their discord, the more I sink low, clutching the seatbelt and cuddling Mish, the elation from my new cluster of medico friends disappearing. We're steering up a ramp, into the even more violent energy of the motorway.

'You okay, dear?' asks Mrs O'Bee.

'I feel really weird.'

'Yes. Stepping back into the world after where you've been can be frightening at first.'

'What's going on with me?' I ask, trying to stop the tremor in my voice.

Reaching over, she pats my knee. A soothing swell of calmness is delivered in her touch. 'Doctor Nick wouldn't have mentioned anything about it, but this is common after you've had a near-death experience. You went home to where we're all from and where we're all going. To where part of us always exists – even when we're here on this planet in our bodies.'

I know she's speaking of the mist that felt like bliss – where Traveller's surety held me, as did my knowingness of my absolute wholeness. My total oneness. It brought with it a sense of fearlessness even. Briefly.

'You were already opening up when I met you, but let's just say the Great Power has fast-tracked your awakening.'

I nod, only gleaning a slight understanding of what she's saying.

'The Donovans' will be the perfect place,' she says. 'The living energy of the land there is heaven on Earth. Truly.'

'Even with what's going on with them and Doctor Nick's mother?'

'Even with that. They're the sort to see things from above, so to speak. What Nick's father did was wrong, but they won't hold a grudge.'

'Wrong! It was appalling!' I blurt. 'I mean, telling his manager to aerial-spray like he did, knowing full well it would affect the Donovans' organic status.'

'I know,' soothes Mrs O'Bee.

'Nick told me about the genetically modified seed his dad ordered the next sowing season and how he sowed it on boundary paddocks, letting it go to head and blow across their land.

'Plus the dairy pollutant run-off, and altering the course of the river. Surely people can't do that!' I feel myself winding up, taking me straight back home to Sunnyside and my pain with my own father.

'Yes, Connie. But there are so many in the world like him. Don't let it impact you. The Donovans are so respected and within their rights, Nick's mother hasn't a chance. Edward O'Meara can only do so much from the grave. He's no longer around to coerce his legal and government power-pals to pull strings in the fight.'

'Still, I'm a bit nervous now about turning up to their place, seeing as I'm Nick's, um, friend,' I add.

'Oh love, don't you be troubling yourself with that. The Donovans know Nick's a good egg. They'll have you working for your keep anyway. They're interested in the rare breeds project you'd started in Australia. They're keen to have you.'

'They are?'

'Oh darling girl. Stop.'

'Stop what.'

'Doubting yourself. Here's your chance to change the story of your life. Past. Present. Future.'

I look to her puzzled.

'Indeed we can, if we choose, rewrite our history and create new futures. Time is so flexible. Really it is.'

'Mrs O'Bee, how long have you …' I falter searching for the right words, 'been able to *see*?'

'Oh, since I was a little girl, dear. Growing up in rural Ireland, it was easier. There were the old crones … the wise women who taught me the secrets and the powers of the Sheela Na Gigs. Of course, when I moved to Dublin as a young woman, the modern world shut it down for me. That and drinking and chasing men with Shauna!'

She laughs, re-gripping the steering wheel. 'My late husband, Ronan, didn't go in for me holding any kind of ancient power – his upbringing conditioned him to that. Religious strictness like you've never known. I kept a lid on it, until I had my babies. Then I'd use the charms and the balms, and the ointments and the tonics and the energy healing on them, all helped from my own garden. The results have been wonderful. I've raised a healthy buck and two beautiful does with barely a visit to a doctor.'

I think of Mum's angst-ridden trips to old Doctor Wilmot, and in my teen years, Doctor June and always to Mr Crompton for medicine.

'If it hurt in our family, my mum just dished out Panadol, like it's a one size fits all.'

'That's no good at all. But a word of advice, if you'll take it. Don't be blaming your parents all your life, dear. Often one child chooses to be born into a family to heal what has been passed down for generations. The child who remembers the light often selects the worst kind of families before their souls enter a body. You are that child. Many of the unawakened ones can't stand being in the presence of those who see and who remember. So they try to shatter them early in life.'

'Remember what?' I ask, sensing she's walking me towards some great truth.

'That we've been here before. Time and again. To heal. And to simply learn how to love and experience joy while ever we walk this Earth ... so as to bring heaven to Earth.'

Tears begin to blur my eyes as the truth becomes clear within me. In my head, it feels like marbles are falling neatly onto a solitaire board. Entire notions and vast concepts land in my mind. Armies of past negativity and fear seem to be battling this new-found clarity that comes and goes.

'Connie!' Mrs O'Brien snaps me out of my inner tussle, just as Mish resettles herself on my lap. She gestures to the patch of blue sky emerging from the grey.

'You have to look to the light. You have to be vigilant in your thoughts. Otherwise, you too feed the confusion and fear in this world. Love,' she says, 'is the cure for everything. With love, it's not all bad, here, in the dream. I'm not talking about modern-day Valentine's mush, but deep resounding, vibrational inner love.'

Mrs O'Bee veers from the motorway, shooting us off the exit ramp and onto a large roundabout, the road feeding us into subdued countryside. As the leafy abundance of the natural world emerges beyond the car windows, I feel peace settling within me again. We turn onto a country lane into a majestic canopied tunnel of trees as the afternoon sun spears through, flickering the light. Stone fences flanking the road are softened by leafy blackberry and ivy tangling up and through them. Once again, I feel the excitement of this new journey unfolding.

As we drive on past the bird-twittering lushness, it's as if the natural world is a thousand times more intriguing and vibrant than how I saw it before. It is positively glittering.

We turn onto an impossibly narrow lane, driving beside a high stone wall that is at least ten feet tall and makes me think of marauding armies. It runs for kilometres ahead of us, its limestone sides coated in moss, with massive oak, elm and ash trees draping their branches over the top. I'm about to ask what's behind it, when Mrs O'Bee clicks the indicator on, changing down gears, and rolls between two massive open black wrought-iron gates.

A brass sign set on the stonework reads: *Donohill Dairy*.

'Your new home for the coming weeks,' she says. 'It's where you're meant to be.'

Chapter 34

Entering a leafy wonderland, tyres crunching over white gravel, we curve through woodland interspersed with meadows that are divided by shaggy hedges and stone fences, passing wildly lush fields where a herd of the most mottled looking dairy cows I've ever seen graze. They are drifting across pasture, tearing mouthfuls of the meadow, their calves, gathering in little gangs, or lying like dark puddles under shady trees.

'This is what farming with love and awareness looks like,' Mrs O'Bee says.

'It's beautiful!'

'Yes. Wait till you're out in it and standing on the earth. You can *feel* it! The thriving creatures in the soil vibrate up into your body. It's amazing.'

We roll onwards into a cloistered grove of pines before blasting into the sunshine beside a vast ornamental lake. It is sculptured by more beautiful old stonework and gleaming discs of lily pads surround the water's edge with late summer pink blooms.

'Water lilies!' I say brightly. 'I love lilies!'

'Me too. The Donovans are using plants to filter the contaminated water that was running onto the property upstream, compliments of Nick's father. Since, it's invited a return of the dragonflies, the fish, the frogs and the sticklebacks. The scientists are going bonkers about it. Common sense really, in my book.'

We drive on past a copse of ancient oaks where a herd of mixed-breed maiden heifers graze, before sweeping around the lake and rumbling over a cattle grid towards an expansive lawn.

'Wow!' I say, when a large, raggedy but still-elegant country house reveals itself from behind a massive wall-like hedge. Framed by ancient trees, the three-storey house has an aged beauty to it that can't be denied. The main circular driveway steers us towards the house's large wide steps. Mrs O'Bee switches off the engine and pops the boot as I look to the entrance flanked by huge stone lions, worn by weather and time, gifted now with lichen and moss in their muzzles and manes.

At the top of the vast steps a wide front door swings open and a short, curvaceous young woman in jeans and a soft rose-coloured jumper emerges. Her curly black hair bounces on her shoulders as she jogs down the steps, followed by two tall lean men, identical in looks and almost in dress. The men have the ruddy cheeks I'd expect of Irish farmers and are wearing plaid shirts with cord pants and sturdy lace-up boots. They are far more handsome than their photos on their website. One wears an Irish flat cap and swipes it off his head, revealing shaggy strawberry-blond hair. He hugs Mrs O'Brien as we get out of the car.

'And you must be the famous Connie Mulligan!' he says, as Mrs O'Bee lifts Mish from my arms. He takes my hand. 'Declan Donovan of Donohill Dairy. Lots of D's I know. And this is my brother Devlyn who adds even more D's. And my wife, Grainne, who shoulda been called Donna.'

Grainne, backlit by the glint of sunshine and abundant green of the trees, looks as if she could be part woodland goddess and part my long-lost beautiful sister. She is solid Irish stock and yet ethereal and light.

'Welcome, Connie Mulligan! Now come. Let's get you inside. I know what emerging from hospital is like after I had my twins! You feel altogether out of sorts.'

Mrs O'Bee says, 'Well, Connie, now I've got you here, Mish

and I must push off. I'll leave you in the Ds' capable hands.' She gives me a hug and kisses my cheek. 'Mind yourself, lass.'

Then she gracefully places Mish on the passenger seat, and drives away. At the top of the stairs, Devlyn wheels my leopard bag past the lions sitting beside the large front door like guardians.

'I hope they won't get in a fight,' he says then winks at me.

I grin back at him. As we pause at the door, seeing the twin brothers close up, face to face beside each other, is transfixing. I take in the fascinating miracle of human genetics. Same smiles fold the wrinkles around their weathered faces and illuminate their gentle aqua eyes. As they usher me into their home, the sound of dogs whining behind a door escalates.

'It's a bit overwhelming to meet all of the family all at once, but here's some more of us,' Declan says, swinging the door open. A delighted pack of dogs made up of an assortment of breeds burst out, sniffing at me, grinning, wagging tails. I'm introduced to chocolate lab, Gordon, and deer hound, Wolfgang. Then Hector the pug, and Hugo the wire-haired dachshund, and lastly Mrs Hobson who is a little white fluffy bitzer, so old, her cloudy eyes look like foggy brown marbles about to plop out of her head and roll along the stone flagstones.

'This is the half of them. The working collies are in the courtyard,' Devlyn explains as I try to pat as many as I can all at once. The dogs hover long enough to say hello before bounding out of the front door to run on the lawn, except blind Mrs Hobson, who stands at the top of the steps, wagging her tail and barking as if she's still part of the action.

'If you think the house feels rambunctious now with the dogs, wait till the kids get home from school,' Grainne says. 'It's not unusual to have an orphan lamb wandering about and the occasional chicken inside. But I'm sure you'll fit right in.'

As Declan disappears to put the kettle on, Grainne, Devlyn and I climb the stairs. My eyes fall to the floral worn carpets – gentle blues and greens, the patina of age weaving stories of many comings and goings over time.

'Wow! This house is beautiful. It must be so old!'

'That it is. There's a book on its history beside your bed, so you can read up on it,' Grainne says.

On the first landing, lugging my case up behind us, Devlyn says, 'Yes, I hope you're not afraid of ghosts.'

'Don't tease her,' Grainne says.

He indicates for me to keep going up the next wide set of stairs. 'That's why I live down at the gatekeeper's cottage at the main entrance. Less ghosts there,' he says.

On the next landing I'm frozen to the spot when I come face to face with a suit of armour. It dominates the space beside the window, the stance certain, visor closed, dagger held in both gauntlets. Immobilised, my breath is stolen. Chills flood throughout my body.

'You look as if you have just seen the first of the ghosts,' Devlyn says.

I offer a weak smile, but can feel perspiration on my palms.

Devlyn looks to the armour. 'It's something handed down in our family. A victory spoil, taken from the aggressor who had ruled our land for centuries.'

'I can't stand it either,' Grainne says, laying her hand on my forearm.

Her touch makes me tremor, as if something has entered my body, shimmying throughout my whole being.

Instantly, I'm in a smoky hut. Herbs of all kinds are hanging from the wooden rafters, bound neatly in drying bunches. Around me wicker baskets brim with freshly gathered plants and flowers. I look up and across from me sits Grainne at a wooden table, head bowed over, her hair longer, plaited and falling past her thin waist. She is weaving and tying the dried cornstalks into the shape of a vulva. Looking up, she smiles at me ...

Just as swiftly I'm back on the landing, standing before Devlyn and Grainne and the knight's armour.

Grainne steps towards it, lifts the empty visor and says, 'You don't scare us, you old goat.'

Chapter 35

When they leave me in the quiet of the bedroom I sink onto the bed, running my hands over the embroidered quilt of daffodils in buttery yellow and gentle green. Paintings hang over what was once opulent wallpaper, now faded and peeling in places. There's scenes of cows in fields, and shire horses carting hay stooks and a dainty miniature of snowdrops. Above the fireplace, a large portrait of a noble-looking woman with dark ringlets, holding a single-stemmed white trumpet lily, gazes down at me, her eyes knowing and seemingly alive. On her slim hands, she wears a silver ring on her little finger. The Claddagh. A flicker runs through me, the hairs on the back of my neck rise. There's a familiarity to her. I smile up at her.

The same portrait from 1822 can be found in the history book of the estate as I flick through it. The woman's name is Aoife Donovan. The book's cover – a black and white of the country house in its heyday. I open to the centre and fold out a complex family tree. My finger traces the lineage from Declan and Devlyn, roaming back and back in time to a name I know so well. *Mulligan*.

Stars shimmer my skin and I feel slightly dizzy as I close the book and get up. I topple my case, unzipping the lid, revealing neatly packed op-shop outfits. I smile picking up the red cashmere cardigan. Shauna and Mrs O'Brien have jazzed it up with a little silver cherry brooch. Discovering a plastic bag tucked under the clothes, I look inside. It's my one red gumboot. Only one? Running my fingers over the sequins, there's a tug of homesickness for Megan and my new friends in Lilyburn who sent me off on my journey with such flair.

What a mess I've made of that version of the trip they were sending me on. I know Raylene will be binning my boutique and rare cattle-breeds project and a universe of genetic preservation will likely now never make it out of canisters I helped store in the Global sheds. Inside the gumboot, I discover a note.

> *You only had one boot when they brought you to the hospital. Someone must've souvenired the other at the yards. You may find it on eBay selling for thousands perhaps? Or maybe a prince is searching the land to find you and fit it to your dainty dairymaid foot! Beware though! Don't let any fella take your life arseways because he's really a gobshite. Make sure he treats you as the flower-crowned queen that you are.*
>
> *Look forward to meeting you in a meadow in Australia one day.*
> *Your loving Irish soul sister,*
> *Amber (aka Grumpy Nurse).*

'Sneaky bugger,' I say, realising she must've snuck the gumboot into the case when I was showering at the hospital. As I fold the note, storing it carefully inside my sketchbook, another marble of realisation drops into place – that it's only my fragile old personality telling me I've made a mess of it. The other part of me knows that all the big trudging lost gum-booted steps I've taken in life have actually led me to exactly the right place at exactly the right *time*. Here I am!

Outside the window the undulating land rolls away to a sunset sky, like a postcard scene of rural Ireland, and suddenly I'm ecstatic to be here. I can feel I am drawing something to me ... a swelling up of something big. A knowingness that I *can* make a difference to the world! I change my clothes quickly, eager to find out all I can about the Donovans' farm.

On my way downstairs, the empty shell of knight's armour on the landing seems to hold no power over me whatsoever. Taking Grainne's lead, I blow it a flippant kiss, before making my way down the last flight of stairs into the large entrance way, still a little head-spacey but too excited to slow down. The all-sorts dogs hear me, bursting out from the direction of the kitchen, bringing with them an effervescence of life energy. They soon lead me to where the Donovans are gathered with tea, waiting for me.

*

The conversation on cows and the cosmos draws us beyond lunch and soon it's milking time. Outside, the Irish mist curls my hair. Since escaping Mum's scissors for the best part of three months, it's grown fast. My fingers roam under my beanie to the shaved area where a ridge of stitches line where my scalp split. There's still an egg on my forehead where the gate got me, throbbing a little, but soon my mind is dazzled by a rain droplet. It's shining in my peripheral vision, like a bright silver star settling on the tip of one of my dark curls.

In the cobblestone farmyard, Declan and Devlyn are looking at my feet, laughing at my one red boot with its dazzling sparkling hearts and one of their white industry gumboots that's too big for me.

'The cows are going to love you in those,' Declan says.

'I promised my friends I'd wear them. One is better than none.' I grin at the twins.

Devlyn sets his hands on his narrow hips, his plastic overwear crackling, and shakes his head. 'Oh you're a riot, Connie Mulligan. They should make more of ye.'

It's taken me since lunch to work out Declan wears the flat cap in blue tweed tones, and Devlyn the green. The pair of them, with their long, lean faces and ruddy cheeks, look like they belong as handsome comperes on a country reality TV show.

Together we set off to bring up the cows with a surprising spring in my odd-booted step, given my recent head knock. Before me, the sun is settling down for the day like a dull blob of cream behind a curtain of cloud. The fields and hedges are so lush, and richly, deeply green it's hard to fathom, even for a northwest Tasmanian who's used to verdant hillsides in spring.

'Most of the farmers our age razz the cattle in with quad bikes. But me 'n' Devlyn and our team like to do as much as we can on foot with the dogs. Keeps us trim. Keeps our girls happier too. And we think it's quicker in the long run. Plus, we get to really see and feel what's going on in our soil and with our plants.'

'We'll take the scenic route,' Declan suggests, and begins to climb up and over an old fence stile into a stone-walled field, followed by their collie farm dogs, who remind me tenderly of Nick-nack.

'How can it get any more scenic than this?' I counter as Devlyn offers his hand to help me over.

The dogs launch themselves into the meadow and disappear into long lushness. My boots land upon a thatch of meadow plants, grasses, broadleaves and dainty flowers. It's as if I am walking upon clouds in heaven. As we wade through gumboot-high pastures, starlit with yellow and orange buds on the brink of bloom, the slight headache that'd been knocking at my temple dissipates from the meadow-scent. Soon we're standing before an amazing herd of Droimeann cows and a diversity of breeds I've never seen.

There's about two hundred mingling around the gateway, and I'm in awe that their calves are at their flanks. Seeing us, some cows low gently, others are more vocal, turning their faces upwards and delivering concertina bellows from their open mouths. They are like nothing I've ever seen before. Their sides and legs are patched and speckled in splats of blackish blue and many have a broad white stripe down their backs. Their adorable charcoal noses glisten from the wet grass. Some have dark fluffy ears that nestle below upturned horns – the sort you'd see in children's story books – and all of the milkers are wearing the latest tech in electronic collars.

'It's so amazing to see the calves with their mums!' I say. 'And they're so nuggety! Not at all like Dad's giant genetically wired ladies!'

'Aren't they beauties? And tough! We out-winter them here, unlike the rest of the farmers in the district who keep theirs in barns. No need to shed these when the cold comes. They cope just fine, don't ye, girls?'

Declan grabs the yellow insulated gate handle and allows the herd through to the lane. They flick their ears forward and eagerly walk on quickly towards the dairy, some hesitating as they call up their calves.

'They're content to head in to be milked, and don't at all mind their calves going in the overnight shed,' Devlyn explains.

'Wait till you see a morning milking. The reunion of the mamas and the bubbas is our favourite part of this calf-at-foot system,' says Declan. 'Come. We'll show you how our homemade creep race works, where the babies sort themselves out as they flow through the dairy.'

Excitement thrills through my body. Leaving the calves on their mothers in the dairy system is something I'd only ever dreamed of witnessing, but here I am!

'I'll go on ahead, get the parlour prepped, and leave you in Devlyn's capable hands,' Declan says.

As we walk, Devlyn explains about the cows. 'The Droimeann breed traces back over a thousand years to the Celtic era and has famous songs and poems written about it. The poem "Bó Bithbhliacht Meic Lonan", and songs like "An Droimfhionn Donn Dílis" and "Áilliu na Gamhna".'

I have no idea what he's saying, but goosebumps trail over my skin to hear their ancient native tongue. It sounds so foreign, yet deep within me, *so familiar*. I feel my heart warming.

'You'll have to sing it to me sometime,' I say, glancing at him.

'No time like the present,' he answers, and for the first time in my life I'm serenaded, not by DJ Dean-O into a dairy, but by the deep baritone of a gorgeous Irishman singing in Gaelic as the cows *and their calves* come home.

Chapter 36

'Shall I do udders?' I ask, indicating the spray bottle and paper-towel roll on the shelf in the dairy pit.

'Oh no,' Declan says. 'If you hadn't noticed, there's still a lemon on your forehead and you've only just cut a hospital tag off your wrist! You just watch and learn.'

He waves the bottle under my nose. A lovely waft of eucalyptus and lavender rises, the scent seduces my eyes shut and infuses a smile on my face.

'Nice hey? It's a la natural antiseptic for their udders,' Declan confirms. 'Nothing but botanicals as medicine around here. My Grainne is our wonder-witch who concocts our brews. She's genius – from a long line of plant women. Only brave enough recently to come out as one. You know how the old story's gone.' He elbows me with a smile. 'Worse than being gay in some places, being a wise woman.'

A flash vision comes to me ... of a sooted chimney and a swingle where a black pot hangs, steam rising from it. Of a low ceiling beam. Of herbs hanging in bunches – wolfsbane, belladonna and black henbane.

A rush of sound like a hailstorm startles me and brings me back. An auger spins, Declan tugs on a pulley rope, and the leader cow's daily ration rains into their trough.

'All organic and regenerative,' he says, pointing to the mix as the cows tuck in. 'We grow some of our own fodder and some we source locally to give them variety. Then there's Grainne's herb plants blended in it as well, which varies with the seasons. The girls love it.'

'I can tell,' I say.

Declan begins to wipe udders with the antiseptic brew – some udders are hairy, some swollen, some slightly flaccid, all with teats sucked loose by calves. It's clear that udder perfection is not a thing round here, unlike Dad's obsession.

As the cows single-file in, I watch their calves ducking through a creep race, and beyond that I can see Devlyn in the yards, whistling as he works. It's all so calm and quiet compared to home. Declan points at the calves.

'They know their Mama Grainne is in the barn with milk in the feeders and some little medicinal garden treats to get them experimenting with their tastebuds. They get quite used to the self-draft after a few days.'

'And the cows?'

He points to the calf race that runs past the muzzles of the milkers. 'We discovered the cows let their milk down better if their babies are within reach in the morning, so the calves have the option to hang about with Mama as she eats her ration. It was all trial and error, and a lot of tears at first, but we've nutted it out now,' says Declan over the whirring milk pump.

He holds up a set of milking cups before he gently attaches them to a cow.

'The other point of difference at Donohill is our tubing. The moment we learned that warm, fatty milk and plastics don't go so well together and the plastics contaminate our dairy products, we spent a bomb on new tubing and milk cups.'

I nod, impressed, looking more closely at the innovative marriage of high-tech and basic old-fashioned practicality. The place has a charm and a flow, along with a peacefulness that reminds me of the old days with Grandad. Here, the Donovans don't so much 'produce' milk, rather 'create' it with a sense of the alchemy. The magic of nature exists in here in a new system that is still anciently wise. The health and contentment of their cows is palpable, striking on some kind of magic mix from the soil up to the people. I realise that this would be possible on Sunnyside. The hairs on my arms lift. I have at last found them. Ethical and holistic thinkers. My clan! And I've found my answer to my question of how we can do this better at home.

Devlyn arrives to the pit and gives me a grin. 'Enjoying yourself?'

'It's amazing! But I can hear what my dad would say.'

For the twins' benefit, I parody his deep critical voice. 'Aren't you draining your milk profits by leaving the calves on their mothers and running the risk of high cell counts doing it this way? It's so irresponsible you're not combating mastitis with antibiotics in the rations. That's against health and safety regulations!' I finish with my hands on my hips and jaw jutting.

The twins share a mirror-image wide smile.

'Ah, the naysayers,' says Devlyn. 'We get it. But they always ask the same things. They don't get that people are giving up on dairy altogether because of the intensive industry and health worries.'

'Not to mention the environmental costs,' adds Declan.

'Yes,' continues Devlyn, 'at first our milk profits fell, but it was balanced out by hugely lowered input costs. And yes, we had to work hard with the old original cows to counter mastitis, but once we got the right kind of cattle and the nutrition in the paddock right via healthy soil, the mastitis stopped being a problem. The authorities have tried to shut us down many times with their regulations. But as you can see, we monitor closely, so we can educate the knockers about our chem-free existence.'

He indicates the state-of-the-art computer screen collecting data on each cow.

'Once the cattle got used to it, and we began building our brand to a premium price point, we stopped going backwards,' Declan says. 'Five years in, our calf-at-foot ethical products are making us such a profit, we've gone from being the craziest farmers about to the richest.'

Devlyn grins. 'It's not just about money, of course. We're rich because we have the best living soil and the healthiest cows. All our products are tested regularly, and compared with conventional products, we're out of the ball park on nutrition. The profits can't help but come with that.'

His brother continues, 'We've had every robotic and machinery sales rep in here trying to make us upgrade to something bigger, but we reckon they're snooping with a mind to copying our yard design.

'The big lads are wanting to cash in on this new cow-friendly management that customers are demanding. The number of people who care about where their food comes from is on the rise. How land and water is cared for is on their radar. The boys in big business are cottoning on. Luckily we've found the perfect partner to expand into the retail area ...'

Declan stops talking when from somewhere in the dairy, Grainne calls, 'Connie, are you ready to come see this?'

Declan flicks his head in the direction of her voice. 'Off you go,' he says.

When I find Grainne in the add-on barn, she greets me with a smile and says, 'I believe this is why you ditched your conventional conference to visit us.'

Inside, speckled, blotchy and freckled calves stand lined up at a feeder, suckling on teats, the milk frothing at their muzzles. Unlike our poddy shed where there's almost constant calling, the barn is calm, quiet. Entering by a small gate, I join Grainne where she's stroking the spine of a little calf that's arching his back cat-like, stretching in his nest of warm straw.

'This little fella's always last in,' she says affectionately. Grainne's hair is done up in a pale pink cowgirl-style bandana and she's wearing lipstick and groovy denim overalls under her heavy farm coat. Her lashes are lifted upwards with black mascara, dark eyes as pretty as the dewy-eyed calves that she stands among. My mother was wrong – the dairy can have room for glamour. Grainne epitomises it. I'm glad I wore Megan's colourful red polka-dot scarf around my neck today, to match my one bling boot.

'They're so robust,' I say, indicating the calf. 'Our Holstein calves are taken from their mums after just a few hours and some scour themselves to death in sorrow. The antibiotics and expensive milk powder never seems to get them to thrive. They get so frantic to find a teat to suck, some take to each other's ears, tails or nuts, suckling until the skin becomes a weeping red raw wound.'

Grainne nods. 'Yes. We had the same issue when the twins' dad ran the place. We looked into the technology of sexed semen, but to me that was getting us further and further away from nature. Now our customers know if they buy our milk products, they must also commit to buying our veal. It's given our neighbour a good business, growing out our little lads and setting up an on-farm butchery for us and other dairies. Then he supplies the meat to our Portlaoise shop. And the inedible offal, blood and wastewater is used for composting to put back on our paddocks.'

Grainne turns the tap at a large stainless-steel trough, rinsing out buckets just as Devlyn and Declan begin singing loudly from the pits.

'They are so much nicer to listen to than Dean-O on the radio at home!' I say to Grainne.

'They sure do have a talent for many things.' She points to the rafters out in the dairy. A small black box with a green light is suspended from the shed's roof.

'Wave! It's our internet cow cam. Customers can watch a live feed of the milking and the calves mothering up as they leave the parlour in the morning. That's the real reason the boys put on such a musical show. I think they want to be discovered on *Ireland's Got Talent* or something.'

I laugh. 'Aren't you worried about animal activists?' I ask, thinking of the mob who raided the saleyard.

'We've had our fair share of fully angry people, and even vandalism because we're so open about what we do here. But a few of our friends who aren't meat or dairy eaters, actually applaud us. They understand it's all down to personal choice and individual philosophies, provided it's kind. In fact, I was going to cook our veal tonight for dinner.'

'Oh yes, please!' I answer. A surprise sweep of emotion lifts in me and shockingly I'm suddenly crying.

Grainne circles me in her arms, warm hands soothing my back. 'Oh love,' she coos.

Swiping my eyes with the backs of my hands, I sniffle. 'Sorry. It's just … I don't know. I see what goes on here and then I think of what goes on at home. And I've tried to get my dad to see it. But … he …' I lose my words in a small faltering breath. 'Sorry.'

'Don't be. I get it. Totally.' Grainne looks to the roof and then back to me. 'It's almost broken us, just for being different from the mainstream. Thank god for the bond between brothers. Just Declan and me alone, we would've folded.'

She takes my hands, hers slim and warm, mine cold and square. 'You're tired and you're fresh out of hospital. Now these guys are fed and bedded, let's get you back to the house.'

We head into the milking parlour where the twins are hosing out as the cows mosey back to a new field. I inhale a steadying breath deeply into my lungs and an awareness strikes me – the smell!

'I've only just figured it out!' I say excitedly to them.

'Figured out what?' Devlyn asks.

'Your poo! Your poo smells so bloody beautiful!'

Declan, who's scrubbing the railing, guffaws. 'I've never had anyone compliment our poo before!'

I laugh. 'At home in our dairy, the dung smells rank. *Off.* Like the deceased. Like the diseased. I know it's from all the fake pastures the cows eat, the high nitrates. The lack of healthy soil microbes. But your manure smells like the sweetness of life itself. The perfume of a living meadow that's been chewed up a bit.'

The men turn to look at me, their blue eyes crinkled at the sides in amusement.

'That's lovely of you to say! It's the happy microbiome of our perfumed cow poo that keeps it sweet. We love it too … it's also going to cook your dinner tonight.'

'It is?'

'Come see our bio-digester tank. The manure from the dairy goes into it, the bacteria works its magic, then whoosh – natural gas. Enough to run both houses. It's the perfect system. No need for offshore rigs or fracking, just natural renewable gas.'

'As if my day could get any better! My dinner cooked by cow poop!'

And soon we're walking back towards the big old country home, the green leaves of Irish trees helping to bring a new-found freshness to my mind.

Chapter 37

A few nights later, at Devlyn's old gatekeeper's cottage my mobile rings. I'm seated at an old wooden kitchen table the colour of honey, made even warmer by the glow of a yellow-toned lamp hanging from a rafter, hand-split over three centuries ago. Declan on my left, Devlyn on my right and Grainne seated opposite, pretty in a dusky rose cashmere jumper with her black hair tumbling down. Her three children are happily engrossed in Lego on a rug in front of a wood heater – twin girls, Molly and Mary, and little Conor. They look like a Christmas card, so cute are they in their knitted jumpers over pyjamas, nestled fireside with the dogs.

'I think it's the hospital,' I say, looking at the number on my phone. 'Excuse me.'

'Here, take it in the office,' Grainne says, opening a low door and ushering me through into a cluttered but cosy space.

'Hello?'

'Hello, Doctor Nick O'Meara, here. Sorry for the after-hours call – catching up on night shift. Just a quick follow-up to see how you're getting on?'

A smile finds me as my hand flies to my chest. 'Fine,' I say, 'and you? Your mum?'

'Fine, fine. But this call is not personal,' he says, and then proceeds to ask me a series of doctorly questions finishing with a rather brusque, 'and you will need to come to the hospital for approval to fly. Admin will be in touch about an appointment.'

He sounds a little tense.

'I might not want to fly home,' I say. There's a pause.

'How are you getting on at the Donovans?' he asks abruptly, off script. Ah, I think, maybe that's why he's slightly guarded.

'Brilliantly. I've been working in the calf sheds and soon I'll be learning the ropes at their shop. Getting ideas for home.'

My excitement is met with silence. The door opens and Declan waves a bottle at me.

'Oh, Declan's here. He's offering me a drink.' I squint at the label. 'A Bertha's Revenge. Apparently.'

'Gin,' says Doctor Nick. 'Connie, you have recent head injuries. I would not recommend alcohol.'

I shrug at Declan. 'My doctor says I can't.'

'Tell your doctor to pull his head in. Surely one won't hurt,' Declan counters.

'Declan says one,' I relay to Nick.

'Tell Declan to pull *his* head in, and stop corrupting my patients. Don't you let him get you completely wankered, Connie.'

I laugh at what seems like rekindled, familiar banter, then Nick says, 'I've done my fair share of stumbling home from the gatekeepers' cottage. As a doctor I say no. But as me? Go easy.'

I raise my thumb and index finger to indicate a small sip to Declan.

'Tell Nick if he'd like to come for a drink,' Declan says, 'we'll ignore the fact his Ma is being a ...' Before he can finish, Grainne dashes in, cupping her hand over his mouth and dragging him back out of the office.

'I think he's a little merry.'

'That he might be,' Doctor Nick agrees.

'Well, the invitation's there. A Bertha – whatever that is awaits if you change your mind.'

When I arrive back in the kitchen, Grainne asks, 'How is he?'

I shrug. 'He sounds stressed.'

Grainne bites her lip and frowns. 'You know Nick offered us to lease the farm right after his dad died,' she says. 'But when he read the will, he realised his father locked the estate up in a weird family trust for the next sixty years, so Nick has no say in how it plays out. No wiggle room whatsoever.'

'I tell ye,' Devlyn says, 'his father was a megalomaniac, and his mother and the farm manager are hellbent on doing the evil old man's bidding for the rest of their lives.'

'Nick needs to grow a set,' Declan says.

Grainne whacks him on the arm.

'Ouch!'

'Dec, enough gossip. Pour Connie a drink.'

Grainne turns to me. 'Since his wife died, then his dad just a few months later, Nick's not been himself.'

'Wait, his wife died?'

'Yes. Horse accident. German.'

'The wife. And the horse,' Devlyn says, setting a small tumbler in front of me.

'That's awful.'

'Blessing in disguise, if you ask most,' mutters Declan. 'She liked jumping fences as much as her horses. Made Nick's life miserable. Only married him for the stables.' He attracts another sharp whack from Grainne.

'And they say women gossip! Well, bottoms up!'

My eyes widen when I taste the drink. 'That's a bit schmick!'

'It's milk gin,' Devlyn explains. 'Named after Big Bertha, the most famous of Droimeann cows. Guinness World Record holder for the world's oldest cow at forty-eight years old, and she had thirty-nine calves in her lifetime.'

'Thirty-nine!' I say, thinking of Dad's cows that conk out as breeders after just a few calves.

'It's made from whey alcohol, and they forage for local botanicals at Ballyvolane House, which in Gaelic means "the place of springing heifers". So I consider it healthy as well as supporting dairy farmers! Which is why we'll soon need another.'

Devlyn narrows his eyes, regarding the clear liquid, then looks up at me. 'To your good health,' he says before tipping the gin back. 'But not too much good health. You're proving to be so handy in the calf sheds, Connie Mulligan. And all your thinking outside the square and your outta space ideas mean none of us wants you headin' home just yet.'

A flash vision of the Global Genetics office and Raylene arrives. I flinch slightly.

'Stay as long as you like,' Grainne says laying her hand on my arm.

'So, to Big Bertha and to cow-loving Connie who'll talk cows with us till the cows come home!' Devlyn toasts.

The Donovans repeat his words and raise their glasses.

'If Devlyn wasn't so hopeless with the ladies, I'd get him to marry you. Make you stay,' Declan adds.

This time instead of firing comeback banter, an awkward chasm of silence opens up. Grainne shoots Declan a look and sadness settles over Devlyn's face. Thankfully the moment is moved on when squabbling between the children erupts.

'Time for bed, raucous little calfies,' Grainne says, rolling her eyes and getting up to gather the children, 'I'll come back and get you Dec, after the kids are down.'

'I'll come help,' I say, wanting to evade the family tension.

Grainne ushers Molly and Mary over the stoop, me carrying little Conor, and we trail along on the dimly lit path towards their old Land Rover. The littlest twin, Molly, points to the stars in the inky night sky. 'Look! St Brigid's cloak, Mummy! She's magic.'

'Yes, darling. There's woman's magic everywhere in the world and beyond!' Grainne says, kissing her daughter's crown before helping her into the car.

As we drive back to the main house, I ask, 'What happened, with Devlyn and his wife?'

Grainne glances at me sadly. 'Siobhan was his world. His one and only.'

I think of Uncle Larry and his woman in the paintings.

'Why did she leave?'

'It wasn't all Siobhan's fault she, y'know … strayed. Devlyn … you know … couldn't …' She gestures towards her crotch.

'Oh,' I say, embarrassed that my question has led somewhere so personal.

'But he has children, doesn't he?' I ask thinking of the clutch of mini-me clones I'd seen him with in the photos at his gatekeeper's house.

'No. Not his. My Declan was the donor.'

Involuntarily, my eyebrows lift in surprise.

'It made such sense,' Grainne continues. 'It's just so sad they're no longer here on the farm full-time. They're week on week off. It's so hard.'

She glances at me. 'Dev still doesn't forgive himself for not being able to give Siobhan children. Before he came home here he worked as a spray contractor. Slapped and slathered the stuff about like it was water. It was Doctor Nick who helped him get to the bottom of it all. Apparently Dev's endocrine system is knackered for good.'

'Oh, I'm sorry,' I say. 'I sometimes worried about my own brother, Patrick, and what we do on the farm. There's something going on in our own district, in fact.'

'It's too big to face, isn't it? As women, we kinda know it innately. But doing something about it seems too big.'

We round a sweeping bend and the house comes into view, downstairs windows glowing gently.

'Do you ever want children, Connie?'

Images of destruction ambush my mind. Of the logging decimating our valley. The sting of chemicals in my nostrils after Dad's bought up big from the farming catalogues that announce 'Springtime is Spray Time!' The slip of the scarred hills grazed and bare. The topsoil dusting out to sea. Our giant machines tearing up soil and plants. Land razed and smothered with concrete and energy-hungry houses. Turner's touch burning my skin. My father's fury. My mother's slap.

'Never,' I say as we pull up at the house.

Chapter 38

The next morning, I find Grainne in the farm kitchen clutching a mug of tea in front of the old wood stove that is draping the room with a comfortable warmth.

'I was just about to leave you a note,' Grainne says. 'The lads and I are going to the farm shop today to meet Nancy, our retail partner, so why don't you have the day off? I don't think you've had a proper one since you got here.'

'Are you sure? Can't I do some cleaning or something?'

'Not on your Nellie. If you have to do something take the big dogs for a walk. They get terribly jealous when we take little Hector and Hugo with us to the shop office.'

Soon, I leave old Mrs Hobson snoring in her doggy bed on the wide kitchen hearth, and Wolfgang, Gordon and I set off. We're at the top of a domed grassy hill when Wolfgang hits an invisible scent trail. Like a slingshot, a hare hurls itself up and out of a hedgerow. It sends the dog hurtling off and away over the meadows.

'*Wolfgaaaaang!*' I call, but he's deaf to me.

Clambering up and over the prickly hedged fence sty, I set off at a jog, Gordon at my heels. Entering into a woodland where I last saw Wolfgang's rangy form cantering into the thickets I begin to worry I've lost him for good.

So, on I go, into the woods. Darker and darker. Quieter and quieter. The trees, eerie, reminding me of Doctor Cragg's cushions. A slip could come so easily to me here. There's an echo of familiarity about the place that sits uneasily with me.

'Wolfgang!' I call again, sending the ravens flying from an old moss-covered ruin. The coldness shudders through me. My lips, too dry to whistle. Even Gordon looks like he's given up enjoying the walk and has clamped his tail down.

At last I find a sty that crosses over a thick stone fence. Climbing it, I know I'm on someone else's land. The ground feels harder. The pasture grazed short. It doesn't hold the same life force energy as the Donovans' land. Coaxing Gordon over the sty, I search the valley for a huge grey dog, loping over green, but there's nothing but the sound of the wind and a knowing that I've been here before.

*

Across the way, the land is crisscrossed with blindingly white horse fences. Grazing inside the handkerchief squares of perfect green are long-legged thoroughbreds rugged from ear to tail. Neat tree lanes divide an unfolding patchwork of fields that sweep all the way to a blue-tinged mountain ridge in the distance.

Before me in the valley, beside a tree-lined river, a majestic stone mansion stands. The imposing house is draped with green ivy, topped with several wonky stone chimneys, and straight modern ones in a tasteful blend of old and new.

The dwelling and outbuildings are nestled in a neat garden and the formality of the place is enhanced with a circular pond, a stone statue at its centre of what looks from here like some important man from an era past. Impeccable lavender hedges and immaculate lawns curve around picture-perfect garden beds. With relief I see Wolfgang frisking about on one of the lawns with another dog – a golden retriever waving a plumed blonde tail.

'Wait till I catch up with your mate,' I say to Gordon as we set off in his direction. 'He's going to be in the poop, big time.'

As I clamber over yet another fence towards the gleefully playing dogs on the vast lawn, a grey BMW slides towards me along a gravel road. As it nears, I call Gordon to me, ready to deliver my apology to the driver about the runaway naughty giant dog. I plan to be polite, yet witty – like a friendly Bridget Jones, and not at all like a Tasmanian trespasser in odd gumboots.

The window screens down. 'Holy smokes, it's you!' I say clunkily when I recognise Nick.

'And it's you! What are you doing here?' he asks, surprise on his face. His eyes slide down to my one red and one white gumboot. His eyebrow cocks slightly. I'm not sure if he's amused or judging my questionable style.

'Um, I'm here because of him ...' I say, gesturing to Wolfgang who's doing a giant-limbed splayed-paw play bounce with the rather exhausted but over-excited golden retriever. Gordon, now joining in with the dog party, is starting to get a bit humpy.

'He just took off. I'm so sorry!'

Nick waves the dog discretion away. 'It'd be Daisy that caused it all. She's such a tart. I'd say she's coming on. Ma isn't one to pay attention to those sorts of things. Won't hear of having her fixed.'

'I should've put them on a lead. I'm so sorry.'

'Not at all. It's good to see you. Here, I'll give you a hand to catch them. I don't think we're in need of pups – and that particular cross could be a bit ... confused.'

'Not to mention hairy.'

Before I know it, he's out of the car, shrugging on his big black coat. He sets off at a cracking pace so I have to gallop a bit to keep up. When we get to the dogs, they're spent, lying on the grass, tongues extending fully, panting fast.

'C'mon you,' he says, grabbing Daisy up by the collar. 'Enough flirting.' He catches my eye and smiles.

'Shall I drive you and your friends home?' he offers.

'Oh we can't put those dirty scruff bags in your clean car. I'm fine. I'll walk back.'

Nick pauses. 'Listen, since you're here, why don't I give you a quick tour?' He runs his large hand over his stubbled jaw.

'No, really. You don't have time to–'

'Time? Oh I do have time. To be frank, I'm avoiding my mother for as long as I can. I'd appreciate the delay. Will you walk with me for a bit?'

I look to his beseeching eyes, the way his eyebrows are pulled low with vulnerability and sincerity.

'Sure. Let's walk a while.'

We whistle up the dogs and head through a gate to a tree-flanked muddy path that dips up and down to a burbling brook. Pausing on a tiny foot bridge, I'm mesmerised by glistening water that chuckles over river pebbles of silver, gold and amber. Daisy finds herself a stick and looks at us imploringly. I oblige, throwing it into the water.

'She'll have you do that all day, if you let her.'

As the dogs cavort in a doggy game in the stream, above us birds flit, sun sparkles through tree branches and the smell of life rises up from the fecund woodland soils.

'I've just resigned,' he says abruptly, staring ahead.

'You have?'

Before I can ask why, he sets off from the bridge down the track. I frown after him. We arrive at another wooden gate, which he opens for me, letting me pass in a gentlemanly gesture, before striding off again out into a field that has an unyielding compaction to it.

When he at last stops I ask, 'What will you do?'

'Well, as I can't change what's going on with this place, I'm clearing out to America. I'm going to work with a former medical oncologist who's connecting with farmers to raise awareness about the links between human health and soils.'

'Sounds awesome.'

'It is. You gave me the idea. After our talks, I did a bit of a google search about people working in the area of diet and regenerative agriculture. I emailed his organisation and I was in like Flynn. It's all happened so fast. So easily. Like it was meant to be.'

'And your mum?'

I watch Nick's jaw clench. 'She's known for a while now that I'm not sticking around. Duty to the estate and all that be damned. Not while she's still targeting our neighbours and backing our manager.'

Nick gestures to a hillside where black and white cows are making their way across the face of the hill, like sailboats on a stiff breeze heading into harbour.

'Unless she caves, Dad's got it all stitched up with an international dairy company for decades. And the horse syndicate pick their managers based on who plays by Dad's rules.'

'Can you challenge the rules?'

'I've tried.' He looks down at his boots. Then glances up at me. 'But shall we have another crack at changing her mind?'

'What?'

'Maybe with your ideas along with the agricultural science you know, maybe she'll listen to you?'

'To me? Wait? What?'

'Maybe, just maybe, she may hear reason from you.'

My mouth drops open, then closes. Then opens again. No words come. I must look like a fish out of water.

'C'mon then, let's go meet my mother.'

Chapter 39

'I'm in the conservatory!' sings a voice as we enter the gargantuan house from a side door. With the dogs now safely contained in a courtyard, I shed my coat and kick off my boots.

'You're continuing the theme,' Nick says, gesturing towards my socks – one purple, one green.

'Setting the trend, I am.'

I try to walk elegantly beside Nick, but succeed only in a sock-slippy gait. Glimpsing into each room as we pass, not a thing is out of place. The formality is stifling, yet intriguing. Gold chandeliers in floodlit stairwells, fresh flowers in huge ornate china vases on spindle-thin polished wooden plant stands. Above our heads gleams fancy gold and white cornicing, while hand-painted birds flitter on flowers up the walls. Regal marble fireplaces shelter gilded fire dogs, with mirrors above the mantel to match. On the antique couches sit plumped cushions in tasteful tones. Every inch screams of class. And every inch within me screams, *Tassie dag*. I think of home with Mum's synthetic Kmart cushions, tractor teapots and faux wishing wells. Dad's Hawthorn garden gnomes lining the path. And at Christmas, tacky plastic lights and inflatable Santa on top of the roof. Her collection last year expanded – thanks to the *Innovations Catalogue* – to solar-light meerkats in Santa hats.

My heart thumps. I want to run. Instead, Nick turns. His kind smile encourages me to follow.

He leads me into a glass conservatory where plants moisten the air with the energy of their living breath. Rattan furniture is gathered invitingly around coffee tables, but it's clear no one ever has much time to sit here.

'Ahh, Nicholas,' comes a voice, and a thin, immaculately dressed woman steps forward in a cappuccino-coloured silk dress, light longline cardigan, wearing pearls and holding pruning shears like a dagger.

'Oh, hello,' she says, surprised to see me, eyeing me up and down.

For a moment I feel shabby in my charity shop polka-dot skirt, tired-looking leggings, wide belt and white cardigan, pinned with my cherry brooch.

Nick's mother looks down to my socks. She offers her hand. 'Mrs O'Meara,' she says formally.

'Connie,' I answer.

'Connie? Just Connie? Connie who?'

'Mulligan,' Nick adds. 'A patient of mine.'

Mrs O'Meara presses her hand to her throat as if shocked. 'A patient?' Then she looks at me with an iced stare. 'He's starting to make a habit of getting close to his nurses and his patients. Just recently he came home with the most dreadful homespun portrait that someone had given him, didn't you, dear?'

My cheeks colour. Nick flashes me an uncomfortable glance. I want one of the giant plants to come alive and swallow me whole.

'Um, Wolfgang, um, the dog. He ran away. And now, um ... here I am.' My speech staggers. And stops. And starts. The Connie of old is here in the room. The woman's energy is so much like my own mother's.

'Shall I go make us some tea,' Nick says. 'Connie, come help if you like.'

'Oh don't have your guest do that, Nicholas,' Mrs O'Meara commands. 'Connie, do sit. Nick can manage on his own.'

I feel like a dog compelled to obey. Heat rises to my face.

'Back in a tick,' he says, looking at me apologetically.

After a time, still devastated from her jibe about my art, I point to a photograph of a striking horse that sits upon a mantel.

'Beautiful horse,' I say.

'Summertime Showoff,' she says.

'And does he?' I ask.

'Does he what?'

'Show off?'

'Well, if killing my son's wife is showing off, yes, I guess he does.'

I colour. My eyes trace to another photograph with the same horse impeccably turned out in formal equestrian tack. A woman stands next to him in gleaming white jodhpurs covering lithe long legs, a tailored coat hugging a trim elegant figure. She's holding the reins of the giant bay with a whitewashed blaze. The shape of her face ideal.

'Really, I should be putting them away,' Mrs O'Meara says following my gaze. 'But I'm not ready to let her go. Helen was perfection.'

The old Connie Mulligan, snarky and insecure, would quip to the snooty Mrs O'Meara that she wasn't 'perfection' – but she'd be close. If you did the mathematics and the stats on Nick's wife, she'd have a golden ratio beauty phi up there in the ninetieth percentile. But this Connie Mulligan simply remains silent and soaks in the truth, that the painting was crap and that my convict genetics are radiating out of me before this vastly superior woman. I don't belong here. Someone like Nick could never truly be my friend. He's clearly just being kind.

'Of course, given Nick's situation, the poor man's been inundated with fortune hunters, with Helen barely cold in her grave.'

When I don't respond, she smooths down her dress and lifts her eyebrows at me. When Nick returns with the tea tray she asks pointedly, 'So, Connie, when are you leaving Ireland?'

My jaw drops at her rudeness. I glance at Nick. 'You win,' I say to him.

'Win what?' his mother asks.

'Nothing,' he says as he sets down the tray. 'But Connie's not the one leaving.' He stands before his mother. 'It's me who's going. I've quit. I'm going to America.'

The silence after his statement soars around the room until it begins to scream a muted fury, and all I want to do is run for the door.

*

A few days later Mrs O'Bee drops me off outside the serious facade of the large hospital for my final doctor's appointment. I gaze up the wide steps.

She leans across Mish, speaking through the open passenger window. 'I'll meet you in the cafe across the street when you're done.' Then she flips her scarf over her shoulder and zooms off to find a park.

In the waiting room, the plastic chair bites the back of my legs and I fall into a zone of my own, blocking out the noise of TV on the wall. Soon a nurse arrives, with a clipboard, smiling with no warmth in her eyes. 'The doctor will see you now.'

She leads me along a seemingly endless corridor and places her slim hand on the door handle. The sign on the door says *Doctor Nicholas O'Meara*.

Swinging the door open, a young Indian woman in a white coat stands up from the desk, indicating a seat. 'Hello, Connie. I'm Doctor Patel. Unfortunately, Doctor O'Meara sent his apologies for today. Take a seat. I'll just bring up your notes.'

As she clatters on the computer keyboard, disappointment brims that Nick's not here. I feel my body slump slightly.

Doctor Patel draws me back with her sharp questions about the state of my head and health. After she's looked at my scans and examined me, involving squeezing both her hands and

264

standing on one leg with my eyes shut, she says, 'Everything's looking good. You are absolutely clear to fly home.'

'Home,' I say absently. 'Yes, thank you.'

'Oh, and Doctor O'Meara left this for you before he flew to the States.'

'He's gone already?'

She smiles a distracted yes, then passes me a brown paper bag and, with a lift of her cool eyebrows, sends me out the door.

*

Mrs O'Bee is gazing at me from across the cafe table with her twinkling eyes, teacup held aloft.

'Go on! Open it!' she says like a little kid on Christmas Day. I reach in and pull out a beautifully wrapped gift. As I peel the paper away I discover White Witch Connemara skin care products. There's a pulse of botanical energy captured within their bottles as I handle each one as if they are diamonds.

'Oh wow. They're beautiful.'

'Is there a card?' Mrs O'Bee asks.

I investigate the bag and find one. I read aloud the words captured in Nick's typically messy doctor's hand.

Dear Connie
Sorry I didn't see you before I left for America. It was all
a bit of a rush. But thank you … thank you for being such
an amusing patient and persian.
Fond regards, Nick.

'Persian?' Mrs O'Bee asks.

I squint at the slanted letters. 'Person,' I correct. 'Patient and person.'

'Well, that makes better sense.' Mrs O'Bee chuckles.

'*Amusing*?' I ask. 'What on earth he find so funny about me?'

*

When I get into bed that night, slathered in Nick's beautiful scented creams, I tell myself not to be disappointed he didn't say goodbye. Instead I tell myself I'm the happiest I've ever been in my own skin. On my own terms. The potential of an entirely new future now swirling in the stars. It's then I decide I shall stay on in Ireland. Sunnyside and Lilyburn can wait. The woman in the painting holding the lily looks down at me and I'm certain she too is pleased.

Chapter 40

Weeks on, the leaves of Ireland turn from green to rust and crimson, dropping like confetti when the wind stirs. Today I'm driving the Donovans' little green Jeep past their winter bones, that are now revealing their angles against the grey sky. The heater's turned on flat stick, as I make my way up and over the craggy mountains, gliding past green fields, whizzing beside stone walls and ivy-wrapped trees that shine silver when the sun emerges. There are patches of snow in the shade cast by buildings and stone fences on the higher lands. As I pass the Mary Magdalene grotto beside the little bridge, I breathe in the wonderland, barely believing I've been here three months already.

At the Donohill Dairy store in Portlaoise I park and enter through the green side door for staff.

Eileen is chinking glass bottles of fresh milk from a crate, Gerald is packing delectable cheeses into fridges and Maeve is setting up mounds of butter in the display counter, glowing like gold bullions.

'Morning!' I call, carrying in the boxes of documents Grainne asked me to bring. The young staff – who call themselves the Dream Cream Team – chorus a greeting.

'Grainne's in the office,' calls Maeve. She sidles up to me and whispers, 'That philanderer lady's here already.'

'You mean philanthropist?' I ask.

'That's what I said. She reckons your coffee idea was the best yet.'

Centre stage in the shop is the new beast of a coffee machine, red and silver like a race car, recently installed and doubling turnover in just a few short weeks. A few FaceTime sessions with the happy chappies and an expert barista up from Dublin, means most of us are now friends with it.

I find Grainne in the back office.

'Ah, Connie,' she says, 'You're just in time to meet our partner, Nancy Fairchild.'

The woman stands, shakes my hand warmly, and with her thick New York accent says, 'Grainne's been telling me about you, Connie Mulligan. Creative ideas. Clever mind. Genius move with the coffee.' She raises her cappuccino, its frothy top decorated with a heart.

At a guess she's about Mum's age, but soft in her demeanour and stylish with her sheened black bob that catches the lights above.

She hands me her card. I look down to it.

Nancy Fairchild, CEO
Shiva Revival – Ecosystem Economics
Collaborative Creation in Earth's New Doughnut Economy.

Smoothing down her black loose-fitting boho dress, she says, 'Grainne tells me you're from Tasmania.'

The word Tasmania slides out of her mouth as a very American 'Taaaaaz-may-nia'.

She indicates for me to flip her business card over.

'Shiva Revival has been making headway in Australia.'

The reverse side is a photo of Melbourne's smog-filled CBD skyline, where pewter skyscrapers intimidate the atmosphere. Wedged between the masculine lifeless walls of steel and glass, a towering turret of green plants rises like a vertical jungle, breathing, photosynthesising, living.

'Wow! Is that photoshopped or real, for real?'

She laughs. 'Real. It's some building!' she agrees. 'We've spent three years creating our Melbourne centre. We have another in

New York and one on the go in London. Those plant-slathered buildings are sending a clear signal that the feminine is rising.'

'And doughnut economics?' I ask, looking at her card and thinking of the time I tried to raise the concept at a uni debate in relation to agriculture and humanity not outstripping the Earth's supply.

'It's time to reach the greedy assholes in the boardrooms and egomaniacs in the science labs,' Nancy says. 'We need to very, very quickly inspire them to know that partnering with nature is the only way. Not technology alone. Not economics alone. But also, mostly, the Earth's ecosystem.'

A scintillation runs across my skin. As I drink in the image of the outstanding, upstanding natural building amid the steel grey of the city, I can feel Granny Mulligan looking over my shoulder, smiling that her wish for cities to be dreamed up by women is emerging. Cities designed not just for money-making mindsets, but for nature too.

'Hold on to that card,' she says. 'We're looking for more people on the ground in Australia. People just like you.'

*

That night at the Donovans' house I sleep deeply.

I awaken into fog, seated upon Traveller on a thick felt saddle blanket of lily-pad green. His rump is draped in an emerald silken cloth, embroidered with a gold thread border, bells on the fringes. They jingle with every solid, feathered-hoofed step. Yellow and purple meadow flowers are woven throughout his mane that falls over his curved dappled neck. My gown is as sheer as the fog, and over my shoulders, a red cape lays, heavy and warm. We ride on through a leaf-carpeted trail in a woodland. Rounding a giant aged trunk, a knight in full armour on foot appears. The moon-gleamed figure does not step aside but instead stands, feet apart, dagger in one hand, white lily in the other. The knight also wears a red cape, draped over steel shoulders.

I draw in a jagged breath but remember that I'm not to let the fear of the past draw me backwards in time. Instead, I focus on the future, the meadow flowers, my inner woman's wisdom guiding me. The jingle of the golden bells plays a merry tune of joy, the safety of my steed, the sheathed dagger strapped by deer leather against my thigh. I look down to the knight.

'Allow us to pass, sir,' I say boldly.

The knight does not move. I sit back and Traveller halts.

'What business have you here?' I ask in a voice as deep as a she-wolf's growl.

The knight lifts up the lily, offering it to me. I hesitate, but something calls within me to take it. I leg Traveller over. I take the flower. Slowly, the knight hinges the visor open.

The face within has shadows cast by metal. In the moon's light, I recognise her immediately.

'You!' I say, laughter rising in me, sweeping joy that ignites me from the inside out like a burning star soaring across the black sky.

'Yes, me!'

I slide from Traveller, then stand barefoot before the knight, my heart beating inside the cage of my ribs, reaching my fingertips towards the face. My face. My very own face, that is looking back at me from the armour. My smooth pale skin, my dark mole, my red lips. I am smiling lovingly, knowingly, at me.

'Me!' I say.

'Yes, you!' she says and we're both laughing with relief and happiness, so hard that we can barely catch our breath. We mount Traveller and together we ride on through the forest until its edge. The mist at the forest fringes clears and soon Traveller is stepping through a flowered meadow of grasses and blooms rising up to his belly. Me with my arms around my own steeled waist of the warrior maiden I have become.

Something causes me to stir in the night. My mobile phone vibrates with insistency over on the dresser, illuminating the room. I pad over to it, groggy from my dream.

'Mum?'

'Oh Connie!'

'Yes?'

'Your father's had a heart attack.'

Chapter 41

The curvature of Earth is captured in the plane's oval window frame, revealing an ethereal glow as the sun dips golden into a vast sky-sea. Running my fingertips over the puckered skin where the stitches were, I feel the fuzz of my hair around the scar – such an unusual souvenir of Ireland.

Thoughts of Dad arrive. I wonder how he's doing. When I begin to worry I hear Mrs O'Bee's steadying voice: 'Worry is a prayer for failure. Simply don't entertain it, dear. Everything is always working out for our highest good. Always.'

Now, after hours held captive in a bubble of distorted time, I'm feeling claustrophobic, but I know it's only my mind that needs changing. Nothing else.

A bell eventually pings, and a flight attendant's stringy nasal voice follows. 'Ladies and gentlemen, we will begin our descent into Melbourne shortly …'

As the passengers unfold themselves from the plane and drift through customs, I eventually emerge on the other side of the auto doors. Following the arrow leading to Domestic Departures, I turn my gaze to a monitor searching for my connecting flight home. One more plane trip, less than an hour in the air, and I'll be back on Tasmanian soil. I feel a sadness for what I'm leaving behind, but also an excitement that I'm heading home to Uncle Larry and his over-the-river haven, along with my Lilyburn group. Even my brother feels more human to me, thanks to the amusing text exchanges and FaceTimes we had with Amber in the hospital.

Flashing letters on the monitor catch my eye.

Launceston – TA 1323 – Flight Cancelled.

I groan, check my boarding pass. Yep, it's me who's grounded. Finding an information desk, I cluster with the other stranded people surrendering to the altered universal plan that must be unfolding.

A 'mechanical issue' with the plane is explained and because bugger all people generally ever want to fly to Launceston, there's no more flights for today.

After a short taxi ride to a Melbourne airport hotel, I find myself in a room as bland as a beige brick. Perched on the bed staring down at the few straggly gum trees planted in concrete, I brace myself as I dial Mum's number. My homecoming buzz begins to flag and jet lag snags on the reality that I'm headed home to *them*. She answers.

'Mum?'

The sound of the car in motion backgrounds the static of her judgemental energy emanating through the phone.

'Aren't you meant to be on a plane right now?'

'The flight was cancelled.'

A strangled groan of frustration follows. 'That's just typical! You can never be relied upon, Connie! I'm already on my way. What time is the next flight?'

'It gets in at eleven … tomorrow morning.'

There's another angry moan. 'I've been in and out of Launceston to your father at the hospital. Your brother's grumpy and downright rude. I've barely had any time at home. Now this!'

I look to the planes taking off outside the hotel and have an urge to get straight back on one, heading anywhere but Tasmania.

'Don't worry, I'll get a bus. Patrick can pick me up from Lilyburn.'

'Don't be silly, Connie.'

'I'm not being silly, I'm being practical.'

273

'Practical? Did you stop to think who might be milking?'

'I'll ask one of my friends then. It's no drama. Unless you want it to be, Mum?'

I can sense her fury that I've answered her back.

'How's Dad?' I ask quickly before she can hang up on me.

'Oh! Him! So typical. He's milking it for all it's worth. He's had the operation. He's home now and fine.'

'He's home?'

'Yes.'

'He's *fine*? But you said it was urgent. That I had to come home.'

'Oh, Connie, how was I to know how urgent it was? Turned out it's a fairly standard condition. Are you complaining your father is no longer on death's door?'

'No!'

'Typical. So selfish!'

My unlived Irish future drains like dark, dirty water, whirlpooling the wrong way, into the tired-looking Southern Hemisphere airport-hotel carpet.

As I hang up, I shiver my shoulders in a hope of evicting my mother's neediness, like a dog shaking off an upset, but the sorrow remains like a damp stain.

In the bleak hotel room, I contemplate turning on the telly but have no heart for the unconsciousness of mainstream TV. Behind gauze curtains, city lights begin to illuminate in the smoggy sky, the colour of a sick salmon.

Too early to order Uber Eats, like the poster suggests on the back of the door. Too late to go for a dismal walk along a weedy pavement beside the eight-lane highway. Too financially challenged to get a taxi to drive by and gawp at Nancy's plant tower. I pick up the compendium and notice there's an advert for the Skyline Bar on the top floor.

'Glamour plus,' I say looking at the tacky photos. A glimmer of fondness for my time in Ireland ruffles through me. A drink, though? Why not? To both celebrate my trip and drown the sorrows of the circumstances of my return.

By the time I've travelled up in the lift, reached the bar and slid into a black vinyl booth, I regret coming. I turn my face to the window, my reflection a shadow in the glass, peppered by the coal-fired powered lights of urbanity insanity that masks the night's arrival. My eyes follow the blinking wings and tails of the planes that heave upwards and soar downwards in the darkening sky. Spinning my drink around, I sigh. Whiskey. Irish. Neat. I take a sip. It burns. It doesn't taste the same. My heart aches.

A voice shakes me from my solitude.

'Of all the airport hotel bars in all the world.'

I turn towards the accented voice. A voice so deep. So rich. So recently familiar.

There stands Nick O'Meara, travel-rumpled in a chambray shirt and jeans, tousled hair and stubbled jaw. His dark eyes rich with joy in his discovery of me, his former patient, here on the other side of the world.

'What the heck are you doing here?' I blurt, my face lighting up. 'I thought you were in America?'

'I thought you were still in Ireland?'

Standing, we lean together in a brief hug.

'My flight to Tasmania was cancelled. Till tomorrow. So here I am.'

'We leave tomorrow too.'

'We?'

'There's a few of us headed to New Zealand. We're on a speaking tour organised by Farmer's Footprint. We're delivering presentations on the links between holistic agriculture and human health.'

'Oh wow!'

'I know oh wow!' He glances around, lifts his eyebrows humorously. 'So this is our temporary salubrious accommodation until we reorganise our plans.' He slides into the booth seat opposite me and smiles. 'Of all the bars,' he says again.

'In all the world,' I finish.

We laugh, my body tingling, knowing that universal synergies are at play here, bigger than us. The hairs on my arm lift. A pulse between my legs flourishes and I tell myself to stop it.

'Drink?' I ask, pointing to my glass. 'Same as me?'

He nods a yes, our eyes still bright with surprise. As I make my way to the bar, I have to hold my breath to stifle the girlish squeal that wants to escape. Two sips in and a flood of talk begins about Nick's new work researching microbiome in plants, soils and stomachs. On his next whiskey shout, we journey on to Dad's condition, my plans for my imagined Sunnyside Dairy Farm revolution based on the Donovans' business, the challenges with my family with my changed headspace, then on to talking about Mrs O'Bee's extraordinary intuitive diagnostic talents and her need to dress dogs and people up in charity clothes.

'And your mum?' I ask. 'How's she now about you leaving?'

'Oh, you know ...' Nick says defeatedly. 'And yours about you arriving?'

'Oh, you know ... same.'

I clink my glass with his and our eyes meet in mutual understanding. Hunger rumbles my stomach.

'I think we need to eat,' I say, lifting the empty glass.

'We do indeed.' He scans a laminated menu. 'The bar food looks shite!'

'Shall we find somewhere else?'

He looks out the window. 'I don't think we have many options. Taxi to the city?'

'Too far. Too crowded.'

'Maybe in-room dining, then?' he suggests, then looks away shyly. 'Just being practical, y'know.'

'Well, I don't fancy hiking all the way into the city and it is a practical option.'

I look down to my fidgeting hands at the suggestion of going to a room together. When I look up, he's staring deeply at me, placing his hand over mine to steady them.

'Connie Mulligan,' he says in an altered voice. 'I can't believe you're here. Right here in front of me.'

My body buzzes from his touch. I fall into his eyes knowing there is now an irrefutable magnetism between us. 'Let's go for in-room. Shall we?' I add, desire rising in me so fast I feel as if it will drown me.

'Yes.'

We head out of the bar and enter the lift, the doors sliding shut. As natural as breathing, we fall into each other's arms, lift sailing downwards, Nick's large body pressed against mine. A longing surges so powerfully in me, I'm surprised by the velocity of my passion.

Pulling back from me, his brow creases as he looks into my eyes with such deep sincerity that it reaches directly into my heart. I fall towards him, pressing close to his chest, turning my face upwards, seeking his kiss. It arrives with the rough rub of his stubble on my face, his warm whiskey-tasting tongue inside my mouth, his large hands roaming over my body. The lift door dings and opens. It's my floor. I take his hand. I lead him to my door, wave my key, and we fall inside.

Murmuring my name with desire, he pushes my back to the wall. Over his shoulder, I catch our reflection in the large mirror. The flex of his muscles under his shirt, a torso of triangulated masculine gorgeousness. My strong legs, shaped nicely by a lifetime of walking the steep Lilyburn hills, one hooked up around his lean hips so I can draw him in as close as I can, the press of his erection in his jeans against my verenda. His passionate kisses send me into a frenzy. With confidence and conviction, I drag him to the bed. Now is my chance to satiate myself with one of the most beautiful men I've ever met – from within and without.

Our clothes peel away, and soon we are skin on skin. Desire rushes throughout my body like a wind gust as Nick traces his fingertips over my belly, prompting a flash vision of the fullness of the bellies of the Sheela Na Gigs. His fingertips find the softness of my inner thighs, releasing a gentle moan from me.

His touch roams over me, exploring, stroking, then eventually sliding his long fingers into me, caressing me into a high state of otherworldliness. I buck against his hand, orgasming for the first time ever with a man. I lie back for a moment, as if the cloak of Brigid has fallen heavily over my whole body, covering me in stars and a blissful blackness. After my first shuddering orgasm, he kisses his way onwards, downwards, as my palms enjoy the feel of his muscular shoulders.

I groan as he roams his tongue around in the valley of my feminine place, I feel a deep melting within. An arrival for the first time into my own body. Mid tongue-stroke he looks up at me, his brown eyes locked on mine, his black hair Irishman shaggy.

'Oh Connie. You are truly beautiful.'

He gets busy again, kissing me so tenderly on my valley garden, and pressuring me into ecstasy, my head falls back upon the pillow, and I cry out as another sweep of orgasm travels through my body. I draw him upwards, urgent now to have him plunge his stone-god phallus into me.

'Protection?' he asks desperately.

I flounder but then remember Jane's parting gift of the knickers along with the small bag with *Mile High Club* written on its tag and three condoms within.

'Only three?' Shirley had joked.

'Just a sec,' I say as I dash to the bathroom and back. Naked in front of him. Not caring. Just living.

As he pauses to roll on the condom, I feel the swollen rose between my legs desperately flower for him. As he enters me I relish the weight of his chest upon me. As we begin in a blissful rhythm, I drift out beyond the ceiling, floating amid the black nothingness of space. When he shudders and we both meld into orgasm, he falls upon me, stroking my hair and kissing my face, there's nothing but us and our breath and the roar of planes as people from all around the world come and go. As I drift my fingers over the smooth skin of his back, I wish this moment in time would remain forever.

Chapter 42

The next morning on the short flight over Bass Strait, I smile with nostalgia for that time of rumpled sheets and the incredible one-nighter with Nick. Naked and warm against the solidity of his body. Me. Altered. All freshly loved-up and feeling purified, instead of shamed. Then with a twinge I recall the way I'd panicked when he'd put his number into my phone. Images of perfect Helen flashed. The face of his disapproving mother. Him so countrified gent and doctorly. Me so Tassie bumpkin and dairy farm damaged.

Southern Connie stammered, 'You don't have to keep in touch. It was a lovely fling. Let's leave it at that.'

Now on reflection, I grimace. Had it been a shadow of hurt that had crossed Nick's face? Or, in fact, relief? The crackling voice of the captain comes on and the flight attendant, wafting cologne, sweeps by collecting water bottles and checking seatbelts. Tray tables up, luggage stowed, my leopard in the hold.

As the plane dips towards home, I push the Nick-fling from my mind and instead choose desire for my new Lilyburn future to run fast in my mind, like burgeoning floodwaters, gushing over that conventional farming dam wall Dad has built so solidly during his lifetime. The wall that is now showing cracks. That may sound cold or callous, but isn't a changing of the guard normal through time? However, in Dad's mind, the baton is handed to sons, not to daughters.

As I gather the in-flight magazine to place back in the seat pocket, I stare at the cover. It's an artfully drawn map of Tasmania. Our little island is apparently (according to the headline): 'The world's hottest tourist destination'. Tracing my finger along the island's edges, it's only then that the coin in my mind – that has been spinning in the air for so long – drops into my inner wishing well, sending out ripples of realisation.

Looking at the illustration, I fully absorb the significance of the actual geographical shape of my island and its symbolism. The island where I was born and bred is shaped like the sacred feminine triangle, the same as the ones depicted in Megan's art and on the ancient walls behind Mrs O'Bee's shop. As I digest my realisation, I stare through the window, down to the plumed line of white breakers kissing the fringes of the northern Tasmanian shore. My gaze returns to the magazine cover. Tasmania, Lutruwita.

'Trikona!' I say with love and an awe I've never fully felt, running my finger around the edge of the illustration, taking in the delicious, forested, lush, natural triangle. An island of untameable wilderness. An island that mirrors the sacred wildness of women. The area of my body that leads humanity to the portal of human life.

'Show us your map of Tassie,' I whisper. It was a taunt the boys at school threw at us girls, sliding out of their mouths like a dirty smear, 'Showuz yer map ov Tazzie.'

I realise now how young we all were as little girls, being coerced culturally into shutting out our very deep power and taking on shame. But not anymore! Now that power is mine to claim!

As the plane rattles through cloud, an image of the stone Sheela Na Gig flies to mind. Now I see my return as a reclamation. On behalf of my long-gone sisters of the island, it is my time, as a woman, to really show them my map of Tassie! It's time to face the future of our family farm as an equal. I close my eyes. As the plane wheels hit the tarmac, I know I'm returning home with the full force of my geography as a woman firmly in place.

*

'Mum!' I call and wave, but she's looking right through me. She's thinner, her face pale and anxious. I stand right before her. 'Mum!'

She startles, then looks me up and down. Taking in my boots, stretchy black tights under a black broderie anglaise skirt, and the leopard-print body suit Mrs O'Bee smuggled back into my shopping bag all those weeks ago. I have redone my Shauna-red lipstick and tied a black ribbon in my hair.

'Connie? You've got lipstick on? And what on earth are you wearing?'

'My travel outfit. We thought it would be fun if I matched the luggage,' I say brightly. On the carousel, my giant bag sails towards us and I capture it.

'See! We're a *puurrrfect* match!' I say, modelling my suitcase with my outfit.

But Mum doesn't smile. 'We?'

'Mrs O'Bee Wan Kenobi. Sybil. A friend.'

She simply rolls her eyes and shakes her head.

I draw her into a hug. 'I missed you, Mum,' I say, meaning it. 'How's Dad?'

I try with all my newly awakened self to see beyond her testiness and tension, and her withheld love for me. But Mum's having none of it. She stands unyielding in the circle of my arms.

'He's fine. Of course it was stress-induced. Those months with your legal university business. Then what you did in Ireland. Letting us down like that.'

As she targets me with her words, I recognise my own bile-like bitterness that I hold for her. She's syphoned me back here for her own egotistic needs, to entwine me once more in her dramas with Dad.

'Come on,' she says. 'The cows won't milk themselves this afternoon. Patrick said it's your turn.'

*

On the drive home, Mum seems different. Small. Vulnerable. Dark rings under her eyes, her skin like dried white pastry on the places the foundation missed, and her clothing isn't its normal crisp perfection. Her red lacquered nails shorter now she's back milking. She would by now be bantering her bullshit. Gossiping. Telling tales. Today she is utterly silent.

'Is everything all right, Mum?'

I can sense her vibration is as shuddery as the roadworks base we're slowing for near Devonport. She pats her hair and twists her mouth, which tells me it's not.

'Yes, fine. But we do need to have a talk with you when you get home. A family meeting.'

Like a black hole in space, I can feel the pull of her negativity. The trauma of my last 'family meeting' crackles like static. I turn the radio on to stop my mind being sucked into the past. As we move up a hill, the auto tune picks up SAND FM. Dean-O's voice permeates the car as he voice-overs a promo for his morning show, and fondness lifts in me. No matter how flawed, Dean-O is the sound of home, so I turn up the volume. I'm hoping to drown out the negativity that seems to be spinning around us.

'Have you still got a crush on him?' I ask, like I'm talking to Amber.

'Who?' Mum asks, irritated.

'Dean-O! He had a *thing* for you. At the Plaza. Remember? If you squint your eyes, he's actually not bad-looking.' I grin.

For the first time since I've seen her, a small smile twitches on her face.

'He didn't have a thing for me! It's his job to be friendly like that.'

'Rubbish! He was *mad* for you!'

'No! He wasn't!' she says but her cheeks are like bunches of blooming red roses, not helped by the fact Dean-O is now saying, 'A reminder ladies, our Do Dinner with Dean-O competition closes soon. Just go to SAND FM's website to enter. I'm looking forward to doing you for dinner, my darling ... whoever you are.'

'He's talking about you, Mum,' I tease as the ad ends, and The Weather Girls' 'It's Raining Men' fills the car.

My spirits lift. I know it's a sign! I'm in the right place! I've arrived home with my power, if I choose. Memories of the op shop flash. Me laughing, dancing with Mrs O'Bee and Shauna. Turning the dial louder I start singing.

'C'mon Mum!' I wiggle in my seat. 'Hallelujah!'

As the song blares, Mum turns her face away. Tears swim in her eyes and she bites her lip. She jabs the radio off.

'Stop being so *stupid*, Connie! I thought travel might have grown you up a bit. You seem to have no idea of the messes you've made. This last stunt you pulled in Ireland has *ruined* us.'

Her words cut me. Spinning tyres and the car engine fill our silence. I see for the first time how I have a well-practised habit of holding a deep sense of shame for things that aren't mine to be ashamed about. We don't speak for the rest of the journey.

Chapter 43

As we near Lilyburn, Mum pipes up. 'We need medication for your father.'

She steers us off the highway. In the main street the sun dances silver brightness over the cafe tables that are chockers with people. A few locals, but the rest are blow-ins. There's a buzz. Even the strutting seagulls seem happier.

Mum parks her RAV outside Mr Crompton's and gets out, sending a bird winging up and away in the direction of the white wave shoreline. My Northern Hemisphere body-clock niggles, stomach rumbles. I'm tempted to rush over to say hello to the guys and grab something to eat, but I know Mum is in no mood for dallying.

'What are you doing?' she asks when I get out of the car too.

'I need to stretch. Long-haul flight body,' I say, then think happily to myself, *Sore from hot sex body.*

'It's really bright and boiling compared to home,' I say, peeling off a layer. 'I mean Ireland. Here's home. Right?'

She rolls her eyes and disappears inside the pharmacy. I decide to quickly duck in to see Megan so head to Verenda's door.

Counselling session in progress. Come back later, the sign says. All in good time, I think. I must not go grasping for others, when all the support is within myself. I just have to hold my mind steady in these first hours with my family and all will be well. *Breathe, Connie.*

Walking on I take a look at Dawn and Dick's window, crowded with ads for local properties. The pub across the road is still up for lease or sale. It's been years languishing, waiting for someone to care for it. I turn towards it, standing double-storey tall across the road from me. The building looks to me like a proud old woman, wearing her row of attic dormers as a crown. Just a few blocks up from the sea, she's begging to be loved again. I see her with fresh nostalgic Irish eyes. A true old beauty, with her touch of wrought-iron elegance revealing itself like a lace camisole, her curvaceous bull-nosed veranda, still charming and never out of style. After my time with the Donovans and Nancy, she's whispering, *Community potential.*

Taking my phone out of my skirt pocket, I snap a photo of the listing, then one of the actual pub. I text a note to Megan, smiling to myself: *I'm back! How's this for an idea – Local Food Community Collective? Regenerative meat and organic dairy and grocery shop? Cheese-making? Women's commercial kitchen? Endless possibility. Can't wait to see you. Xx.*

I send the photos with a heart emoji and smile again. Then I flick a similar message to Nancy Fairchild into the iPhone ethers. Sowing seeds, I think to myself.

Satisfied, out of curiosity and on the hunt now for more opportunity, I scan the rest of the properties in Dawn's display. I pull a face reading the extreme prices for Tassie real estate.

With my mind stomping off with its own indignations about the wealthy 'land-banking' properties they've never been to, it takes a moment for me to recognise an aerial photograph of Sunnyside Dairy Farm. *My farm!* Captured by drone on a vibrant, blue-skied day. *For Sale* typed above it. My heart seems to stop, while the world continues to revolve without me. *For Sale?* Sunnyside? There has to be a mistake. The dot-point listings catalogued in such a cold economic way confirm my despair. The text swims before me.

*902 ha quality land with 1500 mm rain annually
*Current permit to convert a further 80 ha of bushland to
  pasture
*Red basalt soil ranging to river silt loams
*Bores for stock and Lilyburn river frontage throughout
*Four-bedroom homestead with workman's cottage
*New 50 unit rotary dairy
*300 yearling heifers and older cows available at
  valuation
*237 ha runoff block upstream with permit to clear
*Timber sale potential
Tenders to Dawn Donaldson at Dawn and Dick's Real
Estate Agency.

Despite the day's warmth, I'm chilled to my bones. The listing blurs before my eyes. Running to the pharmacy, I shoulder the door open like a rugby player in a tackle, bellowing, 'Mum!'

*

When we emerge from our furious stand-off in Mr Crompton's, Mum will barely look at me, embarrassed by my public tear-washed face and cries of 'How could you?' and 'Why?'

With Mr Crompton being as deaf as a post, and with no other customers, I can't understand why she's claimed the right to get the shits! Before I can crumple myself into Mum's car, the squealing of rubber on road at the war memorial sends the seagulls screeching into the air. Slugs's ute flies around the war memorial towards us like Brockie on Mount Panorama. One of his mullet-headed duck-shooter mates is driving, camo trucker's cap on backwards.

Slowing almost to a stop outside the cafe, Slugs and two other hefty guys rise up from the ute's tray, and like chariot-riding Romans, release guttural roars. Holding aloft slabs of red meat, they chuck their carrion hard at the vegan outdoor diners, as if they're slinging rocks. The steaks fly through the air, landing with heavy meaty splats on the patrons. A bit of round steak lands on one woman's lap and she screams as if she's just given birth to an alien. Slugs and his mates reload from a bloodied bucket. From the stench on the breeze I can tell the bucket's sat for some time in the sun. Piffing meat rapid fire – sausages, livers, hearts and guts – they shout, 'Go home, ya stupid vegan dickheads!'

As raw flesh rains heavily on the tables, the diners cluster together sheltering. A couple of men try to shout Slugs's crew away, like you would an aggressive dog. Others panic and dash indoors. The wheels smoke. The ute roars off, leaving carnage and chaos behind.

Vernon and Fenton rush out to the melee. A woman in a flowing skirt has crumpled to the pavement, sobbing and swiping blood from her face and hands with a paper napkin as if her family has been gunned down by the Mafia.

'Onya, Slugs. Not helpful,' I groan, then I turn to my gobsmacked Mum. 'Shall we go help them?'

'Help them? Don't be ridiculous, Connie.'

I sigh. I want to cry. I want to lie down and die.

When I get into Mum's car, I say, 'Yep. It's so fucking good to be home.'

'Language, Connie. Language,' she growls.

*

The shock of the things I've just discovered and witnessed have barely settled in my body when we swoop upwards towards David and Raylene's Waterbright Dairy, and there looms large a Dawn and Dick's sale sign.

'No?' I breathe, brow creased, turning to Mum. 'The Rootes-Stewarts' farm's for sale too? What's going on?'

'I don't want to talk about it.'

A few minutes later, turning onto Mulligan Lane towards Sunnyside Farm, I see another huge sale sign has been staked into the long-dead glyphosated grass beside our gate. An involuntary sob escapes me.

'Stop being so dramatic, Connie. It's been on the cards for a long time, you know it. I just can't keep doing this anymore! So don't you start on *me*! This is *all* your father's fault. We'll talk about it when we're inside.'

At the wishing well, Mum gets out, slamming her door. She waits at the garden gate, holding it open for me, impatience creasing her brow. Still absorbing the shattering news, I remain in the car, looking out beyond the house's ugly brown bitumen-coated roof tiles. Glowing golden and silver clouds scud over the range. A sheer curtain of rain is sweeping a rainbow across the face of the largest mountain to the west. How could this place, *our farm*, be for sale? The luminescent trees on the other side of the river blur through my tears. A cloud-filtered sun on Uncle Larry's paddocks blazes orange-gold kangaroo grass to life. The sun is captured by the old windowpanes of the apple shed and seem to wink at me, signalling a sad, secret 'welcome home'.

My gaze sweeps along the dry river flats, revived only a little by Dad's inefficient irrigation on tired soils. Now, after being at the Donovans', I can overlay the valley's agricultural destruction with a healed version of the meandering river flats. It causes my heart to swell with love and then shatter, knowing I could turn this farm around the way the Donovans had theirs if I had the chance. But, it's too late, I think as I gaze at the compacted paddocks, threaded by the bastardised river, dotted with our black and white cows. All now for sale.

'Hurry up, Connie,' Mum calls. As I get out of the car, I scan Granny M's cottage paddock and see Traveller dozing under his one gum tree, back hock kinked, hay net half full. He looks well. The mobile fences are all in order, set up perfectly. I'm momentarily puzzled. Who would do such a thing for him? For me? Someone has been diligently rotating his grazing using the electric white tape.

Nick-nack barks once from her kennel under the broody pine. I wish she was here tangling herself up in my legs, waving her homecoming flag for me. I realise Mum would've made Patrick tie her up. She wants no distractions from the theatre she's performing now at the gate. She seems eager for her big family drama moment inside at another of her 'family meetings', sucking all the air of joy out of my arrival, filling it instead with her lost-dreams bitterness. Around her is a swirl of vindictive energy – the same that she was emanating on the day she summoned me to the kitchen to tell me I was sacked.

'You coming?' She rolls her eyes as dramatically as a Bass Strait swell.

Like a brave little boat, I push on through her giant waves of tumultuous energy. *Her patterns can no longer impact me*, I tell myself.

Walking towards her in my Irish fun and freedom clothes, there are no eagles, soaring noble and wise in the sky. Nor are there calls from the black cockatoos. Not a single hawk or falcon signals me home.

At the back porch I ask, 'Where's Paddy-whack?'

'He was on his last legs. Your father shot him. Always under my feet. Smelly old thing.'

'Wait? When? Why didn't you tell me?'

As I follow her inside, the reality of my family hits me like a boulder avalanche. I now see just how hardened these people are. How loveless. I can read their energy field now. Shrunken and unawake. They are people who choose fear and greed over compassion and gratitude. They choose to count their tainted dollars instead of breathing life into lucky stars and love. It's they who are insane. Not me. I don't see this fact with judgement. I simply see it with a raw realisation that these are the choices they have made in their lives. And I, for all of my life, have been seeking a different way of being in a different world. Except the problem is, we both exist in the *same* world. I realise with clarity, that this open-hearted, *seeing* little child within me has endured their flawed thinking all my life. Taught by them. Fed by their beliefs. Judged by them. That little girl was almost crushed by them ... *Almost*.

*

The mudroom's familiar earthy smell draws me inside to the kitchen where the bite of Mum's faux flower–scented cleaning products assaults my nostrils. Dad is sunken in his armchair looking smaller than usual, his face grey.

At his seat at the kitchen table, Patrick rises to greet me. His hair has been cut neatly, mullet gone, and he's clean-shaven. He looks thinner, gaunt even, and his sharp blue eyes set against his pale skin seem haunted. Mum cuts him down with one of her singeing looks. He sits again.

'Dad.' I move over to him, not knowing what to do. He *never* shows any affection, and it seems even a major health scare hasn't softened him to a hug or even a handshake.

'What's going on?' I ask. 'The farm? You're selling it?'

He won't look me in the eye. 'Hello to you too,' he says.

Remembering all I've learned in Ireland, knowing I hold the answers for turning the farm around, I soften my energy towards him. I need him onboard with me.

'How are you feeling? You're up and about. That's a good sign.'

He grunts in disagreement.

'Dad, just because this has happened doesn't mean it's the end of the road! Patrick and I can–'

Dad frowns. 'Oh so you've been home five seconds and you're already making claims!'

'No!'

'I'm sick because of all this.' He sweeps his hand around. 'And I'm sick because of all of you.'

Without warning a plate flies through the air, slung by Mum like a test-cricket outfielder, missing Dad's head by a hair.

290

It smashes on the wall. Shocked, I look to the broken pieces scattering on her perfect floor. Then I look to Mum's broken face while the Holstein wall clock ticks insistently.

'What's going on with you all?' I ask.

'Don't pretend, Connie,' Dad says coldly. 'You know what's going on.'

A memory of the fogged-up windows of a jiggling Volvo arrives to me.

'*She knew?*' Mum exclaims, recoiling, then turning to me. 'You knew about Raylene?'

I pause, looking to their faces: Mum's stricken, Dad's cruel, Patrick's downcast. Mine, most likely guilty. In my mind's eye, I fold my knight's visor in front of my face, shutting their negativity out. Shielded. Whole. Complete.

'Oh no,' I say, standing my ground. 'This time I'm not getting drawn into your drama. I'm not being made the family scapegoat. This is your dysfunction, not mine. I'm unplugging from you, and *don't you dare come at me* with your judgement. Do not try to dominate me. Or belittle me. Or gaslight me. Or use me as an excuse for all your miseries. Those days are done.'

There's no shortness of breath, no flaring vision, no sweating palms or pumping heart. Instead, self-love and compassion swell within me, along with a certain steady pulsing power. As I stand amid this sad, angry, misguided family, Patrick adjusts his body uncomfortably in his seat. Dad looks momentarily startled too, not so much at what I've said, but *how* I've said it. It takes him a beat to regain his mettle.

'Well, after everything your mother and I have done for you!'

'Your *mother* and I?' mocks Mum. 'Is that all I am to you? A breeding cow? Now that you've made your bed, Finnian, with that ... desperate old slut!'

'For fuck's sake, Mary, stop being such a bitch.'

'That's enough,' I say sternly, flinching at their words.

Dad looks at all of us, with his yellowing eyes and turned down mouth. His classic manly jawline failing to reveal any of the handsomeness of his youth. 'You lot can all go to hell! I can't wait to see the back of you!'

Getting up from the chair he skulks to his bedroom, banging the door shut. He's so tortured, I wonder if his poor heart will falter again.

Mum turns to me. 'How could you? How could my own daughter betray me like that?'

'Me? Betray you? Where were you and Dad in protecting me from *him*?'

She stares at me. 'You always make everything about you.'

'I was virtually a child, Mum. A naive country kid straight out of boarding school. You were more worried about what other people thought. Not about protecting me.'

She tries to stare me down, but her face crumples. She makes a wounded sound, hurries from the room, slams my old bedroom door from where muffled howls then shred throughout the house. The clock ticks on tiredly.

'Welcome home,' Patrick says.

'Home? *Home and Away* more like. Drama, drama, drama,' I say flatly.

Chapter 44

Later that afternoon, Nick-nack and I walk behind our skyscraper cow ladies, labouring up the lane from the crackling dry paddocks for milking. As we lump over the rock and hard-pugged ground, I smell their rancid breath generated from the toxic irrigated pasture they've just ingested. Some have ringworm marring their sincere faces, some have raised warts on their dull summer coats, others have sores on their udders. Many are lame. All of them have an absence held within their deep, kindly eyes. My own eyes now see them and this place so differently. Until Ireland, I'd endured this as normal enough to tolerate, too worn down to change it.

When I join Patrick in the pit, he turns and surveys me. 'Despite all the shit going down, you look good. Different. But good.'

'Thanks, brother,' I say, touching the soft pink cowgirl bandana Grainne gave me to wear in my hair. 'How are you about all this? The sale?'

He looks at me openly for the first time in years. 'Gutted,' he says, then swipes his large dairyman hands down over his face to erase emotion pooling in his eyes. 'It's been hell, Connie.'

His voice is thin, the energy of his pain clutching in around him.

'I can imagine.'

We get busy with the cows. With the computer. With the cups. With the hosing. With the monitoring. And my heart longs for Ireland. I can now see the ways of the Donovans' dairy in here, in this very milking parlour. When cow 1761 – Five Teats – comes onto the platform I say, 'I'm relieved Dad hasn't culled her yet.'

Patrick blasts some manure away from the railing. 'Me too. She's a nice cow.'

'That's the first time I've heard you say a kindly thing about them, Patrick.'

He looks at me darkly. 'Since you left and this whole Dad roots Raylene fucked-up-ness exploded, I've seen how I've been acting like a prize tool. Chatting with you and Amber, watching that farm in Ireland on the live cam – it's made me realise there's a whole world outside of this place away from Mum and Dad's shit, and I don't have to buy into it.' He gestures around the dairy. 'I'm not cut out for this. Not with them anyway.'

Patrick lifts his cap and runs his palms over his clipped hair. 'I've been a prick of a brother.'

'Well, it takes two. I've been a smart-arse sister. And a bit of a fruit loop.'

'Who wouldn't be with that pair? They've been at each other all our lives. I used to be jealous of kids at school who had divorced parents. I'm relieved the shit's hit the fan. But to be honest …' His voice chokes. 'I just don't want to lose this farm. I don't want to leave it. What the hell else would I do?'

'We. What the hell else would *we* do,' I say.

We hug. It feels awkward. But necessary. There's a silent understanding that as kids, both of us have had to behave in the way that we needed to, in order to survive Mum and Dad's toxic, anger-filled marriage. The endless push of the farm. The constant complaint about money. It was always about lack, not prosperity, even when natural abundance was all around us. If only Mum and Dad could've seen it, they would've shaped our lives so differently.

Patrick's phone buzzes. Our togetherness moment in time passes, but I know it's pivoting us both in a new direction. He looks down to the screen and a smile awakens his face.

'How are you getting signal?' I ask. Patrick gestures to the eastern wall of the dairy.

'New tower. On Knocklofty's hill. Only went up last week. You still can't get signal anywhere else on the farm. Just the house, and the cottage on the northern edge of the veranda. But the internet now works in the dairy, mostly.'

He chuckles, looking at the screen. 'Amber,' he says holding up his phone.

'Amber?'

He shows me a photo. I squint.

'What is it?'

'It's someone's toe they had to cut off at the hospital last night.'

'Oh! Gross!'

The phone beeps again. He reads it.

'She's asking if my lovely sister's home safe.' He hooks an arm around the back of my neck in a gentle headlock. 'Smile! Thumbs up.' He snaps a selfie then presses send.

'She's a right craic,' I say.

'That indeed she is,' he says in a perfect Irish accent, clearly learned from Amber herself.

'So, it was you who's looked after Traveller so well?'

Patrick slides me a glance. 'Amber made sure I did. Bossy bloody nurse.'

I smile. 'Thanks.'

'No wuckers,' he says.

'I reckon it's time for us to get bossy now too. With those two.' I flick my head in the direction of the house. 'We're adults, for crying out loud, Patrick! They've kept us behaving like kids. What are we gunna do?'

'You're the brainbox, Connie. We'd better think of something, quick. Dad's already looking for buyers for the herd, and that lady Dawn, from the real estate, has *three* foreign investors interested in the place.'

'Three!'

The reality of the farm being snapped up by people detached even more than my father from the land's sacredness hits me, along with a surge of overwhelm. 'Seriously?'

'Yup,' Patrick says gravely. 'One Canadian and Chinese consortium, another Chinese company, and some Kiwi corporates are kicking tyres.'

Tears surprise me. Grandad and Granny M, and Uncle Dougie and Auntie Sheila come to mind. Our roots. Our family. Our home. 'No! We can't allow this to happen.' I search his eyes desperately.

Patrick looks at me concerned. 'Are you having another one of your ... you know ... *episodes*. Is it a Doctor Cragg thing?'

'No!' I laugh, realising I'd forgotten all about Doctor Cragg. 'But tomorrow, you and I will head into Dawn's office and hatch a plan to stop the sale!'

'Tomorrow?' Patrick echoes. His brow knits. An impatient cow kicks. 'I haven't told anyone yet ... but tomorrow after the morning milk, I'm leaving for Ireland.'

*

That evening as I ride over the brittle grass to Larry's, Traveller gets up on his toes. He's been well fed in my absence and with his gleaming coat he's behaving like a green-broke. I have to check him gently with his nose band to slow his jog to an amble. It's as if he's in a rush to get over the river to Larry. Then I realise it's me who is in a rush. So I breathe, land my mind in my body, and the horse settles.

As we near the broken bridge, I think to myself that nowhere in Dawn's harsh real estate lingo was the mention of the important things about this place – the value of the roar of the winds, the rich call of the birds, the abundant songs of frogs. The hum of silver-winged insects in summer from the bush. The medicine of the river's music as it tinkles in dry times and roars during flood.

Nor does the price factor in those echoing remnants of my great-grannies with their hardship and wisdom. The money doesn't regard the value of the once thriving Indigenous sisterhood and brotherhood who lived in this very place. The original land-keepers are not just sorrow shadows in the deep fern glens of the river bends. They are not gone … I can feel their presence. Our ancestors are still here. They remain forever upon the land in another dimension, a land of plenty where calendars were told by the rise and fall of the sun and moon, the sweep of stars and the plants, quietly moving along with the seasons.

As I invite Traveller into the rushing shallows, I can picture in my mind's eye the women seated on the riverbank, all grounded around a fire, smiling with love at the chubbiness of their babies, when money was a far-off distant figment of modern man's imagination. And time respected them. But not now. This time, my time on Earth right now, seems like civilised brutality. On the other side of the river, I ride on towards Larry's track and soon find him standing amid tall corn like a benevolent scarecrow from a storybook. Relieved to see him, I return a smile.

'Ahh! She's home!' he says, weaving through the maize and stepping over rows of early summer beans. I notice the expanded garden now runs the full length of the apple-pickers shed and curves beyond it. It's bursting with fruit and vegetables as butterflies flit over flower-sprinkled greenery. It's a living, thriving feast. At the fence, Larry holds up two corn cobs either side of his face. 'Tell me about your trip. I'm all ears!'

I laugh, and Traveller nods his head as if he too shares the joke. Nick-nack trots to him, her plumed tail painting joy between us.

'It was awesome, thanks.' I point to the expanded garden, complete with a new possum-proof fence. 'I like what you've done.'

'It wasn't so much me. Those clowns you sent to check on me kept wanting to pitch in. Help in exchange for my vegetables. The skinnier one reckons you've put him off commercial cauliflowers for life. And the dark-haired one can't keep his hands out of the soil. And that other one – Megan – she's always bringing cakes and biscuits up to me. Her shelter women keep turning up and insist on helping too. And kids! So many kids. There's a cast of bloody thousands coming and going, thanks to you.'

He says it like he's grumpy, but I can see the light in his eyes – an altered man to the one I'd left behind.

After I slide off Traveller and set him to graze about the cottage, Larry and I meet at the back porch. Kicking off our boots, Larry teases, 'I heard you had a good trip. Literally.'

'How did you hear?'

'How could I not? Your vegan friends had it all over their phones. You – a bloody animal activist!'

'Well, I am in my own way.'

He looks at me knowingly, and his eyes crinkle as he smiles. 'Same.'

Inside, the kitchen is enlivened with ultra fresh fruits, vegetables, plants and flowers, gathered in wooden crates lined up on the central table.

'That's the next order for Megan's lot and the happy chappies,' he says, gesturing to boxes. He reaches for the kettle. 'Word's getting out about how good the cafe's fresh tucker is, so they order more and more each week. Even after I showed them a thing or two about soil and took them up to meet Glennon and the gang. Set them straight.'

'How'd they take that?'

Larry shrugs. 'Not good at first. Went silly over the piglets. But now they're slowly getting the full picture of how Mother Nature likes to run the show, and how the natural world turns. They're starting to see the whole.'

I glimmer from the inside out, until I remember why I've come. 'Have you heard about over there?' I ask, flicking my head in the direction of Sunnyside.

'Heard what?'

I swallow, the words like rocks in my throat. 'That Dad's selling the farm.'

Larry doesn't seem to react, instead busying himself with the tea, his back to me. I press on.

'I was going to stay in Ireland, but Mum called to say Dad had a heart attack.'

Larry stops mid-pour.

'He's fine now. I think. Recovering.'

Larry's pouring resumes.

'But … the farm's on the market. They're selling.'

'Debt got too much for him?' Larry asks tightly.

'Well, maybe? But not exactly. It's because he … um … cheated on Mum. With Raylene. So it's over. Mum's pulled the pin.'

In the gap of silence, I feel a chill run through my body. Even without seeing his face, I can feel Uncle Larry's upbeat demeanour dissolve into a black angry swirl in the room. He holds the kettle aloft.

I speak into the frosty gap, 'I thought you might know what to do?'

Thumping down the kettle hard, sizzling water splashes wickedly into the air. Larry propels himself from the bench, slamming through the side door towards the packing shed.

'Come with me,' he orders angrily over his shoulder.

Following him gingerly as he storms into his art space, he reefs a painting from the wall, sending the hook flying and panicking dust particles into the air. There's a furious gleam in his eyes.

'See this? See her?' he demands, turning the oil of the woman to me. He flings his arm out to point over the river. 'See that? See that farm? See Her? *She*, the land?'

I nod, mute.

'Your father is the reason things are like they are.'

He holds the painting so close to my face the lumpy oils blur. 'Annabelle,' he says forcefully, then turns the painting to himself. 'Annabelle,' he repeats more tenderly, staring at her image.

'We were going to take on the farm after we got married. Your grandparents had it all sorted, but he …' Larry jabs a finger towards the other side of the river. 'He waited until I'd gone away to some bigwig art prize on the mainland. Jealous prick.'

He sets the painting down, glancing at me. 'He got full of grog one night and tried his luck with Annabelle. She told him no. She tried to fend him off. He wouldn't listen. Forced himself, y'know.'

I look to him in horror, but his eyes remain downcast to the wonky floorboards.

'It broke her, knowing he'd ...' He struggles to find the words. 'He'd violated her. Pig of a man. A pig with women.'

My mind rushes, trying to catch up with what Larry is revealing. 'You mean, Dad ... *raped* her?'

Larry's eyes ghost upwards to the other paintings on the vast walls and he presses his fingertips to his eyes. 'I told her we'd get through it. But there was no coming back for her. She said she could never get over it. The shame of it ... my own brother. So, eventually she left. And then ... then a few years later, she took herself ... off. *Away.*'

He goes to the drawer and takes out the yellowing newspaper clipping from the pile I'd found earlier. He hands it to me. I read it. That a woman had been found drowned in a loch in a freezing place in Scotland. Annabelle. The tragedy of a beauty, an artist, a love story gone wrong, all bleak and black. Suicide.

Reaching out, I touch Larry's arm, thinking he will pull away, but instead he turns to me and he folds into my arms. As I hold him, his body lets go. Shuddering. Juddering. Until sobs come. Years of pain, up and out. Tenderly, I lead him to his painter's stool, and sit him down. He speaks to the floor in a rasping whisper.

'She was my life. She and I were going to take farming and art to a whole new level. Your dad broke someone so beautiful. Just because he could. Then he set about breaking the land. I've watched her slowly dying, for years. Watched him desecrate another beautiful being.'

As he says the words, my heart chills. My father. Professor Turner. The energy of them. Those men. One and the same.

Chapter 45

The next day, pre-dawn it's already unseasonably warm and I know the flies will be buzzing after the sun gets up. Numb from Larry's revelation yesterday and knowing Patrick is leaving today, I resolve to take myself gently as best I can.

'Top of the mornin' to ye!' I call over the sound of the pumps, entering the dairy. Patrick already has the first of the cows up and Dean-O is in full force promoting his Do it with Dean-O competition. Nick-nack shines her God-dog eyes at Patrick and wags her tail.

'All packed? Excited?'

Patrick nods and points to the leopard-print case waiting at the dairy office door.

'You're not taking that thing?' I laugh.

'I sure am. Amber says it has its own fan club back in Ireland. I can't wait to get outta here. Shit's getting really twisted round here!'

'You sure you don't want me to drive you to Lonnie airport?'

'Nah,' he says. 'Got me mates lined up. You'll have to go see Dawn yourself. See what's goin' on.'

'Me? Today? Might leave that little meeting until after I've slept.' The computer releases the head bails and the cows back out, seeming so large to me now I reckon they need reverse alarms, like trucks. Patrick jet-blasts a pool of noxious manure on the concrete, as the auto-gate triggers, letting more cows up.

'Maybe we can put in an offer to buy the farm?' I continue.

'Us?' Patrick pulls a face. 'As if we'd be able to afford it and as if Mum and Dad would let us buy it! It's already *waaaay* up in the millions now the corporates are on to it. Dreamin',' Patrick says as he checks the computer data.

'Yes, Patrick. Dreaming. That's what it takes.'

He shakes his head. 'There's no way.'

'There is a way. The happy chappies would be on board. Megan has a battalion of women at Verenda. They're already enlisting themselves into Larry's land army. Keener than mustard. Then there's Nancy Fairchild.'

'Who?'

'A businesswoman I got to know in Ireland. A woman with fancypants connections. She helps people who have lots of spondoola to choose ethical investments. We could ask her? Crowdfund or something? Set up a co-op? Form a community collective? I dunno, but I do know. And she'll know. You know?'

'No I don't know. Connie, you're forgetting,' he looks up to the clock above the office door, 'I'm outta here in two hours and forty-seven minutes.'

'So? You're visiting the Donovans right? They'll be on board to help us. Once you see the community spirit they have over yonder, and you see business booming because of customers who back them, you'll change your tune. People are loyal when they know there's truth at the heart of what they do and it's good for the world.'

'This is Lilyburn we're talkin' about, Connie. I reckon Dad's porked most people's wives over the years with his wandering willy. We Mulligans aren't too popular round here.'

'Irk! Please don't talk about Dad's willy!'

'You know he was on the job with Raylene when he had the heart attack? That's how they got sprung. Raylene called an ambo out into the bush – so Mum caught him with his pants down. Literally.'

'Enough!' I say covering my ears.

We continue working in silence, me trying not to think of Dad's willy, but I can tell Patrick is ruminating on what I've said about the Donovans and Nancy holding keys to retaining the farm. After a while he indicates in the direction over the river. 'What's he like?'

'Larry? He's great. Bit grumpy but I wouldn't blame him.'

'Why?'

The story of Annabelle and Dad pours from me as we work. Patrick's cheeks turn increasingly pink as he listens, then he eventually says, 'So Dad's been lyin' to us for years.'

I shrug. 'Yeah.'

Soon the oldest, cleverest cow Norma ambles out the gate, number 63, always last onto the milking platform.

'And not just lying about his marriage ... also lying about this farm.'

'What do you mean?'

'We don't have to struggle like he makes out we do. See Miss Norma,' I say, gesturing to the departing cow. 'Dad labels her an old cull. But he's been looking at this whole farm the wrong way. She's a cow who has quietly got on with it for seven years. Never our top producer but never had a sick day in her life, and given us a calf every year.'

I turn to Patrick. 'When Norma finishes slaving for us, she gets her head chopped off. No gold watch. No send-off party. With the foreign-owned abattoirs the way they are we get nothing for her.'

Patrick pulls a face. 'What are you on about?'

'Well, customers now see how many dairy farms are just factories. That the animals are simply part of a brutal system. Dad blahs on about what a good farmer he is, but is that really true?'

Patrick rolls his eyes. 'But we do care for our cows.'

'Truly? And our land?' I push. 'Once you see the Donovans' you'll see this is no way to treat a lady.' I gesture to the old dame Norma who is trailing the herd. 'They keep their retired girls on to enjoy a few years out on grass, just doing their thing. No more traipsing to the dairy daily. Then their loved, old cows are processed on-farm as ultra-valuable aged beef for their shop. The pure foodies go nuts for it. And really, ethically, it's better, more truthful, isn't it? So why can't we do that here? Change things? Change how we think? How we see things? Be honest about what we're *really* doing to these animals and this land.'

I can tell Patrick is listening intently as he starts cleaning up the teat-dip cups, which are emanating a disturbing tang. I want to tell him how the chemical concoction he just used to wash the cows' udders is another endocrine disruptor in humans. And that the teat-wash chemicals mimic oestrogen so it ends up in our water and even landing in milk powders, like baby formula. But instead of sending my energy that way, I hold on to a vision of using Grainne's teat-dip recipe with compostable udder wipes, right here in this very dairy, in the future, soon.

'Chin up, Patrick. This shake-up may be just what we all need. You'll be in Ireland soon. Amber will take you to the Donovans'. You'll see! Times are a changin'. People are onto it, and we could be too.'

Patrick winds up the hose, now with a gentle, hopeful smile. On the radio, Dean-O begins wrapping it up too, fading out a lame 80s love song.

'That was an oldie but a goldie,' comes Dean-O's voice. 'Hang in there, because I'll be phoning up our Do it with Dean-O winner, after the neeeewwws headlines ...'

Gesturing to the radio, Patrick says, 'Ooo! The Do it with Dean-O comp!'

He reaches to turn up the volume. A stern newsreader's voice dominates the dairy.

'Yesterday's attack on a Lilyburn vegan cafe is now being handled as a police matter. Witnesses say a gang of men caused emotional trauma to patrons and the cafe owners by throwing meat and offal at diners. The accused have been identified but are evading police. More coming up in our full bulletin.'

'Bloody hell, Slugs!' I say. 'He's not helping himself.'

Patrick shakes his head as Dean-O's voice arrives with gusto into our space.

'And now to the winner of our Do it with Dean-O competition. A last-minute entry caught my eye and stole my heart. I'm about to call her now … the winner receives a night out with yours truly and a free all-you-can-eat buffet dinner at Franko's Plaza diner. Hold tight listeners while we get her on the line.'

I wince. The sound of a phone ringing comes over the radio. As he waits, Dean-O jokes wryly, 'Hopefully she's not a vegan. I love a woman who loves meat. Oh, dear. That came out all wrong.'

'Oh, for fuck's sake!' I say. 'Can we switch it off?'

'Leave it,' Patrick says batting my hand away. 'I sent in a bogus entry. It could be me.'

'You did? But how can it be you he's calling if your phone's not ringing in your pocket?' Patrick looks downcast as if he wanted the dinner with Dean-O. Eventually someone picks up.

'Hello?'

'SAND FM's DJ Dean-O here. Would that be Mary? Mary Mulligan?' Dean-O inquires. My mouth drops open. Patrick turns to me in horror.

'Yes?' comes Mum's voice.

'Holy fuck,' says Patrick.

'Are you ready to do dinner with *meeeeee* at Franko's Plaza Diner?' asks Dean-O.

'Oh, oh, oh!' Mum gasps, sounding like she's orgasming over the phone. 'Yes, yes, *yes!*'

'Congratulations! Hold the line, little lady. It's song time!'

As the music blares throughout the dairy, Patrick and I remain mute, not knowing if we ought to laugh or cry.

Chapter 46

The next morning, by the time I wake, the lead cows are already making their slow procession up from the river flats, calling to the rest of the herd.

Nick-nack and I set off to my parents' house in search of Mum to see if she's coming milking. At the porch, it's so odd not to step over Paddy-whack. I wonder if they buried him, or more likely, if Dad just dumped him in the offal pit to rot down with the calves. I grimace as I cross the dog-less threshold.

Mum's not in the kitchen in her usual 'first thing' place unstacking the dishwasher, so I pass the gilded frames in the hallway of gawky-awkward, forced family studio portraits. This time, the school photos of me and Patrick fail to haunt. I look into my old bedroom, where I know she's been hiding out from Dad. The bed's made and the calf-placenta-colour cushions in place. I shut my bedroom door on a past I no longer need to revisit.

'Helloooo?' I call. Dad coughs from his bedroom.

'Just going milking. Need anything?' I call through the closed door.

'Wouldn't matter if I did,' he barks.

I lean my head on the door. This feels impossible. I inhale. 'I'll come back after then. Get you some breakfast, yeah?'

'You'd better get to and start drying off the cows.'

I feel my energy sink. Drying off the cows means antibiotics shoved into each quarter of their udders and a teat sealant. Industry standard. The old Connie looms.

'I'll stop feeding their concentrates then,' I say despondently, 'and I'll arrange the drugs.'

I now know in sixty days' time, the dairy will be still and silent with no more cows to milk. The farm may be sold by then anyway. On my way out, knowing I'll need the vet's number for the drying off, I open the office door.

There's Mum, invading Dad's space. The new internet connection must've cranked her compulsive shopper habit up a notch. I'm in no mood to stir her along about Dean-O. Nor is she giving away she's off on her daggy date. She remains with her back to me, clicking the mouse, zoning in on apartments in sunnier parts of the world, with clear skies, aqua seas and smug models showing off their sliding doors that lead onto sun-drenched balconies.

'Morning, Mum. Milking time. Coming?'

'No. I'm not,' she says bluntly. 'I'm no longer living my life for other people. As far as I'm concerned, you're all grown and now Patrick's gone, I get to live my own life. No more cows. No more kids! Movin' on!'

The vinegar in her tone tells me otherwise. She is marinating in her hurt right now but I'm not going to join her. I soften my voice. 'Well, if you are movin' on, go see Megan, Mum. She'll help you. She did for Shirley when her marriage went bung.'

Mum turns to me with fury. 'Go to see some hippy-dippy at a women's support centre? Why on earth would I go see *her*? You and your father have got me to the point where I need Doctor Cragg! I'm going insane with all this.'

'Doctor Cragg? Really? I'd steer clear of her if I were you,' I say, folding my arms and leaning on the doorway. 'At least with Megan you get cake and a laugh along with her universal wisdom – not pills and a patriarchal point of view.'

'Whatevs, Connie, whatevs!'

Patrick's clearly made an impression on her.

Leaving her in her emotional blackberry tangle, I feel compassion for her, but no sorrow and no attachment. If she's intent on unravelling this land and selling it out from under Patrick and me, so be it. She's unaware of the revolution that I'm planning in my head.

I declare to the waiting Nick-nack at the back doorstep that it's milking time. At the words, she dances before me, reminding me to judge-not as we walk down the path together, and to surrender to all the good that can come. How? Who knows? My Higher Self does. Choosing joy, I manage to retain my good vibes all through milking and resetting the fences, where the gold pastures radiate heat from compacted soils that I now know I can help heal. With optimism in my heart, it's soon time to go see Dawn.

In Grandad's old wooden garage, I find Poo Brown parked where I left him all those months ago. The car door creaks a welcome as I dive in, turn the key, engine spluttering, car shuddering. My nose wrinkles.

'Jesus, Connie, it smells like a Coles dump bin in here!' I say to myself, looking down at the flotsam of old takeaway wrappers and chewed chicken bones – the mess belonging to the diet and lifestyle of the old Connie.

I look at myself in the rear-vision mirror and see a different person looking back.

'A holiday is as good as a change,' I say to myself, before spinning tyres on gravel just for a laugh, then burning out of the farmyard, flinging stones. In the distance, the dark steel of the sea cuts a flat line with the quiet sky. Cockatoos swirl like white confetti above a giant dead grey gum. Over the top of the desolate agricultural landscape that I drive past, I layer my coloured dreams, knowing I could help heal this land. Dreams born in Ireland. Dreams that could become dust if I don't find water for them soon. I've barely had time to digest all that's unfolding on the black snake road, when Poo Brown gives a giant fart and dies. I think of the unchecked oil and water as I roll on engineless, tyres crunching to a stop on the verge.

Yanking on the handbrake, I refuse to berate myself as steam slithers from under the bonnet hissing. The steep snaking road falls away to the valley and beyond to the coast. There's nothing left to do but walk on.

Despite everything, out here in the bush, I am so, so happy. Joy-filled. Richly content. My mind is so still. *Am I on drugs?* I ask myself, wondering how I can feel this way despite the current state of play in my life. Then I realise I am on drugs! My own naturally manufactured dopamine, generated by my breath, my disciplined thoughts and the awareness that I am utterly one and part of the nature that sings around me. I am utterly whole. Utterly complete.

It doesn't last. Around a blind turn, I'm jolted out of my walking meditation to discover Slugs's ute emanating the smell of rotten meat. It's parked under a large peppermint gum on one of the few pull-over places on the treacherous road. Alongside it is a second rural rig. Like Slugs, someone's gone the whole hog – aerials, spotties, huge roo bar suited better to a Mac truck.

Must've gone for a shoot, getting more meat to chuck at vegans, I think wryly. Out of the blue, shouting rises up. A ruckus is unfolding somewhere in the bush on the steep drop below the road. Inching closer to the precariously leaning fence, I can see down to Slugs in a small grassy clearing, crouched over shielding his head with his arms for protection.

'Leave me the fuck alone! Please, guys?' He's begging, kneeling before three men who are standing above him, two pointing guns.

At first I think they're just larking about, but then I realise Slugs is terrified. My mind races – they're most likely pissed, or worse – on that ice stuff or something? I think of the useless phone in my pocket. I can't leave Slugs like this. There's nothing else to do.

Cupping my hands around my mouth, I shout, '*Police!* Freeze! Nobody move! Lay down your weapons. Place your hands on your heads.' Sure, they're lines out of a movie, but it's the only thing I can think of.

They glance up.

'Cops! Let's get outta here,' says one.

One of the shooters moves to get a clearer view of me through the scrub.

'Hang on,' he says. 'That's not cops. It's just some chick in a skirt.'

Some chick in a skirt? *Just some chick in a skirt!* I'm over it! The eruption of 30,000 years of quashing the feminine power cracks open within my ribs. The warrior woman within awakens, that brave she-knight arrives. A swamping of all the years, all the moons, all the eons of injustices lift in me. The grief, pain, torture, disregard and drudgery of women surges like a tide, filling my chest cavity with furious anger until a howl erupts.

Shamelessly, mindlessly, I clamber through the fence. Roaring, I hurtle down the embankment, sliding and slipping, grabbing at branches, angling feet sideways to slow the momentum so I don't tumble and fall. The steepness propels me downwards, so I crash through the bush arriving in front of the men in a blast of rage.

'I'll give you "some chick in a skirt",' I shout. I charge at them fiercely, shoving them away. I don't care if they have guns. I don't care if I get shot. *I am so over it all.* Ancient memories of the armies of women claim me. I shimmy my skirt at them and scream like a banshee.

'Fuck *ooofffff*!'

With a guttural she-wolf roar I cry out to the sky, to the trees, to the wind, to the water, until all the air has gone from my lungs. Decade upon decade of repressed female anger released into the men's space. It stirs horror on their faces. These guys must have never seen a woman and her fully expressed rage and I can tell it's terrified them. If I wasn't out in the bush and I was carrying on like this in public, I'd be institutionalised for my display, like so many passionate, enraged women before me have been.

'She's fucken crazy,' says one and I can hear the tremor in his voice. They turn and scamper back up the hill towards their vehicle.

Breathless, I'm left knowing that other women, on the other side of the world, have felt me roar. Chest heaving, hands shaking, I call after the men. 'And never come back!'

Slugs looks up at me with a tear-stained, shocked face from where he's kneeling. It's only then I notice what's behind him. Spread out in a row on the tufting kangaroo grass as if they've faced a firing squad, are four massive wedge-tailed eagles, dead. Beside them, five black cockatoos, the gloss of their midnight feathers capturing silver from the sunlight, claws curled, the soft yellow of their tails no longer fanning out in flight. I draw in a devastated gasp at their fallen glory, the stillness in their blank eyes.

'What the fuck have you done?'

'I didn't do it!' Slugs yells, his cheeks red, his cap skew-whiff, spittle and snot shining his face. 'I told them I wouldn't be part of it! It was those bloody new duck-shooter blokes!'

'But why?' My voice is thin and shredded as I take in the heartbreaking beauty of the slain birds.

'Them dickhead farmers in the valley said they'd buy the boys a carton if they took out the eagles before lambing. And then the arseholes started on the cockatoos … just for fun.'

'And you let them?'

Slugs's voice breaks, breath heavy. 'You seen them! They fucken pulled their guns on me.' He swipes his palm over his face, his hands shaking. 'We've been on a bit of a bender.'

'I can fucken see that. Come on,' I command.

He looks at me in agony. 'You're not gunna–'

'Take you to the police. You bet I am.'

'They talked me into some stupid shit. I'll probably go to prison.' He shakes his head ruefully, swiping his face again, merging tears with sweat. 'All that cafe crap – just so we'd go viral.'

Anger flaps its wings in my heart and gives me flight. The bird messengers, the carriers of song, hope, and seed to the land have been slain by mindless men and my fury is palpable.

'Shut up, Slugs. Get up,' I insist.

We stand shoulder to shoulder staring at the magnificent birds. Feathers so glorious, but so still.

Slugs cries openly. Like he did at school.

'C'mon,' I say, this time more gently. 'Let's get them up to your ute.'

Before we lift them, I take a few photos of them for the police, saying, 'I've had it with the blokes treating this place like a toxic tip and a war zone.' I tuck my phone away and stoop to stroke the sheened feathers of an eagle. 'They've no respect. None of them do. No respect for the soil, for the air, the water, the plants. No respect for Mother Earth herself. I'm done with it. I'm going to make some changes around here ... And you're going to help me!'

'Help you? How can I help you from jail?'

I jut out my chin. 'Where there's a will there's a way.' I haul him into a hug. 'It'll be okay, Slugs. I promise.'

He feels like a treated-pine post in my arms. I don't think anyone aside from his mum has hugged him in a long time. I feel the denseness of him, smell the pungency of his sweat and the bitter scent of stale animal blood and booze. I pull away and look into his eyes. I recognise the pain of so many, lost, in this crazy world. In silence we carry our grim cargo up the treacherous embankment, laying them gently in the back of his ute, our breath labouring from each climb.

'You over the limit?'

Slugs shrugs.

I open the passenger door and invite him in. Settling into his driver's seat, we head off towards Lilyburn with our gruesome load. I have a knowing, deep within, that from this moment on, Slugs is now fully enlisted in my land army and there's no turning back.

Chapter 47

Gearing down at the T-junction and indicating onto the highway, I notice a slim young man traipsing along the verge, his shoulders hunched under his black jacket, hands jammed in pockets.

'Isn't that the guy from the servo?' I say.

'Yeah,' Slugs says. 'It's Pie Face guy and judging from his pie face, he's one unhappy camper.'

I pull over and lean out the window. 'Aarav? Right?'

He nods, looking self-consciously at us with his divine chocolate eyes, pulling down impressive eyebrows and wiping his outstanding nose.

'Seems like you could use a lift?' I look down to his grey uniform trousers and work shoes, evoking memories of my own highway hell walk.

Aarav looks cautiously at us.

'We're not serial killers, in case you were wondering.'

An empty spud-harvest truck roars past, rattling us all. When he sees what's splayed on the ute's tray, his rich eyebrows lift in shock, backing away. 'What have you done?'

'We didn't do it!' Slugs fires.

'We're on our way to the police to report it. It's beyond awful, we know!' I add. 'Where are you headed?'

Aarav shrugs, then turns to look back in the direction of the servo. 'As far away from my family as possible.'

'Lilyburn do you to start with?'

He shimmies his head sideways in agreement, tugging open the door. Slugs swivels around to drag away jump leads and camo waterproofs to make room.

'I'm Connie Mulligan. This is my friend, Slugs Meldron.'

'Friend?' Slugs retorts. 'What kinda friend drives you straight to the lock-up.'

'Shush, you.' I grin as we merge into the traffic. 'You'll make our passenger nervous. He'll realise you are in fact a notorious criminal on the run from the police.'

'Give it a rest,' Slugs says, glancing to Aarav.

'Yes, I've seen you on the news with the throwing of the meat,' Aarav says. 'And I have seen you at work.'

'You make a good pie,' Slugs adds quickly, aiming to gloss over the meat throwing bit.

'I noticed you never tried the vegan pies?' Aarav jokes as he indicates the scope on the dashboard.

'Nope,' Slugs says. 'Don't trust what's in 'em. Plus them things would make me fart for a week.'

'So, what's your story Aarav – when you're not at work?' I ask.

'There is not much of a story around me,' he says. 'It's my family's business. So all there is is work.'

'Ah – working for family. It sucks sometimes. We're with you brother,' Slugs says kindly.

Aarav delivers a small grateful smile, then Slugs – who I swear is still slightly drunk – launches into an amusing account of all the crap going down in his life, impersonating his father communicating in broken English and sign language with Anong, and how he's become her personal manservant. By the time we're coasting off the bypass and onto the old Lilyburn road, he has us both laughing despite our distressing cargo.

'So what's got you on the run?' Slugs asks bluntly.

In the rear-vision mirror I see Aarav's expression cloud.

'My parents are expecting me to marry a girl I don't even know or like.' He leans forward, poking his head between the seats and whispers loudly, 'She is the type of person who likes the Kardashians.'

We all make noises of distaste.

'Are arranged marriages really still a thing?' I ask, surprised.

'In my world, they are. My parents say the marriage will help get the rest of her family out from India. And build bigger our business. But ...' He stalls. 'She hates my nose. And ...' He stalls again. 'And I don't like girls. Not like that.'

There's a pause. We read between his lines.

'She doesn't like your nose?' Slugs asks. 'Your nose is bloody awesome, mate. I've always loved it.'

There's more silence.

Slugs looks momentarily panicked as we take a moment to absorb what he's blurted out. 'Yes,' he begins with a little more restraint. 'I've always liked coming in to see you and your nose, mate. Why do you think I eat so many pies?'

There's more silence. I'm wondering if it feels awkward, but with a glance in the mirror, I see that from the way Aarav's face has softened, Slugs's comment is being absorbed without offence.

As we near the Lilyburn police station down near the wharf, our collegial mood drops, knowing what's ahead of us. We pull up outside the humble 70s brick building that has a no-frills state government budget ugliness to it. Inside we find Constable Tony at the desk with his cocker spaniel, Neddy, sleeping at his feet. As we approach the counter, Constable Tony lifts his portly self from his office chair, pushing up with his giant bear-like hands.

'Ah, Slugs. I've been looking for you. Come to turn yourself in, have you?'

After a brief explanation, we lead him outside, where Neddy sniffs the bloody scent. Tony shakes his head when he sees the carcasses.

'For fuck's sake, Slugs.' Hands on hips, he turns to us. 'You're in deep shit already. And now this.'

Slugs swallows nervously.

'Just last week,' Tony begins, 'a couple of clowns got caught on the mainland injecting farm chemicals into dead lambs. They killed hundreds of eagles. The stuff they used was harmful to humans too. Big charges for them – and the media storm. You've already set one off with your vegan stunt. What were you thinking?'

'I tried to stop them,' Slugs begs. 'I'd never do this. I know them birds keep the rabbits and hares in check. A lamb or two is a small trade.' He gestures at the beautiful birds, tears coming again.

I look beseechingly at Constable Tony. 'He's telling the truth. They pulled guns on him,' I add. 'It's them who need charging.'

Slugs begins to cry and Aarav sidles near to rest a comforting hand on his shoulder.

'Ease up, mate,' Tony says. 'We'll just take one step at a time. I'm afraid I'm going to have to deal with all this formally. I'll have to charge you. And you'll need bail if you don't want to stop here for the night.'

Slugs's face crumples as he looks to his boots.

'I can't be locked up. I know Mum won't have the money and Dad won't pay. He'll kill me.'

We feel his panic surging.

'I will pay the bails,' Aarav says quickly.

The young men exchange a look.

'You sure?'

Aarav nods.

'I'm gunna do the right thing from now on,' Slugs says. 'I promise.'

'We will be holding you to this,' Aarav says.

'We sure will,' I add.

*

Later, a sharp onshore breeze is cutting up the centre of Lilyburn's main street, blowing all the diners inside the Happy Chappy cafe.

Policemen in blaring hi-vis cluster in the doorway as if raiding the place.

As we pull opposite at Dawn and Dick's, Slugs slumps low in the passenger seat, pulling his cap down. 'What are the cops still doin' 'ere?'

'You've turned the main drag into some kinda Spaghetti Western,' I say, then I sing the *wa-wa* sounds of *The Good, the Bad and the Ugly* tune, half expecting the sea breeze to push a tumbleweed past. 'Slugs and his steak and lentil shootouts.' Firing a few finger pistol shots, I add some daggy *ka-pow-pow* bullet sound effects. 'Go ahead, vegans. Make my whey! Get it? Dairy/ vegan pun. Make my *whey*!'

I thump Slugs's arm.

Aarav catches the Spaghetti Western wave with a very good Clint Eastwood impersonation. 'I tried bein' reasonable. I didn't like it.'

It prompts Slugs to smile.

Satisfied he's cheered, I say, 'Now, I'm going to see Dawn. Then afterwards we can grab a bite.'

Slugs glances at the cafe. 'No way!' he says.

'Yes *whey*,' I pun. 'You can't hide forever.'

'I'm not hidin', I just don't like their tucker. And I reckon what them vegans say about meat is bullshit.'

'So you're saying massive cattle feedlots supplied with fossil fuel–hungry genetically modified grains or fattening animals on sprayed crops and noxious monocultures for cheap meat isn't bullshit too?' I ask. 'As long as everyone is shunting animals and plants along corporate timelines and making money and people can drive through and get fries with it, who cares!'

The tension of the morning is winding me up. 'Let's all just keep eating, drinking and not thinking! If we don't band together and change the way we grow food here, we're all up shit creek under a toxic cloud. Vegans, omnivores, carnivores, giant bores.'

I realise the old Connie is back in the ute and my monologues are not helping, so I pause and breathe and ask her to leave.

In the space, Aarav pipes up. 'In India my family were tanners of the cattle hides. It was a small family business – in a place where the cows are sacred – so it was done slowly. Honourably. But my uncle sold to a big company. Now it is greedy. And very dirty. And bad.'

'But isn't leather better than poxy plastic shoes that won't rot down for a bazillion years,' Slugs counters.

'Too hard basket for today,' I say reaching for the door handle. 'I'll leave you two to it.'

When I get out, Slugs is looking wistfully at the seascape. 'I love doing my own tanning. It's the best.'

'You do?' Aarav replies, his face lighting. 'When I was a boy, my uncle used to teach me.'

As I leave Slugs and Aarav to talk skins, I marvel at what looks like the most unlikely of friendships made in heaven. Their energy is so bright combined I almost need to dive into Mr Crompton's for some sunnies. Then I remember the real reason I came to Lilyburn today. To fight for my family farm.

Chapter 48

As I walk into Dawn and Dick's Real Estate Agency the electric door buzzer zaps the air. The front desk is unattended so I ding a silver bell.

Dawn's cigarette-shredded voice comes from the hallway. 'In a meeting! With you in a minute.'

I look about the office. It's a boring space. Tidy. Unimaginative. I wonder where the Dick part of Dawn and Dick has got to? There's two austere chairs but I'm too keyed up to sit. While I wait, a print on the wall catches my eye. It's the Great Western Tier mountains appearing as if floating in cloud. I could point out the photo to Dawn and say that *all* land is sacred and would she reconsider, but I understand that's not going to cut it with her.

Glancing at Dawn's desk, a glossy publication captures my attention. The title, *Sunnyside and Waterbright Dairy Farms* overlays a drone photo of our irrigated river flats. The prospectus has *DRAFT* and *CONFIDENTIAL* stamped over it. Looking about the empty office, swallowing nerves, I open it.

In gold type on the inside cover shines, *International Consortium – Vancouver Lucrative and Yingli Naizhan Investments (VL&YN Investments)*. There's a photo of their CEO, a spectacled man with sleek dark hair standing beside the Chinese flag, and a photo of Dawn, smiling in a power-woman red jacket and coiffured hair. She is named as Investment Project Manager.

I feel a cold sweat arrive.

Flipping over to the next page, my stomach churns.

VL&YN Investments plans to pool its available funds raised under the offer by purchasing and aggregating Australian broad acre dairy farms subject to the investment criteria under section 5.4 and will focus on diversification across vectors to help mitigate risk and earnings volatility.

What the fuck does that mean? I need Nancy here to interpret, but I think what they're aiming to do is buy up as much land as they can. And that all they care about is the returns to their shareholders, not the land, not the animals, not the water. Not the local people, or the customers who ingest their 'product' – aka industrialised food.

As I flip to the next page, there's a photo of our premier, wearing the same old scholars pin on his lapel as Professor Turner did. Reading the spiel, he's offering support and a welcome to the potential foreign investors, saying it's fantastic for the Tasmanian people.

I recall when some of the foreign-owned dairy farms were exposed in a scandal. Animal cruelty and environmental breaches were splashed over the local paper. From the photos and rumours, it was a shitshow, overstocked to buggery and cow crap running into the rivers. The pictures of the skinniest bags of bones I've ever seen still haunt me. And I know the editor who printed the article was 'let go' soon after. A bit like Doctor Amel.

On the next page the board members are lined up. Headshots of businessmen from all over the world. Not one female among them. I turn to the next page. Professor Turner stares back at me, smug and clean-cut. Sensible black-rimmed glasses and suit – his new corporate look.

My stomach rolls. I want to heave.

The headline reads: *Proposed Pharmaceutical Animal Byproducts Laboratory – Meet Our Scientific Team Leader and Geneticist, Professor Simon Turner.*

Animal byproducts! Scanning through the text, my hand involuntarily arrives over my heart. It's not just dairy farming they're interested in! They're planning to build an on-farm experimental laboratory on Raylene and David's property. A lab that not only harvests gelatine from skin, bone and tissue, but is for genetic modification development.

My brain kicks into gear. I know they use gelatine and cows' blood for stabilisers in vaccines, and they'll use the lactose and cellulose for creating binders and fillers in tablets and capsules – Big Pharma, basically, that never pay farmers for the use of those cow innards. But the experimental genetic modification bit feels so creepy when it's all tied in with human medicine and with Turner. I know how far he goes.

I run my eye down the list of products VL&YN Investments are planning. They'll use extracts to manufacture the cows' pancreas, liver and bone. They're also going to develop products from fatty and stearic acids for industrial production. They list potential affiliations with companies that produce tyres, antifreeze, asphalt, and glue in car bodies – all standard industry stuff – cheap cattle byproducts converted into profits for giant companies, but there's that vague referencing to GMO of cattle *and* human medical products. It's so well disguised, but alarm bells sound in my mind. I realise that not only is factory dairy farming fully invading Lilyburn, like the supermarket vegetable industry has, but now pharmaceuticals and genetic manipulation – potentially in humans – is here! Along with Turner ... on what will be my *former farm*.

The old me would run, but the newly emerged Connie sets the document down calmly.

'Healthy soil, healthy food, healthy people,' I whisper the mantra. The words calm me, giving me enough presence of mind to whip out my phone and quickly photograph the pages.

With a growing sense of doom, I realise maybe my parents have already gone too far in negotiations. Why would the premier be bestowing his blessing on a draft proposal if it wasn't already done and dusted? Surely Dawn would have to be in the clear from any conflict of interest if the premier's supporting the venture? But I know, after my experience in Tassie's judicial system with Turner, how the big end of town look after their own.

Sneaking along the corridor, I realise with a sinking heart it's too soon to confront Dawn. I don't have enough information.

Through venetian blinds, I spy Dawn seated at a shiny wooden table in a meeting room. Next to her is Raylene's daughter, Nikki. She is as sleek as ever and miraculously uncrumpled in a taupe sleeveless jumpsuit, her concentration fixed on whatever Dawn and she are discussing. Her timber-tall husband, Tobias, is standing near her, their baby strapped to his front in a pouch. He's jiggling up and down to soothe the child.

Seeing her rushes me straight back to childhood and my inadequacies. The impossibility of it all storms at me. The dark bird of memories around Turner rise up and nausea claims me like a swamping wave. Rushing out of the office, I find the nearest street bin and vomit violently into it. The burning in my throat and belly, the throb in my head almost unbearable.

*

'This is the stuff of futuristic nightmares,' Megan says as she scrolls through my phone reading the draft proposal. She has me seated on a couch with a glass of water and cool face washer on the back of my neck.

As she reads, I gaze out of the newly installed French doors to the garden where the gnarled old pear tree is offering a summer canopy of lush green. The leaves are dancing filtered light over the garden. Women and children drift about, pushing swings or just sitting. Many have a numb quietness to them. Some of them are here due to assaults and violent relationships. They are micro mirrors of the relationship mankind seems to have with the Earth. I try to connect with the peace of the tree for calm. Deep within though, I know Professor Turner has declared his revenge on me.

It's too much of a coincidence that he's stepped into the realm of the dairy pharmaceutical industry. Of course he'd know it's my farm and my valley that he's targeting for his big dream lab. I shudder, realising his assault continues on me.

'What can we do?' Megan asks, thinking aloud.

'I've sent the document to Nancy and the Donovans,' I say. 'Perhaps they'll have some ideas.' I was on the brink of sending the distress beacon out to Nick, but I deleted my text. Too complicated. And I'd contemplated telling Patrick, but not wanting to spoil his arrival in Ireland, I decided to leave it until later.

Slugs and Aarav are sitting on the couch opposite us, Slugs only just finished with his rant about the Tasmanian government selling us out. A handful of the women have joined us and are also on a roll of indignation.

Megan passes me back my phone. 'C'mon, you need something to eat.'

'I'm really not hungry,' I say. 'I've got to get home, start drying off the cows. Plus Poo Brown is stranded on the side of the mountain.' Jet lag swirls.

'Drying off the cows?'

'Dad said. So we can sell the herd when the property sells.'

'I wouldn't be too hasty on that one and I wouldn't be caving in to your dad's orders,' Megan says. She turns to the women who are sitting opposite.

'You like cows, don't you, Nadine? Debs?'

The women's faces light up.

'I've always wanted to hang out with cows,' says Nadine, bouncing her son Tyson on her lap, swiping his hand away from her earrings.

'Connie here needs some milkmaids.'

'Pick me!' says Nat, raising her hand and jabbing the air enthusiastically. 'I've loved it at Larry's with the animals. I want more.'

'Me too,' choruses Debs. 'I'm getting bored off my scone just hangin' about here. Put me to work.'

'Get in line, ladies.' Megan grins and pats me on my knee. 'See, Ladies Dairy Army – sorted.' She hauls me up from the couch. 'Now, food for you. To the cafe. We need to enlist the boys.'

'You too Slugs and Aarav,' I say.

Slugs looks at me.

I cock an eyebrow. 'You know you're not getting out of this one, Slugsie.'

On the street we find Shirley coming as we're going.

'Connie! You're home!' She drags me into a bosomy hug, Slugs pretending he's invisible by standing behind the tall, lean Aarav. 'You look fantastic. Frilly knickers mission accomplished, I'd reckon,' Shirley says, eyes gleaming in amusement. I can feel my blush.

'I know you're there, Nigel,' she adds dryly. Slugs steps out, head hanging like he's seven years old again.

'We've been to see Tony. Now he's just on his way to apologise to our favourite barista boys,' I say.

Shirley's eyes blaze at her son and she clips him on the back of the head. ''Bout time! Where the fire truck have you been, Nigel? Ya bloody goose! What were you thinking?'

'Mum, I'm … sorry.' Tears well and she draws him into a rough hug.

'I'm glad you're safe, but I'm gunna tear strips off ya later. Time to call it off with them duck fuckers!'

Slugs bites his bottom lip, nodding. 'Right-o, Mum.'

Shirley fixes her focus on Aarav. 'And you? I know you from the servo, right?'

He nods.

'Aarav, meet Slugs's mum, Shirley,' I say.

'What are you doin' with this motley lot?'

'Running away from his family,' Slugs answers for him.

'Well, looks as if you could do with some feedin'. I'm sure you can fit under my wing too. Now that I'm outta work, I'm looking for more lads to mother hen. Whaddya reckon?'

Aarav smiles a little nervously, but seems happy with the suggestion. Shirley takes my arm, and with that, we step off the kerb and cross the street, me filling her in about Dawn and the investment plans. As she digests the information and starts to swear like a wharfie, I feel the revolution rising. It's arriving, *becoming*, and I know all of us are headed for a rebellion, right here in Lilyburn.

Chapter 49

It's packed when we walk into the funky space of the Happy Chappy Vegan Cafe. Chic Latino music overlays the loud buzz of patron chatter. Two new staffers are scribbling orders and barista-ing with flourishes and smiles. Several police sit at one of the large tables, sipping coffee and eating pastries as if crime does not exist. From behind the wooden bead curtain bursts Fenton, carrying plates, today in denim overalls and a tight red t-shirt, looking younger now he's de-moustached. His face lights up when he sees me, calling as he passes, 'Connie! You're home! Look at you! You're glowing.'

He heads for the table of a young cool-cat couple, the type you never see in Lilyburn, sets the plates down, saying, 'Enjoy!'

When he turns, he notices Slugs for the first time and freezes.

'Don't worry! He comes in peace!' I say, holding up both Slugs's hands as if in surrender.

Slugs offers a handshake. 'Sorry for being a pissed idiot the other day, mate.'

Fenton looks to his extended hand. 'You're making alcohol the excuse?' he challenges.

'No! Shit-carted or not shit-carted, I was a dickhead. I'm really sorry.'

After a beat, Fenton reluctantly shakes. 'Apology accepted. What you did was really shitty, until it turned into the *best thing*. Look at the place!' He gestures at the throng. 'After your media stunt, we're at long last on the foodie roadmap. Plus, once the police tasted our coffee, they're all coming off the byway to get our special blends on their rounds now. Then there was Connie here who created a miracle for us.'

'Me?'

'You gave us Uncle Larry. His veggie produce is *amazing*! Next level. No more caustic caulies!'

The kitchen bell dings demandingly.

'Sorry! Gotta get that!' He dives away.

We settle into a booth being vacated by an elderly couple. Fenton reappears, clearing and wiping the table efficiently, then returning swiftly with his order pad and a smile.

'What can I get you?'

'An army,' I say.

He frowns. Megan quickly explains about the draft prospectus.

'What? A laboratory using animals in trials? Human–cow genetic experiments?' Fenton grimaces.

'We're not exactly sure just how far they're going with that. But, like the salmon industry where they've genetically fucked about with the fish, they're taking this to the next level with humans and cattle – they're playing God and line-blurring with the backing of Big Pharma,' I say. 'But if *he's* heading up the science bit, it's going to be dangerous for humanity and downright cruel on the animals. Trust me, he's done it before.'

'He?'

'Professor Turner. He's one of their main science directors.'

'No!' Fenton lays his hand across his heart as if to protect it.

'We've come to ask if you'll join us.'

Before he answers, Vernon arrives, his cheeks pink from being under the pump in the kitchen. 'Some one said *he* was in here. What the hell is going on?' He casts Slugs a furious gaze.

'Vern,' soothes Fenton, 'he's come to apologise'

'It's all very well to apologise to us, but what about the poor people yesterday. Felicity will be in therapy for years because of him!'

'Please,' Slugs says, 'I want to explain.'

Vernon folds his arms across his chest. 'We're very busy.'

'Let him explain,' I urge. 'Please.'

Vernon relents with a roll of his eyes.

'I'm sorry for what I done. I was angry,' Slugs pleads.

'Angry?' Vernon counters. 'About what? Us having a different opinion from you? Making different lifestyle choices?'

Slugs grimaces. 'I thought I was angry about the vegan thing, but now I reckon it's more about people coming here who don't get it. Don't get *us*. You mainlanders gotta see we have a Tassie culture here different from yours.'

'It's not like it's another country,' protests Vernon.

'It kinda is,' I suggest, 'if you were born here and your family goes way back, especially if you've lived off the land and the sea like many Tassie originals have.'

'It's true,' Shirley says. 'My grandad's mob, they all lived basic like. And the early white fellas too. Rich, but not with dirty money. When I was a kid we had a woodpile that made us rich. And we was rich with grains, plants, fruits, but also meats 'n' that. Plenty of meats – roo, cray, birds, fish, shellfish. It wasn't about ... what was that word them animal activists always use, Connie?'

'Exploitation?'

'Yes. That's it,' Shirley says. 'It wasn't about *exploitation* of animals. For your grandad, Connie, and Dougie's and Sheila's mob, it was about livin' with the place. About takin' only what you need.'

'It was the same for our convict rellies,' I say. 'They were displaced people, just trying to survive, so they ate what they could from the land and passed that down the line to us – make do and mend – until Dad's generation at least. He turned his back on the old ways. There *is* a different culture here with our food. But it's the corporates and the money-fixated who are the threat to the place now. Everyone wanting their cake and eating it too. Not you guys. Slugs gets that now.'

Slugs looks at the chappies with such gentle sincerity. 'Just cause I shoot and eat meat don't mean I'm your enemy.'

Shirley looks as if she will burst from pride.

'You may think I'm a dumb local, but out there in what you mainlanders call "the wilderness", is our way of life. The bush is part of me. I'm not into killing things for the sake of it. Or chopping shit down just coz. But I'm also into *not* wasting good food. And I sure as hell ain't into losing more of Lilyburn to outsiders wanting to trash the place more than it's getting trashed.'

'Fair enough,' Vernon concedes. 'Connie here was the first to open our eyes to that. Then Larry. We had no idea all the animals – birds, lizards, snakes, snails and insects – had to die for the supermarket plants we were dishing up. And that so many animals were shot to protect those crops.'

'The corporates stop at nothing to grow their bottom line,' I add. 'They don't give a toss about community. I'm talking all community ... from a soil-microbe community, to a wallaby community, to a town community.'

'Yeah,' Shirley says. 'Them big bastards don't care. Barry's closed down. Sellin' the trucks. All them years we worked on the milk run, now gone. The international companies have taken over. They got tankers comin' from the mainland next week and a dehydration plant goin' in at Devonport so they can ship milk powder overseas. And everyone round here's gettin' sicker. Government's sellin' us out. It's about bloody time we all said somethin'! Did somethin'!'

'So true!' Fenton says emphatically.

'Well I'm in,' says Aarav. 'In my country, farmers die from suicide every day because of the chemical companies. And every day nearly two million people are going hungry. We all have to do something!'

'Yes we do!' Slugs says.

'So what I'm hearing,' I say, spreading my hands on the table, 'is that we're all on the same page. We all want to claim our food sovereignty – be in control of our own food systems and environment. But we need to do it intelligently and with a powerful kindness. So the bottom line is, are we joining forces? Are we going to try and not just stop this sale ... but create something amazing for Lilyburn?'

I look at their faces, all ignited with passion, all nodding, all replying a resounding, 'Yes!'

*

Twenty minutes later, with a bellyful of pumpkin turmeric soup made from Larry's very own garden, I find myself driving in Shirley's car through the lemony light of a blustery sea-breeze afternoon. We are chattering like galahs in the car, covering as many potential land-reclamation strategies as there are guideposts passing by. Aarav and Slugs follow behind in Slugs's ute on our way to give Poo Brown a tow home.

When our odd convoy rolls into Sunnyside, Nick-nack dances and barks a welcome. Getting out of the car at Mum's wishing well, Shirley folds her arms, frowning.

'That bloody car of yours, Connie. No point fixing it. It'll make a nice home for a tethered goat one day I reckon.'

'I'll just have to borrow Patrick's ute, I suppose,' I say, knowing Mum will be royally pissed to see my car parked where we've left it.

'Oh? What's going on?' comes Mum's voice now. She's tottering down the path in her white strappy Melbourne Cup shoes and is dressed to the nines in an orange floral frock, hair pouffed higher than normal.

'Car broke down,' I say.

'Oh, that's no good, dear. Hello Shirley, nice to see you. Boys.' She nods a greeting.

I look at her incredulously. She's not hammering on about leaving the car near the house, or sneering a snide comment to Shirley about Barry's new Thai wife, like I *know* she would. Or quizzing Aarav about why he's here, and asking pointedly where his 'people' come from.

As I help Aarav detach the snatch strap from the tow ball, I say, 'We'll shift it later.'

She waves my words away. 'All in good time.'

I frown, puzzled. A kookaburra laughs. A cow calls from the valley below, setting off the others in an impatient chorus.

'Oooh, the girls are restless. Time for milking,' she says, widening her eyes at me.

'Clearly you're not today?' I reply, nodding at her outfit. 'You look very non-dairy ... very nice.'

'Yes! Thank you!' she says, smoothing down the front of her dress, her eyes bright. Nick-nack barks. A car engine can be heard winding up the mountain. Mum breathes out, more excitement than nerves, and sets her purse in the crook of her arm.

'He's here! I don't know when I'll be home. Late I'd say. Toodles.' Then she walks a little way off to wait. Along the drive, a sleek powder-blue Mustang convertible glides into Sunnyside. Top down, music throbbing as the sound of 'The Final Countdown' approaches. My nose involuntarily scrunches at the hideous 80s sound.

'Dean-O?' I ask.

As he cruises nearer, Mum flips a Grace Kelly scarf on to cover her hair, and slides on her giant Dior replica sunglasses. From behind the wheel of the imported left-hand drive, DJ Dean-O gives us a Top Gun salute.

He gets out, kisses Mum's hand, does a little bow, then opens the door for her.

'Don't expect dinner!' Mum calls as she gets in, then waves as if she's setting off on a luxury oceanic cruise. 'I'm doing it with Dean-O tonight!'

Dumbfounded, we watch as the car drives away.

'Well I'll be buggered,' Shirley says.

'Stone the crows,' I add.

'You're shittin' me,' Slugs continues.

'That's your mother? Going off with the DJ Dean-O? Oh *ghanta*!' Aarav says.

Our gobsmacked ogling is interrupted when Dad comes rioting down the path in his slippers. I'm relieved Paddy-whack is no longer with us. By the look on Dad's face, the old dog would be getting a kick in the guts.

'Where's your mother?' he barks. Dad doesn't seem to register that there's others here. Nor does he seem to have come to terms with the fact that lowering stress is a major factor in heart care. He frowns down the road.

'Fuck them,' he mutters, the public version of himself as the upstanding local dairy farmer absent. The hair that roams over his ears is sticking out at all angles and his dressing gown is undone, revealing a work jumper over a striped pyjama top, and grey stained trackie daks.

Limply I point in the direction of the road. 'She went that way.'

I can tell he's more furious than hurt. Huffing, he swings around to head back inside.

'Nice to see you up and about, Finnian,' Shirley calls after him, turning to give me a sympathetic look. 'So things are pretty crook around here too, then.' She draws me again into her signature bosomy hug.

'Boys, you go inside, see what you can find to make us some dinner,' she says in a non-negotiable tone. 'Connie, I'm comin' to help you milk.'

'Go inside there?' Slugs protests, glancing at the house like it's a vasectomy clinic.

'We're an army now,' his mum says. 'Armies take over places. We're taking over. Isn't that right, Connie?' She grins at me, winds her arm in mine and we set off. It's milking time.

Chapter 50

A few hours later, our work done, the smell of curry emanating from the house leads Shirley and me home. Nick-nack trots in front of us, her nose tipped in the air as if on a string tied to the aroma. It's so delicious, saliva swims in my mouth.

When we enter the house, it's like a different home. Aarav has a tea towel over his shoulder, laughing as he lifts a lid from Mum's big pot, stirring the contents with a wooden spoon. Slugs is busy setting the table. Rice is bubbling in the cooker. I glance up at the wall to see what time it is. It's something I'd practised all my life, to gauge how late I was and how much trouble I'd be in. But tonight I realise the clock has stopped.

As I arrive at the table of an entirely new family, I watch the collage of colour and fun swirl in the room with Slugs, Shirley and Aarav here. When I sit in Dad's chair, head of the table, I feel like I'm committing sacrilege, but my anxiety is short-lived. The curried lamb and rice melts in my mouth. Nothing has ever tasted this good at this table. Ever.

Soon ice cream and Larry's raspberries pilfered from my cottage kitchen are plonked down in front of me, like Christmas has come early. Slugs and Aarav are animatedly talking cricket, from Big Bash to Tests to IPL. Shirley continues to debrief me about her disastrous nano-second on Tinder.

'Made me toes curl and me pubes go grey, seein' the stuff on there! They can have their hook-ups. I'll stick to me chooks!'

'Hey Mum,' Slugs says, waving his spoon her way, 'speaking of your chooks, tell Connie about what you're thinking of doin' next year.'

'Well, since the business and Baz have gone, I'm going to start "Shirl's Cock in a Pot Show" and put it on that boob-tube, or whatever it is you young people watch on the computer.'

'Your cock in a *what*?' I ask, face scrunching.

'Pot!' Shirley laughs. 'It was Debs' idea, you know, the preggers girl from Verenda. I love raising me chooks, but I get all these annoying little rooster fuckers in the process. So, every so often I put a few of them in the pot.'

'Better than them getting dumped on the roadside like dickheads do nowadays,' Slugs pitches in.

'And better than the munted ones you eat from KFC, Nigel,' she adds flatly. 'Debs wanted to learn how to, you know, "do 'em in". So she came over and helped. She did a great job. Didn't upchuck once at the guts bit. Got right into it. I hadn't laughed that much in years. She videoed a bit of me, you know, doin' my thing. And it went influenza – you know, viral.' She chuckles. 'It got us to thinking. She wants to start up a series about it! Starring me! A food series on what tucker we throw away, but could eat instead. And me veggie garden. I love me garden.'

'Yep! Mum's gunna do it!' Slugs adds proudly. 'Aren't ya, Mum ... teach people how to kill 'em kindly. Then recipes and stuff. Have others on it – like me and you and Aarav.'

'Yeah, and share what I know about chooks.'

'And cock,' Aarav adds innocently and we all laugh.

With our laughter comes a vibrant energy blaze that seems to fill the room. I realise collectively, creatively, just how powerful we are. We are outshining the old ways and finding new paths. I smile, just as my phone buzzes.

'It's Devlyn!' I read his message. 'Aww, look! A dot-point strategy on how to dry off the cows without having to use those chemical nasties.' My phone beeps again with a video clip he's sent. I press play and we watch him being the cow king, revealing all his cow wisdom and insight into udder health.

'Oh those Irish accents.' Shirley swoons. 'I could quite get used to having a Baileys in bed with that! He's worth a bit of carry on with. Must get him on me new show!'

She elbows me and I flush, thinking of one-time Irish Nick. As we clear the plates, clattering and chattering and roaring with mirth, I sense Dad's fury emanating from the bedroom. I'm not entertaining that old obligation to soothe him. It's up to him to deal with his own stewing anger and it's up to me to be the container of my own energy.

'Pipe down, would you?' Dad says now, surprising us, his face haggard.

'Fun police has arrived,' says Shirley, flicking a tea towel in his direction. 'You could've brought your tray in with you, Finnian. Ya lazy git.'

Dad flares a look back. I know she's pissed he's selling us out. And he's pissed there's a woman challenging him in his own home.

Before the verbal fire ignites, the mudroom door swings open and in walks Raylene. She's wearing a striped navy top and white pants like she's going on the *Love Boat*. Except from the look on her face, there's no love sailing in her seas. She looks us all over, puzzled at the invasion of Mum's kitchen with such a motley lot. She sniffs the air.

'Smells like a refugee camp in here.'

I almost reel back from her racist toxicity.

'Finnian,' she says, ignoring her chance to berate me about the Global Genetic trip. 'A word. Outside. Now.'

Dad, caught in his daggies, turns pink, does up his dressing gown and attempts to smooth down his side hair. Raylene turns on her heels and marches outside, Dad following like a little kid bracing himself for a belting.

Soon a car engine roars. When Dad doesn't return to the house, and with the dishes done, Shirley shrugs. 'We'd better get on and get home. Just so you know, Megan sent me a message. Nat and Nadine are rostered on for milking time in the morning.'

I feel the spread of stars across my skin. The old Connie would normally protest about such help ... but not anymore. We are on a collective mission.

When I show them out, I gasp. Dad is slumped at Mum's wishing well, lying on the gravel like a pile of old clothes.

'Dad?' I call running out of the gate, the others following.

Hearing my voice, he pushes himself up from the ground to sit and sway as if he's drunk.

'She's left me. She's gone!' He sobs, head in hands.

I look down the drive to where Raylene's just whizzed away, then to the skies, asking for strength. It's disconcerting seeing this stone wall of a man crumpled on the ground.

Shirley stoops. 'Get up. Get your shit together, Finnian. What did you expect from someone like her?'

He glares at Shirley but gets up, steadying himself on her shoulder. I step in and take his weight.

'C'mon, Dad, back inside.'

'You all right, Connie?' Slugs asks pointedly.

'Yes. I'll take it from here,' I say.

'Call us, if you need,' Shirley says. As she hugs me, she whispers, 'Bide your time.'

Reluctantly, they leave me there with my sullen, broken father.

'C'mon,' I say, softening my tone, leading him back along the path. 'It's never as bad as you think. You just need to come inside. It's all good.'

He flinches away from me. 'Don't treat me like I'm some kind of invalid. I don't need your help,' he sneers.

'Yes, Dad, but maybe I need your help.'

He gives me a sideways glance, his blue eyes illuminated madly in the sliding light of the day, irises pinpricked black.

'Help *you*?'

'Yes, Dad. Patrick and I don't want you to sell. You're not only selling our family farm but you're also inviting Turner into our space. *Here!* Why would you do that to me, Dad? *Why?*' My voice is shredded with hurt. 'What sort of father doesn't protect his own daughter?'

Pink galahs shuffling under the silo squawk, as if sensing the conflict between us.

Slowly, like a bear coming out of hibernation, he stands to his full height beside me. For a blissful moment I think he's moving to hug me, but instead, he staggers a bit, leans on the porch and says coldly, 'Everyone's gotta learn to look out for themselves in this life. You're on your own, Connie. I was done with you a long time ago. You crossed the line and you betrayed me,' he says.

'Betrayed you?' I gasp. 'You abandoned me! What about what you did to your own brother? And Annabelle.'

An eagle soars above us. Then another. A pair. I find my voice. 'I know what you did to Annabelle.'

Shock registers on his face for a microsecond. 'What would you know? You've only heard his side of the story.'

'Oh no I haven't. Patrick and I have heard your side for years. It's all lies. You've based everything on lies, Dad. It's time the truth came out!'

'Truth, huh? Do you want some truth, do you, Connie? Well then, here's some truth ...' He pauses, then with a coldness that chills my soul, says, 'The truth is that Larry is your real father.'

The words hit me. The world around me flares. Galahs scatter up into the blue, as if shrieking indignation.

Dad delivers the last blow. 'Didn't he tell you about the revenge root he had with your mother?'

Satisfied, he turns, and goes into the house, slamming the door.

*

Curled up as small as I can in Granny M's chair, my mind spins. Larry is my *father*? My dad *is not my dad*? My memories run in reverse, winding back in time. Everything about my life starts to fall into place.

Dad's looks of chilling disdain. Mum's cold bitterness towards me. Had I arrived into the world with my tell-tale dark hair and Uncle Larry's eyes, exposing Mum's 'indiscreet' encounter? Dad must've known then. He used Mum's dirty secret as power over her for the rest of their marriage. Now I understand the misalignment with this family.

Nick-nack has given up trying to cajole me out of the chair, lying listlessly at its base, her eyes shut but the dabs of her tri-colour eyebrows giving her the appearance of alertness. I'm not sure how long I've stayed in this stare-into-space state, but my phone buzzing jolts me out of it. I head outside to the veranda where I'd left it in range of the signal.

It's now almost dark, plovers giving their last calls of territorial claim down on the flats. I grab up my phone. Patrick's WhatsApping me. The reception's glitchy, but there emerges the faces of Patrick and Amber. Northern Patrick ducks his head into shot too. They swing the phone to capture Captain sitting at their feet. My heart glows seeing them together at The Farmer and the Folly.

'Hey!' they all chorus, smiling as bright as the moon that is lifting here in the indigo sky.

'Hi,' I quaver. My Patrick instantly knows there's something wrong.

'He hasn't hurt you again, has he?' he asks, his smile fading.

A sob escapes me.

'Connie,' soothes Amber. 'What's happened?'

I look to the moon, willing the strength to speak it out loud. 'Dad just told me the truth.'

'The truth?' Patrick prompts.

I can feel my bottom lip quiver, scrunching my eyes to find my voice.

'Hello half-brother,' I whisper, looking at Patrick, before my face crumples in tears.

'What?' Patrick urges.

'Breathe, Connie. C'mon, love,' Amber encourages.

'Apparently, according to Dad, um, Finnian, Larry is actually my father.'

'What? Uncle Larry is your dad? He ... with Mum?'

'Yes.'

'*Faaaark*,' exhales Patrick. Amber settles a hand on his shoulder.

'Oh Connie, that's shite!' she says.

'Kinda explains things, though,' Patrick says.

'Sure does.'

Amber leans close to the camera. 'Connie, you're in shock. Make yourself a cup of tea with sugar, or honey and lemon, then off to bed for you. It'll all feel more settled in the morning. We promise.'

I shrug. 'What does it matter, anyway? What's done is done. The past is the past. I still know who I am – "Connie of the Meadows and Occasional Confusions" – regardless of parental genetics!' I aim to find the funny side. But I know I'm really just trying to make them feel better.

'That's the spirit,' Amber says.

After I hang up, I look out across the valley. As the day fades to black and I look to Larry's cottage lights on the dark mountainside, the hurt of my family's lies ease, and a gap emerges in my mind large enough to let love in. Love for the new-found knowledge that *Larry is my dad*.

*

The next morning, Nat and Nadine arrive at the dairy exactly on time in their still-creased King Gee overalls, straight from the packet. Buzzing with their 'first day on the job' enthusiasm, I have no time to dwell on my double-dad dilemma. As I introduce them to the cows and the process of the dairy, I realise that with Dad absent, I can make this milking parlour my domain – at least until the land is sold. The women before me are blank slates when it comes to cows. I decide then and there to train them Donovan-style.

As the women coo gently at the cows, and I get them underway with the repetitive yet skilled nature of the work, I dig out an old CD, and instead of Dean-O I play the soothing tune of Jack Johnson's 'Better Together', as if we're all headed to the beach for a surf and a lounge around in a hammock. The girls start to gently groove. The cows ease into their mood.

I get to thinking I'm a chip off Larry's block. *I am* the artistic creator of my world. A creative, I decide I'm going to design my own movie of my life, starting here and now, property sale or no sale. Once Nat and Nadine get the hang of the work, I whip out my phone and get the women to pose, cups in hand, laughing, drawing in joy from the newly captained dairy.

I capture the moment and text, *Virgin milkmaids no more! Thank you!* and send it whooshing to Megan in Lilyburn.

She texts back a thumbs up. Then she writes, *Got a roster going with the women. Shirley up on the weekend to train Etsy and Debs. We can get Aarav and Nigel up to speed this afternoon. Free your energy up for the rebellion.*

I send emojis of gratitude. Then, looking to the giant cows lining up in the bails, I make a decision that could reap rewards – or land me in jail.

I message Slugs: *Hey. Thanks for offering to help milk. What might you be doing afterwards, late?*

Not much, he texts back straightaway.

Meet me at the back of the Ulvie basketball courts 11 pm. Wear something black.

What?

I have a plan. Step one in the revolution. Don't tell anyone.

I press send knowing his curiosity will bring him to me.

Chapter 51

After Nat's and Nadine's first milking morning, instead of letting the cows along their normal track, I block the lane with an electric wire, and open a sagging wooden gate to a southern-facing hillside. Dad had the bush block logged when I was about ten when there was a milk-price slump. The cattle are at first confused, the lead cows fussing and mooing a bit. I talk to them gently, inviting them to follow. Nick-nack chaperones.

The self-seeded re-treed hill has been holding on well over this last dry spell, thanks to the shade. There's native grasses in some patches, a lot of it rank with under-grazed phalaris and cocksfoot. Where the bracken ferns aren't taking over, the rest is getting choked with wattles, gorse and blackberries. The cattle, pliable in nature, begrudgingly accept the change, but they are so used to the monoculture flats they seem at first nonplussed being funnelled here.

However, soon they explore, rubbing on dappled gum trunks, roaming through the wattles, taste-testing plants, self-medicating with a nibble here and there. Their calls ring out excitedly around the mountains at the diversity of their new surrounds and menu.

Dad's linear thinking ruled out the block as unsuitable for the cows. He reckons bush plants would drop production and taint the milk. I reckon glyphosate and high nitrates taint the milk worse. Believing it was bad to run cattle in the bush too, I had reckoned the cattle would damage the native landscape, but looking to the thistles and blackberries, the native landscape is no longer. It needs managing now.

Based on what I've seen on Larry's side of the river, where his bushland is infrequently, periodically grazed, I now know it will do both the land and the cows good. To help the girls adjust to their new diet, I fork some hay bales with the tractor and place them on a ferny patch. Repeating the same with a silage bale.

I set the trough, check it's filling and shut the gate. Just sensing how happy the cattle are, I realise things are landing into place in this present moment. There's at least three days grazing ahead of the cattle and I know there's another unused bush run to be had further along the track after this one. There's at least two months of diverse, nutrient-dense tucker for them so I can rest the main paddocks, and there's plenty of supplementary feed on hand. I don't need to think about what's unfolding in the future. Right *now*, things are being set right.

Soon after, Traveller and I head off across the cow-empty river flats, soaking in the sounds of the river, swollen overnight from a surprising summer storm. My mind is like the incessant river … it wants to flow fast and snag and tangle itself on whatever grievance wants to bubble up: Turner's involvement with the buyout, the farm sale, Mum and Dad – who isn't my dad – even Nick who hasn't been in touch, despite the fact I asked him not to, and who I've not messaged. I shut my eyes, breathe, thank my mind, then ask it to stop. Instead, I pull my focus onto the swaying motion of Traveller's strolling walk, looking to the mountain peaks, sending a prayer of advanced gratitude like Mrs O'Bee taught me. A prayer of thanks that things have already worked out as they are meant to, and I am to simply *let go, and be*.

The ground is revealing tiny changes to the landscape. Teeny tiny shoots are emerging from the moist soil where water has been captured in the wheel ruts where Dad's machines and spray rigs once rolled daily. Dad would see the seedlings as weeds taking over, but I know they are just succession plants passing through temporarily as medicine for the land until we help Her correct Herself.

Just by leaving the river flats to themselves for a rest, nature will make her claim once more. I know her command and healing will come faster than we predict.

By the time I've crossed the busy river and arrived at Larry's, I'm so spellbound by the beauty and vibrancy of what Sunnyside Dairy Farm could be, I almost forget the reason I've come.

'Hello, stranger,' Larry says from under a big tattered felt hat. He's carrying a crate of green and yellow beans. 'Where have you "bean" for so long?' he jokes, tilting the box at me.

'Funny. Not,' I say, with a new style of awkward near him knowing *he's my father*. Complete with dad jokes, it seems. I slide from Traveller, winding his lead rope under his neck, setting him free to graze.

Larry nods in the direction of Lilyburn. 'How's it going with our mob in town? Did they have another party to welcome you home?'

'It was more like a political party.'

'Political?'

'We're launching an army. We're at war.'

'War?'

I fill him in on the document I saw in Dawn's. Then on Turner's involvement in the giant dairy and pharmaceutical scheme. Larry shakes his head. Then I tell him about Mum and Dean-O. He shakes his head again. I relay Dad and Raylene are busting up and he shakes his head some more.

'Dad wants the cows dried off for the sale, but I'm not going to. I've put them on the logged block to get it and them a bit healthier. A drop in production is a small price to pay in the long run. Megan's Verenda women are helping milk.'

He nods this time. And smiles. I hold myself back from telling him about my plans with Slugs tonight, in case he talks me out of it.

'So you're managing the circus over the river okay then? Good on you,' he says, then heads off with his bean cargo. It's odd knowing that I'm following my father. I soak in more details about him than I've ever paid attention to – his square-set shoulders, the weathered back of his neck, the young-man tone of his legs. He seems decades younger than when I first found him. Gentler. Happier. Open.

We walk into the shade where crates filled with fresh produce are awaiting pick-up for the chappies.

Standing beside him, I feel shy. I want to study his face closely and place his hands next to mine to read the similarities. I want to compare our feet. Our toes. Compare our eyes. Our smiles. Then I realise I simply want to just hug him and feel for the first time in my life I have a father who cares about me. Because surely, he does? He seems to?

He sets the beans down and bends to grab an empty crate. I bite my bottom lip in contemplation. There's no way I'll get him inside to get the kettle on now and dump my new-found knowledge on him with the comfort of tea. Not when he's in work mode like this. No time like the present.

'Larry?'

'Mmm?'

'Dad told me. I mean, *Finnian* told me.'

He inclines his head to one side, curious. 'Told you what?'

I draw in a deep breath. 'That you are my father.'

Larry frowns. Nerves keep me talking. 'He said that you had an affair with Mum. He made it sound so classy – a revenge root, he called it.'

Larry drops his shoulders and shuts his eyes, tilting his head backwards, groaning. 'When will that man stop lying through his teeth!'

For a moment my imagined world of Larry and me being father and daughter begins to drop like a deflating balloon. I want to desperately fill it so it can float once more.

'So, you're not my father?' I ask in a childlike voice.

He seems to register my anguish, so he sets the crate down, laying his soil-stained hands on my shoulders, then stoops to look directly into my eyes. 'I didn't say that.'

'So? What do you mean?'

'It wasn't an affair,' he says. 'I never slept with your mother.'

'Well then, who am I? The second coming of virgin-born baby Jesus?'

He chuckles sadly and shakes his head, opening his palms to me. 'Do you really want to know?'

'Of course I do!'

Larry sighs. 'Okay.'

He invites me to park my backside on the work bench, pausing before he begins.

'Your mum was desperate for a baby. She and your dad tried for a good few years for a kid, but your dad couldn't do the job.'

I think of Devlyn and the anguish it caused for him and his wife.

Well, he did insist on slinging chemicals about the place – the largest cause of infertility in males around the globe, I think, but keep the cynicism to myself.

Larry continues, 'Your mother knew what he got up to on the mainland at the Cattleman's Bar and the like at the Royal Easter Show. And the shenanigans on his dairy industry trips away. Women, y'know.'

I nod. I know full well, now.

'There was this one night he was away, and she got herself pissed as a cricket and turned up here with some of the AI gear from the dairy. Dry-ice canister and such. She begged me for my … you know …' He gestures to his crotch region.

'She wanted your *semen*?' Larry's eyebrows lift and he nods.

I look away in shock then back to him, searching his face. He raises both hands in protest. 'I told her no, straight up, no!'

'Then why on earth did you agree?'

'You know your mother – it's her way or her way. She figured it was still family and Finnian would never know. Turned on the tears, she did. I made her promise me, if the baby took, that she'd make Finnian change his farming ways. I didn't want the child raised in all those chemicals of warfare he uses. The pregnancy was a success. The promise, not.'

'So I was created by artificial insemination? Just like the cows?'

'Well. Not just like the cows,' he says gently. 'But kinda.'

My knees grow weak. I'm a non-natural baby just like Dad's calves in the shed! Then it dawns on me just how sad and desperate Mum must've been – for her to keep Larry's semen in a canister and inject her own vagina with sperm in secrecy! She went through all that weirdness to have a baby ... just to have *me*. Then I turned out how I turned out, and that wasn't good enough for her. I was no Nikki! Tears pool in my eyes, thinking of my angry, sad mother. I know she didn't come home last night from her date with Dean-O, but I realise now, she's never been home – not really.

'And what about Patrick? Is he from one of your ... um ... *donations* too?'

'No. Your dad managed that himself. Apparently, it can happen, even with men with a low sperm count.'

'So, in my case, you just supplied the goods?' My heart feels as if it might shatter.

'Yes. But in my case, I'm so glad I did. You're here in the world. I'm just sorry you didn't know sooner.'

'Why? Surely it means nothing to you? I must be an embarrassment to you, like I am to everyone else.'

He looks at me shocked, then shakes his head. 'Connie, it means *everything* to me.'

I hear the tug of emotion in his voice, prompting tears in me.

'That day you found me down by the river, I believe you were sent to save me. I've been waiting for years for you to figure it out. Surely you can see?'

'See what?' I ask.

'That we're birds of a feather.' He smiles gently at me.

In a sudden rush, he pulls me to him and holds me tightly. I hold him back, drawing in his earthy scent, his love emanating from his chest. My tears pool so that the world looks liquid. Deep within laugher rises up at the irony. I pull away and look at him. 'So I'm Connie Mulligan, an AI baby!'

'Indeed you are.'

'Well then, thank god I'm not half Holstein.'

Larry laughs. 'Thank god you're not, and thank god we found each other.'

As he hugs me again I say, 'In the nick of time.'

*

When we head back out to pick the last crate of beans, there's no awkwardness between us, just a quiet contentment of companionship and love.

'I better not stay too long,' I say, putting the last of the plant waste in the barrow for the animals. 'I've got something on tonight after milking.'

'Right-o, but before you go, come with me for a sec. I've got something to show you.'

I follow him into the apple-pickers shed where sunlight is streaming through the clerestory windows, giving Larry's art studio a warmth and glow. The paraphernalia of paints, brushes and palettes have been tidied up and set neatly on shelves. The half-crazy energy of his art space in the vast shed is now serene, clean, orderly, but still retaining that flair of artistically beautiful clutter. Even Annabelle seems happier as her image repeats across the walls.

'It looks amazing!'

'Megan's been up here regularly. Not just to pick up the produce for her and the boys, but also to help me with my noggin.'

He taps his head, as if by way of explanation. He then moves to the side of his large art table, taking out a new white canvas from a large assortment and setting out a new easel, as yet unchristened by paints.

'I've realised I've let too much in. Paid too much attention to the ones who don't see the beauty in all life. They just disregard it. And spray it, or doze it or concrete it. So you and I aren't to blame for not being able to stand the version of the world most are creating. We just don't fit life the way it currently is. It's their madness, not ours.

'So,' he continues, setting the canvas on the easel, 'now you're home, and there'll be times when you need to escape Crazy Land over there, would you like me to teach you to paint?'

I look from his open, caring face to the empty canvas. Tingles of joy run through me.

'Oh yes please, Dad-Larry.'

My skin shimmers just as a flock of rosellas lift up from a tree outside, dabbing the vista with colour and life as they sail by. It's then I know I must go into battle for all that is precious and dear to me in this life of mine. For this place. For us.

Chapter 52

Later that night, when I pull up in the vast basketball courts carpark in Ulvie next to Slugs's ute, I can see he's joined by two black-clad figures, balaclavas pulled down over faces so only their eyes show.

'I told you not to tell anyone, Slugs,' I say, exasperated.

'Yeah ... but ...'

'Hello, Shirley. Hello, Aarav,' I say flatly.

'How did you know it was us!' Aarav protests.

I roll my eyes.

'Reporting for duty, Captain Connie,' Shirley says.

'Please don't call me that. Shirley, what are you doing here?'

'I knew youse two were up to somethin' – plotting stuff at milking time. I grilled Nigel and he spilled the beans.'

'You really shouldn't be here. I'm about to commit a serious crime.'

'Well, I can't have my son headed for more trouble,' Shirley says, '... without me joining in!' She cackles.

'But you don't even know what I'm about to do!'

'All I know is it's part of the war we're in and I'm on your side,' she says.

'Okay,' I say. 'Just so you know, what I'm about to do won't hurt anyone.'

'Well then, what is it, Captain Connie?' Aarav asks.

'Stop it!'

'Yes, sir,' Slugs says, taking the piss.

When I brief them on my plan, Aarav says incredulously, in the darkness, 'You want us to steal *what*?'

*

Soon, we're creeping around the side of the Global Genetics office in the dark, trying to be cat-like. In truth, our land army are as slinky as wombats. At the back of the offices, I instruct Shirley to keep watch. Gloves on, I lift the rock where I know the spare key is hidden, under the gleam of Slugs's head torch.

'It's hardly a break and enter,' she whispers.

We are lucky security isn't a priority here. Crime in Ulvie mostly involves bottle-shop thefts, recreational drugs and domestic violence. Sure there's been bull-semen heists in Germany and America, but not here. Not in Tassie. Until now.

As I usher the boys into the large shed where the semen canisters are stored, while Shirley keeps watch, I rationalise that this is not even a theft. I'm just gathering unwanted goods that Global Genetics will most likely chuck out. The semen I managed to organise for collection from the diverse cattle breeds before I went to Ireland is really my project. The concept is mine, and therefore it's arguably my intellectual property. That's my justification anyway.

I shine my torch to the area where the techies placed the canisters, praying that Raylene hasn't already chucked out the fruits of my labour. Relegated to the back shelf, there sit my canisters filled with semen straws of the rarest breeds of milking, draught and meat cattle I could muster.

Raylene had argued the canisters of old line bull semen was an absolute 'waste of resources'. She'd pointedly lectured me saying, 'Just ten straws of Holstein semen is enough to attract as much as $67,000. Whereas this bloody stuff is virtually worthless! A waste of money to collect, Connie.'

I shut her voice out of my head as I hand the canisters to Aarav and Slugs. We carry them out to Slugs's ute and as we make our

350

headlight-less getaway, I send a silent request for forgiveness. This act is for the greater good.

The next morning, I call the vet. I cancel the order for the drying-off drugs that I'd left in place as part of my game-plan with Finnian. Instead I ask him to come and help with insemination. It's leading up to Christmas, and I know he blocks out a spot for us year to year. When he asks about Finnian drying off cows and selling the property, I'm vague. People are used to me being vague. He buys it. As I hang up, I send a promise through the ether to the cows that, if I can help it, this will be the last time they will be forced to get pregnant by unnatural means.

*

When Christmas arrives, it's an unusual time of silent warfare in our house, but weirdly things feel more peaceful on Sunnyside. Mum doesn't have Finnian up a ladder anchoring the inflatable Santa sleigh on the roof. Me and Patrick aren't arguing, untangling Christmas lights on the lawn. Even last year's new solar light meerkats in Santa hats are being left to rest in the cupboard.

Mum is way too busy with Dean-O to bother with decorations, Christmas dinner, or us. She's barely home. Breezing in, showering, staying in my bedroom like a lovesick teenager until Dean-O's shifts are done. Waltzing out all dolled up, shooting little darts of hurtful words on her departure to Dad.

Finnian skulks about the house, but isn't coming out onto the farm. When I go into the main house to use the office computer, he asks lots of questions about the people coming and going from the dairy. I just tell him they're mates, helping catalogue for the clearing sale.

He doesn't know we're still milking. He doesn't know I've pulled the landline out of the wall and diverted the house calls to my phone.

Each time the milk tanker is due, Shirley steps in and bosses him out for a drive to Mr Crompton to collect his scripts or to pick up groceries. After that, she takes it upon herself to organise his hospital check-ups in Lonnie, all timed so we can get away with our changes on the farm. Finnian's so used to being served by women, he lets Shirley drive. He lets her fuss over him. He ignores her banter, but tolerates her, using her for his gain.

I reckon not once has he asked himself why the once-hostile Shirley is now being so helpful. He probably thinks she fancies him now they're both 'single'. Nor would he have asked himself why his normally disagreeable daughter is now as compliant as one of his beleaguered cows.

'Subterfuge is easy for women when dealing with a man who runs on enormous ego and can't see beyond himself,' Megan had advised when we'd nutted out our plan.

In the days before Christmas, Finnian asks why the cows are still coming and going from the dairy. I'm vague again, saying it's kinder because they like the routine, even if they're drying off, and that I'm collating stats on them for their impending sale. He mutters that I've got rocks in my head, but accepts what I say, too absorbed in his own poisoned mental cloud and poor health. When he mentions with concern that Dawn hasn't called about the sale, I shoot off a text to Dawn: *Landline is down. Best to email Finnian re sale.*

Bloody Telstra, she'd replied.

Like a diligent daughter, I write out neat messages from other farm-related calls, relaying them like the most efficient of secretaries. He's satisfied with this. I've led him to believe that I'm absconding to Ireland to join Patrick once Sunnyside is sold. I think he sees my behaviour as that of surrender and obedience to his will.

Little does he know, I'm not giving up. He has no clue his cows are now up the duff to the most unusual mix of genetics, rendering them extremely unappealing to the mass-market livestock buyers. I'll refuse to take the calves from the mothers so he'll have no choice but to accept that in nine months' time, there'll be little all-sorts calves here – the foundation herd to our Lilyburn Collective calf-at-foot dairy dream. A Southern Hemisphere version of Donohill Dairy is on its way.

If I can believe it, I will see it, I tell myself as I go to sleep each night at Granny M's, breathing away the tensions and trials of the day and settling into a place of gratitude.

There are days though when those dreams are unseeable. In the pre-Christmas rush, Dawn's emails come thick and fast about the sale. To balance myself, I head over the river and Larry sets me straight with a paintbrush and a meal. Summer days languish. My Christmas is spent with him at a table under a shady tree near the veggie garden, Nick-nack snapping at flies. A feast of lettuce, tomatoes, sugar snap peas and ham, thanks to a Glennon baby and Uncle Larry's smokehouse. A new fan paintbrush for me; a new metal bucket for him. Dessert is raspberries straight from the canes, warmed by the sun. A rare treat of Canopy ice cream for Larry, who devours it like a kid. We feast. We laugh. We chat about what's possible with Sunnyside Dairy Farm and Lilyburn, based on the Irish business model. As the day stretches, we sit in silence and contentment. I have a knowing that the stars, no matter which way they slide above me in the sky, will anchor me here on Earth safely ... together, with my dad.

On Christmas night, a little reluctantly, I venture back to Finnian and hand him a plate of Larry's food. He deduces where it's come from and it winds up slung against the wall.

'I'll call Nick-nack in later to clean that up, then shall I?' I respond without a flinch.

He's been stewing all day that Mum's absconded for two nights with Dean-O to the Country Club in Lonnie. This morning, after wishing us a Merry Christmas, she'd said matter-of-factly, 'For Christmas, Dean-O's given me tickets on the Spirit – a double cabin, with a porthole! We're off to the Gold Coast to stay at Dean-O's flat. Oh ... and they're one-way tickets,' she says with a sniff.

She had set her cases out neatly, ready to roll after Boxing Day, still annoyed Patrick had taken her largest one, the leopard. The luggage sits waiting below the stopped clock. The photo of her and Dad winning their dairy prize is now turned to the wall, like she's turned away from us all. Nowadays, part of me understands.

*

On Christmas night on Granny M's veranda, there's a video call from the cheerful two Patricks and Amber. Then comes another – the smiling faces of the Donovans appear, all wearing silly hats, the kids a riot of giggles and Christmas excitement.

When I hang up from them I start to make ready for bed. On the mantel, Mrs O'Bee and Shauna's Christmas cards stand pride of place. I smile, picking up Mrs O'Bee's card of a snow-covered Christmas scene, and re-read the letter that came with it.

> *Every single time I walk my dear old Mish on our morning path and I think of you, I see a hare. It makes me smile. Cheeky little thing. Not fearful of the dog at all. Interesting. In our old ways, a hare is symbolic of birth, death and rebirth. I get the sense your old Connie has died and now it's time for a new you to be reborn. Shauna and I are off to the stones again in the New Year. It will be cold for my old bones, so I'll have to cuddle up to Shauna. We will ask for you, about the hare. Merry Christmas, beautiful wise one.*

*

The next day, Boxing Day, when I set off with Nick-nack to the dairy, there in the milky morning light a hare sits upright, ears lined black, brown coat rich and thick, bright almond-shaped eyes. She looks at me. She doesn't run.

'Birth, death and rebirth,' I say. I remember the hare that led Wolfgang to the O'Meara estate and me to Nick, and something shivers through my body.

By lunchtime, I'm perched on a colourful beanbag under the pear tree at Verenda, where Aarav and Slugs have set up the TV so we can watch the Boxing Day Test. Larry, Vernon and Fenton are in the kitchen bantering about the two barbecues that need firing up – one for meat, one for not. Megan is lying on a hammock, eyes shut, hands folded over her belly.

Family obligations have dragged away the women who are normally here. I don't miss the fact my family had no Christmas celebrations this year. It gets me wondering what Raylene, David and Nikki's Christmas looked like? Awkward, I expect.

I look to my new-found friends and realise, like in Ireland, I am with my family. I shut my eyes listening to the friendly chatter of the men, the cricket commentary, our soundtrack of summer, and everything feels good at this moment.

The public holiday slowdown allows all of us some reprieve from our underground war, but we know it's a temporary ceasefire. Next door, the wheels of corporate domination will begin to roll again after the holidays, and we'll need to be ready.

Megan has been into Dawn and Dick's frequently, with negotiations to buy the pub with the help of Nancy's Shiva Revival. Because Dawn is being so obstinate in expanding the women's support community in Lilyburn, Megan's had good cause to storm in there unannounced frequently, ears and eyes open for extra information on the farm sales.

My drifting thoughts are interrupted when someone gets out for eight, and Aarav cheers and Slugs swears.

Shirley arrives with a platter of prawns and some dipping sauce. 'I made sure I got all the poop out of them,' she says.

One whiff and my stomach heaves. Rolling over in my beanbag I gag a few times, like a seagull with a stuck chip.

'Aw love!' Shirley says. 'I didn't know you didn't like seafood. Sorry, ducks.'

'I don't. I love it.'

'Well, why you got the spews?'

'I don't know. I don't seem to have ever gotten over my jet lag. Could be stress about everything?'

'Or maybe it's not,' Shirley says, narrowing her eyes at me. 'Have a think what else you may have got up to in Ireland to make you feel sick, love. Them knickers got anything to do with it?'

'It wasn't Ireland,' I say, the world swirling. It was Melbourne, I think to myself. I want to run straight to Mr Crompton's pharmacy, but I know he's closed for the public holiday. At our long lunch table, trees dappling light, I'm quiet. Too quiet. On her rounds topping up water with a big white enamel jug, Shirley whispers in Megan's ear. By the time Christmas pudding rolls around, Megan squats down beside me. She slips a package into my skirt pocket.

'Shirley says you may need one of these. I have them on hand for the women who come here.'

I know without looking it's a pregnancy test kit. I swallow.

*

With the image of two pink lines etched in my mind, before I open the bathroom door, I plan on saying my goodbyes, pleading farm work for my early departure. But instead, Megan knocks on the door.

'Well?' she asks.

I nod. 'I am.'

She folds me into a hug and I begin to cry.

'It's okay. Take your time with how you feel about it. Have a think about what you want to do.'

'Do?' I echo, frowning. Knowing from farm life how precious this new life within me is, a sad smile dawns. 'There's only one thing for me to do. I mean it's not the worst thing that can happen. Right?'

Megan embraces me again, and I fall into her comfort. She takes my face in her hands. 'Don't be afraid. We'll take care of you,' she insists. 'Just you wait and see. It's going to be wonderful. You have an entire village. Oh you're going to be the best mother!'

'Mother,' I echo.

Coming out of the room, I sit back down at the table and with a tremor in my voice say, 'Guess what everyone. I'm in calf!'

Suddenly I'm surrounded by so much love, I begin laughing and crying at the same time as they embrace me over and over.

Not once during that surreal afternoon do my friends ask me, 'Who is the father?' And yet, it takes all my strength not to contact *him* – Nick – the man who, like me, never wanted children.

*

At home on Granny M's veranda, I sit, stunned. I've filled up an old stone birdbath on the front lawn and the magpies are having a fine time of it. Rolling around in it, escaping the heat, flicking starlight drops into the dense summer air.

I tune into my body and realise I've failed to notice the small things. The tiny changes that I'd pushed to the fringes of my consciousness, as if I'd not been ready to know the truth. My swollen, slightly tender breasts, my craving for sleep and insatiable appetite for Larry's steak. I'd put the missed periods down to the Northern Hemisphere swirl reversing itself and the stress of the farm sale. With a big exhale I blow out the confronting fact that I am going to have a baby. There's no turning back. It's simply a 'meant to be'.

Glancing up, outside the cottage fence, I see another hare. She is loping along the gravel. She stops outside the front gate, sits up on her haunches, flicks her paws over her nose, grooming herself, then leisurely lopes away. I realise the cycles of life are not ours to control. They claim us. They move us through time. It's up to us whether we meet them with grace or not.

I pick up my phone. I dial Nick's number, stored for so long in my phone, but never forgotten, like a shadowy presence in my mind. Now I *have* to call.

The phone rings. A woman with a cheerful, youthful voice answers, 'Hello, Nick's phone. Merry Christmas! This is Zara.'

I sit, wordless, my heart contracting. Before she can speak again, I hang up.

Chapter 53

The next day a subdued grey sky domes over the dairy and the world feels different now there's a new person unfurling within me. Because of it, I hold myself with tenderness, wanting to resonate with a state of mind that supports this unplanned, but not unwelcome, life. I want to be a mother who gives wings – not one to enmesh or entangle. A mother who simply, peacefully observes and guides, and learns from the new soul who is crushing his or herself into the density of cells, into a body, to walk with me on Earth's soil. Soils that I hope are enlivening and are on their way to thriving by the time this child is born. It makes me keenly aware that my future on Sunnyside is even more imperative. Retaining the farm now feels even more tenuous and the 'war' now feels unacceptable ... all I want is peace, for me. For this baby.

Shirley and Megan are already gently ushering my mind around to the fact I'll need to get some scans done and offering to help me 'nest' somewhere after the farm is auctioned in March.

Since hearing the woman's voice on Nick's phone, curiosity leads me to click the dairy computer awake. My cheeks prickle as the temptation to torture myself gets the better of me.

'Zara,' I mutter as I pull up a chair and begin Google-stalking Nick. Turns out, the chirpy Zara is a biologist, with a PhD in soils. Of course she is. *Doctor* Zara Heart. In several photos, she and Nick are side by side looking happy at farm field days, giving lectures at ag conferences, hosting regenerative agriculture and human-health movie nights. Shoulder to shoulder with the now-famous leaders of the regenerative movement. My gaze sticks on a staff Christmas party photo. Zara and Nick with felt reindeer antlers on their heads, glasses raised, arms casually around each other, smiles radiating.

A memory of Nick's mother flashes. Her spitting judgement of me. The gilded house and perfect grand estate life. His perfect Helen. Now the perfect Zara. My hand involuntarily moves to my belly as I remember the time Nick had shaken his head ruefully, sitting on my hospital bed. He'd been talking about the state of the world, the collapsing ecosystems, and the health crises, then announced, 'I don't care what my Ma says about "continuing the legacy". I'm never bringing kids into this messed-up world.'

Remembering the conclusion to his dismal speech, I realise I'll be having this baby alone. Nick's trajectory in life is one that ought not be tied to mine. One night in an airport hotel absolves him of any obligation. I was the one who pounced on him. And he's clearly happy now with Zara. Clicking the computer off, I sit listening to the roof tick as the sun warms it. Hearing an engine, I glance out of the office window.

A police car pulls up. Constable Tony gets out, Neddy tumbling to the gravel behind him, unbidden. Despite Tony's commands, the floppy-eared spaniel locks his nose on a scent trail. Off he goes towards the calf shed, the dairy smell sending his brain into overload. Next, David Rootes-Stewart's ute rolls in and I'm surprised when Nikki gets out. From a baby capsule in the back seat, she gently lifts out Sarah, cradling the tiny child in her arms. Shouldn't the baby be bigger than that by now? I wonder. With immense care, Nikki straps Sarah into a front pack.

I expire a long slow breath. Throwing a couple of milking aprons hastily over the guilty canisters, clearly stamped with *Property of Global Genetics*. I breathe in calm then out I go, ready to surrender. I vow that before I go down for semen theft, I'll first challenge Nikki on conspiring to sell off the farms by doing dodgy Dawn deals. Surely she must sense the devastation that will follow to the Lilyburn river catchment and our community? Nikki knows better than most that in the business world 'environmental protection and preservation' is merely a box-ticking exercise on paper and nothing to do with the on-ground actions.

When he sees me, Constable Tony sets his hat on straight. 'Good morning, Connie. I'm here to investigate a theft from Global Genetics.'

'Morning, Tony, sir. What sort of theft?' I ask.

'Semen,' he says, cheeks flushing pink.

Just to draw my confession out, I ask, 'What kind of semen?'

He rolls his eyes at me. 'Bovine.'

I almost snicker at his formality. Then I realise if it's a serious crime, and I have to do time, I could be having a prison baby! I clear my throat to confess, knowing I need to be careful not to drop Slugs, Shirley and Aarav into the effluent pond with me.

'It was …' I begin.

But Nikki's voice bustles over the top of mine. 'Of course, if we catch the person, we're going to drop all charges.'

I look to her in disbelief. So does Tony.

'But your mother …' he begins, frowning.

'My mother has changed her mind,' Nikki says in her clipped voice. 'I saw your car passing our place, constable. I wanted to pass on my mother's message directly, before we waste any more of your valuable time.'

'But,' Tony begins, then the baby mews. It's a pitiful sound.

She looks at him beseechingly. 'I'm sorry, I'm going to have to see to her. Connie, would you mind if I used your cottage for a moment? I think she needs changing. And her medication. It's a little urgent.'

Constable Tony lifts his head as if sniffing out something suspicious. The baby cries again.

'Very well,' he says tersely, opening the car door, calling his dog. It's only then we notice dear little Neddy and Nick-nack outside the calf shed. The dogs are done with humping and are now knotted like a double-headed rather comical beast.

'Neddy!' groans Constable Tony.

'Seems it's a morning for semen theft,' I joke. 'It looks as if Nick-nack has pinched a bit of Neddy's.'

Constable Tony turns pink again.

'Feel free to hang about until they unknot. I'll just show Nikki in. Let me know later – vet needling for an abortion or pups? Personally I'd like pups.'

I leave the suggestion hanging as I usher Nikki into the cottage, wondering why on earth she's protecting me, and what cocker–collie crosses would look like.

'Those dogs are a bit like my mother and your father,' she says, as she follows me along the hall. 'Haven't they behaved *dreadfully*? Carrying on like that over the boundary fence like randy rabbits. And now their big break-up. It's so pathetic.'

'Yes. It's a little hard to get the head around,' I say. 'Cuppa?'

As she settles at the kitchen table, I fill the kettle at the sink, setting the cups and canisters out, trying hard not to start on at her about the foreign consortium deal she and her family are orchestrating with my parents.

Undoing the front pack, Nikki takes the baby out and cradles her. Her dear little face is striking – almost alien in shape, topped with jagged black hair. She's wearing a *Snugglepot and Cuddlepie* suit, her little fist pressed in her mouth. She has such pale translucent skin and her eyes have an otherworldly slant to them. I want to be prickly towards Nikki, but my heart goes out to her. It's obvious the baby has rocked her world. I think of the dividing cells within me, and for the first time register the things that can go so wrong with pregnancies.

'Yes,' Nikki says, reading my expression. 'Some people get a little shocked when they first see her. She's tougher than she looks.' She kisses the baby's crown.

'Normal tea? Or herbal?'

'Normal will do.'

'Milk?' I ask.

She shakes her head. 'I'm allergic to dairy.'

I nod and sigh, not so much at the irony, but the idiocy of our farm systems that create so many allergies.

'I know you know our dear Doctor Amel,' Nikki begins.

'Yes, I do.'

'Well,' she says, cupping her mug, 'after Sarah was born, the local doctors were useless. It turns out Sarah's got some rare genetic condition – so rare they couldn't settle on a diagnosis. So I called June for advice. It was our lovely Doctor Amel who got to the bottom of it. Sarah's been improving since then, and Tobias and I are less freaked out, better parents, y'know?'

I sit on the stool opposite Nikki. Sarah's eyes track my movement. Clearly, she's a round-the-clock-care baby. Nikki looks exhausted. I nod.

'I'm so sorry it's been so rough.'

Nikki shrugs. 'It is what it is. We love her just the same. Thanks to Doctor June, we've found out Sarah's condition is a generational thing. It's linked to the farm chemicals Dad was using when he was a younger man in the eighties. She told us the impacts generally skip the second generation and reveal themselves in the third. It's often just a matter of time before these things emerge, according to Doctor June. And I must say, I believe her. My instincts as a mum tell me this is true.'

As I stare at Sarah, I try not to be sucked into fear, recalling all the artificial toxins my family's exposed me to throughout my life.

Nikki turns to me, her wide brown eyes sincere. 'After I found out Dad was pushing to sell the farm, and Mum's agreeing, I did my lolly with them. With things how they are with Sarah, I fully lost my shit.'

I've never heard Nikki swear before and I almost splutter out my tea.

'Tobias had to restrain me. It wasn't pretty. I went full-on mental mother.'

'Not mental,' I add. 'Justifiably angry, I'd say.'

She looks at me with pooling tears.

'I laid down the law to Mum and Dad. I told them they are not to sell, and if they do, I'll sue them in whatever way I can for wrongdoing. It's a shitty thing to do to my parents, threatening legal action, but honestly, Connie, I can't keep condoning farming this way. Not after Sarah. I told them straight, Tobias and I don't want to raise our babies under their chemical clouds, watching the soil blow or wash away, the native animals die. I told them we are taking over the farm. To run it clean.'

'And they agreed?'

'Well, Dad did. I think they both know once I commit to something, I do it well. And I would take them to court. But apparently it's all gone too far with the deal.'

'Too far?'

'Our parents – mostly your mum and my mum – have rushed the sale through to the next stage.'

'They have?' I reply weakly.

Nikki reaches out and clasps my hand. 'I don't want to lose our farm. I really need your help.'

'My help?'

'Mum told me about your crazy ideas – as she called them – when you were at Global. Then how you took off to that alternative Irish dairy. I got curious, so Tobias and I googled the Donovans' business. Then when Sarah got worse with conventional medicine, I got more than curious. I got determined. The more I looked at their business model and the more I looked at Sarah not thriving, the more I knew whatever you're on to, Connie, I want to be part of it.'

'I'm not on to anything.'

She looks at me sternly. 'Connie, I know you stole those canisters.'

That silences me.

'I know you and your friends have a plan. I want in.'

I look at her, about to deny my part in it, thinking this is a trick, Raylene and Dad are trying to flush me out. But then I note the furrow in Nikki's brow and the way her hand is rubbing up and down Sarah's tiny back a little too quickly, like her anxiety can't be contained.

'How can I do anything? The deal's virtually been done.'

'But why take the canisters?'

'I'm just hedging my bets. If the farm isn't sold, I have a plan.'

'A calf-at-foot kind of plan?' Nikki asks, smirking.

'Maybe?'

She smiles widely and warmly for the first time since she arrived. I look at her beautifully boned face as she bores her determined, lively eyes into mine.

'Well then, we'd better bloody well have a good crack at stopping them,' she says definitively.

'Yes, we bloody well shall!'

Chapter 54

Several weeks later I pull up at the old pub in Patrick's ute, Poo Brown now retired to under the pine. Megan and Nancy are outside ready to greet me, Nancy's arms already outstretched, emotion flooding her eyes. She hugs me, gushing over my emerging baby belly. 'Look at you!'

'I'm not due for a while, but I already look like I've swallowed a wombat.'

'Nonsense, you look wonderful,' Nancy says, touching her hand to my cheek, appearing vibrant in a bright green dress with her shiny black hair.

Megan stands beside her in paint-splattered denim coveralls, her bulky blonde hair done up in a pretty sunflower-print scarf.

Gazing up at the facade of the large Federation-style hotel, I say, 'You're wasting no time in claiming her!'

'We finalised the paperwork with Dawn at nine,' Megan says. 'Keys at five past. Here at nine-ten! Working bee at nine-fifteen. It's all systems go.'

The graffitied window of a dick and balls has been removed and a glazier is on the job. Above us a builder is measuring the broken iron lacework on the sagging end of the gappy upstairs veranda. On the third storey quaint dormer windows sit on an elegant but rusted roofline. Above it, the gulls circle and call, dabbing white on a pristine sky.

'Bit of a fixer-upper,' I say. 'I hope I didn't steer you in the wrong direction when I suggested buying it.'

'She is a little worse for wear,' Megan concedes. 'And Dawn charged like a wounded bull for the place. She sure didn't want Verenda gaining more ground. But it's perfect for what we want to do here.'

'Is she on to us, d'you think?' I ask.

Nancy shakes her head. 'In her mind, a women's community centre and a not-for-profit company like mine investing in local social enterprises aren't a threat. To her it's not serious business. She's so in bed with the big boys and has the dazzle of the dollar in her eyes, she won't see us coming.'

Megan grins and says, 'My intel – aka the kids hitting a six over the fence several times and the mums retrieving the ball – have confirmed the consortium is flying their CEO, CFOs and scientists into the state next week for the final sign-off. The public auction listed in March is merely government smoke-screening – all just for show.

'We've discovered that Dawn has scheduled an investors' farm tour for Valentine's Day too,' she finishes.

Nancy smirks. 'It's ironic. There's nothing they do that's about love. I say we hijack the day as a National Regenerative Agriculture Day.'

As I process the news, the women usher me through the wide front door, propped open with a paint tin. Inside, the volunteers are in full flight – among them, the chappies, Aarav and Slugs, Shirley, the women from the shelter, and even Post Office Jane on her day off is hard at it.

The old pub darling, tainted with cheap layers and poor taste from the 70s, 80s and 90s – is being aired out, purified, prettied up and whitewashed into a classic, cleaner space. The beauty of age and the pub's original features are coming to light.

Nancy and Megan lead me up the creaking stairs two flights into a charming but musty-smelling attic room. There's a single wrought-iron bed, left over from a bygone era.

'Good view,' I say looking out over the back paddock. Beyond that, through the giant decommissioned and rusting mining port infrastructure, I can glimpse the liquid silver waters of Bass Strait. The stillness of the day belies the gusts of nerves within me now I know that the leaders of Vancouver Lucrative and Yingli Naizhan Investments will be coming here, and with them, quite likely – Turner.

I glance into a quaint bathroom as Megan turns the geriatric taps. The pipes clunk to life, the showerhead spits and splutters awake, spraying water into the deep rust-stained bath.

'Works!' she says, delighted.

She wanders back to the window beside me. Nancy also flanks me. I can feel a gentleness emanating from both women and also tension in their silence.

Nancy clears her throat. 'We were thinking if there's nothing we can do about the sale of Sunnyside, could you see yourself moving in here?'

They watch me closely, gauging how the suggestion lands.

'Here?' I look to them, shocked. 'I don't want to think beyond Sunnyside.'

'Connie, it's something we have to consider,' Nancy adds kindly.

Megan gestures outside. 'Look. There's room out the back for Traveller, and it's a great place for Nick-nack and her pups,' she encourages.

'And no matter what happens, you know you already have a position with Shiva,' Nancy says, 'as our holistic dairy and farm co-ordinator when we get this place up and running. As a plan B, I'm looking at some other lovely farms we can invest in to support what Verenda will do here. Your Sunnyside cows, now they're in calf to your wonderful hotchpotch of bulls, can be the foundation. You can still realise your dreams, Connie. Just on a different farm.'

I baulk. 'You haven't given up trying to stop the sale have you? Are you bailing?'

'No!' they both chorus.

'But you know the power of the old boys club,' Nancy finishes.

Knowing they're right, I can't help but feel slightly hurt. I can't yet imagine myself anywhere else.

'It'd be a whole, fresh new start on another property,' Nancy urges. 'Please keep it in mind.'

I'm still having mixed feelings as we make our way to the old beer garden where dandelions are reclaiming the paving. The garden, despite its abandonment, has a charm with self-sown flowers erupting out of the soil and fragrant jasmine and wisteria cascading over a sagging pergola.

'Like my office?' Nancy's set up her laptop out here, where bees are buzzing and mottled sunlight dances on the table's surface.

'Here, take a look at the business prospectus. Came up beautifully thanks to your dreaming, Connie.'

I flip open the document that Shiva's designer compiled after I'd sat down with them to share my vision. There's an artist's impression of the pub, just as I'd described during our gatherings at Verenda.

The hotel is rebranded and re-envisioned as a local food hub. The prospectus invites philanthropists to invest in a Tasmanian Produce Collective–food system that includes a local, fresh calf-at-foot organic milk supply. A large silver vat has been sketched into one drawing. Other images portray women making cheese and selling organic chem-free fresh produce. There are beautiful watercolour drawings of children picking fruits. And of customers filling glass milk bottles directly from a large stainless-steel container. Families seated at long tables in the beer garden eating fresh, healthy meals.

'It's just how I imagined!' I drink in more graphics. The paddock – complete now with Traveller looking over a fence to a vegetable and flower garden where children and women work in the beds. There's also goats, sheep and chickens, and a small orchard. On other pages, delicious fruit and vegetables are displayed in crates like Uncle Larry's, ready for collection. The side of the building shows it converted to a milk receival depot. The document has such a wonderful positivity to it but for me there's that snag – the one of the river, the mountains. My place. My home.

'This is wonderful, but I'm still not ready to give up,' I say. 'I still want to try to retain our farm at the heart of this.'

'We've tried every avenue.' Nancy sighs. 'We're out of ideas.'

Deflated, I look away so as not to reveal my tears. I notice one of the women sanding an old door back to raw wood, the colour of candied honey. The woman has AirPods in and the music is inspiring her to move with vigour. She's wearing Blundstone boots and a skirt printed with possums amid banksia. The skirt swishes as she sands. Watching her, I recall the way the duck shooters had reacted to me in my skirt, in the bushland, scattering from my rage. An idea lands. I turn back to the women.

'Actually, I have an idea!'

*

A week later, I drive Nancy up to Larry's via Irishtown. The further into the hills we climb, the more excited I become.

Nancy looks to me, laughing. 'This is such a crazy idea, Connie, I had to fly back to Tassie for it.'

I glance at her as I change down gears at a bend. 'It's so great you could come. I know we need you in the city, altering the big systems from the top down and changing the minds of politicians and corporates, but it's important you're part of this. Generating change from the bottom up too.'

'Literally the bottom!' Nancy laughs. 'It's a genius idea. Shock tactics are needed. The men coming today don't seem to realise we're in for a shitstorm on this planet soon. It'll at least make them stop and think.'

'I hope so.'

'I know so.'

She pulls her sunglasses down. 'I'll have to lay low though. If I'm seen antagonising what could be considered our "competition", it could jeopardise our pub project. Best I shelter up at Larry's and leave after it's all over.'

'Larry's place isn't that flash,' I warn glancing at her city clothes and polished style.

She waves my comment away, her face illuminating at the mountain rainforest that nestles in shaded groves. 'This place reminds me of my dad and the hikes he'd take me on. I'm not really a five-star girl. I've roughed it often enough. I really don't mind.'

By the time we get to Larry's, the long, delicious summer evening is holding on to a comfortable warmth. I introduce Larry to Nancy, and he takes her hand, greeting her shyly.

'Feel like coming on a bit of a paddock bash now the track's fixed?' he asks. 'I'd love to show you what you and Connie could be saving from up high.'

'Sure!' Nancy says.

At the top of the hill, Nancy takes in the stunning valley, the grand mountain's rise lit by flaxen light, and she gushes over the animals as we feed them. The sinking sun is showing off the best of Sunnyside. The land is selling itself to the one woman I know who could have the power and the pocket to help us scuttle this deal, but for the insider trading.

'Look at my girls,' I say, pointing back across the river. 'They look so much happier on a medicinal banquet.'

'When are they due to calve?' Nancy asks.

'Not long after me,' I say, running my hand over my belly. 'So I really, really hope we can stay.'

She doesn't answer but I can tell from the way she's so spellbound by the vista, she's hoping as hard as me. The reality is this could be the last time I look at the property as my family farm. I think of Finnian holed up in the house and try not to let my frustration with him swamp this moment.

*

Later, after I've dropped Patrick's swag on the veranda for Larry and we've taken Nancy's bag to Larry's room, she emerges from the car with a bottle of whiskey.

'The best Irish you can buy in Australia. For you,' she says, presenting it to Larry at the front door.

We show her into the lounge room, me with my pregnant lady soda water and lemon instead of whiskey. Larry has lit a small fire, taking the chill off the cottage that is rapidly being wrapped in cool mountain air now the sun has sunk behind the range.

Taking a sip, Nancy almost splutters her whiskey back up as she notices the painting of Annabelle above the fireplace – a richly dark oil of her, seated on a milking stool, forehead pressed against the flank of a Jersey house cow, a Jack Russell sitting beside her, looking adoringly up at her. It's entrancing. Nancy's dark eyes are wide with surprise. 'Is that what I think it is?'

'What?' I ask, trying to sound nonchalant.

'Is that an *original Mulligan*?'

She peers at it, then spins towards us, searching our faces. Larry shuts his eyes momentarily and his jaw clenches.

'Is your family related to *the* artist?' Nancy breathes incredulously.

I try to look blank. Then I look to Larry. Larry looks to his socked toes.

'You could say that,' he mutters.

'Oh my god! Do you know how much that thing would be worth?'

'Which artist might that be?' I ask.

'*Which artist?*' She's exasperated, pointing to the signature on the bottom right corner that reads clearly, *LM Mulligan*.

'Just the biggest thing back in my day. Sell-out exhibitions. Outrageous auction prices. But then he disappeared off the face of the Earth, right at his prime. A few people tracked him back to Tasmania, but the story goes he never let anyone near him. A real recluse. How can you not know of him? He must be a relation, Connie!'

Larry quietly looks into his glass which is fast approaching empty.

Nancy stares at the painting, her voice softening. 'Annabelle D'Arcy. The story goes they were deeply in love. When they split, she moved to France. She painted Mulligan's portrait over and over. She must've been heartbroken. Her paintings of him grace the wall of many a leading gallery in the States and Europe. So sad. After her manic creative spree, she moved to England and that's where she died. So, so very sad.'

Larry's eyes moisten at Nancy's words as he stares at the fire.

'How do you know so much about the art scene?' I ask, trying to draw her questions away from the painting.

Nancy flops her hand about in the air. 'Oh, you know. It's the best place to track down people with too much money. Of course I love art, but attending the major galleries was always the best place to network with philanthropists looking to invest in ethical food system businesses.'

She reaches out towards the shadowed painted fabric of Annabelle's clothing, her fingertips hovering but not touching. 'This is extraordinary. The best I've seen of his. Larry, how on earth did you come by this? Did you inherit this painting from him?'

I brace myself, knowing this might sink him, dragging him back to the place I found him in – lonely, cold, heartbroken, sick, and not too right in the head, like my own good self had been.

I'm about to make up some kooky story when Larry says quietly, 'I think you'd better come with me, Nancy.'

When we walk into Larry's art space, Nancy gazes about and promptly bursts into tears. She turns to Larry and unabashedly holds him tightly in her arms for a long time.

'Oh, Larry! How rude and stupid of me not to put two and two together. I'm so, so sorry. Oh my dear man.'

She hugs him again and his body softens into her insistent American arms.

'I can't believe it! You were, *are*, my all-time favourite artist!'

She looks from Larry to the paintings and shakes her head. 'These paintings would be worth an absolute fortune. You do know that?'

Larry shrugs. As she gazes at the paintings in wonder, she says, 'The universe is conspiring, I just know it. Just you wait for tomorrow. It's going to be powerful! We are about to change the future of humanity!'

Chapter 55

The following morning, on our self-proclaimed National Regenerative Agriculture Day I'm nervous as I ride towards the river, running through our plans in my head: the chappies will text us when Dawn leaves Lilyburn with her investment consortium; Slugs and Aarav are on look-out at the dairy; Shiva Revival's social-media person, Kat, is ready with her drone.

Crossing the river, riding past the symbolic talisman the Verenda women have hung in the trees, my mind stills, and my nerves melt away. Seeing their charms caressed by the breeze lifts a sheen of goosebumps over my skin. They may look like handcrafted whimsies, but I'm now keenly aware of the ancient power that lies within these corn dollies, pottery vulvas and breasts, clay suns, stars and feathers. Our female ancestors are being summoned here.

Up at the cottage, the women greet me and Traveller warmly, and Megan flings open her wicker basket saying, 'Now our mastermind Connie is here, welcome to our very first Raising of the Skirts Festival!'

Vibrant skirts puff out of it, like we've opened a new kind of Pandora's Box – this time a box of bloom, and positivity and love.

Megan, in a skirt of bright blue invites me up beside her. 'And now … a little speech.' She addresses our female army. 'Today, thanks to this woman, Connie Mulligan, we make history and join the women who have been raising their skirts for centuries.

We join the ancients of Egypt, Greece, Persia, Ireland, Africa, Indonesia and Japan. This evil-averting gesture that we're about to perform is war! War against the corporate army who have overtaken us. By revealing our hidden core as women to our enemy, we could today be inspiring a massive change on a world scale.'

I feel a surge of energy from the women around me.

'Our ancient sisters knew this act of exposing our female genitalia was potent enough to bring the Earth and all life back from the brink of destruction. So today ... let's demand life, and above all *peace*.'

Megan stands, full force in her boots and skirt.

'Such is our power as women! And in closing my little sermon I'd like to thank you, Connie Mulligan – for your bravery and your truth and for gathering us here. Would you like to say something?'

I look at their faces. Tears spring up. I'm momentarily lost for words.

'Just thank you for being supportive of this. And thank you to the kind men who are also supporting us today.' I cast Larry a glance. 'Now, everyone, my sister goddesses, pick a skirt that calls to you!'

When the basket is almost empty and I'm about to take a skirt from the remaining few, Shirley pulls me aside.

'Here,' she says, handing me a parcel.

Undoing a scarlet ribbon, paper peeling away, I discover a beautiful deep green silken flared skirt. It's stitched with gentle fern fronds and glimmering stars. My fingers slide over the magic of it. It's the most beautiful piece of clothing I've ever seen. I look at Shirley quizzically.

'Anong made it for you.'

'Barry's new wife?'

Shirley grins. 'Turns out she's not a bad stick. We bonded over Barry's prostate problems.' She snorts laughter and elbows me. 'She's got Baz by the short and curlies at last. She can't be with us, but she said to tell you good luck – well, at least that's what I thought she said. Her English is pretty crap. Worse than mine,' she jokes.

I smile, knowing how far Shirley and I have come.

'I wonder if old Finnian's over there right now preening himself for his visitors.' Our eyes roam to the ugly house across the river. 'I sure hope he likes our little show!'

In that moment the sun lifts beyond a cloud over the eastern mountains, blasting the landscape to golden.

My phone pings.

'It's Vernon,' I say, glancing up from the screen. 'They've left Dawn's. Most likely headed here, in a white van. Nikki is on standby at Waterbright, should they pull in there first.'

What I don't say out loud to the group is that Vernon also revealed *he's* with them – Turner. I feel my energy being sucked into a black hole. But there before me are the women in their colour swirl. Jane grinning in a purple skirt, Nat in Orange, Debs in light green, Nadine in egg-yolk yellow, Shirley in Tigers black and gold, Slugs's sister, Nicole, in earthy ochre patterned with gum leaves, Wendy in irrefutable red, Etsy in pink, Dannika in crimson and Claudia in silver, their little kids running about dabbing more colour to the scene.

When I pull on my skirt, it's a perfect fit for my baby mound and me. Wearing it, there's a sudden rush and all of time seems to swirl within me – time back and forward, time still, time flowing. Like I'm in touch with all those who struggled and laughed in wonder and birthed and cried and loved before me and beyond me. As I swish the skirt around my legs and lift my face to the blue, blue sky, I find one constant – the essence of light. It's as if I've again tuned into that frequency of unstoppable, never-ending love. I'm taking this action today, out of light for my baby, and for me. For Mama Earth. Fearlessly.

I'm awoken from my reverie by Nancy and Larry emerging from inside the cottage, and Shiva's social-media guru, Kat. Nancy introduces her to the women saying, 'Might as well make a big online splash!' She beams at us. 'Today we can make history! Like the African women of Liberia did in 2003, blocking the corridors of the presidential palace. Telling the warlords to choose peace or lose intimacy with their wives. They threatened to expose themselves. The men caved. The war ended. That is our aim today. To stop the war on this beautiful landscape and the creatures within it. For the women who can't be identified today for safety reasons please see Larry.'

I catch the fear that simmers in some of the women who have to hide from violent and controlling men. As they step up onto the veranda, Turner looms again in my mind-shadows. But, as Larry squats beside an old chest, he looks up at us, eyes filled with emotion.

'Annabelle would've liked you to wear these today, I'm sure.'

Lifting the lid he draws out the most exquisite collection of masks. They trail silk ribbons of red, orange, yellow, green, blue, purple and violet, gold, silver and white. Each of them is unique, eerie, ancient, made from shells, feathers, fur, river pebbles, bark and hide. They are stitched with coloured wool and brightened with collected coloured stones, old fabrics and the delicate shells of wild bird eggs. They are otherworldly. They are savage. They are beautiful.

'She made them in the months after she was raped,' Larry says bluntly. He passes each woman one so reverently that I melt with love for my father.

On the first hairpin bend down to the flats, we stop, surprised by the shining snake of cars rolling up the mountain in a long convoy, one after another they park on the grassy verge. Women of all ages, all in skirts of many colours, begin getting out of their cars. Some are gathering excited children, in skirts also, no matter their gender.

They rush to us like a flowing tributary of colour and laughter joining us on the track. Among them, in a rich mauve skirt, is the tall lithe figure of Doctor Amel. I cry out just to see her.

'Doctor Amel!'

'June,' she says, drawing me into a hug, then reaching to lay a hand on Traveller's neck. 'Just call me June. It's so good to see you! Nikki told me you were having a festival and an ambush combined. I thought I'd rally a few more.' She gestures to the women. 'If people want to treat us like witches, then let's behave like witches. Let's be medicine for the world. The way women used to be.'

'Yes!' I say, laughing. 'Yes!'

We walk, united, through the greenery, gathering on the river flat like a Frida Kahlo painting in motion. They are family. They are sisters, mothers, daughters, grandmothers, and all of them are seeking a reclamation. The secret whispers of women have found a collective voice. Maybe, just maybe, this is the seeding of a new world. A new world imagined, but not yet attained. A new world that is swirling and becoming, germinating.

I clamber onto a log, Traveller's reins in my hands. I breathe in deeply, and look skyward to the clear blue beyond, knowing that every clunking step of my difficult journey has brought me here. When I speak, it's as if the words arrive from another realm. 'Thanks everyone for coming! Today we begin to crumble the old-world order. Today we claim our right to soil. Our right to unadulterated seed and plants. Our right to pure and glorious food and clean water. And our right to raise our children in thriving, healthy, peaceful communities. Today, ladies, we change the world!'

The women cheer, and after I've instructed them on our plan, I swing onto Traveller to await the signal from the other side.

Soon it comes. A text from Slugs up at the dairy beeps in my skirt pocket. I read it.

'They're here! They're coming!' I call to the women.

Amid the wavering talismans, and behind thick wattles and tea trees, we hide the plumage of our skirts. Megan taps me on my leg and points through the foliage towards Sunnyside. A white van is driving down the lane slowly, navigating the ruts. I know Finnian will bring them here beside the river – the best vantage point of the river and irrigated flats. I can almost hear Dawn's rasping voice pointing out the listed features, an interpreter turning her words into a sales pitch in Mandarin. The women hush, drawing their children to them as the van approaches. The shelter women fix their masks to their faces.

'Undies off, ladies!' Shirley commands, and we delightedly decorate the trees with our knickers, feeling the freedom rush of fresh air to our verendas.

'We no longer have to feel shame!' Megan says to them. 'We no longer shall be silent! We no longer need to keep ourselves small!'

I join in, knowing Turner will soon be here and I must talk myself into bravery. 'We have permission to be angry, and to be fierce. We have permission to unleash our rage, and to transmute that power into *fierce* love. For our children. For our land. And most of all, for our *selves*!'

The van stops on the bank opposite, the door slides open and the investors get out. Some are dressed in full-length black puffer jackets, others in suits with ties. The Lilyburn mayor is here too, and a portly local councillor. Finnian is beside Dawn. And there he is. Turner.

Dawn's tour leads them towards the riverbank and when they are within metres from us, I turn to the women. 'Ladies! Goddesses! It's time to *raise our skirts*! To the riverbank and bare yourselves! It's time for *Ana-suromai*!'

I leg Traveller forward, leading the battle charge, 'Ana-suromai!'

'*Let's show 'em our maps of Tassie girls!*' Shirley adds, cackling wildly beside my horse as she runs.

Our war cries ring out so loud and so clear, our voices climb the mountains. The corporate cluster turns in shock. Deep bawls generated from women's bellies, rising up through angry throats and out through open mouths arrive with such ferocity, my heart pumps harder.

We rush the men, united as a fearful, feral, vibrant mob. A fever of fun, fury and excitement like electricity fills us.

Collectively we splash into the river, with lifted skirts and open lungs. Moving as an army of power we unleash with our outraged vaginal displays. Some women climb fallen logs, others clamber onto rocks or turn, revealing their bare buttocks, slapping them lewdly. Bawdy, unbearably brash. Some are laughing. Some crying, tears melding with river water. Some are exuding immense fury, letting rip with throaty screams, or swearing, at the men. We revel in our nakedness, thrusting our creative, sacred, divine triangles at them in all their glory. Gyrating our hips. Some licking lips wickedly. Jane from the post office, up a tree and the wildest among us.

'Respect your Mother! Respect your Earth! Respect your Mother! Respect your Earth!' Megan begins to chant.

We join in. The sound carries itself upwards as high as the wedge-tailed eagle that soars above us. Ancient memories stir in the ether. Nineteenth-century China is revived on the riverbank, the men's ancestral mothers, who once were the keepers of seed and soil, fly with us too. Our words cast a shadow of shame over the gathered men, who stand transfixed. One businessman begins shouting at Dawn in Mandarin and pointing to us angrily.

I fix my eyes on Professor Turner and chant harder. I know our gathered energy is sending a shock wave *right through them*. Professor Turner tries to settle the men, but they're shielding their faces and backing away. I ride through the river, right to them, my bare legs exposed, my belly rounded and heaving. I see Finnian's eyes land on it. The realisation that I'm pregnant clouds his face in shock. I see him *see* me for the first time. My power. My intelligence. My savage beauty. My wildness.

I rein in the horse before them.

'Connie, what the ...?' he begins, his voice shaking.

Dawn looks as if she could murder me with her bare hands. But it's Turner's face, one of haughty disdain, that enrages me the most. The women gather beside me and Traveller. Finnian's eyes land on Doctor Amel. She lays her palm on my bare thigh, and with her touch, I find my voice.

'You are being warned! This buyout is wrong! Your actions are wrong!' I look to all of the investors gathered. The interpreter begins translating, rapid-fire like a machine gun.

'Whether your corrupt sale goes ahead or not, know this – women from this day are rising up. We raise our skirts to you and demand that you stop the denigration of our land.'

I look directly into the eyes of the government men, on the take. 'We demand our land be protected from overseas sales, from excessive development, from dangerous genetic meddling and from toxic farming.'

I sense Kat near me with her camera. Other women, phones out recording.

'Your old ways are crumbling. Your power is failing. Our Lilyburn community, Verenda and Shiva Revival are already leading the way to a new system. The Divine Feminine has reasserted herself here, today, *now*, and there's no turning back.'

Dawn scowls. 'Get off your high horse, Connie, literally,' she says with mocking bitterness. 'As if you and a bunch of women wearing skirts can sideline a venture backed by the premier.'

Traveller's energy lifts as the drone hovers near. I settle him with my seat. Turner speaks, 'Dawn's right. Didn't you learn the first time, Connie?'

His ice-cold eyes land on me. But with the women around me, I feel my resolve.

'You don't get to silence me again, *Professor*,' I say. 'You're just one of so many egomaniacs in lab coats playing God. You and your worship of money. You and your narcissistic view of yourself. You, predator of young women. Did you tell your business associates about your deviant habits and grooming your young students for sex? Me. Grooming *me* for sex.'

Turner lifts his jaw. 'False allegations from a hysterical, mentally unstable female,' he fires back, speaking to the investors. 'She's nuts. The charges were dropped.'

'We all know which side the law lands on in these cases. Laws made up by men,' I say.

The interpreter's words land, the businessmen's faces reveal their understanding. The Canadian men begin murmuring among themselves.

For once, Turner is speechless. I know he can sense the tables turning. Instead of a panicked ramble, I speak from my wisdom-core, and the groundedness I now know I hold within. High up on Traveller, I am on my high horse. I am in my knowing. The words I am about to speak are going live … to the world.

'What is missing from your "man's world" is integrity. What is missing from your vocabulary and the vocabulary of all the masculinised systems that drive this world is the word *love*. You have forgotten love. You stand only on your fragile egos. And on greed. What you're proposing is abhorrent. It will kill this place. The systems are already killing people. You're set to poison everything and everyone around you. Your actions are at war with the Earth and with each other. It's time for this to end! If you can't see it, you are blind.'

I look to the investors. 'For those of you here to buy this land, look instead to partner with Shiva Revival – that's the future of business. Earth-friendly commerce founded in love and community – not competition and corruption.'

'Love,' Turner scoffs. 'You're mad, Connie Mulligan. Always were. Always will be. You're a nobody. No one is going to listen to you throw a tantrum about losing your already mismanaged farm.'

'No,' I say calmly. 'I think you'll find people *are* now listening. And it's you who's insane. What you do with your science to food *is* insanity.' I point to the drone. 'That thing's recording this for all the world to see. The Truth.'

Turner's face reddens. 'I'm not getting pushed about by a bunch of crazy fucken women,' Turner says, losing his cool.

His comment clearly lights Shirley's fuse. 'Crazy women, eh? Well then,' she says, reaching for her skirt. 'If old Professor Turd-ner here wants crazy, Connie, let's give him some fucken crazy! Shall we, ladies?' Her voice is laden with invitation and infectious boldness.

'Yes, *let's*!' I grin.

'Again. On the count of three ...' she says, turning to the women. 'One, two, three! Show 'em your maps of Tassie!'

'*Ana-suromai!*' I add, for my ancient sisters.

Traveller, unable to contain himself as the women erupt, spins, his rump connecting solidly with Turner. The knock sends him flying. The men look at him sprawled on the ground, but no one moves to help him.

The women around me raise their skirts, roaring, dancing in the faces of the men. Annabelle's masks, fearsome and bold. Howling like she-wolves in a bare-bum pack, kaleidoscope skirts gathered at our waists, raiding the men's personal space with our brashness. Turner scrambles to his feet and I rage at him, chasing after him with a spinning, prancing Traveller. 'Get off this land! Leave this place!'

He and the others scuttle for the van. We shout them gone. The last in, sliding the door shut behind him, is Finnian, his cold eyes cast downwards. And soon those men who had come to dominate this place become mere shadows of the past on the landscape. I swing off my horse, and on the riverbank, we women hold each other and weep.

Chapter 56

The next morning, Nick-nack gives a protective woof from her basket, then comes a knock on Granny M's door. Skidding along the hall in my socks, smiling, I'm expecting it to be one of my skirt sisters. Instead, I find Constable Tony, taking his hat off, tucking it officially under his arm.

'We seem to be making a habit of this,' he says, frowning.

I pull a conciliatory face at him.

'Connie, what were you thinking? You know what Tasmanian laws are like on protesting!'

'Draconian,' I say.

'Seriously, you could all be jailed for three months after the stunt you pulled yesterday. Or at least fined eight-thousand dollars – each.'

'We weren't protesting. We were dancing. It's not a crime to dance.'

He lifts an eyebrow. 'With your pants off? That's indecent exposure. I've seen the YouTube footage. It's all over the web, all over the telly. All over the world!'

'Pixelated I hope.' I grin.

'Connie, it's not funny. Dawn's hell-bent on pressing charges.'

'Oh c'mon, Tony! Whose side are you on?'

'The law's of course.'

I shake my head. 'I know the law.'

Nerdy Connie Mulligan steps in. I jut out my chin and speak

in an ABC radio voice. 'The *Police Offences Act 1935* states that "a person must not organise or conduct a march, rally, or demonstration (political or otherwise) without a permit if it is to be held wholly or partly on a public street". I checked. We were on *private* property. My very own farm. I can't help it if Dawn walked her buyers smack-bang into our ceremonial dancing.'

He delivers the same look he gave Nikki when she steered him away from the semen theft.

'Be warned though, Connie. You're dealing with some very powerful people. If it's taken further ...'

'It won't be,' I say. 'You know as well as I do, Dawn's on the take with this one. Likely, the government and local council too. They won't push it. We've done no harm. I've heard the Canadian portion of the consortium's still nibbling. If we play our cards right, Shiva just may be able to find enough funds to secure both farms for *our community*. Dawn'll get just as much of a commission. There's no skin off her nose. And those old boys in government down in Hobart will come to see just what local doughnut economies run with integrity can do.'

'That's if Shiva can raise the funds,' Tony warns.

'C'mon, Tony,' I urge again. 'Either way, Mum and Dad will get their sale money, so what's the harm in a bunch of women having a little tree-hugger dance? With that particular deal out of the way, we've saved the place from whacko cow gene-splicing and more toxic shit in our river.'

'I've still got a job to do,' Tony says.

As if sent from above, Nick-nack arrives like a breeze from heaven, wagging her love around Tony's legs. She rolls over grinning, as if to say, *Look at my preggers belly!*

'Ned's done his job,' I say. 'When the pups come, one's got your name on it.'

Tony looks at me, surprised. 'Truly?'

'Truly.'

'Ah Connie.' All his policeman demeanour fades and his face softens. 'I'd be gutted if I ever lost my Neddy. I'd love a pup by him.' He purses his lips and looks at me with such intensity. 'Neddy kept me ... y'know, going, after my wife ... y'know, did the dirty.'

Shocked by his candour, I'm about to console him when the sound of a car journeying up the mountain stops me. The car pulls up at Sunnyside gate. Nikki gets out holding a sledgehammer. She wallops the For Sale sign so it falls backwards onto the grass and gets back in the car. The women are still laughing when they arrive to us. June, Nikki, Megan, Shirley and Nancy greet us as they get out.

'What's going on?' I ask.

'Dawn's agreed! We've got a deal on both farms!' Nancy says.

'*Whaaat?*' I reply excitedly.

'Yes!' confirms Megan. 'We crashed the internet. Overnight! The crowdfund went ballistic.'

'Yesterday's consortium have pulled out,' Nancy says. 'Shiva Revival has just now put a deposit on Sunnyside and Waterbright! It's going to be ours! Lilyburn's!'

'Champagne?' Nikki suggests, lifting up a bottle. 'You included, constable.'

He protests.

'C'mon, Tony,' I say, giving him a happy hug. 'Tasering you with love, Tony! We're going to be puppy parents together!'

A smile arrives on his face and we know he's not leaving any time soon.

'So, Mum agreed to the sale?' I ask Nancy.

'Yes. She saw you on the news. In fact, her broadcaster boyfriend got behind the crowdfunding. I asked her to call Dawn this morning, and Nikki's mum did the same.' Nancy's voice softens, 'And, your mum asked me to tell you she's proud of you, Connie.'

The words land as she hugs me.

'The board have just given the green light for building the milk and cheese facility at the pub and you and Nikki can start to plan how to run the farms as one from today!'

'It's all happening!' I gasp.

Shirley raises a glass. 'It gets better! Baz and Anong are putting their hands up to run the tanker to transport the milk. I've started a crowdfund with Debs and one day soon, there'll be enough spondoola to set up an on-farm abattoir service and hide-tanning, run by our boys. Nigel and Aarav have got their hearts set on a custom-built semi-trailer as a mobile processing facility!' she says.

'We'll partner with them, so we at Shiva have put in our offer to Dawn to buy the old butchery and the haberdashery store,' Nancy says. 'Like we'd discussed. Ethical meat sales in one, clean and green tanned animal-hide products in the other. We're all systems go.'

'But surely even an avalanche of crowdfunding can't afford all that over the longer term?' I reply. 'We're going to need to pay people and build the infrastructure, plus changing the farms from conventional to natural systems takes money and time?'

Nancy looks at me, then to the sky above, and grabs both my hands, fixing her intense brown eyes on me. 'Let's just say a major, *major* contributor has come back down to Earth. Literally. He saw you on the internet, Connie Mulligan. You underestimate your power, *still*! In hearing you call to account those men yesterday, he's realised saving the Earth's soil is more important than exploring space. So he called me.'

'Who?'

'I can't say. But we had a good chat, about art, about land, about Lilyburn. About love, about cows and the cosmos. He got it. He's backing our social and economic model as a prototype to roll out in other health-impacted farming districts.'

'So you lot and Shiva Revival are now set to conquer the world?' Tony asks, lifting his eyebrows.

'Not conquer,' Nancy replies. 'Care for it collaboratively!'

'Yes,' I say. 'Instead of world domination it's cross-pollination!'

Suddenly, our euphoria is slayed when Finnian appears, roaring at us as he's making his way from the main house.

'Get off my property! You mad, dirty fucken women. Get away with you!'

His words are slurred. His gait unsteady. Dishevelled, he's still in his 'meet the investors' clothes from yesterday.

'He's got the wobbly boots on,' Tony says, watching him lollop towards us. 'Crook or drunk?'

'Bit of both, I'd say.'

'I'll handle it,' Doctor Amel says calmly, stepping towards him, but he shoves her violently.

'Piss off, you stupid bitch!'

Constable Tony dives in, grabbing his arm, fixing him with his blue-eyed stare. 'Settle, Finnian.'

'Get your fucken hands off ...'

In that moment, like a rag doll, Finnian's legs give way. He drops to the ground, eyes rolling back, head lolling. Doctor Amel immediately kicks in to first-aid procedures and I rush to his side.

'He's dead drunk, but not dead,' Doctor Amel says, glancing up. 'We'll still need an ambulance.'

Constable Tony reaches into his cop car, cool as a cucumber, and radios it in.

'Womanising prick,' I hear him mutter as he hangs the handpiece back in its cradle.

I look to Finnian. Then to Tony. So he's the reason why Tony's wife strayed and why Tony sought solace in the eyes of his dog.

*

That afternoon, alone, the creaking comfort of Granny M's cottage wraps around me and with Nick-nack happily snoring at my feet, I video-call Patrick and Amber in Ireland, lighting up to see them.

'You're a YouTube sensation *again*!' Amber teases.

We laugh. Then I fill them in on Doctor Amel's report on Finnian – stable in hospital, with another heart surgery on the cards. Then I moved on to Shiva's proposed business structure.

Patrick doesn't seem at all fazed that the farm's not technically ours anymore.

'The draft contracts mean we can stay here if we like, Patrick, for the rest of our lives,' I explain. 'Even our descendants.' In that moment I feel the baby kick.

'Speaking of the rest of our lives,' Patrick says, drawing Amber into his side, 'we did it!'

'Did what?' I ask.

Amber holds up her hand, a beautiful ring on her finger, her smile shining as much as the stone.

'We're engaged!'

*

Later, hanging up the phone, I notice there's a missed call. I replay the recording.

'Connie Mulligan! It's all over the news and socials! Thanks to you they're calling for not just one but *two* Royal Commissions into foreign ownership of Australian land and chemical usage in food systems, plus legislation to protect soil health. You did it!'

Nick's deep voice sends electric currents throughout my body. I feel the baby twinge inside me. He sounds elated. Delighted. Excited.

'Go the Sheela Na Gigs! I'm so proud of you, Connie. Getting the message out to the world and leading women to rise up. Congratulations for sowing the seeds!'

Hearing him sends me orbiting around the Earth, somewhere out in the Milky Way, until I remember our impossible mismatch. I lay my palms on my baby within and shut my eyes. Is it so wrong not to tell him? I look to the sky and search for birds. For clouds. For signs. None comes. Just the pesky hare on the track, grooming her thick butter-coloured belly.

Chapter 57

A few days before Amber and Patrick's Tasmanian wedding, I wake to the warble of magpies outside Larry's bedroom window and gentle sunshine draping itself over the bed. House-sitting has never felt so good, particularly on the sunny side of the valley.

Stretching and getting up, I peer into Liam's room, the breeze stirring the colourful cloud mobile above his cot. His dark hair is sleep-ruffled, his little hands curled. Standing over him, watching the land divas of morning light sparkling around him, I smile, stroking his hair. The age of discovery is upon him and I'm so blessed to be exploring his all-new world alongside him.

In the kitchen I pick up the postcard lying beside the ready-packed produce boxes on the table, destined for the Lilyburn Food Hub Pub and the Happy Chappy Holistic Cafe. I flip over the card.

> *Paris lights in full flight on a dark night. Funds flowing in*
> *for more community food hubs and regenerative farms in*
> *every country we travel to. Xxx.*

Larry and Nancy are clearly making a fine old time of it on their world gallery tour and Regenerative Food Networks promotion, judging from the delight contained in their scrawled messages.

I stick the card onto the fridge alongside their other postcards – London, New York, Madrid.

It'd been a warm night, so I'd left the big doors to the art space cast wide open, now empty of Annabelle's image. Larry's works have flown overseas to hang beside her paintings in a travelling show about the timelessness of land and love.

Traveller has made his way into his stall through the double doors, tugging at his hay net. Beside him stands his little bay mate, Dublin, eating from his net. The gentle-souled rescue pony ripples a greeting. I greet him back, excited for the day in the future when he will take Liam up and down the mountain tracks, where the sacredness of the land has the chance to imprint itself upon Liam's soul.

In the treetops, parrots flitter and swoop, like fresh dobs of paint on brand-new art palettes. Liam's toys are scattered beneath my easel, where my painting awaits until after the wedding.

Stepping out to give the garden an early morning water, I look over to Sunnyside where the cows are making their procession up to the dairy to join their calves in a new purpose-built barn. The Verenda crew are over at the dairy, quietly going about the twice-daily rhythmic ritual. Beside the dairy is Granny M's – swept, cleaned, tidied and freshly flowered, ready for the arrival of our Irish wedding guests today. Mrs O'Bee and Northern Patrick are on their way with bride-to-be, Amber, and groom, Brother Patrick, the Donovans following soon after.

Across from Granny M's, Mum and Finnian's house has also been transformed for the newlyweds to move into. Our Lilyburn crew have lime-washed the orange bricks to white, added gentle green shutters, and Shirley's talent for gardening has transformed the place – the faux wishing well sold on Gumtree and all the gnomes gone. Mum's formerly regimented garden is now free to express itself with white flowers and varying shades of luscious green foliage, reminiscent of Ireland so that Amber can feel at home.

Nick-nack trots up to me, tailed by her golden daughter, Clover, one of only three. When the litter landed, we instantly knew Neddy's genes dominated. The pups' ears were signature spaniel with short legs and feathery tails. Two females, like little blobs of butter. The other, the male, with the markings of a mini border collie, a white-tipped Shepherd's Lantern on his tail.

I think of the boy pup, Den, happy with Constable Tony and a playful sidekick for Ned, and love their little backwards–frontwards names.

The littlest pup, golden girl Angel, has fitted in well as a permanent resident at Finnian's care facility. With her collie smarts but cocker kindness, all the patients love her. Finnian too, the stroke he had during surgery impacting his mind, leading him to a softer, childlike place.

When I hear Liam wake, I bathe him and dress him in his little shorts and t-shirt, then head to the riverside. Amber has asked me to collect river stones to paint Celtic motives on as a talisman for each guest's place setting. It's a task I've been looking forward to all week.

As Liam and I journey to our sacred horseshoe bend, him in a backpack, I take my time, allowing him to soak up this bushland world. A grey crane watches us as we pass, stick-legging between pin rushes beside the water's edge, where we've started reinstating the chain of ponds using Natural Sequence Farming methods.

We head to where we routinely come to thank the water sprites for flowing abundance through the world from these headwaters – all connected around the Earth via rivers, glaciers, streams, creeks, seas, rain, mist, dew drops, clouds and oceans.

In the past year, I've washed so much pain into that water to heal. The flashbacks have stopped, mostly. The only one that comes now to taint my mind could be seen as a comfort and I never know if it is real.

The image of a suit-clad newsreader swims into my mind. Behind him on the screen is the corporate photo of Turner, not long after our first skirt-raising. As he reads out his bulletin, the words come to my ears, like bubbles released underwater, pushing up for air.

'*Renowned scientist Professor Simon Turner was found dead early this morning in a Hobart university laboratory. Police revealed Turner suicided by ingesting the agrichemical Paraquet – a commonly used farm chemical. Police say there are no suspicious circumstances.*'

When I have this memory, I feel some sorrow, but mostly it feels like peace has at last arrived. Now, I'm here in the clearing, immersed in the bliss of birdsong. 'Joe Witty' birds chime, magpies warble, perched in a stunning white gum that's perfuming the air with eucalyptus scent. The drifting tune of black cockatoos accompany the river's music as four birds wing past the face of the mountains. An eagle, a speck above the craggy peak. It's my time, now.

When we get to the shallows, I unroll a picnic rug for Liam. He's sure to scoot after the dogs, as if he's another of Nick-nack's lively pups, so I ask her to sit beside him, which she does with all the wisdom of a wise old wolf. I empty out his bag of toys.

Carrying the small bucket into the shallows, the water wrapping around my legs, I stoop for river stones, harvesting each one with reverence and awe.

I'm so engrossed collecting perfect polished stones, that I don't even look up when I hear a vehicle coming over the repaired bridge that now links Larry's to the other side. It will be one of the chappies' crew, come for their vegetables for the wedding banquet. I offer a wave, and carry on with my task.

Soon, I hear a voice behind me. 'What are you searching for? Gold?'

Breath is stolen from my body. My mouth drops open.

'*Nick?*'

The dogs dance towards him.

'Connie!' He smiles. 'They said you'd be about.'

He says it like I'm an old friend. Not a one-time lover. Part of me is relieved. Part of me is disappointed. All of me is shocked.

'What are you doing here?'

He grins at me as he stoops to pat the dogs.

'Duh!' I say, answering my own question. 'Wedding.'

'Yes, but also, work.' He takes a backpack from his shoulder. 'I wasn't coming but your Natural Sequence Farming repairs and the community food supply model are awe-inspiring. I came to have a look, and collaborate, then Nancy offered me work here.'

'But I thought you were in America with the Farmer's Footprint organisation?'

'I was, but ...'

Liam burbles a sound. Nick looks over at my child ... *our child* ... and I'm flooded with guilt.

'Ah! I've heard about this one. You'd better introduce us.'

I look to Nick, floundering. 'Um, this is Liam.'

He crouches down before my son. *Our son.* Nick's hair is now longer, shaggier. A mirror image of Liam's. He's dressed in well-worn farm clothes, looking so different from the shiny-booted, neatly groomed but stressed-out doctor I first met in Ireland. The one who said he never wanted to bring children into this messed-up world.

'Liam,' he repeats, saying his son's name. He scrutinises our baby who is giving him a giggly smile. Something crosses his face.

'Yes,' I say. 'Liam. Capital L for Love, and i, a, m for the great "I am",' I say.

Nick reaches out, taking his tiny hand. 'Hello little man, Liam, I am.' Again, he looks at the child and then to me. A slight incline of his head. 'He's a bonnie one.'

I wait for the penny to drop, but it doesn't seem to. Instead, he says, 'Oh I forgot. Mrs O'Bee said to bring you this.'

'She's here already!'

'Yes. We pushed our flights forward.' From his bag, he pulls out my missing red bling gumboot.

'Oh wow!'

'Mrs O'Bee said someone donated it to the op shop and it was a sign that we had to drop everything and come to the wedding ... and to see you. She's quite taken with your cottage. Says it's the brightest place she's ever been. I think you'll be hard-pressed to move her out. Once she meets this little lad, she's likely to never leave. She's bursting to see you, but is having a rest first. Said she felt upside down.' He laughs as he passes me the gumboot. 'Don't mistake this for a Cinderella-ish moment!'

'No glass slippers round here.' I grin, gesturing to the rocks. 'They'd shatter here. Plus, we all know those stories are never what they seem.' I laugh outwardly taking the boot from him but twisting on the inside. 'Thank you.'

Liam cries out and lifts his arms to be picked up.

'Do you mind?' Nick asks.

I swallow. 'Not at all!' As he gathers up Liam, tears well in my eyes.

'Nick. There's something I haven't told you ... It was so wrong of me, but–'

'Stop,' he says. He sets his deep brown eyes on me. 'You don't need to tell me. I already know.'

It's as if I've had all the air punched out of me.

'You know? How?'

'I just *know*. I went back to Ireland to tidy things up on the estate, see if I could change Mum's mind. They knew I was a mess, so Mrs O'Bee and Shauna took me to the stones in the hill country. They, you know, did their Wicca-woman thing and I ... I can't explain it, but I had a vision. Of a baby. And ... I saw ...' He stops and rubs his hand over his chin. 'This is going to sound weird, but I saw ... you. But not you. It was a version of you. In another time.'

I look into his eyes. I start to cry. Partly with relief, partly with regret, and mostly with guilt that I'd not been brave enough to tell him. 'I'm sorry ...' I begin.

'Stop.'

He sits me down and gently places Liam between us.

'Connie, stop. As Mrs O'Bee says, the universe always times these things perfectly. It took me a while to tell myself it was okay to come.'

The months of tension I've held release with a sob.

He reaches for my hand. 'It's okay. Don't think I'm angry or anything. I'm not here to impose, but if it's okay with you, I'd like to get to know him.'

Through tears I nod.

'And I'd like to get to know you,' he says gently.

His statement sits between us. Uncertainty in me lingers, but I realise there's nothing left to do but be like the river, and go with the flow.

'And your mum? Does she know?'

He shakes his head. 'Not yet. I wanted to see you first.'

I shudder at her memory.

'She's moved to Paris anyway. She lost heart for that big old house once I left.'

'Oh,' I say. 'That's a little sad.'

'Not at all! She's happier in Paris. And she's caved.'

'What do you mean, caved?'

'We've just signed a long-term lease with the Donovans. Devlyn is moving into the big house – we're joining the farms at last. The old manager's long gone.'

A smile shines brightly from me. 'Oh that's the best news!'

'Wait, though. It gets better. Devlyn's Siobhan's back, with the children. They're opening up the house as a holistic hotel. She's born for it.'

'Double awesome,' I say.

We sit in silence save for the river, which carries on with its own conversation.

'Got time to give me a farm tour?' Nick asks.

'Yes! Of course,' I say. 'I'll just finish up here. I need ten more river stones to paint, for the wedding.'

'Okay. I'll help.'

Nick-nack resumes her post as babysitter as we step into the river. As Nick stands near me, in the rushing water, my body tingles with self-awareness. I realise I've been blocking any future potential with this man. I have been blocking love. Potentially, love with a partner that I actually deserve, despite our different backgrounds.

Nick swims his fingers through river sand and rock, silt muddying the white rapids downstream, assessing each stone. We chat about the Celtic motifs I'm going to paint on them. When he gathers the next stone to drop into my bucket and our hands touch and eyes meet, I don't push the emotions I have for him away this time.

'One more for luck,' he says, dragging his eyes away. Nick submerges his hand again, then raises something from the water. He looks at me, his expression that of wonderment.

'Oh my god!' Cupping his hand as if holding a precious baby bird in his palm, he breathes. 'Look!'

When I see what's on his palm, my body ignites as if an energetic flame across time and space is burning in my whole being. There lies a wet and muddied ring. The truth of the colour and design can't be denied. It's unmistakable. It is gold. It is a *Claddagh ring.*

'Do you see?' He looks deeply into my eyes, lit with jubilation.

'Yes! I see!'

'It must've washed down from some old Irish settlement?' Nick suggests. 'Or an upturned buggy back in the day? A buried stash? A flooded Mulligan grave? Pure and simple alchemy? I don't know, but a certain miracle!'

'I think I know,' I say. The paintings haunt my memory. I remember now, the ring on Annabelle's engagement finger. Gold. A Claddagh.

He reaches for my hand and slides it onto my ring finger.

'A perfect fit,' he says.

I feel Annabelle and a long-ago Granny Mary Mulligan hovering near and sense the women from the ages on the breeze, a breeze that has rushed through the high gum treetops to brush against my skin. For a beat in time, my breath stops as the universe swirls. The stars of time and timelessness rush within my body and it's as if my entire being extends out beyond the Earth and into space.

'The Claddagh,' I say looking at Nick, smiling. 'Friendship, love ...'

'And loyalty,' he finishes.

'*A Thaisce! Mo shíorghra,*' Nick says as puts his arm around me and pulls me near.

I rest my cheek gently near the place where his heart knocks. Deep in my knowing, I'm aware he's spoken Gaelic words of love. That I am his treasure. That I am his soulmate. Across the skies of time. I turn my face up to his and we swim in our first ever river kiss.

*

Later that night in the cottage, I tell Nick the story of Annabelle, and deep in me I know innately it was she who cast the ring into the waters, devastated by the acts of cruel men.

Nick lies in silence for a time, absorbing the sadness of the tale, fingertips drifting over my skin.

Eventually, he asks, 'Have you heard the old Irish saying that goes with the Claddagh ring? I'm sure Larry knew of it – that's why he would've chosen it for her.'

'No.'

'With these hands I give you my heart, and crown it with my love.' He draws me near.

'I still can't believe you found it,' I say.

'After all this time,' he says.

'Yes. After all this time,' I echo.

When I close my eyes, I hear my heart pulse a river of blood through my veins. There's no longer a throb of fear, just the quiet sense of infinite space and light both beyond and within my body. I now have a surety that the past is at peace, and the future written upon my sharply focused, obedient mind and open loving heart. All guided by my expanded soul, all because I have remembered that *I am.*

Gratitude as deep as the Earth sweeps in me as I settle against Nick, listening to the rain on the corrugated iron roof that has come to kiss the ground to green.

Beside us, the clock ticks uselessly. I am no longer conned by it. No longer bound by it. And whether this man stays, or comes and goes, or leaves, it doesn't matter. The illumination of our love shall remain with me forever. Nature and her rhythms shall now shape my days in this world.

Nick skims his fingertips over my shoulders, kissing me on my crown.

'Would you mind if I stayed for a while, just milking my time with you, Connie Mulligan?'

I answer with a smile and a kiss.

As we merge together, I fall into the joy of exploring the landscape of his body, and he of mine, in the quiet intimacy beneath this old Mulligan rain-smattered roof. I know our journey across lifetimes has begun again. We may be newly partnered lovers, and unplanned joint parents, but deep inside my core I know we are actually long-time travelling companions. Arriving on this Earth, time and time again, weaving our heartbeats and breath together in this ancient, unforgotten, easily remembered dance.

Epilogue

At the end of the main drag, Bass Strait is behaving like she's a mild Mediterranean sea under a glorious teal sky as the Lilyburn street swirls with colour and life. Nick, with Liam on his shoulders, and me, carrying my cargo of homemade ice-cream cones, return to the Raising of the Skirts Festival, diving into the thrum.

The seagulls have never looked so content as they cluster at the feet of the diners outside the Happy Chappy Holistic Cafe where Fenton emerges, his arms lined with laden plates. The chalkboard is advertising Aarav and Slugs's specialty-recipe game meat pies and Sunnyside and Waterbright Dairy veal curries, along with our aged dairy beef. Shirley's famous Cock-in-a-Pot stew has sold out. The Insta star is mingling with her fans, in demand for selfies with her 'Cock Crew', all wearing her colourful array of organic cotton t-shirts emblazoned with roosters and slogans that read, *Put your cock in a pot* and *Waste not, want cock!*

'Proceeds go to abandoned roosters,' she calls out to onlookers, tugging at her top.

'You can buy them online,' adds Debs, now PR officer for Shirley's burgeoning career as part-comedian who oozes Tasmanian-ness, and part-influencer as an economical cook and gardening guide for the millions wanting to live and eat closer to nature and spend less.

Across the street the women of Verenda and Anong are busily selling vibrant handmade skirts to festival-goers before the ceremony. Dawn is there, tossing up between the red and the yellow, holding the pretty skirts out before her. Swishing my green skirt at them I wave. 'Not long till the ceremony, soil sisters!' I gesture to the memorial clock, which is now, after years, set at the right time.

Nick lifts Liam from his shoulders, takes my hand and we merge through the packed street, waving at Aarav's family, who have beautiful leather goods and hides spread out for sale at the former haberdashery store. Next door, Slugs's co-op butchery is open thanks to his old duck-shooter mate, Mr Rowenbotham (now president of the Lilyburn Feral Cat Eradication Association), who has come out of retirement just for Slugs, picking up his boning knives once more.

We duck under the pub's hanging baskets drooling with flowers and enter the beer garden. Here, a lively Irish band is playing beneath the pergola drizzled with purple and white wisteria. Nick smiles and hip bumps me as we weave through the people dancing to the infectious sound.

'You 'n' me, after?'

'To be sure.' I grin.

When little Liam sees Granny B, his face lights up and he runs to her. She takes him in her arms and covers his face with kisses.

'Oh my favourite boy!' she says. 'Are you excited about staying at Granny B's cottage tonight?' Liam laughs a yes as she tickles him.

'Oi! You said I was your favourite,' Patrick quips at Mrs O'Bee as he lugs another crate of milk from the mobile cool store.

'She said *I* was her favourite,' Nick teases, putting on a show for the kids.

Mrs O'Bee puts her hands up in surrender. 'You're all my favourites. Why do you think I moved to the other side of the world for you!'

'So it wasn't just the weather,' teases Patrick.

As I slide behind the trestle tables to deliver the ice-cream cones, Amber looks up. Her cheeks are pink from the sweep of customers, all wanting our natural flavour milk shakes, ice creams and specialty cheeses.

'We've just about sold out of everything,' Amber says.

I lean over a pram to ruffle Finn's red flop of hair that is the same deep shade of his mother's. The baby is mesmerised by a ladybird that is delicately perched on little Sarah's index finger. Tobias and Nikki's daughter, the once pint-sized sickly baby, is now growing into a robust healthy child, thanks to Doctor June's guidance and the nourishment from our Lilyburn food. Sarah leans in to show Liam the pretty insect and we all make a fuss.

'Our mummies have saved the insects,' Sarah says with an air of sage wisdom and pride.

Nikki, who is busy at the till, laughs then looks over to us and winks.

Across the beer garden, June chalks *SOLD OUT* on the board, having handed the last Verenda fresh produce box to a happy customer.

From the pub's kitchen door, Jane calls out, 'It's time, ladies!' The beats from the Verenda drummers call us together.

As Amber, Nikki and I make to leave, Nick stoops to kiss my cheek, and squeezes my hand. 'Go recalibrate the world, woman.'

On the main street, Megan looks larger than life, holding a loudspeaker, her blonde hair cascading down in Viking woman spirals. Like a river, the crowd of what might be as many as two hundred or more begins to flow down the street towards the sea. The women's skirts form a sea of their own, of vibrancy and power. The energy rises, carried further into the ether by the certain beats of the drummers.

At the seashore we make our way onto the sand, most of us barefoot, most already knicker-less, wading into the cool water.

'Sisters!' Megan says into the megaphone. 'This action, the raising of the skirt, that was once used as a warfare tactic by our ancient mothers to shock and bring our opponents to their senses, has had amazing effect in the past few years. Yes, they gave our grandmothers the vote, but we have been voting for broken systems. Since our very first gathering, we are at last overcoming the madness of this world. We have sent a clear message to those in power that their actions against our Mother Earth are outrageous and dangerous! However, thanks to all our efforts, change is upon us. The old systems are falling away. The Divine Feminine – the Truth – has risen. We are the kind and integrous leaders of this Earth now!'

The women emit a cry of affirmation. Instead of the rage, shame and fear I'd felt in the first tentative Raising of the Skirts festival we'd organised, now I feel a peaceful power. A surety. And a grace.

Megan nods at me and passes me the loudspeaker. As I take it, the world swirls.

Suddenly I am the verdant green of Ireland. An inner well of life force seems to be drawing up the power of the Sheela Na Gigs within me. I spin in the centre of the stones. There are flame torches. And sparks that greet the stars. Time. Past, present, future is all blending, swirling.

Then I blink and I am here. In Tasmania. In the sea.

'Today, sisters, we raise our skirts to find common ground. Today we demand that love prevails over all.' I breathe deeply into my body, remembering all that Mrs O'Bee is teaching me on full moon nights, and in new moon darkness in Granny M's cottage with whispers from the ancients and threads leading to the grandmothers of our future.

'Today and from now on, display your verenda in glory, not hide her in shame. It is safe to unveil and unfold and share with others. It is safe to be your True Self. So, let our powerful feminine force, like thunder and lightning, spread across the seas to our sisters and beyond, so that they too can know their power of fertility and fecundity and reclaim our blue-green planet!

'On the count of three,' I shout.

Megan nods, and we spin towards the vast curving blue horizon.

'One. Two. Three! *Ana-suromai!*'

'*Ana-suromai!*' the women call.

Shirley grabs the microphone, screeching like a wild woman. 'And let's show 'em our maps of Tassie, girls!'

Collectively we lift our skirts, the women bellowing and laughing like she-warriors on a high. As we stand swaying our skirts, I turn to them.

'Let this gesture of change spread to all our sisters and kind brothers, so that even *more* people around the world can join this reclamation!'

We have no sooner lowered our skirts than Mrs O'Bee arrives at my side and whispers, 'Look!'

In awe, we watch as a tumbling nimbostratus cloud forms over the wide bay before our very eyes. It sails towards the triangular, delta-shaped mouth of the river to the north along the beach. The cloud elongates as it kisses the land, becoming mistier so that a rainbow illumination appears within its dark belly. It begins to snake and slide its way up the river inland towards our dairy farms.

The beautiful cloud calls us to our future. I feel myself drift upwards so that soon I'm flying within the cloud, seeing the river from above as I glide upstream towards the mountains. The marriage of the farms along the catchment have created a pretty Eden. From up on high I see the landscape is healing, like a beautiful painting, and my heart fills with joy.

I stick my tongue out so that the misty rain within the cloud can drape upon it. The water I taste is now clearer, purer, more life-supporting than the clouds that used to run this river in the old world of yesterday. I feel their cool, moist drizzle on my face and know they are clouds how Mother Nature intended them to be. Pure. Clear. Pristine. And free at last from mankind's ills. Free from the collective amnesia where we had forgotten that this planet and the feminine is sacred. This place can be heaven on Earth if we choose it so.

That I, Connie Mulligan, have rewritten my story anew — milking this time of my life, joyfully and fearlessly, for all that it is worth. This is my time. As it is yours.

Acknowledgements

What a joy to see *Milking Time* flow out into the world after so many years. For me, and hopefully you, this book heralds the potential for positive change and new awareness about country and community. It's been years in the making, through some very tough periods personally and globally.

I could not have completed *Milking Time* without the steadfast wisdom and love of my literary agent of more than twenty years, Margaret Connolly. Thanks for the daily support and love from my creative collaborator and bestie Jackie Merchant. And to my dear, dear grown and almost flown children, Rosie and Charlie, thank you for supporting me every day to be an artist, farmer and a mum! It hasn't been easy, but you are the most loyal and loving humans I could have ever hoped to have in my life. Your kindness and integrity means the world to me.

Thank you to my gentle and genius publisher Catherine Milne who saw the manuscript's potential even when it was a 'big old raggedy beast' and helped bring Connie to the fore. I've never had a better set of novel notes as a compass Catherine! Thank you!

Many thanks to Louisa Maggio for coming up with the most dreamy and delicious cover that practically photosynthesises. Thanks to Caitlin Toohey, Jacqueline Wright, and the entire HarperCollins team, for helping plant this seeds-of-change novel into the world. Now bring on the rain!

Thanks to the sharp-eyed and sympathetic editor Dianne Blacklock for your writer's empathy. And thanks for the help of more eyes on the pages, Rachel Cramp.

So much love and gratitude to the incredible Dr Lorri Beaver-Mandekic who checked in with me weekly, and to Dr Sue Morter and 'the village people' who are all committed to creating a kind and gentle planet of people. The techniques you taught helped me (and Connie Mulligan) more than you'll ever know!

Thank you to the team at Ripple Farm Landscape Healing Hub (Dan, Andrew and our animals) for the opportunity to heal the landscape using all the techniques I'm passionate about, along with the chance to learn the big lessons in life about self as a woman in farming – which fed beautifully into Connie's story. And to Stuart and Megan Andrews, thanks for slowing the flow!

Thanks to Chez at Tasmanian Produce Collective, our fellow farmers and Jen and Ollie at Sprout. You help small producers like me create real-life food-systems change. Our 'clandestine food distributions' and rebellious zeal helped feed the plot. You've shown me grassroots change is not just an intangible dream.

During lockdown and beyond, Regena Thomashauer, the Pussy sisterhood and the Black Lives Matter women, you gave me the courage to get brave, and loud and pussy proud. And a huge thanks to Catherine Blackledge for your book – *Raising the Skirt: The Unsung Power of the Vagina* – which gave me insight and inspiration into how Connie could reclaim herself and her land for all women.

To the inspirational women all around me who helped carry me: Luella, Kath, Manty, Bec and Bec, Cassie, Kirrily, Mel, Ira, Angie, the Langford Ladies, Heidi, and Karen White at Rural Alive and Well, along with the Hoedowns for Country Towns creators Claire and Kate, and legend Shan Whan, founder of Sober in the Country – you all rock ... let's raise our skirts together soon! If your name's not written here, read between the lines. You are on this page – my heartfelt thanks to my sisterhood and the brotherhood of kind men ... Rocket Rod, Grahame Rees and Graeme Bradders the kings among them.

To my Weka Nation legends and my sisters in soil – Nicole Masters, Jane Slattery, and the regen R's – Rachelle Armstrong, Robin Tait and Ros Rees – you are my inspiration.

My friends are my family ... you know who you are. Pete and Sal, Anne and Noel ... the list goes on, I thank you for accepting me as I am, and for holding me in your hearts.

And lastly (but not least) to my animals around me ... Belle, Wattle, Gemma, Bobby, Barbara Gordon, Megatron, Hans Solo, Adventure Chicken, Mrs Brown, Uzzie Kelpwhaja, Dolly Pupton, Aloeburn yellow tag stomper, Floppy and the girls ... and the rest ... you inspire me every day!

And to you, my long-term readers, and to my new readers, a massive thank you for supporting an Australian/Tasmanian grassroots writer like me – who writes purely from her heart. No matter what your gender ... it's time to raise our skirts – reclaim our power. Life is good if you choose it so.